P9-EFI-258

Backyard

Backyard

Norman Draper

KENSINGTON BOOKS
www.kensingtonbooks.com

KENSINGTON BOOKS are published by

Kensington Publishing Corp.
119 West 40th Street
New York, NY 10018

Copyright © 2014 by Norman Draper

All rights reserved. No part of this book may be reproduced in any form or by any means without the prior written consent of the Publisher, excepting brief quotes used in reviews.

All Kensington titles, imprints, and distributed lines are available at special quantity discounts for bulk purchases for sales promotion, premiums, fund-raising, and educational or institutional use.

Special book excerpts or customized printings can also be created to fit specific needs. For details, write or phone the office of the Kensington Special Sales Manager: Kensington Publishing Corp., 119 West 40th Street, New York, NY 10018. Attn. Special Sales Department. Phone: 1-800-221-2647.

Kensington and the K logo Reg. U.S. Pat. & TM Off.

eISBN-13: 978-1-61773-306-2
eISBN-10: 1-61773-306-7
First Kensington Electronic Edition: December 2014

ISBN-13: 978-1-61773-305-5
ISBN-10: 1-61773-305-9
First Kensington Trade Paperback Printing: December 2014

10 9 8 7 6 5 4 3

Printed in the United States of America

For Mom, Dad, and Morrie

1

Groundwork

The inspiration for the "Burdick's Best Yard Contest" came to Jasper Burdick in the steam room of the Directors' Club, in downtown St. Anthony.

Someone had turned up the steam too high. A half-dozen fat, naked patriarchs of St. Anthony and environs yipped and cursed. They yelled for someone outside to turn it down. Nothing happened. No one could hear them.

Finally, the burning steam got too thick to just sit there waiting for someone else to do something. They lifted their jiggling, wrinkled derrieres up off the tiled bench and stumbled blindly toward the door.

But Mr. Burdick stayed put. His sixth sense told him that something of great importance to the future of his business was about to happen here. If his lungs had to get cooked and his body blistered with second-degree burns to witness it, then so be it. He didn't get to where he was in the gardening world by being a shrinking violet.

Curled tendrils of steam ensnared him. They hissed and murmured. Were they trying to tell him something? A vision began to take shape, coalescing at first into a billowing, diaphanous form, then rapidly gaining graphic clarity and definition.

What Mr. Burdick saw emerge from the mists was a snowy upper-Midwestern landscape bursting forth in legions of gigantic early-blooming crocuses and tulips. Tucked within their petals were human faces. That's kind of spooky, thought Mr. Burdick, but at least they're all smiling at me. They looked faintly familiar. Were they his employees? He'd never really taken much notice of them before. As the snow in the vision world melted away, thousands more human-faced flowers of every conceivable hue and size burst forth from the ground. Nonplussed, yet mesmerized, Mr. Burdick leaned closer to the vision and squinted. Who *were* all these weird flower people?

Then, the vision dissolved into something wonderful: all the mutant flowers trooping to Livia, in the suburban south, then into his Burdick's PlantWorld emporium. They waved fistfuls of cash at soaker hoses, tomato ladders, trellises, garden weasels, tillers, and watering cans.

Nearby stood a clot of TV camera crews and intense-looking reporters armed to the teeth with cassette recorders, pens, and steno pads. Mr. Burdick jerked back from the vision and frowned, distrustful as he was of the press. But what if all these media jackals had been put there to serve some helpful purpose? It would be out of character certainly, but then flowers usually didn't have faces either. They were all standing in a circle around a petite, middle-aged, sun-hatted woman who held a huge gold-plated trophy aloft as flashbulbs popped and reporters shouted unintelligible questions.

"I've just won the Burdick's Best Yard Contest," the woman said with what seemed an understated and almost reluctant enthusiasm under the circumstances. "How could I possibly deserve such an honor?"

Show a little more joy, thought Mr. Burdick; buck up and smell the roses, for heaven's sake.

Someone finally found the controls and turned down the steam, which began to dissolve from its stultifying opaqueness into a warm, misty translucence. The patriarchs, having refreshed themselves in the club whirlpool bath, drifted back into the room. They voiced amazement at Mr. Burdick's heat endurance and plotted exquisite tortures for whomever the idiot was who messed with the timer and thermostat. Mr. Burdick ignored them. He was focusing all his mental energy on the revelation that had just burst on him like a supernova.

"I'm going to hold a contest the likes of which the St. Anthony metro has never seen before," he told the disappearing vision, which now wafted into a faint few billion molecules of nothingness. "The mother of all gardening competitions. Our winner will be a celebrity, a hero, an ambassador for gardening and our particular products throughout the land. Business will flourish as it never has before. Burdick's PlantWorld will expand, first throughout the state, then the region, then the country, and finally, the world. I'll be selling yellow jacket catchers and sweet potato vine in Mongolia before you can say 'Buy Burdick's for Beautiful, Bounteous Blossoms.' I'm going to be the emperor of gardening center owners!"

The shadowy shapes at the other end of the bench stared at him.

"Lost your marbles, Burdick?" gurgled one over the subsiding hiss of the steam jets. "Or maybe you been snortin' too much honeysuckle. Ha-ha."

Marta Poppendauber strolled slowly down the brick pathway through her massive gardens with her watering can. She gazed lovingly upon her potted zinnias, impatiens, and lobelia as she positioned the watering can's snout almost into the dirt around each flower to ensure that the water went straight to the roots. It was how Dr. Phyllis Sproot, her friend and gardening mentor, had taught her.

My, wasn't the lobelia spreading out! She loved their dainty little blooms. And the zinnias! How precious! They seemed to perk up the very instant the water trickled into the soil. The impatiens? Well, we'd just have to see; they might be getting too much sun and too little water.

Having watered all her container plants, Marta scanned the rest of her gardens. It was early June, which meant the clematis's blanket of green leaves and violet blossoms was well on its way to smothering the gray-weathered wooden ladders she had tilted to lean sturdily against the house. The hydrangeas had exploded, as usual. Their plate-sized clumps of green flowers were poised for transformation into white masses of grandeur.

Elsewhere were the phlox, peonies, boltonia, and bugbane. The ornamental grasses, and Martin Frobisher roses, planted years ago, were well-established old-timers. Then there were the yew and the trumpet creeper, and the daffodils and dahlias, not to mention the Don Juan and Jasmina roses.

It was only last month that she had added the love-lies-bleeding, larkspur, mallow, and all the others. Each year, she had filled in every available space with big, bright annuals.

Many of her flowers were still waiting to bloom. Another three weeks or so and she'd have a kaleidoscope of a garden, swarming with honeybees, butterflies, and hummingbirds drawn to her sugary summer paradise.

It had taken years to establish her crazy-quilt pattern the way she wanted it. Along the way, Marta had managed to weather Dr. Sproot's contrariness and ward off her insistence to do something far more contained and predictable.

"It reeks of anarchy," Dr. Sproot had told her two weeks ago, on her first inspection of the season. "You're a garden anarchist, Marta. I've been biting my tongue too long on this. You've openly defied every piece of advice I've given you over the past two years and turned your gardens into nothing more than a menagerie. I told you to get this and you got that. I told you to plant this here, and you planted it there. . . ."

"I didn't ignore everything, Doc Phil. Most of what you've taught me, I've done. It's just I wanted to have a garden with what *I* wanted in it, not someone else. And you haven't exactly been biting your tongue on this."

"So I've told you a dozen times. So what! Since you're my friend what you do reflects on me. And look at what you've done! You've turned your garden into a jungle. And don't call me Doc Phil. What is it with you and this 'Doc Phil' thing lately?"

"Ooops." Marta placed her fingertips gently on the offending lips. "I don't think it's a jungle at all, Doc Phil . . . I mean, Dr. Sproot."

"Well, it sure as heck is. Let me help you, Marta. Your gardens are doomed to disaster this year, but there's always next spring. You'll earn people's respect by tearing everything up and starting all over again, using me as your guide."

With that, Dr. Sproot wound a strand of clematis around her forefinger and yanked it hard, ripping two feet off the plant. She pulverized the flowers and vine, and tossed the mushy remains onto the nearest clump of hosta.

"Sorry, Marta, but I just hate clematis. HATE IT!"

"Hey, sweetums!" The shout from the back door interrupted the unpleasant memory of Dr. Sproot's savage delight as she ground the clematis to a pulp with her bare hands. It was her husband Ham. "Dr. Doofy on the phone for you. She says, 'Come quickly.' I say screw that nutcase and make like a snail."

Marta smiled, but found herself dropping her watering can and quick-stepping down the pathway toward the door.

"What in blue blazes is going on?" Dr. Sproot said breathlessly. "You have contacts that I don't, Marta. You should know, shouldn't you?"

"What are you talking about, Doc Phil? What's going on where?"

"Here in Livia. Where else? There is something horticultural afoot right here in our own community or I'm not a fully accredited doctor of horticulture. What is it? I'm sure you know, Miss Snoop. . . . And *don't call me Doc Phil!*"

"I don't know what you mean, Dr. Sproot," said Marta. Her voice trembled with guilt and uncertainty. "I don't know about anything afoot here in Livia. I truly don't."

Marta was fibbing. The Burdick's Best Yard Contest had been underway, though not yet publicly, since last Thursday. Marta knew about it within twenty-four hours of Mr. Burdick announcing it to his assembled staff. She wished she could tell Dr. Sproot, but that just wasn't possible; she had been sworn to secrecy by eight friends who had also been sworn to secrecy. Keeping a confidence might not mean much to a lot of the gadabouts loitering in Livia gardening circles these days, but it *did* mean something to Marta Poppendauber. You gave your word to someone and you kept it.

"You know darned well that something's in the air, Marta. Why did the Rose Maidens cancel their first monthly meeting in seventeen years? Huh? Why won't the board members answer the phone when I call them, or show me the courtesy of calling back? How come everywhere I go, gardeners are working their rear ends off for no apparent reason, especially considering that they're usually slacking off and going on vacations right about now? And how come people mumble and stutter and find an excuse to rudely walk away whenever I ask them what's up? Huh?"

"You got me, Dr. Sproot."

Dr. Sproot sighed. "Oh, all right, at least for now, my little friend. Never fear; I'll worm it out of you somehow. Now listen up, Marta, because there's something else. I've got a job for you. There's a place I want to scope out in the Bluegill Pond neighborhood. New gardeners. Untutored, from what I can tell. No pedigree, which is sort of insulting. I mean, who gave them permission . . . ? No connections in the usual gardening circles. But they've apparently had some little successes and people are talking about them like they just made a new Garden of Eden without the snake. I want to find out what it is they're doing that's got people talking about *them* and not *me*, fully accredited and as accomplished and experienced as I am. So, are you in?"

"Of course, Dr. Sproot. Just say the word. That's what best friends are for."

"I'll be in touch."

2

Of Cockleburs and Redwoods

George and Nan Fremont were on their way back from Burdick's PlantWorld, where they had just gone on a shopping spree. They bought two Miracle-Gro plant feeder refill bottles, a flat of petunias, a new three-quarter-inch and seventy-five-foot-long garden hose to replace the shoddy one they had bought on the cheap earlier, and which was prone to kinking, and a hanging basket of red begonias. George said the begonias looked like a poor man's roses, so why not just get some more roses?

"Because these are begonias and they're not a poor man's anything," Nan said. "Jeez, George, they don't look like roses at all. Well, maybe the blooms do, but not the leaves. I mean, look at the blessed leaves, George! No resemblance whatsoever. You would think you'd know that by now."

"Of course I know the difference, Nan-bee. I'm just yankin' your chain . . . or just yankin' your *stamen,* I should say. Ha-ha."

"I'll yank *your* stamen. So, we'll hang them on the big hook next to the bird feeders. With any luck they'll help us attract hummingbirds before all the phlox, monarda, and lilies take off. I can't believe how crowded Burdick's was today. I haven't seen it this packed since Easter."

"Yeah, Nan-bee, *jam*-packed!"

On the drive home George and Nan detoured, as they often would when not in a hurry, which they rarely were. Their round-about way took them toward Cabot Drive, home to some of their favorite Livia gardens.

"If you were reincarnated as a plant, which would you rather be, an iris or a pansy?" asked Nan. George swung onto Old Dan Troop Drive with a squeal of rubber that signified he was taking the turn too fast, but which he knew would delight the dangerous woman secretly living within Nan.

"Hmmmm," George said. "That's a tough one."

"No, it's not."

That meant this was probably another one of Nan's silly plant riddles. Not necessarily, though. Maybe it was a joke, something like yesterday's chuckle: "How is a philodendron like a tampon?" The answer didn't bear repeating, not even to think about, because it was about the stupidest thing he had ever heard. What was worse was that she had in her stock some *really* lewd plant jokes she'd spring on him now and again. What was the one about the dandelion and the cocklebur? And why was it all the smutty plant jokes had weeds in them?

But back to the riddle, if that was what it was. George squinched his face and puckered his lips as if to seal off any impulsive and idiotic answer that might come spilling out before he was able to give the matter sufficient thought.

Nan regarded him from her perch on the passenger seat with that unnervingly detached look of hers. That signified it was probably a joke designed to make him look foolish. If it was, he'd better remember the punch line, because Nan never told her jokes fewer than a half-dozen times. Was it more the mark of creeping senility that Nan kept telling her silly plant jokes over and over again or that he kept forgetting the answers to them?

"Uh, that's a really hard one there, Nan-bee. Give me a minute or two to think about it, will you?"

"What, you don't remember! Is it because you can't drive twenty-five miles an hour and think at the same time?"

"Something like that."

"Can't you go faster? Step on it, George. There's nothing around here to see."

George applied a tad more pressure to the accelerator pedal and pondered on what it would be like to be reincarnated as a plant. Bad karma or good to come back as a flower? Depends on whether you're brought back as an annual or a perennial, he thought. Come back as an annual, and you've got just one season to strut your stuff. You make that a full-bore blast, holding nothing back and blazing away color all summer long; that is, as long as your caregiver makes sure to plant you in the right place, then water and fertilize and keep those creepy semi-microscopic bugs off you. That's points for the pansy. A perennial, though. Jeez, a peony can live for decades. A schefflera, too. Why, that sprawling schefflera on the back patio had been around for years and, since they'd bring it inside for the winter, it was still flourishing. In fact, it was flourishing a little too well and would soon outgrow its clay pot. Hadn't he brought that as his only plant contribution to their union twenty-however many years ago? Yep, the schefflera might well outlive the both of them. That's points for the iris.

It suddenly disturbed George that if he came back as a plant, wouldn't he be a hermaphrodite? An *it?* Two sexes combined as one? Uggggh! George flinched in his seat, making the leather upholstery squeak. His palms moistened on the steering wheel. He must have looked stricken.

"What's wrong?" said Nan.

"Nothing. Still thinking."

But why limit yourself to measly backyard flora? What if

you came back as a redwood tree? Then you'd live thousands of years. If your seed happened to sprout within the confines of a state or federally protected area, you'd never have to worry about the teeth of those awful, whirring chain saws biting their way past your thick, armor-like bark—which had resisted bugs and blights for generations—and slicing into the depths of your pulpy innards. All you'd have to do is stand there, procreate, enjoy the view, and lord it over the rest of the forest. Not only that, ant-like humans would look up at you, and tell each other that—just think of it!—you had been taller than they are when Muhammad's conquering armies swept across the Arabian Peninsula.

"Redwood tree!" Out it came before he had a chance to stop it. That impulsive-idiot answer proving, once again, that the mouth is quicker than the brain.

"What?"

"Uh, redwood tree?"

"Redwood tree what?"

"I guess that's my surprise answer to your question." George braced himself for Nan's derisive retort.

"What question?"

They were cruising down Cabot Drive now. All of Nan's attention was focused on the profusion of plant life cultivated with varying degrees of skill and on scales ranging from the paltry to the grandiose on both sides of them. In such a state, she wouldn't be able to remember what she said ten minutes ago.

"Slow down, George!" He let his foot off the accelerator. The speedometer tumbled from thirty to five miles per hour, Fremont garden-cruising speed.

"Check out the bleeding hearts on the right," Nan said. "I can't believe they're still in full bloom." From out of the rock garden that had been assembled along both the east and west sides of the cement driveway of the otherwise unassuming green, wood-sided house at 3492 East Cabot sprouted a profusion of bleeding hearts, their pink, heart-shaped blooms dangling in the distance and sparkling in the late afternoon sun.

"Well done, gardener, whomever you might be," said Nan. That was very sportsmanlike, since the Fremonts' own bleeding hearts were just starting to peter out. Gardeners seemed to be out in their yards everywhere.

"What's with all the busy bees?" Nan said.

"No kidding," George said. "And still planting. Shouldn't everyone be going into maintenance mode about now?"

At the corner of Cabot and Fourth, the roses were just coming out, a little early this year it seemed to Nan. Explosions of the deepest 3-D red daubed the greenery at 3600 East Cabot: scores of Mr. Lincolns.

Next door were the red-orange Tropicanas and luscious pink Belle Amours. A few doors down from that, some people they knew—the Knights—were outside busily trimming their dwarf Korean lilacs now that the fragrant blossoms had faded and dropped. George tooted the horn, and they both waved to Gladys and Claude Knight, whose boys had played Livia Athletic Association Baseball with theirs back in Cub- and Midget-League days. Once they had moved on, Nan shook her head and snorted.

"They shouldn't trim those," she said. "They should let them grow nice and tall. Another year or two, then they can trim to make them thicker. Now, they're just going to look stunted."

3

Backyard Undercover

Dr. Sproot was trespassing. It was for the greater good that she did so, but the fact remained that here she was, prowling around in somebody's backyard without first obtaining permission.

She hadn't trespassed since she was a little girl. That was when she ran up to that spooky old unkempt house with the peeling paint and overgrown shrubs at the end of Cullen Street to look in the window. Then, she figured, she'd be able to see once and for all if Miss Fearington really was a banshee. Marta Poppendauber and Jennie Burlingame stood back at a safe distance egging her on. Jennie had overheard her parents call Miss Fearington a strumpet, which Marta said was a type of banshee from Germany that ate small children. That confirmed their suspicions that the house, which always seemed deserted and emitted an eerie red glow, was a banshee den.

Just as little Phyllis was poised to peek through the window into the red room, Miss Fearington, very obviously not a banshee but just as scary nonetheless, threw open her front door. She was dressed only in her bra and panties, with a filmy chemise barely draped over her shoulders, and was jiggling body parts like a Jell-O shaker jamboree. She yelled at Phyllis about being a Peeping Thomasina, and what did she think she was doing?

Phyllis hightailed it so fast she passed Jennie and Marta, who were screaming and throwing up their hands like a couple of born-again somethings, and ran into a tree, which had left a knot on her forehead for two weeks.

Fifty-two years later, here she was with Marta deep into the backyard of people she had not so much as been introduced to and without even an implied invitation. She knew they were the Fremonts and that what they were doing might well pose a clear and present danger to the venerable institution of gardening in Livia. As far as she could tell no one was home, so what was the harm in doing a bit of nosing around?

She tugged on the hem of Marta's short-sleeved blouse.

"C'mon," she said.

"C'mon?" Marta said. "C'mon where?"

"Why, we're going to inspect this yard from top to bottom. We're sleuths. Backyard spies. Won't that be fun, Marta?" Marta cringed and gently pulled away from her.

Wimp! thought Dr. Sproot. I'm stuck with a wimp who has no stomach for the gardening espionage business. If only Jennie were here with me now.

But, of course, Jennie could not be with her now, having passed away in her garden two years ago. She had been stricken with a mortal stroke as she was weeding the area around her Asiatic lilies, balloon flowers, and purple coneflowers just as they were bursting out in all their late-July glory. Her husband, Doob, had found her lying faceup. A limpid smile creased her face. The five-inch teeth of her weed fork pointed heavenward. She was one for the ages, that Jennie was. And died with her gardening clogs on! What a trouper!

"But can't we just look from here? This is . . . private property."

"So?" Dr. Sproot clenched her jaw and clutched at Marta's

blouse again. "So? Little scruples apply to little people, Marta. We are not little people, and we are here on a higher mission. Trust me, the end will justify the means."

"Please don't tear my blouse, Doc Phil," Marta whined. *Doc Phil! Doc Phil!* Dr. Phyllis Sproot hated the name even worse than she hated dandelions and root rot.

"*Doc-tor Sproot,* please, Marta," she said, releasing her pinch hold. She gazed upon Marta with contempt. She had been all agog about coming with her and checking out these Fremonts, Dr. Sproot reflected angrily. Now her natural timidity threatened to ruin the whole project. Look at her, in that stupid little floral-print blouse, with renderings of five particular plants and their names in notebook script spattered over it. How presumptuous to be wearing such a thing. It was as if she wanted to tell the world she was some sort of queen of the gardeners. Why, she, Dr. Phyllis Sproot, was the one who laid out Marta's first garden, and taught her the rudiments of soil preparation, proper mix of plants, and fertilization. And now her gardens were a mess. She had committed the cardinal gardening sin of allowing unwanted and contemptible genera to spread uncontrolled throughout her yard. It was horticultural hodgepodgery, that's what it was!

"What if somebody's . . . at home?"

Dr. Sproot flinched, as if she had just been buzzed by a passing wasp. What if they *were* home? What if they came running out the door armed with trowels, pitchforks, and razor-edged spades to turn these brazen trespassers into human plant mulch? Dr. Sproot squinted as she studied their back door. There was no sign of life. No lights shone through the uncovered windows. She would instruct Marta to keep a wary eye on the street in case someone pulled into the driveway, forcing them to duck for cover behind a tree or a bush. It was time to get moving and to get scared little Marta moving with her.

"So, what are you, Marta . . . a fraidy cat?"

Marta stiffened, then stood bolt upright on hearing that old childhood taunt.

"I am not a fraidy cat, Dr. Sproot," she said, a new resoluteness ringing in her steady voice. "You just go on ahead and I will follow."

"Watch for their return," Dr. Sproot said. "Cars pulling up along the curb or into the driveway. Be prepared to move bunny-quick!"

After a couple of cursory inspections over the last couple of years, Dr. Sproot had decided to get more serious about these Fremonts. She had been studying their backyard ever since the snow melted and the ground thawed.

She would park her car a couple of blocks away to avoid suspicion, then walk nonchalantly past the yard on the Payne Avenue side as if she were just a neighbor out for her constitutional. For a couple of amateurs they had done extraordinarily well. It galled her to admit it. She, after all, was Phyllis Sproot, Ph.D. in horticulture from the school that pretty much wrote the book on all the modern methods of gardening and lawn care. That would be the Honey Larson-Bayles School of Agronomy, which was a branch of the American Topsoil Institute.

When Dr. Sproot received her diploma in the mail from Honey herself after six weeks of studying mail-order materials and taking some really tough quizzes, there was enclosed as well a special letter designating her as top student of the year. The diploma came in a cardboard tube, a rolled-up parchment specially treated to look old and crinkled, and tied up with a gold-tasseled purple ribbon. She had flattened it out with the help of an iron, then framed and mounted it on the mantle over the fireplace. Dr. Phyllis Sproot. Everyone could call her that now.

That also meant it was only right and just that she should have the most beautiful grounds in Livia. So, why was it when people in north-central Livia talked about somebody's gardens it was the Fremonts who got all the attention?

Who were these Fremonts anyway?

Well, for one thing, they appeared to be ignoramuses. From what Dr. Sproot could see so far, they had not yet discovered the magnificence of yucca and the glories of the coreopsis-salvia-hollyhock blend. That comforted her somewhat. Without yuccas, and a coreopsis-salvia-hollyhock blend, they were just gardening hoi polloi.

It had come down in Dr. Sproot's family through the generations that 11 percent of your gardens, minimum, must be given over to yucca. More recently, she had added her own contribution to the gardening canons: the coreopsis-salvia-hollyhock blend! By her own calculation, arrived at after months of arduous study, and by virtue of her own special inspiration, a garden to be considered truly hallowed needed to be 71 percent coreopsis-salvia-hollyhock blend. She reckoned her gardens to have now reached their optimal composition of 87 percent yuccas and coreopsis-salvia-hollyhock blend. She leavened that with a smattering of roses, and four beds given over completely to dahlias. There was no need to go further.

Dr. Sproot realized such practices defied the conventional wisdom. They were at odds with the popular practices of the time. But that was what genius did! Those touched by genius took the knowledge available to them, ingested it, churned it around with their special enzymes, then ejected it as a moist, rich manure the likes of which had never been seen, and which sat there, steaming, for the common rabble to behold and admire.

Now, with Mort, that bozo of a husband, thankfully gone, and a generous life insurance benefit having come her way, Dr. Sproot was able to cut in half her work hours as the expert in high-priced Parisian perfumes at Cloud's department store, and devote more time to perfecting her gardening craft. Who knew what even more stunning wonders she could create if she could ditch that rotten day job altogether.

As Dr. Sproot mulled over this injustice, she realized that she was getting her introduction to another one. How magnificent, but how awful! What she and Marta were walking through reared up everywhere as a threat to her gardening hegemony. The depressing fact of the matter was there was a magical symmetry to the Fremonts' yard, a wonderful blending of styles, structures, and the short and tall and monochromatic and polychromatic that gave it a magnificence she had to acknowledge.

She and Marta continued on up the slope—clearly interlopers at this point—to examine the gardens. Here were all manner of pedestrian flora sprouting everywhere in an explosion of riotous colors. It was really quite remarkable, and it irritated her to be upstaged in such a manner by . . . by parvenus.

What especially bothered her was what Marta had told her after a little arm-twisting and a few veiled threats: that there was a big contest on the horizon, a contest to determine the royalty of gardening in Livia. She wanted in the worst way to win it. She deserved to win it! She was the one who had worked the hardest, at the books as well as the soil. She was the one who had her Ph.D., knew to the hour when to deadhead her finished blooms, and had taken it all so much further by pioneering the concept of yucca and coreopsis-salvia-hollyhock domination. Now, here was this!

"Ooooh, how pretty," Marta cooed. She and Dr. Sproot bent over to study a bed of alyssum that had just bloomed in a small rock garden and was spreading among the crevices between the carefully placed stones. A simple thing easily nurtured. But so lovely! And so well placed to appear as if it sprang naturally from between the rocks! Dr. Sproot wandered on, absorbed in her study.

How had they gained such skill? She had quizzed others

who had seen their gardens, and Marta, who knew people who were friends of people who were close to the Fremonts.

"They're just beginners with beginner's luck," Marta assured her. "As you say, they have no pedigree and no formal knowledge. It's like the time Ham and I went bowling after we hadn't been bowling for twenty-five years. I rolled two strikes in a row to start off, then it was downhill from there. Beginner's luck."

Marta said Dr. Sproot's own stature, her membership in the right clubs, and the path she had blazed across the new frontier of gardening would surely be good for something, maybe even first prize. And first prize would be rightfully hers! She wouldn't stand for second place. Wouldn't stand for it!

Marta kept shooting worried glances over her shoulder. A car trundled by on Payne Avenue, then a clanking pickup towing a trailer loaded with lawn mowers and trimmers.

"Maybe we should go now," Marta whispered so close to Dr. Sproot's ear that it tickled.

"Nonsense! We're too far gone now to turn back. Finish the job!" They approached a trellis. It was artfully constructed and stained with a thin, washed-looking white, smothered in pink and red roses climbing on their canes to the top, the buds ready to burst out in all their glory.

"What a charming trellis!" Marta said. "And it will be covered from top to bottom with such wonderful roses any day now!"

"So what?" said a testy Dr. Sproot, annoyed by Marta's awestruck and worshipful tone. "Anyone can do roses. Just put them in bright sunshine, water them, then let nature do the rest. And no yuccas or coreopsis-salvia-hollyhock blend anywhere to be seen. Who can win a contest without—ouch!"

Dr. Sproot had pushed a finger into one of the cane's sharp thorns until it broke the skin and a drop of blood oozed out. Marta smiled meekly, as if privately enjoying the sight of her blood.

As they continued their slow traverse of the backyard, Marta quietly exulted in the simple, expansive, and varied beauty of the gardens, while Dr. Sproot labored to commit to memory every plant, flowering bloom, and pencil point of green pushing up through the carefully raked soil, and every little arbor and rock garden.

"The judges will see this as a cluttered mess when a carefully conceived and formatted concentration of the proper types of flowers—such as mine on yuccas and coreopsis-salvia-hollyhock blend—is what really matters."

Marta nodded noncommittally.

With the rose trellises on their right, they inspected a luxuriant bed of hosta. Dr. Sproot shook her head in disdain.

"The true sign of a novice," she said. "Anyone can do hosta. You have to almost *try* to kill hosta."

It was at that point that a wonderful thought occurred to Dr. Phyllis Sproot. Since the Fremonts were obviously not connected to Livia's gardening circles, wasn't there a good chance they would not be informed of whatever contest it was that was coming up? Or, maybe, even if informed, they would have no interest in it? Who would be sponsoring this contest anyway? Might it be Burdick's? Really, that would be the only possibility, as Burdick's was the only gardening emporium of the requisite size in Livia. It wouldn't be any of the gardening clubs; she had membership in all of those. It must be Burdick's and why hadn't she been told it was Burdick's? Marta wasn't saying. She insisted that she was bound by oath to tell no more.

They walked on toward a split-rail fence and the rather elaborate arbor and patch of woods beyond.

"What in heaven's name is that *thing?*" said Dr. Sproot, as they both stopped to examine a lifelike, painted woodcarving that reared up suddenly between them and the house.

"Why, it's a tree sculpture," said Marta. "Someone carved it out of a tree trunk. I wonder who it's supposed to be. Isn't *that* something?"

"It is grotesque," Dr. Sproot barked as they continued on through the swinging fence gate. "If that's not stark testimony to these people's bad taste, I don't know what is. To blot their gardens with such a monstrosity. Well, I never . . ."

Having arrived at the strip of woods that marked the end of the gardens, Dr. Sproot and Marta turned to look back in silence on what they had just passed. Spreading out across the hill that sloped gently down to the street was a wonderland of the gardener's craft. Who could do better? Marta sighed. Dr. Sproot scowled.

What was this? To Dr. Sproot's left were two sweet-smelling, medium-sized shrubs, adorned with dozens of menacing, erect, white flowers that looked like wide-mouthed blowguns aiming their poison darts directly at her. And that divine, seductive, and deadly scent!

"Angel's trumpets!" Dr. Sproot gasped.

"Aren't they just gorgeous!" Marta said. "I want them for my garden!"

"Don't be an idiot, Marta! They are deadly poisonous, that's what they are! And mind-altering!"

Dr. Sproot had to catch her breath. She felt faint. She was inhaling angel's trumpet fumes; did that mean she'd start hallucinating?

"Get away, Marta! Quickly!"

Marta scampered to where Dr. Sproot had moved, farther downwind of the bushes, where Dr. Sproot felt they could breathe more freely. Marta was exhilarated and breathless with the joy of discovery. That annoyed Dr. Sproot, who figured it was more appropriate that she should be shocked.

A noisy rattletrap of a car pulled up suddenly along the Payne Avenue curbside.

"Run!" Dr. Sproot screeched.

Then, forgetting her studies, her dignity, and Marta, she clomped clumsily along the edge of the woods down another slope that contoured steeply down to Sumac Street. Halfway down the slope Dr. Sproot heard a thud, then slipped and stumbled. She quickly pulled herself into a ball, which she had read somewhere was a way to avoid serious injury when you're tumbling down a hill, and rolled all the way to the street. She picked herself up, unhurt, at the curb, and brushed off the thatch and pine needles that were clinging to her hair and clothes. Then, she looked around to see whether she was being observed. There was Marta, sitting next to the weeping willow that had abruptly arrested her departure. Her legs were splayed out in a way no one her age could consider demure. She was furiously rubbing her forehead and moaning.

Dr. Sproot could not be bothered by Marta's juvenile antics right now because she was fretting too much about what she had just seen. After another perfunctory brushing off, she ignored Marta's pathetic whimpering and strode off purposefully down the street toward her car.

4

The Tippler's Guide to Gardening

The Fremonts plunked themselves down in the mesh-fabric deck chairs on their backyard patio and eagerly opened a bottle of their house wine, the excellent 2005 vintage Sagelands merlot.

There had been a little excitement while they were gone. Cullen, the younger of their two sons, told them a middle-aged woman he didn't recognize had come to the door rubbing a bump on her head and asking for some ice and an aspirin. She told him she got lost in a daydream, strayed off her usual route, and *blam-o,* walked straight into the telephone pole out front. He obliged and somewhat grudgingly gave her a ride home, which ended up being in cul-de-sac land more than two miles away.

"And her name was . . . ?" Nan said.

"Mrs. Daffodil?" George and Nan snorted. "And she had to think about it for a minute when I asked her. She seemed really squirmy and nervous, too."

"Ha!" George said. "That just might be a pseudonym. I wonder if she was on the lam. Social Security rip-off schemer?

Gray Panthers dropout gone rogue? Maybe she was casing the joint for valuable, hand-woven tea cozies."

Nan chuckled. "Knit."

"What?"

"Knit. That would be hand-*knit* tea cozies, George. You don't weave tea cozies. Hmmm. She was probably just embarrassed about walking into the telephone pole, and wanted to remain anonymous. Remember the time you did that, George?"

"As if it were yesterday, Nan-bee."

"And you were afraid you had suffered a concussion, but didn't want to tell anybody because of how foolish it would make you look?"

"I don't remember that part."

"Proves my point. Memory impairment caused by a collision between noggin and telephone pole. Maybe we should call the phone company. That telephone pole has clearly become a hazard to the neighborhood."

It only took a half glass of Sagelands to burn off the mild vexation of the Mrs. Daffodil mystery. As the wine supplanted pure mental acuity with a much less taxing disembodied buzz, George and Nan looked out upon their backyard and reflected on what a treasure it was. What they had created was a modest chip of hypercultivated real estate, constituting two-thirds of their three-quarter-acre lot in a solid and unassuming neighborhood populated by Livia's middle ranks. If a pale imitation of Delaware's Winterthur, Alabama's Bellingrath, and Pennsylvania's Longwood, it was still a marvel of the gardener's craft, not only to them, but to a small, enthusiastic segment of Livia's aging population.

Neighbors in awe of the handiwork bursting everywhere through the ground approached them meekly for gardening tips and any other dribs and drabs of wisdom that might bring comfort to their otherwise distressed lives. They included such luminaries as Jeff Fitch, Livia's plenipotentiary liaison to sister city Ogbomosho, Nigeria, and *mondo bizarro* hard-drinking local songstress and composer Pat Veattle, who wrote the often-misinterpreted official city song, "Livia Is for Livers."

No one was as magically transformed in the Fremonts' backyard as Deanne and Sievert Mikkelson. The Mikkelsons were a timid, brittle, childless couple on the cusp of middle age, but seeming much older. Their faces sagged and their bodies bowed with unspoken cares and unseen burdens that no one could identify.

It was one day in midsummer last year when they approached hesitantly from the street at the Fremonts' beckoning. George and Nan, fortified into a heightened sociability by a tall glass of strongly mixed gin and tonic featuring the magnificent Bombay Sapphire gin, had to shout, cajole, and almost threaten the Mikkelsons to cause them to swerve from their appointed route, walk slowly up the driveway, and delicately negotiate the pea gravel steps on their approach to what they feared was sure perdition.

Lowering themselves gingerly onto the Fremonts' deck chairs, the Mikkelsons initially waved off all offers of refreshment. They soon discovered, however, that a bombardment of bonhomie coming from the Fremonts was darned near irresistible.

"Well, I suppose just a touch wouldn't hurt us," Sievert said. Deanne nodded meekly. With that, George uncorked a bottle of Sagelands, which the Mikkelsons proceeded to treat like ice water served up in a sauna. They knocked down their first glasses in one big concurrent glug, both of them wiping their mouths with the back of their hands and sighing contentedly, in harmony.

"Could we be so bold as to ask for a refresher?" Sievert asked.

"Oh, yes!" Deanne said. "Oh, yes!" The second glass went down the same as the first. So did a third, which Nan tried to fill only halfway to the lip of their wineglasses.

"Oh, no you don't," Deanne gurgled. "I see what you're up to. Fill mine to the brim!"

"Mine, too!" cried Sievert. "No stinting now. We're your guests."

Nan and George weren't quite sure whether to be pleased and amused, or somewhat alarmed. Here, clearly, was a couple unaccustomed to the grape, but who, given the opportunity, could guzzle it down like Roman sybarites. They could well be perched on the precarious precipice of alcohol poisoning. But how did you cut off these Mikkelsons? They'd been transformed by three glasses of merlot from the shy, vulnerable mice to the bold, blustering lions of the neighborhood. They might be capable of anything!

"More wine, spody-ody!" yelled Sievert, on polishing off his third glass in two big, violent gulps. He slammed the wineglass down on the table, sending a hairline fracture threading across the base of the stem.

"Me three!" cried Deanne with a shrill cackle as she balled her left hand into a tight fist and began punching at invisible targets in the air. "Yep! Keep 'em comin', barkeep." Nan shot an icy, semi-panicked glance at George. That was her signal for him to figure out a solution to this unfolding drunken-Mikkelsons problem. The lightbulb that occasionally went on in George's brain flickered for a moment, then shone forth in all its slightly dimmed luminosity.

"Here's something that just occurred to me," he said. "We have a special vintage we're looking for someone to try. It's very strong and very rare. A wine magazine has called it the finest wine from the best grapes ever grown. The grapes actually come from a very tall hill overlooking the craggy coast of Oregon. They're called winter surf grapes. Very rare."

Nan pursed her lips and arched her eyebrows into one of those quizzical Nan looks.

"We consider you special guests. Would you like to try it? There's a proviso here. The alcohol content is very, very high, so high, in fact, that it's almost impossible for the palate and brain to detect. Also, this is especially fine wine, very precious, and we can only afford to spare it on those who will properly appreciate it."

The Mikkelsons, their heads wobbling like baseball bobble-heads, looked at each other and chortled.

"Of course, damn it!" screamed Sievert.

"Bring it on, mo-fo!" Deanne shouted. With Nan visibly confused, George gathered up the Mikkelsons' glasses and ducked quickly through the back door. He soon emerged carrying the two glasses, now topped off with burgundy liquid, and perilously close to spilling over the rims.

"Al-rrrigght!" the Mikkelsons screamed in unison. They sloshed half their drinks onto themselves and the tabletop, laughed heartily, then dispensed with the remaining contents in a long, noisy gurgle.

"Ahhhh," said Sievert. "That's delicious!"

"Doggonit," said Deanne. "Doggonit. Doggonit. Dog-g-g-gonit."

Nan and George smiled politely.

"More?" asked George, winking at Nan, whose eyes had widened in alarm. After seven rounds and two trips each inside to the bathroom, the Mikkelsons had undergone their second transformation. Perky, talkative, and fidgeting to beat the band, they had nevertheless lost the monster edge that threatened to turn them into droolingly spastic boozehounds incapable of getting up from their chairs without farting or falling over. A certain shy, yet restless demeanor had been restored to them. They began blurting out long-winded and very rapid apologies for their behavior, rose abruptly, almost upsetting the table in the process, apologized some more, and shook hands three times each with Nan and George. Then, off they went, storming down the steps feeling braver and happier than they had been a half hour earlier.

"Good Lord, George, what did you do to them?"

"Nothing. I just filled their wineglasses with Cullen's power drink, Cranberry PowerPressPlus. Twice the sugar, three times the caffeine of a regular Coke. Looks like wine, smells and tastes *nothing* like wine. It's the power of suggestion that did it."

After that, the Mikkelsons were frequent visitors. They eagerly lapped up the Fremonts' hospitality, and even offered to pay for their prodigal appetites, with George and Nan graciously ignoring them. They had not, however, shown up at all so far this summer. Puzzled and perhaps a little hurt and concerned, the Fremonts wondered whether Sievert and Deanne had returned to their abstemious ways or, worse, discovered their own special vintage, pounding it down by the barrel all day and all night, their lives wrecked by that first sally into the epicurean sinfulness of the Fremont backyard.

It was on the previous Tuesday that the Fremonts had finally spotted the Mikkelsons. They were strolling confidently down the street, shyly waving at them, but continuing on their way, despite the Fremonts' beckoning gestures. It was as Deanne displayed her full profile to them that the Fremonts saw why the Mikkelsons would be avoiding them for a while: she was very visibly pregnant.

The backyard that worked such delightful sorcery on its visitors didn't feature anything particularly fancy or exotic. Nan and George had mostly planted an array of flowers, bushes, vines, and grasses that would be familiar to anyone with a rudimentary knowledge of gardening. It was all in the arrangement, the scope of the project, and the health and vigor of all that grew there.

Hostas of four different varieties filled many of the shady places. The split-rail fence that divided the backyard into two roughly even parts was almost hidden on the south side by pink hydrangeas. There were four bleeding hearts and an equal number of jack-in-the-pulpits. Next to the six-foot wood fence that separated them from the Grunions' backyard rose variegated dogwoods, two burning bushes that exploded in scarlet in the fall, and five lilac bushes that were now eight feet high. Nan had to keep a careful eye on George, who had an itch to perform major plant surgery just to show that his circa 1920-model pruning shears could still do good service.

"No hacking away at the lilacs, you ninny, or else they won't come back for years," she would scold him, but every year he'd dig out those old shears. He'd scrape off the rust, sharpen the blades, and approach the lilacs, snicker-snacking away, only to be turned back by Nan, who would have to interpose herself between him and his intended victims.

A flagstone path led to the north edge of the property, divided from the Fletchers' place by a strip of woods. It ended in an arbor where the flagstones were set in a large rectangle surrounded by paper birches, crab apples, and rabbit-nibbled and stunted alpine currants. A simple wooden bench had been set for those contemplative moments that would occasionally arise. Steps fashioned out of pressure-treated-pine railroad ties and pea gravel rose from the driveway to the tetragonal cement patio. The patio, furnished with its glass-topped table, L-shaped bench, four chairs, and outdoor grill, was the heart of the backyard.

Impatiens, alyssum, petunias, phlox, and two varieties of ornamental grasses bordered the steps. Two small arbors with big, arched trellises jutted out from the edge of the patio, where there was ample midday sunlight. As June advanced, climbing rosebushes would any day now smother them in red, yellow, and pink.

On the other side of the patio, where the light was less direct, there was another latticework trellis, also painted white, and covered in the clinging vines of violet-flowering clematis. Two bridal wreath spirea bushes flourished in another one of the spots where sunlight fell unchecked by any obstruction. Then, there were the angel's trumpets, fragrantly seductive, yet appalling to George, who continually fretted over their reputations as deadly hallucinogens.

Other flower beds sprouted more impatiens and alyssum, as well as purple coneflowers, monarda, and assorted irises and lilies. There were additional flowers, planted in accordance with the advice of the numerous texts, magazines, flyers, and Internet postings George and Nan had consulted over the years as their backyard gardens expanded. Even now, they had trouble remembering the names of some of them.

Sprinkled throughout were late-blossoming mums and sedum to ensure the backyard's liveliness as high summer began to drift toward autumn. The idea was that something would be flowering in the backyard at all times—May through August, and sometimes even September. As the season moved toward the middle of June, the first wave of blooms has already passed. They were in the midst of a new one, which would also have its own brief heyday before giving way to the riotous eruptions of July.

Four bird-feeding stations were situated around the backyard. The Nyger thistle feeder for the finches was suspended by wire from a little board hammered into the trunk of the young silver maple bordering the patio and adjacent to the rose trellises.

There was a large, green, house-shaped feeder filled with a variety of bird feed—black oilers, white millet, safflower seeds, and peanuts. This feeder came equipped with an adjustable counterweight so that the perch shield would snap shut over the feeding portals when anything too big—say, a squirrel—managed to climb onto it.

Adjoining the finch-feeding station was a red, bell-shaped

hummingbird feeder loaded with nectar water and hanging from a curved and hooked planter pole stuck into the ground.

Farther away, at the east end of the property, was a tray of orange slices and jelly suspended from a similar pole placed next to the variegated dogwoods. This was meant to attract finicky Baltimore orioles, who always seemed to be finding tastier fare elsewhere.

The Fremonts counted thirty-two species of birds they had positively identified in their backyard and adjoining woods. Most recently, a rufous-sided towhee had made a brief inspection of the main feeder just as George was looking out at it through the kitchen window. His ejaculation of joy brought Nan to the window. Nan then plucked the *Peterson Field Guide to Eastern Birds* from its perch on the windowsill, made a positive identification, and duly noted it in their bird sightings log.

The Fremonts lived on the corner lot, intersection of Payne Avenue and Sumac Street, north-central one-sixth section of Livia. Livia was a large suburb of the much larger city of St. Anthony, fifteen miles to the north. It marked the northern reaches of the Big Turkey River Valley, which divided it from its more populous and affluent neighbor—Macomber—to the south.

Their lot was on a hill that sloped steeply down to Sumac, and much more gradually to Payne. Beyond Sumac, the land dropped down farther to Bluegill Pond, which was actually a lake of considerable size.

Their house had been constructed haphazardly over the decades. There was a central portion built in 1955 over the ruins of an old two-story farmhouse, then two additions were thrown on in 1962 and 1974, respectively. About an eighth of the lot on its north side constituted the strip of woods. At various points along the periphery of the lot and adjacent to the house were silver maples, ashes, a spruce, two sugar maples, which were the pride of the neighborhood when they flamed orange and a rich burgundy in the autumn, and two huge locusts.

Their children were aged twenty (Ellis), eighteen (Cullen), and seventeen (Sis, or Sister, known officially and when in trouble as Mary). The Fremonts voted their conscience, paid their taxes, and rooted lustily for the major league St. Anthony Muskies. They attended the Please-Redeem-Me Lutheran Church, which represented a breakaway sect of the Evangelical Lutheran Church in America that thought the Triune God should include four more parts—earth, wind, water, and agricultural commodities. They complained about the weather, just like everyone else in this part of the country.

They had thrown themselves with much enthusiasm into the college search for Ellis, who had just finished his first year at a good Lutheran school, Augustus-of-the-Prairies, in a bordering state, and Cullen, who was headed to Dartmouth, and encouraged sis's pronounced musical proclivities (she was "allstate" trombonist two years in a row).

All of this was important. What threatened to eclipse all other things, though, was their gem, their precious possession, their fourth child, assuming a purportedly inanimate object can be thought of in such a way: their backyard. They would never have actually *said* such a thing. They would hardly have allowed themselves to think it, though in moments of pure self-illumination they figured it loomed so large in their lives as a way of preparing them for the coming loss of all their children to distant colleges.

"It's going to be our legacy, really," said George that lazy late Saturday afternoon in early June, as they relaxed in their patio chairs under a cobalt sky.

"And they're so happy with what we've done," Nan said. "Just look at their lustrous color, how they assert themselves.

We've given them the confidence to grow. It's a sort of self-esteem that comes through a positive vibration of how we've treated them. Give them the proper care and love and that gives them the inner strength to be what they were meant to be. We've empowered them, George!"

"Hmm," said George, who thought this was all pretty much balderdash, but figured it didn't take that much of a sacrifice on his part to humor his wife in this regard. "I get what you mean . . . yeah."

"I'm going to start working on my Zen. I think it's good for the plants to be in a Zen-like state when you approach them, especially when you have to prune or deadhead. You should probably do that, too. Be at peace with yourself. You tend to be kind of herky-jerky and enthusiastic when you approach them with anything sharp. They could get the sense that you enjoy it and have a destructive impulse coursing through you. Don't want that! Serenity is what they want to feel. They want you to emanate serenity."

"I'll work on my serenity," said George. "Maybe I'm not drinking enough."

"Do you think they can hear us talking?"

"Uh, sure, I suppose they could."

"Of all our plants, which do you think are the most sensate?"

"The most what?"

"Sensate. Being able to have a physical sensation."

"Jeez," George mumbled. "How do I know? Uh, how about the roses?"

"You're right! Very good, George!"

A warm breeze straight out of the west whooshed through the leaves and gently tousled Nan's graying hair. She clinked the ice in her glass and took a healthy sip of gin and tonic, which had been broken out and mixed weakly to supplement the wine. She silently appreciated the added lime juice George had squirted into the drink. And, oh, there was the rock-like cold of the ice cubes and that fizzing freshness of the tonic water. Only real men could mix a drink like that, she reflected joyfully.

She looked around, gathering in the subtle and showy manifestations of her gardening skills, and smiled.

"We need more lilac bushes. And I'm going to get Jerry to build me another trellis right over there and plant a couple more rosebushes."

Nan pointed her drink to a sunny corner of the lot, where woods met lawn, and which had been turned into the compost pile. That was a sore point between Nan, who hated its ugliness, and George, who lived and breathed the need for compost.

"And then, our little Oriental garden will go over there." The drink hand swerved unsteadily to indicate that part of the backyard that was between the back of the house and the shed that housed the lawn mower, trimmer, and any number of tools, fertilizers, bikes, and sleds.

"That costs money, you know," George said. "I'm getting just a little worried about the money situation here, Nan-bee."

"We can do a lot of it ourselves. I've seen books that show you how to do it."

"Okeydokey, consider it done, Nan-bee."

George pushed back his chair, stood up, and clinked the ice cubes around in a drink already in desperate need of freshening. Nan held out her own. Amazing how quickly those damned ice cubes melted, diluting the drink! A stiff breeze kicked up. Partially blocked by the house, the front of which bore the full brunt of any big wind, snowstorm, and downpour, the blunted wind got here by swirling at them from over the roof and around the sides. Nowhere in the world, they both thought simultaneously, was the wind so frisky as in their backyard.

"Can we get moving on that refill?" said Nan, as a cloud, tendrils flying, thrust its purpling base across the sun, covering her briefly in startling shade.

5

Among the Weeds

Bringing Marta back into the fold as her special confederate would take all the diplomatic skill Dr. Sproot could muster. That would be quite a challenge since she had no such skill. Her gifts were more in the area of bullying, tongue-lashing, brittle sarcasm, and other forms of overt intimidation. Had Dr. Sproot been the seigneur of a fourteenth-century feudal fiefdom, peasants who missed a single bimonthly tithe would have been boiled by inches in oil and offending courtiers fed in very small pieces of hacked-off flesh to the pack of household wolfhounds.

Seeing as how this was twenty-first-century Livia, Dr. Sproot had to settle for being the local gardening community's token douche bag.

But how to deal with Marta?

At first, she tried to call her. One message after another went unanswered. Seven attempts left Dr. Sproot furious and itching to sputter insults into Marta's answering machine. She had never been treated by her so-called friend in such an off-hand manner. Clearly, she'd have to try a new strategy.

So, it came to this: Dr. Sproot would have to drive over to Marta's house and apologize for something for which she was utterly blameless. She steeled herself for the ten-minute drive and what she hoped wouldn't be an exercise in groveling. Still, grovel she would if she had to; Marta was too important to be allowed to slip away. She would even drink her stupid tea if that was what it took. Tea, thought Dr. Sproot as she strangled the steering wheel, was for lazybones wimps.

It was from Marta that Dr. Sproot would have to pry loose all the details about the big gardening contest on the horizon and the inside dope on those gardening parvenus, the Fremonts. No one else would do. That's because, feared and respected as she was, Dr. Sproot was also disliked, which didn't exactly invite the confidences of her fellow gardeners. And it was Marta, who either because she was too scared to resist or couldn't break the tenuous but long-lasting bonds of their friendship, could once again be brought in thrall to her and compelled to do her bidding. But some delicacy was required here, Marta being the skittish and sensitive type.

"How could you do that to me?" said Marta, pouring them both tea after motioning for Dr. Sproot to sit down with her on the living room sofa.

Dr. Sproot fought back the urge to sneer at the prissy little scalloped teacups and saucers, which were decorated with stupid little pansies.

"Hmmmmm?" said Marta, who then noisily slurped at her tea in an annoying manner Dr. Sproot judged to be intended as a penance foisted upon her. "How could you just leave me there knocked almost senseless with a big knot on my head, two miles from home, and no way to get there?"

She gingerly placed her teacup back on its saucer, sputtered something incomprehensible, and began to cry. Dr. Sproot took Marta's hand in hers and petted it gently.

"It was an accident, darling," she said. "You didn't see the tumble I took. It knocked me out of my senses. I think I also inhaled some fumes from those poisonous plants. Remember those? Those angel's trumpets. Remember how I saved you from inhaling them, but then I got a snootful myself? That left me acting somewhat strangely, disoriented. I do apologize, Marta; I really do."

Marta's wet eyes flickered. She picked up her teacup by its dainty porcelain handle and took a slow-motion sip from it as her pinkie pointed rigidly toward the ceiling in the most irritating fashion. Dr. Sproot couldn't help but sense that Marta was flipping her the bird in a secret way that only Marta and her fellow gardening nincompoops would understand.

Dr. Sproot smiled and reached gingerly for her teacup. She touched it to her lips, and lifted the cup quickly to pour a big slug of molten lava into her mouth.

Fire alarm! Dr. Sproot waved her free hand in furious agitation as her face went crimson. The other hand flung the offending teacup to shatter against its saucer on Marta's coffee table. Flapping both hands like a pair of stunted wings on a flightless bird, Dr. Sproot managed to spew the scalding brew in a shotgun spray onto the coffee table, the sofa, the carpeting, and even Marta herself.

"Aaarrrgh!" she shrieked, shaking her head now and gulping in pain. "Marta! Marta! Get me some water! Some water, Marta! Why did you make that shitpissin' tea so hot!"

"My goodness!" cried Marta, looking down at her dress, which was blotched with brown spat-out tea. "My goodness! Oh! Oh! Oh!"

"Get me some water, Marta!" croaked Dr. Sproot. "Or milk. Get milk. Hurry, Marta; my mouth's on fire! Or honey! Marta, get me some honey! I'm burned!" Tears of pain and wounded dignity trickled down Dr. Sproot's rouge-caked cheeks as she quivered and sucked in heavy drafts of cooling air, then moaned in pain. Marta jumped up from the sofa and disappeared into her kitchen. About five minutes later, after Dr. Sproot's searing pain had diminished to more of a lingering irritation, Marta reappeared holding a large glass of milk with some light caramel coloring at the bottom.

"It's about time!" Dr. Sproot said. "What did you do, fix yourself a meal while I, a burn victim needing first aid, was sitting out here helpless and suffering?"

"It's laced with honey," said Marta, handing the glass to Dr. Sproot. "Just the thing for a sore throat. I had a hard time finding the honey. You know Ham. He likes to put things back in weird places. The honey was actually sitting next to a couple of rolls of toilet paper in the bathroom. Tee-hee-hee . . . now drink it all the way down. Get all that honey at the bottom."

"It's not a sore throat, you idiot!" said Dr. Sproot, her voice broken into a cracked hoarseness. "It's a damaged one! You damaged my throat, Marta. People get sued for damaging people's throats."

"But you didn't swallow it, did you? It looks to me like all the tea wound up on the rug, and on the coffee table, and on my dress, which I just got back from the dry cleaners."

"Yes, I did, you brutish woman. I swallowed enough of it to damage my throat and my vocal cords and my esophagus, which means I might have to restrict my diet to yogurt and applesauce in the future. . . . I don't know if I can even drive home."

"Should I call 911, Dr. Sproot?"

"No, I'll drive myself to urgent care. Then, they'll refer me to a specialist. Then, God knows what will happen. Surgery? Therapy? How could you do this to me, Marta?"

"But the tea wasn't *that* hot, Dr. Sproot. It's how I always make it."

"It doesn't matter what *you* like!" said Dr. Sproot, her ramrod frame rocked into lankiness with explosive sobs. "It matters what *I* can stand. And through your unforgiveable thoughtlessness, I've been damaged, maybe permanently."

Actually, the honey milk was doing good service. It had

soothed Dr. Sproot's mouth, which had not been burned at all. Her throat was fine; not a single drop of the hot tea had touched it. Inspired by a solution to her dilemma, which had just been handed to her on a saucer, Dr. Sproot chose to ignore these developments.

"I might never sing again," she moaned.

"Sing?" Marta said. "I've never heard you sing before."

"Well, I do. It's only recently that someone told me I had talent of the vocal sort. You wouldn't understand, Marta, not being artistically inclined. Now, I'll never know. One day, who knows, I could have sung at the Met, or maybe even La Scala. Not one of the principal singers, of course, but someone in the chorus. Now . . ." Dr. Sproot noisily stifled a sob she had managed to manufacture with considerable skill. Marta, by now bewildered and scared, stared down at her tea-blotched carpeting.

"We might have been friends for many years, Marta Poppendauber, but you have brought me to harm through your own simpleton's carelessness. I might have to sue you. I'm sure my mouth's blistering right now with third-degree burns. I'd better be getting over to urgent care. If I stick around here any longer, heaven knows what else might happen. I might get killed."

Dr. Sproot rose up from the sofa to tower over Marta, and loomed there, five-foot-eleven-and-a-half inches of calculating imperial rectitude gazing down with implacable contempt upon her miserable friend.

"Please don't sue us, Dr. Sproot," Marta moaned. "Please don't sue us. I swear I didn't think the tea was that hot. I swear it! Please don't sue us, Dr. Sproot. What can I do to make this right, Dr. Sproot? What can I do?"

"Well, now that you mention it, there is a matter in which I could use your assistance, Marta. It's a gardening matter, which I'm sure you will enjoy." She sat back down on the sofa and folded her hands primly across her lap. She smiled benignly at the miserable Marta. "In fact, it's a matter with which you are already quite familiar."

"But . . . but . . . don't you have to run over to urgent care?"

"Urgent care can wait. We've got more pressing matters to deal with."

6

Sprinkling

George occasionally enjoyed the backyard for its value as a latrine.

For some time, he had been in the practice of urinating alfresco when the urge overtook him. In matters such as these, George felt the community standards of acceptable behavior didn't really apply. What was the harm? Going through the doorway, walking across the dining room, negotiating a hallway, and having to open another door seemed like a long way to go and a lot to do to perform such a simple act of nature.

The strip of woods, though farther away than the bathroom in terms of the usual measures of distance, had the advantage of *seeming* closer, and the thought of spattering his bodily wastes all over the underbrush held a particular fascination for him. If he happened to hit an unsuspecting rabbit or squirrel, then so much the better! In fact, once he got to his spot, he would unzip, unravel, then wait for a minute, still and quiet, in case one of the backyard's offending pests would come within range.

To Nan, it was utterly incongruous that someone could pay homage to the aesthetics of a place—a place he had been instrumental in creating!—then deface it in such a crude manner. And how weird! She would no more squat in their outdoors than she would in the middle of Chalmers Square in downtown St. Anthony during summer lunch hour. It was hard enough to imagine the members of the animal kingdom doing their business in sheer ignorance of what they might be befouling. She always tried to stop George before he committed such a desecration.

"It's the woods I'm going to, not the hosta, or the roses, or any of the arbors," George said. "I'm technically out of the backyard. When I go to the bathroom *in* the bathroom, I'm not messing up the living room, am I?"

"It's still disgusting," she said. "Our woods are the backdrop to our beautiful backyard setting. And now, when you do this, it's like squirting mustard on the *Mona Lisa*." George pondered this a moment, not at all sure he caught the gist of the comparison, other than urine and mustard having a sort-of-close color connection, and wasn't there a ficus in the background of that masterpiece? Soon, Nan recognized the telltale signs of an impending pit stop. George bounced the balls of his feet on the cement patio floor, cast nervous glances from side to side, and fingered his zipper.

"No way," she said firmly. "You can go straight to the bathroom, which is closer anyway. You're not an animal, George. What would someone think if they saw you?"

"Nobody will see me," said George, rising from the chair, determined not to give in to Nan when control over his manly discharges was at stake. "I'm discreet. I make sure no one's walking by on the street. I walk a little ways in the woods so I can be screened from the backyard. It's perfectly private."

"What if there are children back there in those woods? The neighborhood children have been known to play there, you know."

"If there are, then I will return, and repair to the bathroom. Anyway, what's the harm in watching a responsible adult perform a natural function? Why should that be threatening to anyone?"

"Not threatening to *any*one. Threatening to you, who could be charged with exposing himself to small children."

"We should live in France. I understand that in France, they're not so uptight about a simple matter of urinating. They do it wherever they need to without being squeamish about it. I've heard they have little kiosks in Paris, right on the sidewalks where you can just stop and relieve yourself."

"When you live in France, you can urinate like Frenchmen do. When you're here, you need to pay heed to our uptight morality and sense of decorum."

"Not now, if you don't mind. I've really got to go."

"George . . ."

"No, I'm going to unload like a free man. I am a child of nature, doing things the natural way. I'm headed to the outdoor privy." Off George strode, leaving Nan shaking her head in dismay and disgust.

"Animal!" she grunted after him.

George was never one, no matter what his free-spirit proclivities, to just cut loose and let 'er rip. He knew he was being a little too daring for the neighborhood and did whatever it took to make sure that when he pulled down his zipper and prepared for action, he would be the only witness to the endeavor.

He walked a good ten paces into the woods, making sure he was being at least partly shielded on all sides. There were no cars coming down Sumac that he could hear, no noises from next door, which wouldn't have been relevant anyway because the Grunions couldn't see him through their fence, and no sign of life in the woods apart from the rustlings of a few birds and squirrels. Down came his zipper and out came the instrument of his purpose. Soon, a line of deep yellow arced across three feet of forest clutter. The relief seemed so much better, so much more palpable, here in the woods. George sighed as the stream subsided into a few final drips he wagged off onto the leaves of a sapling immediately under him. Just as he felt one last, unexpected discharge coming up, and prepared for a final shake and a return to the confines of modern convention, he saw them: two young children, appearing like elves out of nowhere, and staring at him. The sudden apparition startled him into wetting his pants and his hands.

"Hi," he said. They kept staring at him, frozen into a stone-like stillness. He could see that they were a boy and a girl, but not the neighbor kids, and not anyone he knew. Suddenly, their faces puckered and off they ran, screaming through the woods, in the opposite direction. Quickly, and with trembling hands, George resheathed, and fumbled with his zipper, then walked backward slowly toward the backyard, as if retreating from a dangerous animal he'd been warned never to turn and run from. Nan was waiting for him at the fence.

"What on earth was that screaming about?"

"Some kids saw me," George whispered as if afraid anything spoken at a normal volume might he held against him as incriminating evidence. "They're not the Fletcher kids; they're kids from somewhere else. They saw me."

"In the actual act?"

George nodded, then sighed.

"No big deal," scoffed Nan, suddenly, it seemed, reconciled to George's free-spirited bathroom practices. "The Fletcher kids are at camp, I think. These are strangers. They will probably run home and not say anything at all. Or they might say they saw someone tee-teeing in the woods, and that will be that. They probably won't even tell their parents."

They were sitting down at the table again, George having sworn without Nan's prompting to always use indoor plumbing in the future, when they saw the police cruiser approach on Sumac, disappear behind the barrier of their house, then reappear and slow down just short of where the strip of woods met the road and the Fletchers' driveway.

"Uh-oh," said George. "Maybe I should go inside and hide somewhere."

"You're going to stay right here," Nan said. "It's probably nothing. They're probably just cruising the neighborhood on routine patrol. You don't know that they are *stopping* next door. But just in case we do receive a visit, you need to be out here to explain yourself. Otherwise, I'm left here to try to account for your absence." The slow-moving cruiser was blocked by the woods now.

"You could pretend it was someone you didn't know," pleaded George. "You could say your husband is out of town."

"Then they'll just have those kids' words for what happened, and they'll be looking for a guy who exposed himself, and we'll be holding neighborhood watch meetings, and everyone will know the perpetrator is someone who matches your description. . . . Oh, and you probably wouldn't ever want to wear that T-shirt again." George looked down despondently at his gray-and-green Muskies T-shirt, which had a caricature of a big, semi-human, muscle-bound fish wielding a giant bat. "It kind of stands out."

George let out a whimper.

"Someone's coming."

There was a disturbance in the woods. Leaves and saplings were shaking, and the crunching noise of dead leaves, small twigs, and other forest debris being stepped on signaled the presence of something big out there, and getting closer to their yard. Soon, two light-blue-uniform-clad Livia police officers, flanked by the two children and two distraught-looking adults, broke through into the yard.

"Oh, shit!" George muttered.

"Keep your 'oh, shits' to yourself, George," said Nan, trying to smooth out the tremor in her voice. "It sounds bad . . . and you haven't done anything wrong . . . have you?"

"What?"

"Shhhh!"

"What?" George whispered this time. "What do you take me for? I was only out there relieving myself, and these two little kids popped up just as I was about to zip up. They're not going to check my computer, are they?"

"Your computer?"

"Yes, they won't be checking it, will they?"

"What do you mean, George?" said Nan, suddenly alarmed. "What do you have on your computer? Kiddie porn?"

"No! Certainly not! Swimsuit models . . . maybe a few lingerie models."

Nan shook her head.

"George, they're not going to be checking your computer and, even if they did, they don't care about swimsuit models and lingerie models. What kind of lingerie?"

As the approaching posse drew nearer, detouring around the arbor, George and Nan thought it best to rise and walk toward them, affecting surprise at seeing a couple of police officers emerging from their strip of woods.

"Are you the neighbors here?" asked one of the officers, whom George and Nan noted were a man and a woman.

"Well, yes," Nan said, suppressing a chuckle. "We are neighbors."

"Well, you could have been someone else," the male officer retorted severely. "You could have been visitors temporarily residing in a neighboring residence."

"That's very true," said George, who felt complete, unquestioning accord with whatever the police officers said was, given the circumstances, the best policy to follow at this point. "You're absolutely right."

"Well," continued the officer. "We have a report of a male about your age and wearing a similar T-shirt exposing himself in the woods to these young children. These are the children's parents. Kids, is this the man?" The father stooped down and spoke quietly to the children.

"James, Priscilla, is this the man who pulled out his pee-pee and was watching you?" The little girl wiped a tear from her eye and nodded. The boy, who looked older, also nodded, but he was smiling mischievously and appeared to be on the verge of laughing.

"He was pissing," he said. The two parents frowned.

"James, I've told you not to use that word," the father scolded. "You say tinkle, or wee-wee, okay?"

The policewoman stooped over toward the children and adopted an almost childlike tone that sounded as if she were making a joke out of the whole thing.

"James, was the man wee-weeing when you saw him? This is very important now, was he tinkling? Or was he holding his . . . er . . . pee-pee, and looking happy?"

Priscilla wiped another tear from her eye and began to smile. James began to giggle. The giggling was slow, and intermittent at first. Then, it erupted into full-blown laughter. Priscilla joined in. Soon, much to the consternation of their parents and the confusion of the police officers, James and Priscilla were almost doubled over in uncontrollable hysterics. Nan wondered if this family was British, having detected what she thought was the hint of a British accent in the man, and figuring that only in Great Britain would you find a girl called Priscilla. The kids were still laughing when another loud disturbance in the woods marked the appearance of Jeri and Tom Fletcher.

"What's going on here?" said Jeri, a brash young woman who took on the role of neighborhood organizer and community scold to the mayor and city council. Jeri was well known to Livia's elected officials as the one who bombarded them with e-mails, letters, and phone calls at the slightest provocation or delay in a public service schedule of any sort, and who had once taken a bag full of goose poop and dumped it on the carpeting at a city council meeting.

Nan sighed in relief. When Jeri arrived, and as long as she was on your side, you knew you were safe. She was like the cavalry galloping to the rescue. But was she on their side here?

The mother of the two children stifled a sob, then stood up all ramrod straight, confirming in Nan's mind that she was indeed British.

"The children say this chap exposed himself to them in the woods."

"Chap?" said the male officer. "What's a 'chap'?"

"That's Brit talk for a guy," said his companion.

"What's a 'Brit'?"

"What?" Jeri cried, after a brief pause to digest the news.

"Yes," chimed in the father. "Exposed himself while tinkling in the woods."

"Tinkling?"

"Peeing," sniffed the father. "Ur-i-nating."

"This is ridiculous," Jeri said, as Tom, whose soft-spokenness was the perfect foil to Jeri's chattering extroversion, nodded furiously in agreement. "A guy was pissing in the woods. . . . What's the big deal?" The policeman folded his arms and looked sternly at the two children, who were still giggling.

"Now, listen closely, kids, 'cause this is an important question: Was he already peeing when you saw him? Or did he start peeing . . . excuse me, *tinkling* . . . after he saw you?" The policewoman, who had pulled out a notebook and pencil and was busily scribbling away, pursed her lips. Jeri rolled her eyes. George's shoulders were hunched in the posture of abject misery. Nan couldn't help but wonder what exactly it was that the policewoman was writing in her notebook.

"Uh . . ." said James, struggling mightily to suppress more giggles.

"Uh . . . uh," said Priscilla, looking at her brother, and exploding into intermittent, self-conscious snorts of laughter. "He was already there. We scared him."

"Yeah," said James. "He wet himself." More convulsions of laughter.

"Officer," piped up Jeri in her most stentorian damn-the-city-council voice. "I really don't see what the problem is. There has been a misunderstanding here. George was peeing in the woods. He does that from time to time." George's look of consternation turned to one of puzzlement.

"How do you know I . . . ?" Jeri held up an outstretched hand to stop him.

"He's private about it and it's his property. This is not a pervert you're looking at, but a man merely relieving himself in the privacy of his backyard. And look, there's the proof." Jeri pointed at George's shorts, still blotched with a wet urine stain. George blushed, then sighed. "He was surprised in the act and wet himself."

"This could very well be the most humiliating experience I've ever had," moaned George. "Can we bring this to a close, please?"

The policewoman smiled consolingly and snapped her notebook shut. It was then that Nan noticed the sergeant's chevrons on her shoulders. So, *she* is the supervisor here! she reflected with some pride. She looked at the nameplates pinned onto their shirt breast pockets. The sergeant was *Smead*. The police*man* was *Sneed*. Nan smiled, and had to work to hold back the little chuckle welling up inside of her.

"Yessir," the policewoman said. "I don't think there's any further need to draw this out. You don't want to file a complaint I suppose, do you?" She looked at the children's parents, who were now looking sheepish and every bit as disconsolate as George. They shook their heads.

"Good," the policewoman said. "So, what's the relationship?"

"Relationship?" said Jeri. "Oh, these are our cousins from England. Joel and Bernice Forrester, from Yorkshire." Joel and Bernice nodded.

"How do you do," Joel said.

"Pleased to make your acquaintance," Bernice said softly.

"They are staying with us. They don't understand our American customs very well."

What American customs? thought George.

"We won't take up any more of your time, officers," Joel said. With that, Smead and Sneed strode down the slope to the street and disappeared beyond the woods.

"Awfully sorry to have bothered you," Bernice said to George and Nan. "But one can't be too careful, you know, and the children were acting positively shocked. This is our first visit to the States, and we're a little squeamish, I suppose."

"No bother," said George, forcing out a brittle chuckle. "Happens all the time, especially with foreigners."

"Not with the French, however," Nan said. Bernice and Joel laughed unconvincingly. They had no idea what that meant, but assumed that it was a remark designed to bring a little levity to an uncomfortable situation. Following the Fletchers' cue, they turned around to retrace their steps through the woods. George stared forlornly at his stained shorts, then marched silently with Nan back to the patio, where he collapsed into one of the chairs, staring blankly ahead.

"Drink, my poor, persecuted dear?" said Nan, clasping his limp, clammy hand and stroking it.

"Yes," said George. "Straight up. On the rocks. No lime. *Shhhh*. Feeder! Don't move!" Nan straightened up slowly, without any sudden motions, and turned her head to look at their big squirrel-proofed feeder. There, on the perch, pecking away at one of the feeding holes was the biggest yellow bird she had ever seen.

"What is it?" she said sotto voce and out of the corner of her mouth as the bird paused in its feeding to jerk its big head up and fix its beady eyes directly on them. Its head, unlike the body, was dark, with a yellow stripe running across the brow, just above its eyes and beak. "Jeez, it's almost staring at us. I've never seen that before. It looks like a freak goldfinch . . . or one that's been pumping some serious iron."

"Evening grosbeak," said George earnestly. "That's what it is. I'd be willing to put money on it. I've never seen one of those before."

"We saw the rose-breasted grosbeak last month."

"Yeah, once, then it didn't come back. We should probably get a positive ID on this guy." The big yellow bird took one more peck at the seed portal, then took off with a prodigious whoosh of wings, catapulting itself directly overhead before disappearing on the other side of the roof.

"Bird book," said Nan, scampering across the patio and into the house to fetch the Peterson guide.

"You're right!" she said after checking the index and thumbing through the pages until she got to the picture of the big, dusky yellow bird that matched what they had just seen. "Positive ID." She thrust the book at George, who studied the picture and the brief description of the bird, which also had black wings patched with white.

"Sure is," said George, with a big grin. "No question. That's a positive ID. That just made my day!"

Nan smiled mischievously.

"Now that you're in a cheerier mood, I've got a riddle for you, George: What's the difference between a clump of crab-grass and an orgasm?"

7

Digging In

Dr. Sproot sat brooding on her deck, her forefinger and index finger wrapped into a white-knuckle tightness around the handle of a mug that held her fifth refill of fully caffeinated, dark-roast coffee. It wasn't easy to sit there and quietly fume after you've had six mugs' worth of coffee. Dr. Sproot, however, had trained herself to simmer deeply and quietly when that was required. It was no matter that her nervous system was screaming at her to get up and dance or just park herself on the commode doing a couple Sudoku puzzles while her urinary tract cleaned itself out.

She knew that by carefully cultivating resentment and allowing it to grow you allowed its misbegotten suckers to fill every fiber of your being. All that nurturing would eventually boil over into action, which she was beginning to suspect might be required here.

Dr. Sproot was fully capable of action. For all her botanical erudition and middle-class patina of prim respectability, she harbored violent tendencies rattling the cages to be let out. They wanted her to rape and pillage like a floraphobe Hun. How many times had she had to resist the urge to torch her yuccas or snip off a rose and deposit it in the freezer? But there was another Dr. Sproot buried under the layers of viral pride, intolerance, and mischievous pettiness. It was the sweeter, gentler Dr. Sproot. That Dr. Sproot hadn't been seen much lately or, quite frankly, much at all. It was the persona that subconsciously fueled the floral wizard in her. It made her want to love and pamper her little floral darlings and nurture them to greatness with gentle coaxings and an unwaveringly sunny disposition. Without that secret Mother Teresa thumping around in her otherwise blackened soul, Dr. Sproot would more likely have become a demolition derby driver or the operator of a trash-compacting machine.

Dr. Sproot reconciled her conflicted nature by taking a rigidly unemotional, learned, and professional approach to her gardens. That approach allowed her to infuse her gardening ethic with a ruthless efficiency. Underperformers she rooted out and cheerfully burned at the slightest hint of decline no matter how long they had served her. Her demands for perfection resulted in a considerable outlay for sharp gardening tools, fertilizers, lighter fluid, and dozens of new plants a year to replace those that didn't meet her exacting standards.

The result of all this was a yardful of very nice gardens that were in a constant state of restless transition. There were always holes in the ground. Topsoil was relentlessly churned up and augmented with bags of more topsoil. New plants, their clumped roots covered in burlap, littered the yard, waiting to be fit together in the existing arrangements like missing puzzle pieces.

What was that? Movement! Unseen, but plodding, steadily cadenced, and portending damage or destruction. Dr. Sproot ignored her bladder's insistent call to action, and got up from her chair stealthily so as not to alert whatever flower-devouring beast might be approaching. She reached for the BB gun propped against the house she kept handy to ward off garden pests and screeching crows. Hurrying back on tiptoes to the deck railing, she raised the gun, and took careful aim at the corner of the house. What came into view was no garden-defiling beast, but Marta Poppendauber. On seeing Dr. Sproot poised for action, Marta threw up her hands, inadvertently flinging her handbag onto the grass.

"Don't shoot, Dr. Sproot!" she said. "Don't shoot. I'm a friend." Dr. Sproot lowered her rifle and sneered.

"Marta, haven't I told you before to come through the front door and *not* through the gate in the fence? Huh? Why, I could have put out one of your eyes. You can put your hands down now, Marta."

Marta lowered her hands slowly. Keeping a wary eye on Dr. Sproot, who still had her BB gun at waist height, pointed right at her, she retrieved her purse. Luckily for her, it hadn't landed in a nearby stand of yuccas.

"C'mon up. I'll be back in a second. Gotta go to the bathroom."

Marta climbed up the steps to the deck and sat down in one of Dr. Sproot's stiff-backed, wood-slatted Adirondack chairs.

Marta didn't really want to be here, but what choice did she have? Though she had gotten some guilty pleasure out of watching Dr. Sproot go berserk over a little bit of hot tea, the notion of a Dr. Sproot–initiated lawsuit and all its ramifications terrified her. The damage that her reputation would suffer was more frightening. Dr. Sproot could ruin her. Why, one word from Dr. Sproot, and every wholesale buying club in the state would shut her out. The gardening clubs she hoped to join someday would blackball her. It would also damage any chance she had of winning the Burdick's Best Yard Contest. Marta wondered ruefully if her gardens were good enough to stand a chance anyway. Alas, probably not. Dr. Sproot was right: they were an anarchic mess, pure chaos. She sighed.

More details were leaking out about the contest. Marta had

it on good authority that $5,000 was at stake here—an astonishing sum for a gardening contest!—and that could just be the beginning. Marta had spilled the beans to Dr. Sproot about it. But that was under duress, when Dr. Sproot threatened her again in the most indelicate way with legal action and character assassination.

Gazing thoughtfully over Dr. Sproot's grounds, Marta found herself still admiring them. But what was it that was missing? It was some ineffable void that made these gardens too contrived, too consciously manipulated for perfection to *be* perfection.

Marta heard a toilet flush from within the house. She found herself startled at the sound of the sliding screen door and Dr. Sproot's sudden appearance at her side. Marta forced a wan smile.

"Your gardens are looking in peak condition, even in all this dryness, Dr. Sproot."

"Yes, aren't they? Thank you, Marta. But we're not here to discuss the condition of my gardens, as wonderful as they might be, are we."

"No, Dr. Sproot, I suppose we aren't."

"We're here to further flesh out some details of our little plan."

"Yes, Dr. Sproot."

"Let's head on inside. I have something to show you. We're going to turn you into a crackerjack backyard spy or my name isn't Dr. Phyllis Sproot."

Marta stared in disbelief into Dr. Sproot's bedroom mirror. There she was, modeling a brown, woolen, and hooded cowl far too long for her, and girded around her waist with a rope. A large pair of sunglasses covered about half her face.

"It's a crackerjack disguise, don't you see," Dr. Sproot said as a mortified Marta looked at the ridiculous figure she cut in the mirror. "With the hood pulled over your head, and those sunglasses covering your face, no one will have a clue who you are. That is, unless you're caught. If you are caught and detained, you are in no way to reveal your true identity, or mine . . . especially not mine. I have a reputation to preserve, and if it was to be discovered that I was having you run around spying on other people's gardens for me, well, you can imagine the fallout. Now, you, Marta, on the other hand, have very little to lose. You have no real standing in gardening circles, and your own yard is an absolute disaster, and . . ."

The words kept swarming around Marta. She resisted the temptation to make quick, dispelling motions with her hands, hidden in the billowing sleeves of the bulky garment.

"Actually, this is a costume I wore for Halloween one year, oh gosh, twenty-five years ago, when Mort and I were in our wild and crazy years. Ha-ha. It got quite a few comments, I'll tell you, Marta. So, you could pretend to be a scarecrow. Or a monk. There is a monastery in Livia, you know, for those monks whose mission is making those glazed, hard-as-a-rock caramel candies. You could be one of them. Now stretch out your arms."

Marta obeyed mindlessly.

"We don't want those sleeves too long, do we? You will be having to use those hands to write down observations and take pictures. Lots of pictures. Hmmmm, let's see. I'll have to pin those back a little . . . and . . ."

Marta closed her eyes, lost in the self-abasement of having stooped so low and her own timidity in failing to resist this ridiculous charade in all but the meekest, most halfhearted, and queasy-voiced way.

"But remember what you promised me," Dr. Sproot said when Marta balked at her assignment after trying on the cowl. "You promised to help me as penance for damaging my vocal cords and as surety for my not destroying whatever little reputation it is that you have. Remember? Now, this won't hurt a bit, Marta. All you have to do is take your notes on whatever you see sprouting from their accursed soil, take pictures—lots and lots and lots of pictures—and bring them all back to me. There will also be some night duty, and a little snipping . . ."

"A little *what?*"

"Snipping."

"Snipping?"

"Yes, snipping. You will visit the Fremonts' yard late at night—four or five nights' worth of work will probably do the trick—and snip off the blooms and buds of various and sundry Fremont flora. A few at a time so as to avoid notice, but we must, over time, do enough damage to prevent these Fremonts from, by some freak accident, actually winning the Burdick's Best Yard Contest or, more to the point, preventing *me* from winning the Burdick's Best Yard Contest. We can't assume they won't hear about it. We can't assume they won't enter. We can probably assume that, no matter what happens, I will win anyway, but why take chances? We'll call our little snipping exercise the 'death-by-a-thousand-cuts' treatment."

"But, Dr. Sproot, I don't want to do that. That's vandalism!"

Dr. Sproot smiled.

"No, dear, that is *not* vandalism. There will be no great loss to the Fremonts, only a few buds and blooms snipped off here and there. They probably won't even notice. And, by doing so, you'll be preserving the integrity of what I've worked so hard to build and nurture here in Livia. Take that away, Marta, and you have stupid people raised to positions of fame and importance all because of a little blind luck. Can't have that, can we, Marta?"

"Dr. Sproot," said Marta, her voice quivering with uncertainty. "I just don't think I should be doing this."

What Dr. Sproot did next sealed the deal. She walked over to the counter that separated her dining room from her kitchen, retrieved several papers, and handed them to Marta. One bore the letterhead of an attorney and was addressed to Dr. Sproot. It said that she had valid grounds for a lawsuit against Marta and could recover thousands of dollars as a result of such an injury as Marta had caused through her criminal negligence. Criminal negligence! The others were letters addressed by Dr. Sproot to the presidents of Livia's four gardening clubs. They described in exaggerated detail the scalding tea incident and recommended that Marta be excluded from every officially sanctioned gardening event, demonstration, and contest until the end of time. Tears began to well up in Marta's eyes, and sobs shook her frame. Dr. Sproot suppressed a smile.

"I'm sorry that it has come to this, Marta," she said. "You should understand that not only do I have a reputation to preserve, but it's also a matter of time. You think I have time to go gallivanting around in other peoples' yards? I've got my own creations to cultivate, and I can't take it for granted that I'm a shoo-in for this award, even though I probably am, and just rest on my laurels.

"You know how important this is to me, Marta. It's the food I eat, the coffee I glug, and the air I breathe. I don't know what I'll do if I don't win. Maybe something drastic. I've had such a hard life, Marta. Such a hard life. This, this one crowning accomplishment, could erase all that forever. And you could share in the knowledge of how much you've contributed to it. There could even be a little reward for you, Marta. But you are either with me in this or against me. Now, which is it?"

All Marta could do was bow her head and nod in the affirmative.

"I'll take that as a yes," Dr. Sproot said. "Now, Marta, my own surreptitious observations of the comings and goings at the Fremont house have indicated that there are certain days of the week and times when they are least likely to be outdoors. They are few and far between, since these Fremonts do spend lots of time puttering around uselessly in their yard and getting drunk on red wine. But even the Fremonts have to run out and do their errands every now and then. And, luckily for us, they tend to be rather regular in that regard. Come on. Let's sit down and I'll show you my carefully kept logs. Then you can start working. My gosh, I do believe tomorrow, mid-afternoon, could be one of your windows of opportunity. Say, two thirty to five p.m."

An hour later, Marta walked forlornly to her car carrying a digital camera and a large shopping bag that contained the cowl, the sunglasses, additional batteries for the camera, and a thick log book. Dr. Sproot, a big smile creasing her worn and emaciated face, waved at her. This created a new sensation in Marta, a sort of carbonated bubbling up of excitement and joy. When was the last time she had seen poor Dr. Sproot smile? And waving at her, too? The feelings of friendship began to rekindle in Marta as she got in the car and turned on the ignition. The purring engine reassured her and strengthened her resolve. She would do what needed to be done for her friend, and to further the institution of gardening in Livia. It *was* right and just.

Now, here she was in Fremontland, having terrifying second thoughts about her mission, but compelled by some force to keep going. Fraidy cat? She was no fraidy cat.

Beneath her and to the left were some shoots coming up that Marta hadn't noticed before. She bent over, adjusted the lens of her digital camera for the close-up, and snapped away. Then, she moved back to get the broader perspective and took some more pictures. After checking the little flip-open display window on the back of the camera to make sure she had gotten the best lighting and distance to capture enough detail, she snapped it shut, and slung the camera strap back over her shoulder while she proceeded to scribble down notes and a crude map in her small spiral-bound notepad. She didn't know exactly what it was poking up through the ground here, but Dr. Sproot would want to know, and would probably be able to identify it as soon as she saw the pictures.

What an expert Dr. Sproot was! Over the years, she had been such a sisterly helper to her in her early gardening efforts, and had selflessly shared her encyclopedic knowledge of all things botanical without charging so much as a cent.

Things had changed, of course. Dr. Sproot, always the domineering sort, had gotten more so. And so strange! Marta traced it back to when her husband, Mort, died. Mort was struck down in the prime of life six years ago by a stroke that killed him right before their very eyes, as Dr. Sproot was guiding her on a tour of some of her new creations. It was his death that had freed Dr. Sproot to be the true Nazi the good Lord intended her to be.

Mort was a lush and a lout. In that, he was an insurmountable obstacle to Dr. Sproot's ambition of worldwide horticultural domination, and he did manage to contribute to the community's well-being by tamping down Dr. Sproot's baser nature. He was the only person Marta was aware of who could actually intimidate her.

Mort was a big, blustery Bluto of a man. He belched a lot and wore shirts perpetually stained with WD-40, ketchup, and something else that kept dribbling down from his mouth and dripping off his chin, and which no one but Mort could identify, but he wasn't telling. There was the scent of flatulence and grain alcohol that always seemed to follow Mort wherever he went. It easily overpowered the muted but pleasant fragrances that suffused Dr. Sproot's gardens.

Mort had no interest in the floral world whatsoever. He would regularly ravage Dr. Sproot's gardens by running over the edges with his lawn mower, because he couldn't tell a weed from a weigela shrub. This had created some tension in the childless Sproot family. Still, Dr. Sproot put up with Mort's behavior with a meekness that never ceased to amaze those who were well acquainted with the rude, bossy side to her personality. When Dr. Sproot got her degree, Mort scoffed. When she placed third in the first of two annual Big Turkey River Regional Desert Plant Contest competitions, he sneered, even though the third-place prize was a lovely, suitable-for-framing photograph of a giant saguaro cactus with a watering can somehow attached to one of its spiky arms. Marta shook her head sadly at the thought of it.

Maybe Dr. Sproot was scared of him. Maybe she needed someone to push her around the way she pushed others around. Whatever the psychology involved here, she had always been trying to please Mort. That had involved buying sheer undergarments decorated with lace merganser heads, and Dr. Sproot's attendance at the monster truck rallies over at the St. Anthony Hippodrome. Not even that could smooth over the roughhewn, slovenly obnoxiousness that was Mort Sproot.

It was on Mort's sixtieth birthday that Dr. Sproot had made her startling discovery about him. She had decided to surprise him by coming home early from work with a couple six-packs of his favorite beer. She surprised him, all right. She found him cowering in their bedroom, his face all dolled up with makeup and lipstick, and wearing a pair of her pantyhose, her pink, perky, push-up bra, and a pair of frilly, light-blue panties that he must have bought or scrounged from somewhere because they certainly weren't hers. Plus, he smelled all foo-fooey.

Marta chuckled and felt her face flush. Jasmine Bell, a licensed family counselor who had worked with the Sproots and who had no business telling her such things had told her anyway because they were neighbors and friends, and had known Dr. Sproot since they were kids.

Dr. Sproot and Mort mostly ignored each other after that.

They dealt with their deteriorating domestic situation in their own self-destructive ways. Mort took to drink even more so than he had before.

A self-righteously aggrieved Dr. Sproot no longer felt obligated to kowtow to Mort's whims. On weekends, weekday nights, and saved-up vacation days, she threw herself into her gardening with a new, tireless zeal that put all of her colleagues to shame, but added a good ten years of strain to her face and thinned her hair. That was when she invented the coreopsis-salvia-hollyhock blend. Marta believed it to be a truly revolutionary step forward for gardening in Livia, though such a combination had never been quite her cup of tea. Dr. Sproot had dug up more than two-thirds of her existing gardens to make way for the new find. Marta marveled at how she could bring such an energy and breathless resolve to an act of sheer destruction. It was also then that she followed Dr. Sproot's good advice to hire a couple of guys with a backhoe to dig up her deep-rooted Joe-Pye weed. She had planted it five years earlier and it had flourished. After listening to Dr. Sproot, she agreed that it was a hideous blot on her gardens.

Two years after the ladies' underwear incident, fate struck in the form of the stroke.

Marta had been summoned by Dr. Sproot that day to witness the progress of the coreopsis-salvia-hollyhock blend, and arrived to find Mort downing one beer after another and playing with the propane tank attached to the backyard grill. The next thing they knew he was slurring his words and stumbling around in a semi-stupor. Typical Mort. He had taken to inhaling propane on top of his drinking, which, Dr. Sproot had to admit, made him act a little less like a brooding wannabe axe murderer. Besides, if he was willing to poison his organs and shrivel his brain, well, who was she to stand in the way of his cheap-thrill jollies, especially if they were to have the happy consequence of significantly shortening his life span. What you did was just ignore him when the fumes and alcohol took hold.

A dull thud signaled that Mort had fallen onto the relatively soft carpet of thick rye and fescue. There was some writhing, a groan, then stillness.

"We'll just let him sleep it off right there on the ground," said Dr. Sproot, who, despite Marta's protests, continued to direct her attention to a particularly impressive specimen of coreopsis. When Mort didn't get up after twenty minutes, and wasn't snoring either, Dr. Sproot calmly walked over to his supine form. After examining it, she walked just as calmly back to Marta.

"He's quite dead," she said, her eyes sparkling as she emitted a gravelly chuckle. A sneer rippled across her lips. "Now, Marta, I want to show you my new yucca bed and how yucca can be used to accent your coreopsis-salvia-hollyhock blend."

Marta shuddered at the thought of it, and how that stroke had unleashed the psychotic bitch in Dr. Sproot. She shoved her pencil and notebook in her pants pocket and adjusted the sunglasses. Poor Dr. Sproot, thought Marta. Such a sad, sad life. Such a frail individual irreparably broken by years of straining under the yoke of a foul-smelling, burping flower hater, and here I am balking at doing her a little favor or two. Still, did she have to get so mean and threatening over a little bit of hot tea?

Marta was halfway through the backyard. That meant the only escape, should someone pull into the driveway, was to make a quick dash into the woods, then somehow claw her way through those thickets to the road. She pulled the hood of her cowl across her face and tightened the drawstrings, so that only her forehead, nose, and sunglasses-hidden eyes were visible. It certainly wasn't the kind of thing she would normally wear on such a hot day, or on *any* day! And why did they have to make the bloody thing out of wool? For that matter, why, in God's name, did she have to wear it? Wouldn't a scarf and the sunglasses have done the job just as well? Marta wondered whether Dr. Sproot had come up with the disguise in part to further debase her, and turn her into a freak of nature, a true laughingstock. Still, she supposed it was better than being recognized, and there was that Fremont boy who had given her a ride home that day.

A pickup truck clattered by. Marta froze, turning her back to the street and stretching out her sleeve-covered arms crookedly. She hoped this posture would make her look like a small tree to the casual observer.

Once the truck was gone, Marta began to rush her job. She scuttled toward the back, searching for anything new that Dr. Sproot would need to know about. Catching the sweet smell of the dangerous angel's trumpets, Marta inhaled deeply. She wished dearly that she could come back sometime simply as a welcome visitor to drink in the wonders of such a divine backyard. She threw back the hood of the cowl to get some fresh air, and photographed the angel's trumpets. They had spread out since she had last seen them, and were pointing yet more deadly and fascinating blooms directly at her.

A car door slammed. Marta took off full-tilt, camera flapping at her side and her robes billowing awkwardly behind her. She dove into the woods, fought her way through the underbrush, and emerged, breathless, at Sumac Street. Making sure that no one was coming, she laid her camera on the ground, pulled her bulky steam bath of a disguise over her head, rolled it up, and wedged it under her arm.

There were some new things here to report to Dr. Sproot. She would be especially interested to know that the angel's trumpets had grown and were still blooming wondrously. She'd want to carefully examine the roses to determine the quality of the blooms as well as the likelihood that they would still be in full flower when the contest rolled around. There were those new sprouts.

Marta began walking back toward her car. She tried to carry herself with the purposeful nonchalance of someone focused solely on the stroll that lay ahead of her. Deep down, however, she was troubled and confused. She wasn't sure whether she should be reveling in a job well done, or berating herself for sinking to new lows in her service to Livia's gardening gorgon.

8

The Complete Backyarder

Over six years, the Fremonts had put body and soul, and credit card into their backyard. They sank more than $30,000 into scores of garden center purchases and in building their arbor in the back, the arched trellises, and an intricately set boulder wall, which they had later taken down, redistributing the boulders in various combinations around the yard.

They weeded, planted, watered, and fertilized. Once the children had grown into teenagers, they were able to take the tire swing down from the ash tree, and the big, bare, trampled-on spot underneath it was now trying hard to grow fescue and Kentucky bluegrass for the fourth time, with mixed results. Other than that, the backyard had made the transition from jangling, unkempt juvenile playground to restful adult Zen garden.

Mostly, they had been in accord as to how their backyard would look. Apart from the hideous compost compound, there was one jarring note for Nan. That was the five-foot-high wood carving of Miguel de Cervantes, whose Don Quixote was a hero of George's, because, Nan figured, they were both such a mass of stupid delusions and strange heroic notions all endearingly mixed in with each other. They had paid an artist $2,500 against Nan's better judgment to carve that figure into the stump of the silver maple they had had to cut down because its roots had been coiled around it when it was planted, slowly strangling the tree. The carving had been fashioned with a chain saw, chisels, and awls, sanded lightly, and painted in life-like colors, which were fading now. The entire bloody thing was a constant irritant to Nan, who considered it gauche and stupid. She just couldn't get the juxtaposition of something literary and symbolic and the Vermont Castings gas grill. She was also tired of explaining to visitors who it was and why it was there, which she didn't fully understand herself.

"No more compromises," she had said once she beheld the finished product, firmly convinced of her own superiority in the realm of backyard conceptualizing and design.

She sighed resignedly as she glanced at Miguel de Cervantes's trim and spike-bearded form, with a quill pen in one hand and large book in the other, and his weird painted eyes, which always seemed to be looking at her. The good thing was that no further compromises had been necessary.

The backyard was a seasonal thing; the winters in this particular part of the upper Midwest being far too frightful to allow any consideration of spending much time outdoors unless you did something silly, such as skiing or ice-skating. Once the mercury started regularly topping out at forty, George made a big to-do of putting on his sunglasses, shorts, green-and-gray Muskies home ball cap, Jethro Tull T-shirt, and flip-flops, mixing himself a gin and tonic, then heading out to the back patio to officially inaugurate the new season. That usually happened in early-to-mid-March. It was about the same time that Bluegill Pond thawed enough to film over with glistening water and sprout the CAUTION: THIN ICE signs planted in its shallows.

The backyard flourished as human habitat from mid-April to early November, by which time the temperature had plunged, the light had gone, and all the summer life had had its fall color fling and been gathered up for compost.

Nan and George figured November 14 to be the average date they retreated to the hibernating shelter of a spacious house and on that last day, they'd give the backyard a wake, sprinkling a small pile of leaves and withered plant detritus with their remaining gin and lighter fluid, then burning it at dusk, each reciting a few thoughts concerning the highlights of the season just past and a prayer praising God's goodness for providing them with such an earthly bounty. Then, they'd go inside and prepare for the winter by knocking down a couple of shots of the drink they adopted for the long, dark season ahead: Glenlivet single malt Scotch.

The Fremonts had taken no vacations of any particular note for the last four years. The last time was the trip to Hawaii— but the beaches at Waikiki, the volcanic fissures of the Big Island, and the enchanting rain forest of Kauai had left them feeling empty and unsatisfied.

"You know where I wish I was?" said Nan as they dutifully clicked away with their cameras at a giant plume of molten lava that spewed skyward. "Sitting in the backyard, watching the roses open up, with a g-and-t in my hand."

"Yeah," George said. "With a big slice of lime . . . Who needs all this lava stuff anyway?" So, much to the chagrin of their children, who had loved Hawaii, and had wanted to reprise that trip with others to equally interesting and exotic locales, that was pretty much the end of any traveling of note for the Fremont clan.

On average, in the spring and summer, and into the early fall, Nan and George would spend six to seven hours a day, weather permitting, in the backyard. That counted mowing, planting, transplanting, watering, raking, fertilizing, mapping out changes and new features, and just enjoying themselves sitting on their patio, either alone or entertaining guests.

The exceptions were Tuesdays and Thursdays, when afternoons were relegated to running errands. Other than those, a normal day would find George and Nan sipping their morning coffee on the patio and capping off an afternoon with a few strategically timed drinks—Sagelands merlot vintage 2005, of course, and the incomparable Bombay Sapphire gin. If the weather held up and the mosquitoes and yellow jackets behaved, George would fire up the grill in the evening. Then, they'd enjoy an alfresco dinner on the patio with whichever of their three children were free from variable summer work schedules or the lure of their interminable movable feasts with friends.

It was generally between three and four thirty in the afternoon when George and Nan regretfully abandoned the backyard for the squalor of their respective offices. George would pound out greeting card doggerel for any and all occasions, and design inventions. He had sold one of those—The "Whirl-a-Gig Bubble Blower"—to a major toy manufacturer for $350,000 five years ago. Nan toiled away meditatively with knitting needles and yarn as a locally respected maker of custom purses. Her creations had even made their way up the chain from consignment stores to high-end department stores such as Cloud's and Deevers.

The $350,000 wasn't going to last forever. Nan and George agreed that, with children entering college and a big mortgage still remaining on their house, they would have to ramp up their search for some more lucrative ways to earn money than making women's handbags and banging out greeting card prose.

They soon discovered that job prospects for people who want to reserve most of their day for backyard work and relaxation were limited. They would keep looking, they told themselves, at the leisurely pace that best fit their lifestyle. There was no rush; something would turn up. Besides, who had the time when the duties of the backyard grew so demanding!

They made charts that plotted the dates of each plant's blooming and each tree's leafing, from the smallest impatiens to the loftiest silver maple, then compared them with the logs for the four previous years during which they had kept similarly detailed records. Those notebooks also contained dates and times of plantings, fertilizings, and waterings, as well as when and where the Miracle-Gro was applied.

The Fremonts' annual calendar started as soon as the snow melted and the agonizingly slow appearance of buds and flowers began. They watched the big thermometer nailed to the clematis-bearing trellis flirt with fifty, embrace it lovingly, then soar to a balmy sixty. Once the last killing freezes retreated into the past, George opened up the water valves and carried the hoses slung over his shoulder to screw into the outdoor faucets, and Nan surveyed the yard to determine which annuals she would plant this year.

The bridal wreath spirea would need some severe trimming. So would the fast expanding dwarf Korean lilacs, but that would have to wait until after they bloomed, which, at that time of year, would still be more than a month away. Nan would always inspect the concrete patio critically. She wished they could tear it up and replace it with a cedar deck raised maybe a foot off the ground. It was her pipe dream. Having just had the arbor constructed in the far back, near the woods, last year, they couldn't afford much in the way of new construction, unless it involved a little job or two for Jerry Bigelow, their favorite neighborhood handyman.

This was a time of slow change, with much backsliding. A hard frost struck in the middle of April, with the mercury tumbling to the mid-teens. The season's final snow came on the last night of the month. It showered down in a blinding rush of quarter-sized flakes that piled up in the night to five inches, then melted suddenly with the sun's powerful and blinding appearance on May 1.

Spring showers started in late March, and the first thunder—a pusillanimous affair accompanied by low-wattage lightning—rumbled across the backyard on April 27. The leaves on the lilac bushes had started to come out by then. The buds on the silver maples and their lovelier kin, the sugar maple, were swelling. The grass cast off its deadened brown, though it was still not growing. Juncos still pecked at the detritus under the bird feeder; they would be flitting around on the ground another week or so before starting their journey north. Up above, the slaty, snowy gray of winter gave way to the jumbled, billowing cloud masses of May.

During the course of a backyard season, birds, ducks, and all manner of small mammals searched for nests and valiantly attempted to keep the circle of life spinning. The backyard was a place for endings, too. George and Nan once found the body of a yellow-bellied sapsucker at the base of a hydrangea. Baby squirrels fell out of the trees to die broken-boned and squalling on the ground. Bad-tempered yellow jackets died in the jets of bug spray George squirted into their nests on August evenings.

There were friends in the backyard, among whom they counted the chipmunks and birds, and the mallards from the lake that strutted, in mating pairs, or odd-number combinations of males and females, across the yard during the late spring and early summer. There were enemies, too: raccoons and rabbits, field mice, voles, and the swarms of mosquitoes that could only be warded off with a ring of citronella candles lit around the perimeter of the patio. There were things that were neither. A snapping turtle once dragged itself with painstaking deliberation across the yard looking for a place to lay eggs. They approached it, fascinated, but kept their distance; snapping turtles can snap off a finger as if it were a matchstick.

Other, more menacing things passed during the night. Most notable was a teenager accused of stealing a car and fleeing from the police, whose flashlights probed against the walls of their bedroom. Strange voices awoke them to the knowledge that their backyard was not so sacrosanct that it couldn't be violated.

What other things passed that way they could only speculate. Slithering snakes, owls the size of dogs, deer coming up from the river valley to the south and following the creek to their neighborhood. Other people? They tried not to think about that.

One night as the days edged toward the summer solstice, they were given no choice.

9

Things That Go Snip in the Night

There was a disturbance in the backyard.

It had been waking Nan up for the past three nights, and it was waking her up now. It was interfering with the usual life-force sense she had in the middle of a summer's night: that of thousands of little flower souls charging themselves up to fulfill their next day's brilliant destiny . . . with a bit of help from their human friend, of course.

It was subtle. What exactly was it? The unrelenting movement of night toward dawn? A possum poking around at the orange rinds and onion skins in the compost pile? She strained to hear. Was it even a sound? Or was it something about the scent of the night that filtered through the screens of the open windows? Could be. George had often told her that she could smell a dog doing its business in St. Anthony.

Awake, she could only hear the soft collisions of a million leaves in the night breeze and the distant and sporadic engine drone of interstate traffic.

There it was again, this time unmistakably a sound, and an unnatural one at that. Their backyard was being violated. Something was out there that shouldn't be. Nan shivered. After three nights of keeping her own fearful counsel, she determined that some help from what she hoped would be a stalwart spouse was required. She woke up George, whom she knew all too well was not as conversant as she was with the subtle ways of the night, and would have to be told outright what was expected of him. It was three fifteen a.m.

"Listen!" she whispered as she shook him. "Listen!"

"Listen?" said George groggily. "Listen to what?"

"I don't know exactly. I just know there's something out there."

"Out *there?* Where?"

"In our backyard. Go check, please. But be quiet and don't wake up the kids."

"I could scream at the top of my lungs for ten minutes and it wouldn't wake up the kids," he gurgled. With that, he rolled over and adjusted the pillow with a deep sigh. Nan shook him again. Outside, the motion detector clicked on, flooding the patio with light that eerily illuminated the shades covering their windows.

"George, the light just went on!"

George sat up, rubbed his eyes, and gazed at the shades, which flapped against the windows.

"Hmmm. Windy."

"Our backyard is being violated by something. Please go check it out."

George blinked rapidly at the shades, then reached under the bed for his Johnny "Smokestack" Gaines bat. It was a genuine Smokestack Gaines batting practice–used bat, not just some cheap imitation used as giveaways to lure kids to the ballpark. The name was burned in black into the barrel of the 36-inch, 32-ounce Louisville Slugger.

George had bought it from a friend back in 1996, when Smokestack Gaines was just a rookie. Now, the aging star, two-time MVP, and shoo-in for the Hall of Fame was nearing retirement and poised to make another run at the home run crown. The bat was cupped at the top, tapered into a thinness at the handle that gave his lightning swing even more torque. A chip had been torn from the knob on the handle, which made this particular bat useless for Smokestack Gaines but quite a prize for the fan—George's friend—who picked it up off the ground. He already had another Smokestack Gaines bat—this one undamaged—so he sold the marred one to George for $75. Now, it was worth $1,000, easy.

So, what the hell was George doing keeping it under the bed as a homeowner's weapon of last resort against an intruder? He had always meant to replace it with one of those metal bats the boys had collected during their years playing ball for the Livia Athletic Association, but he had procrastinated. Now, he was preparing to ruin his Smokestack Gaines bat by cracking it over the head of some idiot running around in the sacred backyard. Where was the justice in that?

"Here goes," he said, jumping out of the bed, Smokestack Gaines bat in hand. "Coming with?"

"No, I'll just lie here and pray for you."

George rubbed the grit from his eyes as they became accustomed to the gray semi-visibility of the dark. He plodded heavily down the hallway. An intruder! The full impact of the threat he was facing finally breached the wall of semi-somnolence that had kept him moving obediently ahead, and allowed him to open the back door. He stopped. What if it was an intruder?

"Nan!" he whispered hoarsely.

"What?" came the faint response.

"What if there's somebody in the house? Shouldn't we just dial 911?"

"There's nobody *in*side," said Nan in the loudest whisper

she could muster. "There is some*body* or some*thing* wandering around in our backyard. Or maybe it's nothing. And what would we tell the police, that I just heard a weird sound? If you run into something, just hit it with the bat. Only make sure it isn't one of the kids first."

They had seen lots of things activate the flood lamps' motion detectors. Leaves whirling across the field of vision. Steam vented from the dryer in the basement. Bugs. Once, they saw a raccoon prowling among the shrubs and rose-entwined trellis at the far end of the light's reach, and its eyes shone at them, two perfect orbs, mirroring the light, suspended in the black void for a moment until the full animal came into view.

The scariest thing, by a long shot, was the nocturnal creature that had clung precariously to the bird feeder perch, too light to lever up the counterweight and bring down the squirrel shield.

"What the hell is that?" Nan had said as they stared at it through the kitchen window. Its furred head moved jerkily and confusedly sideways, then up and down in the glare of the floodlights. "Squirrel of some sort?"

"No squirrel. Squirrels are diurnal." The tiny creature turned its face toward them, and they both gasped. It looked like the face of a tiny old man, deformed or mutilated into something gray, jerking, and mute.

"It's a baby opossum," George said. "Gotta be. Night creature. They would eat those seeds."

They looked it up in their National Audubon Society *Field Guide to North American Mammals,* and discovered that it was a *flying* squirrel, which they had seen twice before, its shadowy form gliding from one backyard maple tree to another.

All these sightings muted much of the panic the sudden burst of motion-activated light would have ordinarily triggered in them. But this was different. There was no opossum, no flying squirrel, no raccoon, no nothing that George could see through the doorway, though he was beginning to suspect that a flying leaf or twig might be the culprit.

What was that snip? There it was again. *Snip.* And again.

"Hey!" George shouted through the screen. "Hey!"

He could have sworn he heard the sound of scurrying feet racing across the lawn and down the slope to the street, where they padded off into nothingness. The lights went off. It startled George. He cried out in surprise.

"Honey? George?" came the thin but reassuring squeak of a voice from the bedroom, all efforts to communicate via whisper being abandoned at this point. "Quit yelling! What's with this 'Hey!' business, anyway?"

"I thought I heard something," said George. "Maybe it's nothing. Snipping. Something tearing off into the street. Then, the light went off. Whatever was out there is gone now."

"Well, look around anyway, please. I'm coming out."

George waited for the soft shuffling of Nan moving over the hallway carpet. He didn't really care for this notion of going outside on a scouting expedition for something that wasn't supposed to be there in the first place. Especially since all the signs pointed to it being gone—or just about gone—with no intention of sticking around and causing a fuss . . . that is, unless cornered or provoked.

"Lead the way," said Nan, clinging to his pajama top. "I'm right behind you." George slowly opened the screen door. He cringed when it squeaked, and just about jumped out of his pajamas when he stepped onto the patio and the floodlights came on again.

"Well," he said, chuckling nervously. "Whatever it is that's out there, if it's still out there, can certainly see us now, though we just as certainly can't see it." They crept toward the edge of the darkness.

"I don't hear anything," Nan whispered.

"Aliens from another planet. Didn't you hear the snips?" Nan sniggered.

"Aliens don't snip, they beep," she said.

"You said you heard something. It wasn't snipping sounds?"

"No. I heard something. But nothing I could identify as a *snipping*. What I heard was more like something in motion, Very subtle, but out here for sure. Probably just kids screwing around."

"Kids snipping?"

"I don't know, George," said Nan, the need to sleep winning the battle over her initial disquietude. "Maybe kids. Maybe snipping. But snipping about what?"

"Not snipping as in dissing someone. That would be *sniping*. Not being *snippy*. Snipping as in *snipping*. You know. *Snip, snip.*"

"This is getting silly," said Nan with a yawn. "Who cares if it was kids, and who cares if kids were snipping. No sign of any damage done. We'll check tomorrow. If it keeps up for a few more nights, I'll get more worried. But, right now, I need sleeeep."

"Maybe it was *our* kids snipping. I know I heard snipping."

"Okay. If it makes you happy, we'll check the rooms on the way back."

Sis was in her room downstairs, which was a good thing since she wasn't allowed out past midnight. Upstairs, a big snoring lump indicated that Ellis was in. Next door, there was Cullen, curled up under the blanket.

"Hmmm," said George. "So who was it out there, and what the hell were those snips?"

"Just mischievous kids who probably had a few nights of fun in the woods, and won't ever come back again," Nan said. "Now, get back to bed before I decide to get out the loppers and snip *you*."

10

Cutworms

"This is obviously the work of an amateur . . . a *rank* amateur."

Dr. Sproot turned from the computer monitor she had been studying. She focused her squint-eyed stare on the furiously blinking Marta, who fought the overpowering urge to hunch over and lower her head like a cringing animal.

They had spent the morning going over Marta's notes. Those had been carefully arranged by backyard section to fill twenty-seven impeccably typed pages held in a fuchsia-colored ring binder, picked out specially by Marta to reflect Dr. Sproot's favorite non-garden color. There were also five maps drawn by Marta to professional draftsman standards.

Through it all, Marta noticed Dr. Sproot downing mug after mug of steaming coffee without any apparent effect on her damaged throat. Apart from reiterating her threat to sue, she had not mentioned her throat or any sort of medical prognosis or treatment in the week and a half since she had been scalded by Marta's hot tea. Wouldn't someone as coffee-amped as Dr. Sproot find that a natural topic to broach, especially to her alleged best friend and the perpetrator of the injury?

Marta toyed with the notion of bringing up the subject in

some sort of indirect way just to see what kind of response she would get, but quickly backed off: such recklessness could set off another confrontation with her old friend and more threats. At this point, Marta couldn't bring herself to face any more of that unpleasantness and the disturbing ramifications it might have.

Much of their morning's work involved Dr. Sproot tearing apart Marta's efforts. She picked apart her notes for mistakes—of which Marta freely admitted there were probably a few. She shook her head in disgust at the appearance of smudges on pages four and seventeen. She wondered why Marta, on her maps, had drawn the various plants and flowers in mere black pencil, instead of their true colors, seeing as how pencils of every conceivable hue could easily be obtained at Lelia's Artsy Stuff, near the high school, on the corner of Tremblant and 33rd.

Now, as the day approached mid-afternoon, Dr. Sproot wasted no time dashing Marta's hopes that she would fare better on her photographs.

"Look at this, blast it all," Dr. Sproot said. "I mean, some of these photos are out of focus. Some are too close. Some are too far away. What am I going to do with these? I can barely see them. How am I to even tell what's here? Huh? You have failed me, Marta. Failed! Failed! Failed! And just when I need you the most."

Marta leaned in toward the photograph glaring at them from the monitor. There was nothing wrong with it. The detail and perspective were perfect. The clarity and light were all she could have hoped for. She had risked ridicule and worse to take this and scores more pictures for Dr. Sproot. Now, to be subjected to this, even by a flawed, vulnerable, yet towering genius . . . well, this time she wasn't going to sit there and just meekly agree. She would meekly disagree.

"They look crystal clear to me, Dr. Sproot. I thought they were quite detailed and very good, actually."

Dr. Sproot snorted.

"Very good! Very good, you say! Good God, woman, you might as well have sent a kindergartner over there with a box of crayons or an Etch A Sketch!"

Marta cleared her throat and gazed at the photo she had taken of some meadowsweet they had not noticed before. Meadowsweet! An interesting choice. It would require lots of watering, but that wouldn't be a problem for the Fremonts. They were every bit as diligent as Dr. Sproot. What's more, they put their hearts and their joie de vivre into their gardens. She could tell the moment she set foot in them. The flowers and shoots seemed to want to jump out to her in their joy and fecundity. Even in the photographs, you could see that.

Dr. Sproot's gardens delivered no such warmth. They were like wild animals tamed by the confines of their zoo cages into facsimiles of themselves. Suddenly, the whole notion of the yuccas and coreopsis-salvia-hollyhock blend seemed inane to Marta. It was like a parody of gardening, with Dr. Sproot as the chief gardening clown. Marta stifled a nervous titter. She imagined Dr. Phyllis Sproot as Doc-Phil-the-Flower-Buffoon dressed in floppy shoes, moth-eaten hat, and a tatterdemalion suit, with a little plastic flower attached to her lapel that would squirt hot coffee in your face if you got too close.

Dr. Sproot frowned at the monitor, clicking her mouse to move from one photograph to the next. She muttered something, then snarled. That snarling was something new, even for Dr. Sproot. It signaled that she might be reaching deep within her tortured soul for something better left unplumbed.

The depth of Dr. Sproot's knowledge never ceased to amaze Marta. Why, there were shoots that had just barely come up through the ground, and Dr. Sproot ID'd them without hesitation.

After two hours of going through Marta's photos, she had identified thirty-four different kinds of flowers, shrubs, and vines, and four places where freshly turned and dampened soil indicated that something would likely be coming up soon.

"Very well," Dr. Sproot said. "Let's go back and pay special attention to the monarda, the first target of our 'death-by-a-thousand-cuts' campaign, eh?" She clicked back through the images. "Ah-ha, here we are. Now, let's take a closer look."

Marta stiffened. It was bad enough to get all furtive and dressed up in a steaming hot, ridiculous outfit to go snooping around in somebody's yard, but to violate someone's gardens by taking the snippers to them was quite another thing. To say nothing of having to perform the act of destruction with *noisy* snippers that no amount of cleaning and oiling would quiet. It was no wonder she woke up the Fremonts that night and had to go running through the dark down that wretched hill again. At least she hadn't crashed into a tree! Well, she thought, thank goodness the task was finished.

Dr. Sproot blew up the image of the monarda and studied it intently.

"Well, Marta, you've done the job far too *subtly,* I can tell that right off the bat. For crying out loud, I can barely tell where you snipped."

"But wasn't that the idea, Dr. Sproot?" said Marta, puzzled at how Dr. Sproot could suddenly make out the details of her photographs quite easily.

"The idea, Marta, was to make it so the damage was not overly obvious. The idea was not to make it so much so that the blasted flowers will look virtually the same when they bloom. What is the point of that? Good Lord, look at this! It's like looking at a *Where's Waldo* . . . Ah-ha, there's a snipped stem . . . uh . . . and . . . there's another . . . And that's all, Marta?"

Marta squirmed.

"Well, Dr. Sproot, if you look at my photos of the other monarda, you will see that I snipped some of them, too." She clicked on another photo.

"For heaven's sake, where have you snipped? Um-hmm, there's a little snip . . . and . . . there's another, barely noticeable to the well-trained eye, which, of course, is what we're dealing with here. If I can't notice the difference without prolonged and careful inspection, how in God's name do you expect the judges to? And, Marta, these are judges who won't have the leisure that we do to examine each stem so carefully. What do you say to that, hmmmm, Marta?"

"I say that I tried my best, Dr. Sproot. Gracious, you can see where the stems have been cut and I'd be amazed if the Fremonts can't tell. I actually thought I was erring on the side of being too obvious."

Dr. Sproot gazed upon Marta with all the scorn she could cram into a stare.

"You'll have to go back and do more snipping, Marta. This simply isn't enough. I want you to go after the monarda again, then hit some of the roses. It is a fine line between subtle and obvious destruction, Marta, but you have not even come close to grazing that line. This, of course, is in addition to your con-tinued spying mission. Do I make myself clear?"

Marta could only nod meekly in agreement, and hate her-self for doing so. Secretly, she swore to draw the line this time. She would continue her undercover work, as onerous and mortifying as that was, but she would not cut and cripple any more flowers. *Would not!*

"Ugh!" cried Dr. Sproot, who had been clicking through some photographs she had neglected to examine during her first run-through. "Those ghastly angel's trumpets! So lovely and yet so lethal."

She pushed herself back from the monitor, yet continued

to stare intently at the image that would not allow her to look away.

"Do you want me to cut those, too, Dr. Sproot?" Marta wondered. "It would be awful if you did, but I know how you hate them."

"Cut them? Why certainly not! Of course not! That would be too obvious. Far too obvious. That would be the work of nothing less than a top-flight professional. And it would destroy a feeble little thing like you, Marta, or at least scramble your mind beyond recognition. I would not cast you into such a dangerous situation, Marta. How dare you think for one moment that I would do such a thing! And look, look, would you, how they have some power over me. I can't look away! Can't! They've got me in their clutches! Turn off the computer, Marta! Turn it off quickly if you value my life!"

Marta, stunned by Dr. Sproot's reaction to what seemed to her nothing more than a benign image of some lovely, sweet-smelling flowers—flowers she would consider planting in her own gardens were it not for Dr. Sproot's dire warnings—bent over to turn off the computer. Dr. Sproot collapsed in her chair with a gasp.

"Well, it took you long enough," she whimpered. "It took you blasted long enough when you could see that a few more moments and I might have been lost to their hypnotic spell. Why, maybe you're so slow because you've been exposed to them, Marta. Have you ever thought of that? I hope you were wearing an appropriate breathing apparatus when you approached them. Otherwise, there's no telling what might happen to you."

11

What Cold Fronts Do

Sometimes in the summer the wind shifts and blows down from Canada, which is to say it comes out of the northwest. It is a cool, dry wind that sweeps away the murky, heavy-aired stillness that oozes up from the south and so inexorably settles down upon the land, unrelenting and unmovable. This cool air mass comes barreling down quickly, often hard on the heels of thunderstorms, impatient, it seems, to relieve all those who have been sweltering through that wet, stifling swimming weather and conducting their lives in a kind of greasy, down-trodden slow motion because of it.

There is no particular name for this refreshing draft, though there should be, because when the shift comes, every-one notices, and everyone talks about it. Deep, sultry summer becomes bright, sparkling May. The old and turgid becomes new and sprightly. Friendly cumulus clouds, looking like giant, tumbling cotton balls, sail across the sky as brief visitors. Moods brighten. Movements quicken. Some people say they almost feel resurrected. Any researchers doing a study of what happens before and after these Canadian cold fronts come through would undoubtedly find marked differences in productivity, visits to psychiatrists, jogging mileage tallied, and the incidence of friendly and charitable gestures.

It was at times such as these that Nan swore she could see smiles spanning the width of all her flowers' upturned blossoms and leaves. Actually, all *except* the Dusty Miller. Despite showering more than the usual care and fertilizer on it, Nan had been unable to coax the wretched little albino malcontent into anything approaching the brilliance that all the others had worked so hard to achieve. Perhaps, she thought, it's destined for a different fate. Or maybe it's one of those *evil* plants, a sort of secret weed camouflaged as this meek little snowy thing. She would have to watch for signs that it might be spreading its negative contagion to its neighbors, the monarda, purple coneflowers, and balloon flowers. In the meantime, she thought of a riddle for George:

"Why is monarda like a weapon? . . . Because it's a *bee balm!* Ha-ha. Ha-ha."

Cold fronts always brought out the neighbors. Mitzi and Howard "Frip" Rodard were the first. They ambled up the railroad tie steps toward the Fremonts, talking animatedly and gesticulating wildly to each other, as those chatterboxes always would.

George and Nan watched their approach with some apprehension; when the Rodards showed up, you knew you were in for a gabfest that would keep you a good hour and a half, conservatively. What's more, they were the world's greatest contrarians; make any sort of declaration, and they were bound to contradict it. When talking to the Rodards, it was best to never say anything definitive, though George would often play with them, tossing out one observation after another that either begged to be challenged or was so patently correct that questioning it would be comically absurd.

"Fripper, Mitzi," George said. "What's happening?"

"Why?" Frip said. "Should there be anything happening?"

"I don't know of anything happening," Mitzi said. "You must know of something we don't." The Rodards frowned. George and Nan tittered.

"You're right," Nan said. "We don't know of anything happening and there's no reason anything should be."

"Well, there could be," Mitzi said. "There's always something happening."

"In fact, there is," said Frip as he and Mitzi settled into the other two patio chairs, which responded with squeaks and groans from the fabric backing and coiled metal springs. "We're having that big ash in our front yard cut down."

Nan gasped.

"That beautiful ash! That's the biggest tree in your yard. It must be hundreds of years old."

"It's actually quite ugly," Mitzi said. "As for age, I wouldn't place it at more than sixty or seventy years."

"You're right," said George, lifting his drink mischievously. "It's the ugliest tree in the neighborhood. Drink?"

"It's actually much admired by the neighbors," Frip said. "And it has its points. For instance, the leaves turn a lovely yellow in the fall. No, no thanks. Mitzi?"

"Mitzi what?"

"Drink?"

"No, dear, we have to be off in, uh, fifteen minutes," said Mitzi, stealing a quick glance at her watch. Nan and George looked at each other, amazed. If that indeed proved to be the case, it would set a record for Rodard brevity.

"Any other time, sure," Frip said. "But not today. We've got a recital downtown."

"Mippi must be playing," said George, shooting a quick wink at Nan. "Wish I could hear her. She's so talented."

"In a manner of speaking, it is Mippi," said Mitzi, referring to her fifteen-year-old daughter, whose real name was Beatrice. "But, in a way, it's not. Mippi's only part of the recital."

"Talented?" Frip mused as he stroked his chin then threw his arms skyward for no reason that Nan or George could discern. "Well, that's kind of a loaded term, isn't it? She's got a long way to go on that darned cello. I'm not sure I'd call it talent. Perseverance is more like it."

"You must be proud of Mippi," Nan said, lips tightly pursed to keep her from laughing.

"Not particularly," Frip said, as Mitzi nodded in agreement. "A father probably shouldn't be saying this about a daughter, but she is so willful and disobedient at times. And so contrary."

"No!" George and Nan cried.

"She's way too big for her britches," Mitzi said, shaking her head in dismay. "Always knows she's right. The rest of the world is wrong. Her parents are idiots. You know what we're talking about, don't you? Three teenagers . . ."

"Two teenagers," Nan corrected. "Ellis is twenty."

"No, he's not!" Mitzi said. "Ellis is nineteen." George, smiling, took a long, slow sip of gin.

"That's right," Frip said, lurching forward and planting his hands palms down on the glass tabletop. "Since when is Ellis twenty? He is nineteen. I know that for a fact."

Nan took a healthy swig from her glass to fortify herself for the tangled web of conversation she knew she was about to enter.

"I think we would know, Frip, how old our son is."

Mitzi and Frip looked at each other, confused, obviously uncertain as to how they could respond appropriately to such a bold declaration. George looked at his watch; he would time this uncharacteristic pause in the conversation. It lasted seven seconds.

"That's not always true, Nan," Mitzi said, flapping her hands around as if they were flippers steering her crazily through some underwater world. "Parents forget. Parents subconsciously want their children to stay at certain ages, and they're reluctant to keep tacking on additional years. You might want to check your records, Nan."

"You're probably right, Mitzi," George said. "Ellis must be nineteen. We stand corrected."

"Let's not get too hasty, now," Frip said. "He could very well be twenty. In fact, now that you mention it, don't I recall a twentieth birthday not so long ago? Wasn't Ellis's birthday in April?"

George shrugged.

"Hard to say," he said. "What about this weather? Isn't it beautiful? I actually timed a temperature drop of thirteen degrees and a dew point drop of twelve degrees in the course of one half hour. Wind direction: north-northwesterly. Wind speed: eleven, gusting to fifteen. I just took the readings fifteen minutes ago."

Nan rolled her eyes and smiled indulgently. George looked for any opportunity to show off his weather expertise. He had a state-of-the-art Taylor weather station, armed with barometer, thermometer, hygrometer, and rain gauge sitting atop the end post of the split-rail fence, and sheltered (with the exception of the rain gauge, which had to be open to collect moisture) by a wooden frame open at both the front and back to allow the free flow of air. On the roof of the house was his anemometer and wind vane, which were connected to wind speed and direction gauges sitting on top of the desk in his office.

"I don't think the weather's beautiful at all," Frip said. "It seems like we haven't had any rain in weeks, and this is supposed to be the wettest part of the year. You should see the water bill!"

"He's up at five thirty every morning watering," Mitzi said. "That way, you get the most bang for your buck. No evaporation. No chance of overnight rot."

"You're right about that, Frip," George said. "We do need the moisture. This is awful weather!"

"On the other hand, feel that breeze," Mitzi said. "Who could ever possibly want it to rain now and spoil this lovely weather. My gosh, will you look at the time! We gotta go."

"Take care," said Frip with a violent wave as he and Mitzi bounded down the steps, passing and greeting Jim Graybill, who almost collided with them as he climbed quickly and purposefully toward the Fremonts.

"Lovely day." Jim greeted them with a broad smile, his arms akimbo, looking around to take in the wonderful expanse of the backyard. "If you could bottle a day like this and a yard like yours you could sell it for a billion bucks. God, this backyard never ceases to amaze me. How *do* you do it?"

"Nothing to it," George said. "We just let nature take its course while we sit here and drink."

"Ha! Got another one of those, by any chance?" Jim pointed at George's glass.

"Oh, I guess we can dig something up." George rose from his chair with an exaggerated grunt, meant to make Jim feel guilty for putting him in motion, and made his way languidly to the door.

"No rush, of course," Jim said. "I can stay here till the glaciers melt."

George stooped over more and developed a limp that made his progress toward the door painstakingly slow.

"This is what you get for your sarcasm," he said. "You say things like that and my whole body reacts by slowing down."

"So, when do we sweep the yard?" Jim said after George returned with his drink.

"Pardon?"

"*Sweep.* Sweep the yard. When do we . . . uh, *I* . . . do it?"

"I just swept the patio yesterday," said George, who had already downed his drink and was starting to slur his words. "No need to sweep the yard, is there?"

"Ha-ha. I mean sweep it with a metal detector."

"A what?"

"Metal detector."

"You have one of those?" George said. "Wow!"

"That's about enough in the line of alcohol for you, dear," Nan said, pointing her half-finished drink at a suddenly intense George.

"Just bought it a week ago. Top-of-the-line model. When do we sweep?"

"Sweep for what?" Nan said. "What's there to *sweep* for around here?"

"Any metal in the area, such as, oh, the stray quarter or dime, or millions worth of buried treasure."

"Why?"

"Why? Ha-ha. You're such a card, George. Because buried under even the most unassuming suburban backyards could be enough metal to build a battleship. Old pots and pans, arrowheads, coins. Ill-gotten gains."

"Meaning . . . ?"

"Meaning buried loot."

"Be serious, Jim," George said.

"I am serious. Down in Louisiana, a guy swept his backyard and came up with a chest of Spanish doubloons. I read it in my treasure hunter magazine. It could happen anywhere."

"We're a bit off those old shipping lanes, Jim," Nan said in that supercilious way of hers that both George and Jim knew to mean this conversation should be drawing to an end.

"Anyway, it doesn't hurt to check," Jim said. "A complete sweep would just take, oh, forty-five minutes, maybe a little more. Whatever I find, I get, oh, twenty percent. Maybe twenty-five percent. You get the rest. And you can rely on my complete confidentiality."

"No," George said.

"Absolutely not," said Nan. "Nobody's going to go nosing around under our backyard with the thought of digging it all up."

"We'd dig it up only if there was something worth digging up. A little hole. Hardly scratch your gardens. Then, you could spend the thousands you get from the buried whatever to turn this into the backyard of your dreams."

"It already is the backyard of our dreams," George said.

Jim sighed. "Oh, well, give it some thought. And, on another not altogether unrelated topic, have you two heard about the contest?"

They hadn't. Jim explained that Burdick's had announced, in conjunction with Livia's weekly *Lollygag,* a contest to be held in July for the best yard—front or back—in Livia. First prize would be $5,000, a feature in the *Lollygag,* and a big PlantWorld sign in the winning yard for the rest of the summer!

"Whoa!" George said.

"You guys came immediately to mind," Jim said, then drained the rest of his drink with a big *Ahhhh!* "I haven't seen anything that approaches you guys' backyard anywhere in Livia. Not even in the southeast quadrant."

Nan and George doubted that. The southeast quadrant was where Livia's storied rich lived. They could afford built-in sprinkler systems with timers, fancy rock gardens, and swarms of illegal aliens to do all the gardening work for them.

"Yours is better," Jim said. "Honestly. It's so . . . so . . . idiosyncratic. It bears your stamp."

George and Nan hemmed and hawed, and promised to consider it.

"Well, that would be a pretty good time for it," Nan said. "Let's see, the impatiens and alyssum will be out, of course.

The bee balm, purple coneflower, balloon flower, some Asiatic lilies, maybe . . . Hmmm."

Nan quickly realized that one of the several projects she had in mind could probably be covered quite nicely by $5,000 and would be actually done by professionals, rather than that unreliable amateur, George. "We'll look into it. But $5,000 for a gardening contest? In a rinky-dink little suburb like Livia?"

"It's true," Jim said. "Check out this week's paper. They've got all the rules in there. Well, I'm off. Be sure and think about letting me give your yard a good, thorough sweep. I think you might be surprised by what turns up."

"We'll give it careful thought, Jim," said Nan in her tone that meant she would give it no such thing. With that, Jim got up, wheeled abruptly about, and ran off, almost racing down the steps, flinging pea gravel everywhere, and accidentally kicking over the little painted-model wooden chalets Nan had placed so carefully on one of the railroad ties, but which were always getting knocked over by people who were mad, or in a hurry, or who just didn't look where they were going.

Nan made a mental note: I have to move those bloody things before some clumsy oaf kicks them to pieces.

A souped-up orange Camaro that looked as if it had been finger painted by a kindergarten art class, and an ancient Plymouth Duster, eaten away so badly by rust and corrosion that George and Nan called it the "leper car," squealed to a halt on the side of the road by the driveway.

It was Ellis, Cullen, and their entourages. That meant Matt and Steve, Denise, Charlie, Meg, and a beautiful girl burdened with an old-fashioned name, Bertha. Out they piled, flaunting their Metallica and Black Sabbath haute couture of T-shirts, ripped and worn-out jeans, and tank tops that showed too much cleavage, chatting and laughing, giving George and Nan little finger-roll waves before disappearing into the driveway, and entering the house via the garage door.

George and Nan had known most of them since elementary school. They knew the punch-code combination to the garage door, dipped into the fridge for snacks without having to ask, and were considerate enough to make old-person small talk when they couldn't avoid the senior set.

Lately, though, cigarette butts had begun to appear along the roadside, and cans of super-fortified, high-octane caffeine-and-sugar drinks were getting dumped in the recycle bin. George wondered whether it was only one more small step to joints, condoms, and Magnum .357 handguns loaded with hollow-point slugs manufactured to rip apart lungs and blow away brains.

"They're good kids," said George. "Right?"

Nan shrugged abstractedly. "I suppose so," she said.

George frowned, then lifted his glass in salute to Phil and Ann Boozer, who were walking down the street and waving, yelling something barely audible about "working too hard." The Boozers were not terribly spontaneous folks. When they went for a walk, or devised a plan to do anything else, for that matter, they stuck with the blueprint. They would not be doing anything so rash as to go bounding up the steps to chat with the Fremonts unless they had made the requisite arrangements beforehand. Nan raised her own glass to the Boozers, who were just passing out of their sight lines, and who, she reflected with a smile, were the only ones of their friends who didn't drink.

"Nan-bee, you *do* think they're good kids, don't you?" George had turned in his chair to look at her. Nan saw that his face was a sad mask of silly, niggling concerns, and that he needed her to focus him on the new challenge at hand.

"To hell with the kids," she said. "What do we have to do to win that contest?"

12

How to Win Big at Gardening

The cool, dry spell lasted longer than anticipated. While that made things comfortable outside and kept the mosquito population at bay, resulting in what condominium and apartment dwellers and happy-faced television weatherpersons would deem a string of "perfect days," dry was not what the Fremonts wanted it to be. They were more than willing to put up with the irritant of a few whining pests in exchange for the natural lushness adequate rainfall would bring to their backyard at this time of year.

The sprinklers were on nonstop during much of the morning. George would fit the tap with a dual spigot attachment to keep two hoses going at the same time. "Double headers," he called them. He'd set them on full throttle just before the sun came up, then turn them off as the kids hit the showers in expectation of full blasting streams to come shooting out of the showerheads. That was for the lawn and whatever flowers could get soaked at the same time. Then, Nan would resume the watering for another three hours with the hand-held sprayers and soaker hoses for the remaining flower beds. They finally turned the water off for good at about eleven a.m. as evaporation began in earnest, negating much of the value of watering from that point on.

So, while the front yard spawned all manner of dandelions, weeds, and burrs, and gradually burned into a uniform crispy, fried-brown color, the backyard shone through as a well-watered, tranquil, and quite serenely beautiful oasis amid a desert of drought-stricken neighbors' yards. The water bill that arrived that week detailed charges of only $100 for April and May. The next bimonthly bill, they figured, could be as much as five times that amount.

"We need to do more," Nan announced one cloudless morning as the sprinklers whirred away. "We're not doing enough to win this contest, and I want to win this contest. I want to win this contest so badly I can taste it."

George frowned. On the rare occasions when Nan made such pronouncements, they generally preceded relentless bursts of energy, which invariably sucked him in to their vortex. That meant a lot more work. On cue, a pain spasm shot through his lower back to remind him that the musculature entangled around his spine, ribs, and pelvis was not keen on big backyard projects that involved a lot of lifting and bending over. He kept frowning, having thought that all the big work that had to be done to the yard could now be safely relegated to the past.

"Why?" he said. "We're watering all the time now. You're putting on the Miracle-Gro. The place looks great even in the middle of this drought. What else do we have to do?"

"Lots," Nan said. George moaned.

"Besides, something's been snipping some of the monarda, or chomping it off very cleanly."

"I *told* you I heard snipping that night."

"And I was wrong to doubt you, George. But it's seeing that's believing. Look at these monarda over here. Not blooming, of course, so harder to tell, but cut off very cleanly at the stem. What could do that . . . or who?"

"*Who?* Who'd want to cut off our monarda? What possible reason . . . ?"

"I don't know. But we're damn sure going to monitor the situation, and next time you hear snipping, you're out there with your baseball bat pronto."

The conversation moved on to what, for George, was the unsettling proposition of major improvements to the gardens. As stunning as their backyard might be, Nan was now thinking it didn't quite measure up to her new, higher standards. It certainly would not be good enough to garner them first place in the Burdick's Best Yard Contest. Now, she saw their backyard in its true light, as something that, while it was testimony to hard work and dedicated maintenance, was actually quite predictable and rather commonplace. With the exception of the wonderfully perilous angel's trumpets, which were her own inspiration last month, there was nothing unusual in their gardens, which probably meant nothing that would cause the judges to stop and take notice. Basically, she reflected, everything they had planted in the backyard would scream to the judges that this was the work of novices who had mastered only the basics of gardening, and had not shown the guts to take chances, to really do what it took to turn it into a masterpiece. New areas would have to be cleared. Turf would have to be dug up, and earth turned over in preparation for planting new, as yet undetermined, things. But what? It was getting well past planting season, and deep into summer.

Nan and George decided they needed to spend more time methodically scouting out the competition. It wouldn't be hard to find the other contestants. Their names and addresses had been listed in the *Lollygag,* and on the website of Burdick's, which figured it would heighten interest in the contest if residents could see what yards were being entered, and how they were being improved in preparation for the judging.

Contestants were issued big green lawn signs that read: OFFICIAL BURDICK'S BEST YARD ENTRY, then a contestant number. George and Nan yelped in amazement when they handed in their $25 entrance fee and were issued a set of official rules and a lawn sign bearing #73, having underestimated the number of competitors by about four dozen. They were appalled when they later learned that 148 signs had been handed out.

"But don't a lot of those people just have a few flowers and shrubs?" George said. "I figured the real competition is probably limited to about a dozen or fifteen people."

"And we won't be one of those," barked Nan, "unless we see what other people are doing and make some big improvements ourselves."

George lapsed into silence. He had not seen resolve and passion like this out of Nan since they first began their backyard remake, and that meant the fires of her energy and drive were being rekindled. Even their college searches for Ellis and Cullen had never reached the fever pitch of excitement and determination that now seemed to be building alarmingly in his wife. Nan had lately seemed such a contented and unexcitable person. More wine-relaxed than coffee-driven. And now, an adrenaline-addled, workaholic, garden bitch-ass was going to be loosed on the world. Look out!

Livia is a simple suburb with unremarkable attractions among which wonderful gardens and immaculate lawns have never been counted. It can boast Mound Park, a twenty-five-acre green space featuring a dozen old Indian burial mounds. There is the Prairie Hills Mall, with its bargain-basement outlet stores. Perhaps the suburb's crown jewel is the 200-acre

Billings Lake Park, with its sandy beach and beautiful surrounding homes.

For those seeking the cosmopolitan touch, there is a Tunisian
restaurant started up by a guy from Paramus, New Jersey, that
used to be rated nationally as a four-star undiscovered gem. It had
suffered from its brief fling with fame, and expanded too quickly,
allowing quantity to trump quality. Now, it catered primarily to a
lunch crowd of businesspeople for whom pretty decent North
African fare was plenty good enough.

Because they had some pride in their community, Nan and
George had been pleasantly surprised to find, as they followed
the contestants map supplied by Burdick's, so many lawn signs
sprouting from properties they ordinarily would not have sus-
pected to be in the running for any kind of landscaping recognition at all. They also felt somewhat threatened and deflated
to discover that many of these gardens, often fronting the
streets, were pretty darned good. Many were on streets seldom
traveled by the Fremonts.

Then there was the Billings Lake area. What they found
there was a revelation that gave them new hope. Many of the
yards were too gaudy and pretentious. Others had not been
properly cared for, and were showing signs of drought damage.
Some were quite lovely and tasteful, but others were so often
garish quilts of mismatched plants and flowers. Repeated visi-
tation revealed that many used hired labor, which disqualified
them right away, and would probably double disqualify them if
the hired labor was of the illegal sort.

As they branched out into virgin territory, a new world of
Livia yard horticulture opened up to them. In fact, they found
threats galore to what they had always assumed was their un-
contested place among Livia's landscaping elite.

The curving cul-de-sacs of south-central Livia, known
only to them because Ellis's best kindergarten friend lived on
one of them, were a special discovery. Here were at least eight

lush gardens swimming in moisture. Black soaker hoses snaked everywhere, their mist turning the landscapes into mysterious, wet-climed fog gardens. All manner of exotic annuals and perennials sprouted from these gardens. Even Nan was at a loss to identify many of them. After two such scouting missions, they decided to bring along a digital camera, so they could surreptitiously take their pictures, return home, plug the camera into their computer, and search their gardening books for the appropriate IDs.

It was easy enough to spot the roses. In one garden, four different varieties swallowed up six giant trellises at the front and side of the house. God knows what was in the back, because, at this point, their scouting expedition scruples did not allow Nan and George to trespass on private property. That left them cursing the absence of alleys, which would have allowed them access to what was *really* going on, and frustrated them with the knowledge that what they were seeing was probably only the tip of the blossom. The rose house they were able to dismiss as "too one-dimensional," though it certainly made a vivid impression. With any luck, the Fremonts figured, those roses would have shot their wad by the time of the contest.

It was harder to ignore the house on Waveland Circle, a long, hidden-away cul-de-sac perched on the bluffs overlooking the Big Turkey River Valley. Due to the way the houses on the cul-de-sac were constructed on their plats, Nan and George were able to get a good look at the backyards as they followed the circumference of the cul-de-sac circle. What they saw stunned them. Here was the sort of garden that made theirs look like an HO scale model by comparison. There were at least four varieties of phlox, which would likely burst out just in time for the judges' visit. Lots of peonies, but those would probably be past their prime by then. There were lilies and amaryllis everywhere throwing out beautiful blooms. Would they still be blooming at contest time? Nan wasn't sure. Her own lilies, she knew, would not be, darn them!

Spreading clematis splotched an aging, weathered-gray section of fence with scores of violet-and-white blooms and, right next to it, a huge hydrangea with green flowers would go white in about two weeks. Perfect timing, drat it all! Someone had shown the presence of mind to plant lots of big annuals, which would bloom all summer: sunflowers, which hadn't come out yet, and might not by the time of the contest; love-lies-bleeding, larkspur, and mallow. The ornamental grasses, though, were really what hit Nan because they were so well placed, breaking up the annuals and perennials: Scottish tufted hair grass, huge pampas grass, switchgrass, and purple fountain grass.

Most of those names George and Nan wouldn't even know until they were able to blow their pictures up on their computer and match them with photographs in their four illustrated gardening books.

"Oh, and of course, they have their token roses," harrumphed Nan as she aimed her camera at an eight-foot-tall curved trellis smothered in the ruby red and pink of scores of Don Juan and Jasmina roses in full bloom. "Wow!"

"I don't know; that yard looks awfully busy to me. There's too much going on there. There's no theme."

"Are you kidding! It's spectacular! But, yes, George, if simplicity is considered the top virtue of a yard by our judges, then we can rest easy; these guys will not win. Somehow, though, I think spectacular might win some points. And we're only seeing about half to two-thirds of the backyard. Let's move around the curve here."

They followed the curve around to the other side of the driveway, but the house blocked the view of the backyard from that angle. It was at this point they noticed that a man and woman were watching them through the house's front picture window. They waved and the Fremonts waved back. Then, they moved away from the window.

"Better scoot before we have to answer some pointed questions," Nan said.

They got in the car just as the man came out the front door. He watched them impassively as they drove off.

"I hope he didn't get our license plate number," said George, who had burned some rubber as he shot out of the cul-de-sac.

"Now, why would he want to do that?" said Nan, who was busily scrolling through the photos she had taken on the viewfinder screen. "He was probably going to ask us what we were doing, then invite us into the backyard when we told him. No big deal."

"Can't take too many chances," George said.

As they pulled into their driveway, they were surprised to see a woman dressed in a burnoosey-looking thing and carrying a camera scurry across their yard, then run down the street, get into a white sedan, and peel out with a squeal of tires and engine.

"Loony!" George said. "People just go goddamn loco about some things. What do we have to do, fence in the yard? Keep that car in mind in case you see it prowling around again."

"No problem. I bet only fifty cars matching that description come by here every day."

13

Revenge of the Spurned Gardener

Dr. Sproot didn't appreciate her coreopsis-salvia-hollyhock blend mocking her. It wasn't so much that she could communicate with her flowers as it was knowing when she was being made a fool of, whether by animal, vegetable, or mineral.

The way they were acting! Just look at them! Going to pot after all she had done for them. Why, it was mutiny, that's what it was! Clearly, today, every bloody flower in her gardens was treating her like the world's biggest gardening sap. How could that be?

Here were the coreopsis, all curled up and tinged with brown. And the salvia! Wilted! The hollyhocks were getting duller by the hour. The dahlias looked lackadaisical, uninspired, washed-out.

And as for the wretched yuccas? Why, she had pricked her finger on one of their pointed tips, then sliced her thumb on the edge of another. Dr. Sproot dropped her watering can and pulled back from her flowers in disgust mingled with fear.

"What on God's green earth is happening here?" she muttered. "Am I not the master of my own gardens? Is this the payment I receive for such hard work?"

She inspected every shoot, every leaf, every stem, every blossom, armed with magnifying glass, tweezers at the ready to crush every pest that might turn up, but found nothing. No bugs. None of the usual signs of blight. Nothing indicating the damage resulting from too much sun or too little.

She took soil samples and did her own chemical analyses. Every test from every section of her gardens showed her topsoil to be in flawless, nutrient-rich condition. She read and reread the instructions on every bag of specially-prepared dirt and fertilizer she had applied and found she had followed them to the letter.

At her wit's end to figure out what was happening, Dr. Sproot turned to Cleon Broadmind, an old acquaintance from childhood with whom she had occasionally exchanged Christmas cards and a few brief telephone exchanges. Cleon had gotten various degrees in horticulture and now served as one of the experts-in-residence at the state university extension service. Cleon, who had had a crush on Dr. Sproot during high school, and who was now divorced, eagerly agreed to personally inspect Dr. Sproot's gardens, especially upon learning that she was widowed.

When he arrived the next day, he noticed that Dr. Sproot looked much more drawn and haggard in the face than he had expected. But she still had that trim shape, and so tall! Had she grown since he last saw her? Amazonian! Cleon noted with delight the continued presence of pronounced curves in the hips and the nice way Dr. Sproot filled out her form-fitting jeans.

"Gosh, you look great, Phyllis," he gushed, taking her limp, cold hand into his own and squeezing it.

"I didn't call you to exchange compliments," said Dr. Sproot, yanking her hand out of his clutches. "And I did not intend it to

be a social visit. I called you to give me your professional opin-
ion about what the Sam Hill is happening to my gardens."

Not utterly immune to the charms of the opposite sex, Dr.
Sproot nevertheless could not find anything to admire in this
particular specimen. He was overweight, borderline obese,
with a good-sized gut lapping well over his belt. He was bald.
He had a bulbous, veiny nose that was approaching uncom-
fortably close to hers. Cleon had obviously gone to pot over the
intervening forty-five years or so since she had last had day-to-day
contact with him. Even so, there had never been that much raw
material to work with. In high school, he was a stubby little
greaseball, a moonstruck wallflower who was always annoying her
with weird notes and longing gazes. Besides, he was four inches
shorter than she was, an unacceptable differential for her in any
prospective beau. She eventually had her boyfriend—a basket-
ball player named Johnny—slap him around, and generally
scare the crap out of him, and that ended that.

"Come outside," she said. "And please do address me as
Doc-tor Sproot, as that is my official title."

"Okay," said Cleon with an ingratiating smile. "Dr. Sproot
it is. I'm a doctor, too, you know."

Same old stuck-up bitch, Cleon thought. But not bad
looking in a withered sort of way. Figure's still there, and that's
what matters.

Walking around in the yard, Cleon found his old affections,
half-buried and semi-forgotten for all those years, bubbling up
again. It was the way she walked—sort of slinky-like—and the
way she talked in that hard, uncompromising way that screamed
out dominance. She looked so strong in the arms and legs and
buttocks. Pictures of Dr. Sproot as no one had ever seen her before started forming in Cleon's tortured psyche. He saw her as a
gaunt, powerful, primitive warrior who tied him to a rack with
prickly, skin-gouging rope and lovingly caressed his ample,

naked back with a few choice strokes of the cat-o'-nine-tails while singing out, "Does it hurt Daddy to do that?"

Put her in a studded, sleeveless leather jacket and spiked, crackling leather gloves. Give her a pair of stiletto-heeled stomping boots she could pull all the way up to the crotch, and a chastity belt made of iron with a skull and crossbones on it that he would burst blood vessels trying to rip open. Then, you've got the perfect woman. The woman of his wildest dreams. And now, a very available woman after all these years of secret subliminal yearnings.

"Well?"

"Well?"

"What do you make of all this?" At this point, lost in his reverie of Dr. Sproot as his personal dominatrix, Cleon could only gaze disinterestedly at all the vegetative carnage around him.

"Looks bad," he said.

"I KNOW it looks bad, Cleon. WHY does it look bad?"

After asking some perfunctory questions of Dr. Sproot, and satisfying himself she had done all the things she should do to create a healthy home for her flowers, Cleon found he was at a complete loss to explain anything except his passion for her, which he would be more than willing to expound on for the rest of his life.

"Do you love your gardens?" he asked.

"Do I *what?*"

"Do you *love* them? You must coddle them. Tell them how much you care for them. Play soft music to them. Caress them. Stroke them. Stroke them again. And again. Let them know you're always there to keep them secure and safe."

Dr. Sproot was aghast.

"I certainly don't do anything of the sort!" she snorted. "If I had wanted to oversee a bunch of brats, I would have had children. And I decided not to have children because I hate the idea of having obnoxious little persons running around pestering me with their fickle affections, their yammering conversation, and their tantrums. Isn't it enough that I do what's necessary for any garden to flourish and apply the latest in scientific methods and my own inspiration to their health and well-being?"

"Well, then, have you tried screaming at them and humiliating them? How about whipping them, or slicing their buds just enough to cause endurable pain. You could grab them in hand and squeeze, squeeze, squeeze them until they think you're going to crush the very life out of them. But then you stop. It's the kind of treatment that can create excitement in any organism, present company not excepted.

"And maybe if you could dress in a certain way when you care for them that could perk things up a bit. Say, going topless, or wearing a loose-fitting, wiggly bra made from chain links and old hubcaps."

"What?" screeched Dr. Sproot, raising her arm toward the salivating Cleon as if to ward off an expected blow. "How dare you unleash your putrid perversions on me! Out! Out! Out, you quack!"

With that, Cleon scuttled across the yard toward the fence and fumbled with the latch on the gate, half hoping that Dr. Sproot would follow and whale the living daylights out of him. Instead, she just stood there and glared as he slunk through the gate to his car, reveling in the rather modest helping of humiliation she had dished out.

Dr. Sproot's shame and despair over her gardens were such that she turned what few friends she had away from her door. Same for those craven acolytes accustomed to turning to her for advice or inspiration.

Finally, one day, her gardens looking more than ever like brittle, rusted, and corroded metal, it dawned on her.

"Edith Merton!"

That could be the only explanation. The black arts of Edith Merton. Dr. Sproot shook her head in disbelief. After all, Dr. Sproot was a woman of science who had gotten a B- in biology and B in chemistry in high school. She subscribed to *The Homebound Scientist,* which she now made a mental note she would have to renew because the last issue came Thursday. Every gardening move she made was testament to what you can see, touch, and smell, and apply chemicals to. But what else could there be to explain all this? The flowers were perking up now, but only to laugh at her, pointing their wretched, decomposing blooms directly at her to highlight the object of their scorn.

Good God! thought Dr. Sproot, something's turning my gardens into mobs of horrid little people.

"This is Edith Merton's doing," she whispered.

She hardly dared admit it to herself, but what other explanation was there? Edith Merton casting her spells. Edith Merton, gardening witch!

On the surface, Edith Merton was a middle-aged businesswoman, who, with her husband, Felix, owned Mertons' Liquors on 34th Avenue and Mertons' TV and Appliance Mart on Jursfeld Street. Mostly, she kept the books in the store offices and left all the customer dealings to Felix and his sales and repair staff. From all accounts, she dressed normally, and was a dues-paying member of the Livia Business Fellowship. She walked her springer spaniel punctually at six ten p.m. every day, rain or shine. She had no tattoos or body piercings. As far as people could tell, she never even dyed her hair.

Edith Merton cultivated a modest little garden that gave her great pride, but which, otherwise, could *not* be taken seriously.

She had some snapdragons, which she interspersed with Dusty Miller and milkweed. A few morning glories. A smattering of ornamental grasses. All contained within one eight-foot-by-ten-foot patch of front yard bordered by a wall of decaying rail-road timbers. For years, her flowers were perpetually drooping underperformers, sadly under-watered because, when you kept the books for a couple of small businesses, who had time for plant care?

It was last year that things changed. Something had super-charged her garden into healthy, brilliant vivacity. The morning glories and snapdragons were glorious. The dusty miller had grown to gigantic size, threatening to overreach the mod-est gardening plot. The milkweed was lustrous, and the orna-mental grasses had truly become living ornaments.

Edith's newfound talents as a gardener had led her to seek membership in Livia's most prestigious gardening club, the Rose Maidens. It was the club for which Dr. Sproot served as secretary/treasurer and president emeritus.

The officers of the club had scoffed at the very notion of admitting Edith Merton to their hallowed ranks. Despite her recent successes, she didn't come close to meeting even their minimum requirements, and she had no gardening pedigree. Besides, their president, Dawn Fisher, hated snapdragons with a zeal that the members were led to believe was connected to some traumatic episode of her childhood. Some said that Dawn had once pinched a snapdragon to get that dragon ef-fect. The effect she got was a bee popping out of the flower and stinging her on the upper lip, which had swollen to three times its normal size.

Dawn had torn up Edith's letter of application. She sent back a curt note of refusal cosigned by all the other officers.

Edith Merton did not take this rejection lightly. She barged in, uninvited, during one of the club's monthly meetings and demanded admittance. When snubbed by the absolute silence of the members, she stormed out, knocking a potted Boston fern off its pedestal, and swearing that she would somehow get back at "you dried-up, old-biddy, gardening bitches."

Lately, Livia's gardening snoops, among whose ranks Marta Poppendauber could proudly count herself, had been hearing disquieting rumors about Edith Merton. It was said that she had been pursuing a blasphemous study of necromancy and communing with spirits of the dead. Livia's dead. Mostly, she restricted her practices to household pets, specializing in crickets, turtles, goldfish, and guinea pigs, but occasionally stretching herself to handle opossums and mourning doves. Rumor had it that she had even made the big jump to dogs, cats, and Shetland ponies.

All of this was harmless enough from a gardening standpoint except for one recent development: Edith was branching out, practicing her newfound black arts on her own gardens, which flourished as never before. By funneling the powers of flora long gone into those that still lived, she felt she could control the destiny of any flower, any vegetable, any plot of cultivated land. She had actually acquired a couple of customers for this new service, and was charging them for it, but surreptitiously, because how many people would want to buy their microwaves or fifths of vodka from a store co-owned by a professional witch?

The scary thing about all this was that Edith had those old gardening scores to settle. When Marta warned Dr. Sproot about all this in an oblique and mysterious way that indicated she really didn't put much stock in it, Dr. Sproot had hooted in derision. But now, faced with inexplicable blight and pestilence, and with a major contest and her future as Livia's preeminent gardener at stake, Dr. Sproot was forced to face new, not-very-scientific gardening realities.

A quick drive over to Muffy McGonigle's house was all the evidence she needed. Muffy was the outgoing president of the Rose Maidens. At any given time of day or night, she could be seen outside in her woven straw hat, inspecting and reinspecting her gardens for the slightest blemish and so much as a single dandelion or strand of stray fescue. It surprised no one when

Muffy suffered mild heart attacks on the occasion of early, hard frosts ravaging her mums in September 1996 and October 2005.

Dr. Sproot stared at Muffy's gardens in disbelief. Something awful had turned them into masses of crinkled, brown mulch-in-waiting. Before her very eyes, petals and leaves broke off and fell, pulverized into thousands of motes to be wafted away by the breeze. It was plant Armageddon, that's what it was! And there was Muffy, vigorously watering, her hat askew and her sunglasses perched crookedly on her sunburned nose. Dr. Sproot noticed that the plant food mix attachment had not been correctly screwed on to her hose, which was dribbling fertilized water all over her bare, bronzed legs and sandaled feet as she wobbled weakly from one dying plant to another.

"Muffy!" said Dr. Sproot, startling Muffy into dropping her hose. "What in heaven's name has happened here?"

Muffy wavered, then steadied, and stared at Dr. Sproot.

"Awful," muttered Muffy so softly that Dr. Sproot had to lean in closer to her and ask her to repeat herself. "Everything dying. Don't know why. Been up for three days straight. . . . Where's my hose? Where's Jock?"

"Jock?"

"My husband. You know, Jock. Did he have a coronary or something?"

"Who cares about Jock right now, Muffy? There's your hose." Dr. Sproot pointed to the ground, right at Muffy's feet. "Now get a hold of yourself and pick it up."

Muffy bent over to pick up the leaking hose, which suddenly spurted water all over her gardening apron as the fertilizer attachment loosened even more. Dr. Sproot jumped back to avoid getting soaked. As she did, a gust of wind lifted Muffy's hat off her head and carried it all the way to the fence that separated the McGonigles' yard from their neighbors', where it stayed pinned halfway up one of the fence posts as fast as if it were hanging there on a hook. Muffy didn't notice. She just kept on pointing the hose in the general direction of some for-get-me-nots, though she was mostly watering herself and her very healthy, and apparently unharmed, lawn.

"Muffy, listen carefully: have you heard from Dawn?"

"Dawn?" said Muffy, groggily.

"Dawn Fisher. Our president, you dodo. Has anything happened to her gardens? Anything bad?"

"Dawn? Gardens burned brown. Destroyed. Awful blight. Don't know. Dawn distraught."

With that, Muffy McGonigle keeled over. She flung the garden hose out toward the open lawn, and landed facedown on her turf, which was a combination of rye, fescue, and Kentucky bluegrass, with a little buffalo grass and Bermuda mixed in.

Dr. Sproot raced to her car. She roared out of the driveway, knocking over a watering can that had been carelessly left by the curb. When she got home, she wasted no time in calling Marta.

"Marta!" she gasped. "Marta! I've got to talk to Edith Merton. Got to! Can you get me in touch with her? Marta, you know Edith. You might even be friends with her for all I know. Marta?"

There was an ominous silence on the other end of the line.

"Marta! I must talk to Edith. Could you get her to talk to me?"

"About what, Dr. Sproot?" came the soft, halting voice over the receiver.

"You know damn well about what, Marta. You're the one who warned me in the first place. I didn't believe you then, but now . . . I need to talk to her about her spells. I want her to take her little witch's curse off my gardens and put it on to somebody else's. Do you hear me, Marta? Huh?"

"Why don't you just call her yourself?"

"Marta, you know darn well you don't just call somebody you don't know and ask her to start performing witchcraft for you. She'd tell me she didn't know what I was talking about. I don't even know what she looks like because I don't drink and I get my vacuum cleaner serviced at B&D Appliances. When she burst into our meeting like some . . . some . . . some criminal that night years ago, I wasn't even there. I was having the house fumigated to get rid of Mort's stench. She could walk right by me, Marta, and I wouldn't recognize her from Eve. Besides, she hates me because I'm an officer of the Rose Maidens. I need an intermediary to get my foot in the door."

"I'll see what I can do, Doc Phil."

"*Doc Phil!* Don't call me that again, Marta. Haven't I told you . . . ?"

But Dr. Sproot was ranting to no one. Marta had hung up the phone.

14

An Angel's Trumpet Is the Devil's Kazoo

Sis and her friends Freida and Colleen were sitting around the patio table trashing boys, wondering whether they should break out the cigarettes Colleen had in her purse, and which she had stolen from out of her older sister's dresser drawer, and debating which of their parents were the worst.

"I only have one parent," Freida said. "And she never lets me stay out past nine o'clock, even on weekends. And I haven't seen my dad in three years. I think he's in jail for starting a fencing operation. That pretty much makes mine the winners, hands down."

"Jesus!" Sis said. "What's a fencing operation?"

"It's where you say you're going to make fences for people but make them pay in advance, then keep the money and leave town without making the fences. The worst thing, though, is my mom makes me read books. One a month."

The other girls groaned.

"My parents are always tipsy," Colleen said. "They don't even notice when I get home. They don't set any limits on me. I come home whenever I want and stay at anybody's house I want to. Even though I like that, it makes them bad parents. I've seen them drunk at least fifty times. That's why I'll grow up emotionally stunted and never able to love a man. My dad hit me once."

The other girls drew back in shock.

"It's true. He hit me. You're the first I've told."

"Where?" said Sis.

"Right here," said Colleen, tipping her head forward and pointing to a place of no apparent significance on her scalp. "He made a fist and rubbed it really hard into me right here. You might still be able to see a mark."

The girls leaned in to look.

"I don't see a mark," Freida said.

"Well, if it was four years ago, you would have. That's when he did it."

"I think he just gave you a noogie," said Sis.

"A what?" said Freida.

"A noogie. Just a playful little jab. It's supposed to hurt a little. Otherwise, it wouldn't be a real noogie."

"But it hurt a lot," Colleen moaned. "It hurt so bad I can almost remember the feel of the hurt."

For a few moments, the girls just sat there, silently pondering the iniquity of parents. Then, Freida and Colleen looked at Sis, whom they called by her given name, Mary. Mary had perfect parents, at least on the surface. They knew that because, when they came over, Mr. and Mrs. Fremont were so nice to them and were always offering them something to eat and drink. They were *so* unlike Jaime's parents. Or Natalie's. Or Jake's. Those were parents who were seldom home, spoke little when they were, and *never* offered you anything. Sometimes, those parents' gazes would follow you through the house, as if they expected you to filch a billfold or a stray quarter.

The Fremonts, on the other hand, were usually home. They

were always smiling at you and wondering how you were doing. At least on the surface, they were the parents from heaven.

But what terrible things did they do in the privacy of their home after all the friends had gone home?

Sis tilted back her head and thought for a while. Her parents had never hit her. They had hardly even yelled at her. They set reasonable limits on what she could do at night and how late she could stay out. They supported her aspirations to be the next Kai Winding or J. J. Johnson by getting her private lessons with Bob McKenzie, who played trombone for both the Northland Jazz Stompers and the St. Anthony Symphony.

"C'mon," Colleen said. "Nobody's perfect. Not even George and Nan Fremont."

"I don't know; they're pretty close to perfect," Freida said. "You've pretty much got the neatest parents. That means you lose."

It annoyed Sis to know that her parents were so admired. She racked her brain for some little chink in the armor that would reduce her parents in her friends' estimation.

"I know," she said, sitting bolt upright. "They're obsessed. Goddamn obsessed. They spend so much time working on this goddamn backyard, they hardly have time for anything else. You wouldn't goddamn believe how much they obsess over it."

"But it's so pretty," Colleen said. "My mom and dad say your parents are what keeps the property values up in the neighborhood. They say your backyard is a neighborhood treasure."

"But you wouldn't believe how much they goddamn obsess over it," Sis said. "Jesus goddamn Christ, it seems like it's all we goddamn hear about these days. The backyard *this* and the backyard *that*. It just swallows up every goddamn thing."

Sis had just added *goddamn* to her vocabulary. She was fitting it into conversations with her peers, especially those such as Freida and Colleen, whenever she could. She was the first of her really good friends to be using profanity in earnest, and she wanted to show them that once she took the plunge into something new and daring, there was no turning back no matter who might disapprove of it. She had even vowed to debut it to her parents at some point, though the opportunity had not presented itself so far.

"Anybody want to smoke?" Colleen said, poking through her purse for the pack of cigarettes. Freida and Sis hemmed and hawed.

"Ah, come on; I didn't rip off Janice's cigarettes just to have them sit in my purse."

"Okay," said Freida meekly. "I guess so."

"Let's do it, goddamn it," Sis said. "I gotta have a smoke. . . . Maybe we should go back in the woods. Somebody might see us from the street and tell goddamn Mom and Dad."

"What is it with you and this 'goddamn' thing?" Colleen said. "It just sounds stupid. . . . Goddamn it, I don't have any matches."

"Shit!" Freida said.

"Goddamn it!" Sis screeched. The Fremonts' pale-blue Ford suddenly appeared cruising down Payne toward the driveway. "It's Mom and Dad. Put 'em away, quick!" Colleen stuffed the pack back in her purse. They waved at George and Nan as they got out of the car and climbed up the steps to the patio.

George and Nan were generally not that pleased to see Colleen and Freida hanging out with Sis, as their reputations among Nathaniel P. Kelley High School parents were somewhat suspect. There were insinuations that they were loose girls who liked to moon people from cars and who sloughed off their studies. They were known to have attended parties where bottles of three-two supermarket beer were passed around. They had parents who didn't seem to know or care what their children were up to, or how late they stayed up at night. Worst of all, there was a cloying smarminess about them that made George and Nan think they were trying to hide something.

Colleen and Freida flashed sparkling Pepsodent smiles as Nan and George paused to greet them on the patio.

"Hi, Mr. and Mrs. Fremont," they sang out in their best rendition of an angelic chorus. "So good to see you." George and Nan nodded and smiled, waiting for the effusion of baloney they knew would be coming.

"Mr. and Mrs. Fremont, your backyard looks so beautiful," Colleen said. "My parents say you have the most beautiful gardens in the city. They say you have a gift. Just look how beautiful it is."

"How are Cullen and Ellis?" Freida said. "Is Ellis enjoying college after his first year?"

"I hear Cullen's going to Dartmouth. Isn't that nice! You must be so proud!"

"Mr. and Mrs. Fremont, how do you manage to look so young?"

"Could you teach me how to garden, Mrs. Fremont?"

"How about those Muskies, Mr. Fremont?"

Sis sat through this interrogation slumped in her chair, looking as if she was about to gag. Ten minutes later, after George and Nan had calmly and affably answered each question, it was finally over. When Freida and Colleen got tired of slinging the bs, it happened abruptly, with no transitions to ease the way toward whatever new subject had captured their attention.

"Well, I gotta go," said Freida, sliding out of her chair in a way that made its metal runners screech annoyingly on the concrete patio. "I need to get a Freddy Burger. You coming, Colleen?"

"Yeah," Colleen said. "You, Mary? C'mon. Burger, shake, fries. Perfect diet for the growing girl." She winked at George and Nan, as if letting them in on a little private joke. They both chuckled politely.

"Nah," said Sis, slumped and despondent looking in her chair. "I'll just stay here and eat."

"Suit yourself," said Freida. She and Colleen sashayed down the steps in a manner that George, against his better nature, appreciated, but which Nan found unduly provocative, especially for two seventeen-year-old girls.

"Where are your other friends, Sis?" Nan said. "Margo and Taylor."

"They're around. But I like hanging out with Freida and Colleen, too."

Nan and George nodded gravely. Sis, they feared, was at a watershed point of her life, where she could choose the good crowd, good grades, and constructive activities, or the bad crowd, flunking out of school, getting pregnant, and turning into a community college deadbeat. Too much parental interference, they feared, could backfire on them, but they had to offer at least some guidance.

"Honey . . ." Nan began gently.

"Sis," George interrupted. "What are you hanging out with those two for? They're nothing but trouble." Nan's jaw clenched. When would this moron of a husband ever learn to appreciate the arts of subtlety! She held out her hand magisterially for George to halt whatever calumny he was about to spew out next, then cleared her throat.

"We just feel, Sis, that while Freida and Colleen are very nice girls, and we love them dearly, Margo and Taylor are just super-nice, wonderful girls, and we'd sure love to see more of them."

"Great girls!" George gushed. "Just great!"

Sis sat there pouting. She wondered why she was allowing herself to be subjected to this parental harangue and hadn't gone out with Freida and Colleen for Freddy Burgers. Besides, this was nothing any parent had to tell her anyway. She was beginning to see Freida and Colleen for what they were—losers—and was reconnecting with the old crowd; which, as it happened, was the one her parents approved of. She entertained briefly the notion of debuting her new word, then thought better of it. But there was something else that needed a public airing, and it needed it right now.

"Mom, Dad, I want you to quit calling me Sis. I'm seventeen years old and you guys and Cullen and Ellis have been calling me Sis ever since I was a baby. I can drive now. I will be able to vote in a year, and my reproductive organs have for some time been capable of bearing human fruit. I have changed from a little girl into a woman, in case you haven't noticed. Would you mind if you started calling me Mary?"

She lifted her eyes from the rippled glass texture of the tabletop and looked at her parents. They were muttering and looking at something. In fact, they weren't paying any attention to her at all!

"Mom! Dad!"

"Excuse us, dear," said Nan, finally looking at her daughter. "We've got something we have to go check." With that, they stalked off purposefully toward the far reaches of the yard. Sis watched as they stopped to look at that plant with all the white flowers and the perfumy fragrance, and which Nan had told her not to touch, and to never, ever, under any circumstances eat because it would kill her. Sis had thought that so strange. Why would she want to eat a goddamn plant! Now, they were inspecting the leaves and the flowers, talking about something she couldn't make out, their faces turned into masks of concern.

So where is their concern for *me?* Sis thought. How come I don't measure up to a plant in your eyes, huh?

"Ob-sessed!" she hissed as she stared down at the tabletop, then squashed an ant with a quick stab of her fingertip.

★ ★ ★

Something had been nibbling at the angel's trumpets.

The rustling noises from that corner of the yard had alerted George and Nan and when they turned their attention in that direction they noticed one of the plants quivering in short spasms.

They arrived at the angel's trumpets to find something they couldn't see careening through the woods on their left and a scene of the most awful plant mutilation on the ground before them. Several of the horn-shaped flowers had been torn. Two spiky seed pods had ripened and burst open to spread their seeds. Or had they been torn apart? Pieces of leaves had plainly been chewed off. Some fragments lay on the ground at the base of the plants.

"Who could have done such a thing?" Nan wondered. "Or *what?* A bird? A squirrel? A little child?"

Why in hell, George wondered, had they ever thought to introduce something to the garden that, although fast-growing and beautiful, was considered by many to be one of the world's most poisonous plants? But, if a plant was poisonous, didn't that mean that animals and birds would be deterred from eating it? And surely humans had the common sense not to eat any old thing sticking out of the ground. At least, *adult* humans. George shivered. The evidence was quite plain; something had been mucking with the plant.

Since they had planted the angel's trumpets in May, they had exploded into fragrant bushes throwing out lovely, cylindrical flowers with flaring ends. They gave that part of the yard a much-needed flair for the dramatic. But their lethal reputation caused George no end of anxiety. What if the Grunions, who were grouchy and solitary folks, were to dangle over the top of the fence, eye the lovely flowers and seed pods below them, figure them for fruit ripe for the plucking, then pick a few and drop them onto their cornflakes one morning? The

Grunions also had grandchildren, who could occasionally be heard romping about without parental supervision in their backyard. In fact, George had once seen them climb up to the top of the fence, and look down directly into the maw of the angel's trumpets.

"Get down from that fence!" he shouted, waving his hands frantically at them. "Get down from that fence!"

That prompted a visit from Old Man Grunion, whose visage, George and Nan agreed, resembled a statue of hard, cold granite so poorly sculpted you wouldn't necessarily recognize it as a human being's.

"Say!" bellowed old Grunion as he moved as ponderously as a three-toed sloth across the grass toward the Fremonts. "What the hell is wrong with my grandkids climbing that fence, eh? It's my fence. Why'd you tell them to stop? You can't tell them to stop climbing that fence. It's my fence. I put it up with my own hands."

George and Nan had decided a while back, as the first fears of the angel's trumpets' poisonous potency began to prick at them, not to tell the Grunions what it was that was caressing the other side of their fence. Otherwise, rude, inconsiderate neighbors that they were, they would order them to cut down the plants or face legal action from the Grunions' son, an evidently underemployed lawyer who had sued the city four times over Grunion property complaints, real or imagined.

"I was just a-a-a-afraid they might f-f-f-all over the fence," said George, gnawed by guilt at having such a hazard growing in their backyard and neglecting to call a meeting to alert the neighbors, and the press, should they want to attend.

Old Man Grunion, who had approached no closer than thirty feet from them, snorted derisively, and frowned as he looked around and took in the glories of the Fremonts' backyard. Here was a guy who would much prefer this whole space to be paved over, thought Nan, irked that Grunion would so wantonly tromp over the grass, instead of climbing up the steps in a civilized way, as all the other neighbors did.

"What did you say? Well, you leave my grandkids' safety to me, you hear!" he thundered. "Just makes me wonder if somethin' fishy's going on over here. Sunbathin' nude maybe. You sunbathe naked, do you?"

"Only when it's sunny!" Nan shouted, noticing that Grunion had tilted his head slightly and cupped his hand around his ear.

Grunion snorted again, and trundled back toward his house. It took him ten minutes to clear the Fremonts' property. Nan, who tended to entertain hypothetical anxieties at a far lower level than George, dismissed his worries about the Grunions, who could eat all the poison berry pods they wanted as far as she was concerned. And if they weren't responsible enough to watch after their grandkids, then what could she do?

"They could just as easily get into some fertilizer and eat that," she told George, to keep him from doing too much hand wringing. "Or the toilet bowl cleaner. Or the gas-oil mix for the weed whacker."

Nan was far more concerned about the wounding of their precious angel's trumpets, dangerous as they might be to whatever it was that inflicted the wounds. Fairly certain that no human was involved here, she had begun to fix her suspicions on birds as the culprits. What if the birds had started eating the seeds?

"Then wouldn't you see bird bodies scattered around here?" said George as they continued their inspection of the nibbled-on plants. "And if birds ate poisonous plants, there wouldn't be many birds left in the yard. I thought birds and animals steered clear of poisonous plant seeds because, otherwise, how could the plants reproduce? Then again, maybe there are some species around here that are prone to mental illness and don't know any better. What if there are raccoons, say, that are retarded?"

"If something in the animal kingdom is born retarded, then it stands to reason that it wouldn't live too long. Mother Nature is unforgiving in that respect."

"So maybe it's something out on its own, and really stupid, and it decided to try out something any ordinary critter wouldn't come within twenty feet of."

"It just doesn't make any sense," Nan said. "But there's the evidence. Shaking plant. Leaves torn. Flowers ingested. And plenty of seeds there for the taking."

George, in order to add fuel to his inflamed anxieties, had done some research on the angel's trumpets, and discovered that the whole bloody plant, not just its seed, was poisonous. He had read stories about people crushing the seeds between their fingers and getting sick. He had read stories about people actually eating the seeds on purpose and completely flipping out. All a bird had to do, he figured, was take one little peck at one of the seeds and it would be a goner.

Whatever was eating the angel's trumpet plants, or might be tempted to use them as a food source in the future, was no matter anyway; Nan had no intention of cutting them down or altering them in any way just because of a few safety concerns. It was, far and away, their most striking and unusual plant. Without the angel's trumpets, she thought, their backyard was only lovely and well maintained, with nothing to make it truly stand out in a judge's eye.

It took quite a bit of daring to plant angel's trumpets and lovingly nourish them to their perilous grandeur. What was life without risks? Who else but the most seasoned and brilliant gardeners dabbled with something so fraught with potential pitfalls?

In fact, not only was Nan convinced that keeping the angel's trumpets—seed pods and all—was the right thing to do, but she began to wonder about planting something new and equally daring, something that would cause the judges to gasp in amazement. If that entailed a few risks, and possibly a few dead birds or animals, or some irksome, tripped-out neighbors sent to the hospital to have their stomachs pumped, then so be it. That was life. Life is risk if you are really living it. Why ever get on a plane? Why take a plunge off a diving board? Why even get out of the bed in the morning, for that matter, if you don't want to face any risks in life?

As the plants expanded, George had grown increasingly squeamish, looking at them in his worried way, wondering whether they should at least *tell* the Grunions about them. Or maybe make some teensy-weensy alterations.

"Couldn't we just remove the flowers and the seeds?"

"Remove the flowers and seed pods!" Nan cried. "Are you insane? They're beautiful, and without them, you've just got some ordinary-looking plants. They're part of the plants. Remove them! Not on your life! What would the judges think if we were to prune off everything just because it entailed a little danger?"

George pondered this for a while, then opened his mouth to a degree that would be described as "gaping." He did this when his brain began to percolate with some startling new idea, either remarkably stupid or sensible.

"Rabbits," he said. "It's rabbits. They'll eat anything, the little buggers. But most of the seed pods are too high for them to reach, and that's where the real potent stuff is, isn't it? So maybe the flowers and leaves aren't poisonous enough to kill them, and they're just freaking out and having a lot of weird visions. It might just give them gas and indigestion. Too bad; I wouldn't actually mind seeing a few dead rabbits around here."

If there was anything that was the bane of the Fremonts' backyard, it was *Sylvilagus floridanus,* the Eastern cottontail. Nothing got George into more of a rabid frenzy than the thought of one of their legions of backyard rabbits layering the ground around the shrubs with their poop pellets and ravaging their gardens of everything that suited their gastronomic fancy at the time.

Rabbits had feasted continuously on the four alpine currants after George and Nan planted them at the base of the far trellis. They tried to protect them with chicken wire and mesh fabric coverings, but nothing seemed to work. Every year, rabbits had taken some of their hosta all the way down to the ground, and nibbled away enough at a few of the others to give their smooth leaves a ravaged, serrated look.

George had hoped the last hard winter—three years earlier—would have taken its toll on the miscreants, but they had survived and flourished, especially in the ensuing mild winters. At one point, George wondered whether buying a pet python and letting it loose in the backyard would solve their problem.

"Just one of the smaller varieties," he told Nan. "Not big enough to take on dogs, or cats, and certainly not humans. Well, maybe *small* dogs and cats. We could fence in the yard."

Nan rolled her eyes, but didn't bother to take issue, being reasonably certain that this was George's first step toward solving a problem: starting out by floating an utterly absurd solution, then never acting on it, and gradually working his way toward something that a rational human being might reasonably concoct. When George suggested that they buy a rifle, Nan figured she had to put her foot down.

"Are you out of your mind?" she shrieked once it became evident that this idea fell within the realm of what George would consider a rational solution to their rabbit problem. "You would be firing a rifle in this yard, bullets flying into neighbors' yards, and potentially killing and maiming our friends! What are you thinking?"

"I was thinking only of a twenty-two," George said ingenuously. "That could kill a rabbit or a squirrel, but a lot of times the bullets only bounce off humans. A quick trip to the hospital to treat a concussion or bruised rib. Besides, I would always be sure and aim it toward the Grunions'."

"That's tempting," said Nan, who, after twenty-two years of marriage, reflected that she still didn't know for sure when George was pulling her leg with a sense of humor as dry as the Sahara, and when he was dead serious. "But, no. You are not firing a gun anywhere around this house. That is an emphatic no."

"A pellet gun?"

"No!"

"Bow and arrow?"

"Absolutely not! Same principle."

"Not even a high-powered slingshot?"

That might have sounded a lot more reasonable under ordinary circumstances, but once Nan got into one of her negatory modes, there was no turning back.

"No! N-O, no!"

So, the rabbits had continued their pillaging of the Fremonts' backyard.

One day, though, George struck a blow for rabbit haters everywhere. He came out onto the patio early in his pajamas, and there was a rabbit calmly watching him, its mouth furiously grinding on a white-and-lavender blossom. One of their petunias! An anger he had never experienced before swelled up in him. It was an odd sensation, beginning in his face and contorting it into a mask of rage, expanding his rib cage to allow for the extra heartbeats and deeper breathing that would come with the burst of adrenaline that was already fueling his brain, then moving like a surge of electricity through his arms and legs and out into his extremities.

George reached for a rock of an astonishing roundness used to decorate the border around a bed of annuals that edged the patio. He twirled it in his fingers until he got the right grip, reared back, and let it fly. The missile didn't fly straight. Instead it was headed on a trajectory that would take it four inches to the right of the rabbit. Then, it broke suddenly to the left and hit the blissfully unaware rabbit squarely in the forehead.

"Dang!" whispered George, as he always did when talking to himself. "I just threw a major-league slider!"

He went inside, changed into his shorts and his favorite outdoor T-shirt—that Jethro Tull 2005 American tour one with its "Broadsword and the Beast" motif—walked down the steps to the garage, and fetched a shovel. You couldn't be too careful. Who knew what a wounded cottontail might do? He found the smitten animal lying still and quite dead on first glance, with barely a twitch of the muscle to indicate that it had been alive and rapturously laying waste to the Fremont backyard only five minutes earlier.

Then, George did something that he would always regret, at least just a little: in his rage, he brought the shovel down hard on the rabbit's head.

"That's for the hosta!" he snarled. Then again.

"That's for the . . . the . . . oh, yeah, the alpine currant!" Another blow.

"And that is for all the petunias, the phlox, the radishes I tried to plant two years ago, and everything else you've ruined around here!"

He had raised the shovel over his head for one more blow when something clicked in his brain.

"What am I doing? Good gawdawmighty, look what I've turned into!"

He lowered the shovel with trembling hands, inserted it gently under the supine corpse, lifted it up, its mashed, flattened head dangling like a puppet's over the edge, and deposited it on the edge of the woods next to the compost pile, at a spot where he had seen rabbits on numerous occasions.

"Let that be a warning to the rest of you," he spoke to the rabbit kingdom at large. "This is what happens to those who trespass into this yard on destructive raiding expeditions."

"What, you think that's going to keep the rabbits away?" scoffed Nan when he told her what he had done. "That's the most ridiculous thing I've ever heard of. Maybe you should just post a sign: Rabbits Keep Out, On Pain of Death! That would work much better."

"Well, nothing else has worked, and you won't let me get a gun."

"Please dispose of that rabbit back in the woods, if you don't mind."

But that was then. Now, as they stood there staring at the stark evidence that the angel's trumpets were being nibbled, wonderful new animal control possibilities came immediately to mind. Just to make sure the rabbits got the point, they would lay out a feast for them.

"I guess we can cut off one seed pod . . . okay, two, if it makes you happy, George, and lowers your angst level a little bit," Nan said. "Maybe a couple of leaves, too. But I gotta tell you, I don't think it's the rabbits. Otherwise the population would have been wiped out by now. I'm thinking maybe deer up from the river valley, and too big to be killed by the stuff. Still, if there's a chance of it going to the greater good of diminishing the rabbit population hereabouts, I guess I'm for it. We'll need gloves for this kind of work, and goggles."

The goggles, Nan explained, because it just wouldn't do to have some poisonous seed juice or powder come blasting out into their eyes when they cut them.

"What we need to do is cut off the seed pods and put them on the ground so they can't miss them. Then, we'll mix in some basic rabbit goodies to make sure they take the bait."

When Nan and George emerged from their garage, they looked as if they were preparing to shear off the end of a steel

I-beam with industrial plasma cutters. They had on welders' face shields, thick gloves, and leather aprons that Nan bought, along with an expensive electric grinder, back when she dabbled in tool sharpening through a continuing education class at Livia Community College.

The operation, using loppers to cut the flowers and the seed capsules and a few leaves from the plant, was a delicate one that mostly involved Nan trying to figure out where on the stems to cut. It lasted a half hour. Once the delicate surgery was performed, George and Nan inspected their gloves yet again for any sign of rips, tears, or holes that might allow the smallest speck of dust or drop of liquid to enter. Finding none, then adjusting their goggles, and lifting them up to get rid of any condensation that might impair vision, they gingerly placed the seed pods at the one of the plants' base, and surrounded them with baby carrots and a five large leaves' worth of shredded iceberg lettuce.

"Now, we wait," said Nan through her visor, which had been fogging up from her breath and the high humidity.

"What?" shouted George, unable to hear the normal range of a speaking voice when it was being blocked by a piece of plastic.

"Now, we wait," said Nan, lifting up her visor. "In the meantime, now that we're appropriately attired, know of any tools that need a little touch-up work?"

15

A Midsummer Fête

Nan's birthday fell on July 1, and George's, July 7. So, they decided three years ago, as their backyard began to assume the role of a neighborhood landmark, to hold a midsummer fete-cum-birthday party event on whatever Saturday happened to coincide with either of those two dates or, barring that, the Saturday that came between them. They called it FremontFest in a burst of public relations inspiration, and the name stuck.

They still mailed out the invitations two weeks in advance, but, at this point, that was only to note the date. For many of their friends and acquaintances in the Bluegill Pond vicinity, the Fremonts' midsummer party was now a firmly established companion celebration to the Fourth of July.

It wasn't just the neighbors who came. There were friends from other parts of the city, and acquaintances from church and Livia Athletic Association sports. A few low-level politicians and school board members, who had identified FremontFest as a golden opportunity to garner votes for the coming fall primaries and elections, made cameos, or sometimes worse. There had even been, over the past two years, a modest turnout of teachers from Kelley High, for whom the Fremont brood had proved to be an active (Ellis had been the star pitcher on the baseball team, and Cullen, the senior class president and Homecoming King; while Sis was one of the school's standout musicians) and academically accomplished family continuum.

Highlights of the afternoon would be the usual FremontFest menu—root beer floats, hot dogs, deli-prepared sandwiches, pop, and potato chips—and the private tours of the backyard, which was now bursting with blooming day lilies, clematis, roses, and cup and saucer vine. Interested parties would have to return in a couple of weeks for private showings, when the balloon flower, monarda, and purple coneflower hit their stride.

As a special surprise treat this year, Pat Veattle promised, via gilt-lettered card hand-delivered to the Fremonts' mailbox, to sing, for the first time ever, her new composition.

It was a satirical piece. She called it "The Men of Livia Are Drunken Wife Beaters." George and Nan wondered whether Pat had been hitting the hooch pretty hard when she came up with that title, because she certainly had been when they called her to firm up the details on her special appearance. There was some cause for alarm here. They had drifted away from Pat over the past three years or so, put off by her artiste's airs and boisterous mannerisms. They hadn't seen her at all in at least six months. Rumor had it that she was turning into a drink-addled fool and lapsing into debilitating mental illness. For the most part, she had disappeared from public view, even disbanding her sextet, "The Vignettes (featuring Pat Veattle)," which she always used as the vehicle for introducing her latest compositions. The "reclusive artist," Nan and George figured.

But there was always a small place in their hearts for Pat Veattle. It was Pat who brought them their only housewarming gift basket when they first moved in, and Pat who gave them the skinny on the new neighborhood. It was Pat who was there to offer loud and effusive encouragement when their backyard efforts began in earnest.

But what really distinguished Pat in their minds was her

exquisite taste in wine. It was Pat, after all, who introduced them to Sagelands merlot. For that incomparable act of kindness alone, George and Nan might be willing to cut her some slack.

After giving the matter much thought, and finding that a glass and a half of Sagelands did nothing to lessen their concern, they decided to call Pat again and set some ground rules. They asked deferentially if they could get a sneak preview of the song just in case there might be something in there that wouldn't quite work as well at an all-ages-invited neighborhood gathering as it would at, say, a brothel or a gathering of Ripple Pagan Pink–soused frat brothers. Pat demurred with a couple of hiccups, citing artistic integrity.

"I'm an ar-thist," she slurred over the phone. "An ar-thist . . . a-r-t-s-z-c . . . ar-thist. Ya don't preamble with an ar-thist. I will perform . . . preform . . . I will perform preform. Itsh my song, and I'll cry if I want to. Thou wilt not wilt on me."

Nan and George figured that was probably okay, given the fact that whatever she had written probably wouldn't be that much different from her other songs, which were either only marginally funny and perhaps occasionally just a tad risqué, or utterly innocuous. Besides, their audience was mature enough to handle a little adult humor that their kids wouldn't understand anyway.

But that title! They asked her if she could change it.

"Not in a trice," she said after a loud belch forced Nan to yank the receiver away from her ear. "Not in a smidgeon. The show goes on. Itsh good for all ages . . . young, old farters, young. Hic . . . hic . . . That whash the hiccups that never came. . . . Never . . ." She mumbled something else Nan couldn't understand, but, on the whole, sounded reasonably agreeable. But would she be sober?

"She'll be one soused sister," said Nan after hanging up and indulging in what for Nan was an unusually active and prolonged exercise in hand-wringing angst. "I'm going to call her back and cancel right away."

"Hang on there before you do that," George said. "Pat's never been drunk at a performance that I've seen, and, besides, she's our big featured act. Everyone knows she's coming . . . even though it's supposed to be a surprise."

Nan relented against her better judgment. They rented a microphone and a little thirty-watt amplifier for her, and called Pat back to offer their own Sis Fremont as accompanist on the trombone.

"Nuttin' doin'," said Pat with an explosive belch that rang in George's ear for twenty minutes afterward. "I's sholo, shtricly sholo. Got that? Sholo as shit . . . Dun need no acupitnist."

From what George was able to cull out of the aural assault of slurred and garbled English that followed, Pat would accompany herself with a "juice herp" (Jew's harp) and "cushy tits" (castanets). She also said she would charge $15,000, which she quickly burbled was actually 15,000 "shents." George calculated that to be $150, which still came as something of a shock, seeing as how Pat had been a friend of theirs for years.

The guests arrived as they always had: the early birds came early and the latecomers came late. The in-betweeners came in between.

The Boozers stayed for a couple of diet Cokes, looked around the gardens, then cheerfully departed at three thirty p.m., in accordance with their plan. Mitzi and Frip came fifteen minutes into the party, talked up a storm, knocked a few things over with their wildly flailing appendages, and managed to offend at least six people with their loud and ridiculous contrariness. Steve and Juanita Winthrop, whose kids and theirs grew up together and remained best friends, were already on their second round of root beer floats; they'd stay until closing time. Alex and

Jane McCandless, dear friends with no particular qualities good or bad to distinguish them, were off on vacation to the Canadian Rockies, and had offered their regrets two weeks ago. The Fletchers were hit-or-miss. George hoped for a miss this year as he had no intention of revisiting his outdoor pit-stop episode, which Jeri no doubt would spend the entire afternoon hectoring him into doing. He was reasonably certain Jeri had already recited every detail of the unfortunate episode to every homeowner within a four-mile radius.

The Grunions would *NOT* be there, though Old Man Grunion was always a threat to call and yell at them to stop all that racket. They would ignore him sweetly, with an invitation to "come on over and join the fun." He would call the police, who by now knew that if they drove over to investigate, they would find assistant police chief Fred Face (whose kids had played L.A.A. baseball with Ellis and Cullen) enjoying the festivities, and would be directed to bugger off and move on to the next call.

Lots of neighbors used the occasion to get a firsthand look at what the Fremonts had been up to in their yard. Nan and George were always happy to oblige them with individualized commentary on whatever segment of the yard they wanted to talk about, although George occasionally had to turn to Nan, the true gardening expert of the family, for help. The Fremonts met the effusions of praise that were heaped on them with a false humility befitting their Midwestern roots.

What came as something of a surprise to the Fremonts was the buzz Burdick's Best Yard Contest had created. At least a dozen of the earlier arrivals mentioned it. After quick inspections of the yard, they assured the Fremonts that their efforts were nonpareil and that they were shoo-ins for the grand prize. But one, a bizarre, middle-aged, noisily opinionated nuisance of a widow named Earlene McGillicuddy, warned them not to get too cocky about their chances for success.

Earlene was a former neighbor who had moved to the Murphy Lake neighborhood and whose passions were roses and the literature of the Maldive Islands.

"In my roses club are two women whose gardens will put yours to shame," she said. "One is Vanessa Stevenson. Remember that name, because it might come back to haunt you. The Stevensons are in the southwestern part of the city, near the new Lampkins grocery store, just off Carstens Avenue.

"The other is Yelena Diggity. She and her husband, Kaldo— isn't that an odd name, 'Kaldo'?—live on that long cul-de-sac near Idylwild. They will do anything to win. Believe me. They're not spending their Saturday afternoons having a party, like you folks are; they're working, working, working every minute to make their backyard better. Beware! I'm telling you. There are folks who know who you are and they've been checking out your grounds, without your permission. I assume that because they're doing it on the sly. I know; I've seen them. Just remember, they'll do anything to win."

"That's just ridiculous," Nan said. "That's about the silliest thing . . ."

"Don't you want to win?" said Earlene, shoveling one spoonful after another of root beer float into her maw of a mouth.

"Sure, I want to win."

Earlene leaned closer, spattering Nan with an ice cream spray that came flying out of her mouth like liquid grapeshot whenever she talked. She held out a strong, grasping hand as if to grab Nan by the lapels of her blouse and fling her with a sudden, amazing burst of strength over the house, over Sumac Street, and into Bluegill Pond, and poked a thick, long-nailed finger at Nan's bosom.

"Then you'd better get crackin' 'cause the Diggitys will do whatever it takes to beat you, and you're sitting around here on your rear ends. You've got to take action, young lady! You need help! You could hire me as your consultant. I only charge fifty bucks an hour and you would get half your money back if you don't place in the top thirty. How's that for a deal? I hate Yelena Diggity. I hate her for reasons I don't care to disclose right now. But how 'bout it? Fifty bucks an hour for one of the best gardening consultants this side of St. Anthony?

"And ask yourself this question." Earlene moved her eyes shiftily from one side to the other. "Do you know everyone here? Huh? There could be strangers here . . . strangers you don't want prowling around in your backyard, strangers who mean to do mischief."

Nan took a sip of Sprite and pondered Earlene for a moment. She was not one to be stampeded into anything, not even by a human hurricane named Earlene McGillicuddy.

In spite of her resolve not to do it, Nan peered stealthily over one shoulder. There were a couple of strangers examining the clematis. Then, she peered over the other. More strangers. These were bending over a bed of something that hadn't even come up yet. But so what! Strangers showed up every year for Fremont-Fest. Why should this one be any different? She chuckled to herself at the thought of being called a "young lady," especially by someone her own age, then wondered who that might have been running around snapping photos of their yard. She asked Earlene.

"Oh, that's Phyllis Sproot. *Doc-tor* Phyllis Sproot. Or maybe it's someone associated with Phyllis Sproot. Of course! How could I forget Dr. Sproot? I have seen her grounds. *Im*pressive! Yuccas and coreopsis–salvia–hollyhock blend . . . those are her gardening passions. Yuccas and coreopsis–salvia–hollyhock blend. Strange choices if you ask me, but I've seen stranger. Not in Livia, of course. That Sproot's another one who wants to win at all costs. I've heard that she told someone if she didn't win life would cease to have meaning for her.

"So, she heard about your place, and decided to do some research. She's got a pal, too. Marta something. Popcorn? Nice woman. Kind of quiet and furtive, though, if you ask me. One of those still-waters-run-deep kind of people, I bet. Speaking of whom, gosh, you should see *her* gardens! Magnifico! She could easily run away with first prize. She's another one of that cul-de-sac crowd."

"So," said Nan. "This Phyllis Sproot, or one of her buddies, has been trespassing on our property like some criminal while we were away?"

Earlene chuckled.

"These are high stakes we're talking about here," she said. "People will stop at nothing to win this. *Nothing!* Which is why you need my help. Not only will I consult with you on your gardens and what they need, and from what I can see at first blush, they need quite a lot, but I'm also an expert garden spy, and I've dabbled in gardening sabotage."

"Sabotage!"

Earlene drained her float hastily, as if she needed to fortify herself for what was to come, then beckoned Nan to lean closer. Nan held back, not wanting to be assaulted with another shower of airborne root beer and melted ice cream molecules.

"We don't need everyone to hear this," she said in a hoarse, frothy whisper. "But I have what's needed to, shall we say, take a garden *down* big-time! Whaddya say, fifty bucks an hour to have Earlene on your side? I've got to warn you, dear, that if you don't hire me, others might, but I like you, and I know you need help, so you get the early bird discount."

"Very kind of you," said Nan, who wondered whether the root beer was spiked with something mind-altering, causing her to imagine what she thought she had just heard. "I'll give it some careful consideration."

"Don't wait too long," Earlene said. "My price goes up in two weeks, and, by then, I could be working for somebody else anyway."

"Ah, Earlene, one more thing: I don't mean to sound accusing, but you haven't been snipping off our monarda, have you? A couple of weeks ago, I found about twenty stems cut off of several different plants as cleanly as if someone had taken pruning shears to them."

Earlene closed her eyes for a moment as she worked a gob of melting ice cream around her mouth.

"Not me," she said after swallowing her load of float with a satisfied *ahhhh*. "You're sure it's not animals?"

"Reasonably so. It's too high up for the rabbits to get to. This has happened over time, not all at once. And my husband George heard snipping noises."

"Hmmmm. Sounds suspicious, all right. And smart. Take 'em out little bits at a time and before they bloom to make 'em harder to spot. Not me, that's for sure. But, of course, I wouldn't tell you if it was me, would I. Ha-ha . . . Now, what I want to know is this: Who the hell is horning in on my sabotage business? Hmmm? And here I was thinking I had the monopoly."

With that, Earlene McGillicuddy walked off to further inspect the backyard, sometimes smiling smugly and, at other times, shaking her head in dismay.

"What's *her* problem?" said George, who had been surreptitiously listening in on the conversation from just within hearing range.

"She thinks we're going to lose . . . to those folks on the cul-de-sac we visited last week. The rest doesn't bear repeating. At least not now."

"Well, sure, their yard is spectacular, if it's the same one I'm thinking about. That one where the couple looking out the window spooked us. Old news. We'd already pretty much pegged them as the winners, hadn't we?"

"No, whatever gave you that idea, George? And if that's what you're thinking, then it's our job to make ours spectacular, too. As soon as this party's over, we start working. We're planning on winning this thing. Or didn't I make that clear?"

George sighed. By the time the party ended, he would have knocked down a couple of sandwiches, three bags of thick-sliced, extra-greasy potato chips, five root beer floats, and three plastic bottles of water. He would hardly be in condition to start wielding a rake and a shovel.

He walked over to the cartons of ice cream, which were packed in ice buckets to keep them from melting too fast, and the aluminum root beer kegs, which had been lifted onto a couple of borrowed picnic tables. He scooped himself out three giant hunks of vanilla ice cream, then kept lathering them with root beer until the foam started cascading over the side of his cup.

Children and teenagers began arriving. George moved to the back so he could keep a closer watch on the angel's trumpets. It simply would not do to have children wandering around back there, testing out the pretty flowers and seeds. Why the hell hadn't Nan allowed him to cut off all the flowers and seed pods and commit them to the flames? And, of course, he had forgotten to post the DO NOT TOUCH signs on the plants, as he had originally intended.

The yard was swarming with people now, and Sumac and Payne were lined with cars for two blocks in every direction. George kept his head tilted toward the angel's trumpets as he ambled over toward the patio to perform the duties of host. He saw that Nan was playing the part of perfect hostess, manning the food and drink tables, circulating from one clot of guests to another, then giving Steve and Juanita big hugs.

"You know, George, I think you're going to win this thing."

"Thing? What thing?"

George's reactions and mind had been fuzzed somewhat

by the root beer floats. He looked skyward, wondering if he was the lucky recipient of a secret message from either the Almighty or some other cosmic force.

"What do you mean, 'What thing?' Why, that stupid backyard contest, the dumbest contest in history. What else?"

George felt the clap of a hand on his shoulder, and wheeled around to see Ellis and Cullen, almost wedged against him by the crush of people congregating on the patio. They were laughing.

"Dad, you're so gullible," Cullen said. "Couldn't you tell right off it was me?"

"No," said George, confused and ashamed to put such dumbfoundedness on display in front of his sons. "You disguise your voice well, Cullen. And how did you two know about this contest? I don't recall your mother and I talking to you about it."

"You didn't," Ellis said. "But it's all over town anyway. The Abramses are in it. The Spearmans are in it."

"The Johnsons, the Gilders, the Messersmiths," Cullen added.

"And the Hardys and the Hoosenfoots. Hey, that's alliteration. Pretty good, huh?"

"Gosh, I didn't know about the Hoosenfoots? Come to think about it, I didn't know about the Messersmiths and Hardys either. There must have been more folks entering since Mom and I looked at the entrants' list. Jeez, there must be hundreds of entrants now."

"It's a pretty big deal, Dad," Ellis said. "But we have full confidence in you and Mom winning and bringing great glory to the Fremont clan."

George smiled wanly at his two sons, whose Cheshire Cat grins reeked of sarcasm.

"And have you heard, Dad, that other sponsors have jumped on board, and the prizes have been increased . . . a lot?"

"A lot? How much?"

"Well, Livia Farmer's Bank and Trust is now a sponsor. And Jeepsons' Family Restaurants."

"And Carpet King," interjected Ellis.

"Yeah, Carpet King. And Consolidated Industries."

"And Johnson Marine."

"And Johnson Marine. Shut up, Ellis. New World Semi-conductors."

"New World Semiconductors?"

"New World Semiconductors."

"And a couple of anonymous rich people who are putting up $20,000 each."

"What?"

"That's right," Cullen said. "So now, not only does the winner get the $5,000 from Burdick's PlantWorld, but there's another $75,000 in additional prize money."

"That is the most astounding thing I have ever heard," said George.

"And it is absolutely true," Cullen said. "It's that Burdick guy. Very rich. He wants to get his name on the map some-how. So, this is his big rich-guy project. He will spare no ex-pense and twist every corporate arm he can think of to make this the biggest blowout garden contest in history."

"So, Dad," said Ellis, wrapping his strong pitcher's arm around George's shoulder. "We are now four-square in sup-port of your obsession. We might even help you . . . well, at least lend moral backing. You and Mom gotta win this thing. We know you can do it."

George walked off in a daze, and soon found himself in-specting the far reaches of the yard. He wondered forlornly whether the backyard could even hold a candle to some of the magnificent gardens he and Nan had seen on their scouting expeditions.

Their gardens began to look to him like the work of feckless novices: modest, uninspiring, and showing no particular original pattern that would stand out to judges who really knew their business. He sat down on the arbor's bench to recover from a bout of wooziness; the result of either a contemplative moment coming on or a little too much sugar and fat partying their way through his nervous system; hard to tell which.

On the way back to the patio, George detoured over to the angel's trumpets. It was a good thing he did! The seed pods had been broken open and scattered about. In a panic, George searched his memory for the picture of what the seed pods had looked like when he and Nan placed them at the foot of the plant. Was he just imagining that something—or somebody—had gotten into them? Could his own irrational fears be causing him to hallucinate? No. The iceberg lettuce and baby carrots were gone.

George examined that part of the yard and the area surrounding the compost pile and bordering the woods for something dead or dying. There was not so much as a dead blade of grass. Then, he remembered: death from angel's trumpet poisoning was not instantaneous. It could take days to kill you. What about animals? They would presumably die sooner since they were smaller, wouldn't they? He had not inspected the plants up close since yesterday. A rabbit might have come in the night, gone away feeling sated, and now be dying miserably in its warren out there somewhere in the woods.

George began to think of their campaign against the rabbits as a persecution. After all, they were only doing what nature instructed them to do. And here he was conking them on the heads with rocks and battering them to bits when he couldn't control himself, and now poisoning them horribly.

How much different were rabbits from humans anyway?

They felt pain, didn't they? It was only one step up from pain to feelings of filial and paternal love. Rabbits were fathers and mothers. What if that rabbit's kids were watching as he smashed Dad's (or Mom's) head with the shovel just last week? Might there be some fellow rabbits ministering to the one out there dying, wishing to whatever deity they had that a miracle would be performed?

George grimaced and ground his heel down hard into the remnants of the scattered seeds and pods and little vegetable bits until earth and plant were all blended together in one squashed mess. Then, he ground it around some more. He kept on working his heel into the earth around the plants until it was indented into a little inch-deep basin. There are people in this world, he reflected, who would call him a murderer. George looked around, half expecting to see hordes of SPCA and PETA police bearing down on him.

What he saw was a crowd in motion, gravitating at the sound of Nan's urgings and some amplified static toward the patio, which was now one big clot of people. Pat had arrived. Another amplified squeal from the patio, then a hoarse sort of croaking, broke through the sad, self-mortifying spell. George kneaded his forehead to rid himself of the last traces of these terrible, enervating thoughts, but something more was needed, something with the kind of narcotic value that would take his mind completely off all these unpleasant things. He would have another root beer float.

George would not be able to get to the root beer and ice cream. The crowd gathered on the patio had swelled to even greater numbers as he passed through the fence gate and entered the inner sanctum of the backyard. He found himself part of the migration of outliers drifting toward all the squawking and crackling that was coming from the patio. The crowd was five deep. George nodded warily to friends and acquaintances who, like him, were harboring some vague apprehensions about what sounded like a breakdown in the electronic equipment.

As he scanned the crowd that was following behind him to join the packed-in group at the patio, he was at least gratified to note that their visitors were respecting the sanctity of the backyard, carefully picking their way through the gardens, and detouring around the flower beds and plant clusters. Nothing was being trampled, bruised, or even casually brushed against. The crowd, wedged in by the arbors and their trellises, was so thick now that he couldn't see Nan, though he could hear her voice—what would be called a very average voice, but which had projection and the carrying power to be heard over many other sounds. Then came the grotesquely amplified thump of someone tapping a microphone to make sure it worked. Several in the crowd chuckled.

"One, two, three," came Pat's booming voice, assaulting the crowd, then crashing into the side of the Grunions' house and bouncing back again. "Twenty, forty-seven, eighty-six. I guess it works."

George could only see the top of Pat's head bobbing up and down, her raised, gyrating hands and snapping castanets. The castanets cracked across the backyard like rifle shots, and Pat's gravelly contralto began to make a noise that was somewhere between a hum and a groan.

The castanets established a slow cadence, and Pat's hum-groan grew louder. Could this be the debut of "The Men of Livia Are Drunken Wife Beaters"? George flinched. The groaning grew louder. This sounded like something sort of Mediterranean and Egyptian. Pat had mentioned that she was getting interested in the music of "the rest of the world." But this groaning? The castanets clacked faster and louder.

It's some kind of flamenco music, only without the guitar

player, thought George. He was relieved to think that this debut number was to be a harmless rhythmic chant rather than an actual song about depraved Livians.

George had to admit that Pat was wielding the castanets with authority. Then came the wail, a long, deep, guttural lamentation that, in musical circles, might be called "dissonant." It rose in pitch and volume to the level of a shriek. Then, it stopped, and the castanets clacked, more slowly now until they settled into a monotonous andante.

After about two minutes of this, there rose up a thick, fluttering groan the likes of which George had never heard. Pat was twirling her hands around now, forming little pirouettes in the air as she clackety-clacked away. Words were coming out of the groan, and George listened intently for anything that might signal Pat steering her music in a drunken, wife-battering direction. He couldn't understand anything, though it sounded like something he heard once when he was watching a Travel Channel show about East Timor. As he scanned the crowd, he could see that others were straining to understand. A lot of them looked confused and a little annoyed, perhaps perturbed by the shriek, but not quite ready to walk away.

Then came the change. In the front, people gasped, giggled, and turned to one another with looks of surprise and consternation, maybe even *acute* consternation. There were a few cries—more evidence of surprise—and some male tittering, which indicated, what? Guilty pleasures better left in the closet or swept under the rug?

People farther behind began to shift their bodies and crane their necks to see better. At this point, George could still just see Pat's weaving hands working those castanets like nobody's business. What else might be going on he couldn't tell. The very tall Jim Thebold, the very wide Martha Vinson, and five or six others he couldn't recognize from behind were blocking his view.

Louder gasps came from the front, and the crowd parted, allowing a red-faced, sputtering Caroline King to burst through, dragging along her twelve-year-old son, Jens, who was pulling back but losing the tug-of-war, behind her.

At this point, George decided that, as one of the principals responsible for whatever was happening on the patio, he had to get up there to find out what was causing such a hubbub. He nudged past Jim and Martha What's-Their-Names, and then Sarah and Bert Vines, who cast disapproving glances at him as he pushed past them with a whispered "Excuse me," and a wink of recognition. There was Harry Adams (What was *he* doing here?). George struggled to squeeze between Harry, on the right, and Jenny Perkins and her boyfriend, Phil Grough, on the left. Jenny and Phil were both frowning with their arms crossed. He finally broke through the mass, into the vanguard of the semicircle of humanity that had formed a tight curve around Pat Veattle, the microphone, and the amplifier.

At last, George could see what all these signs of an impending fuss were about. Could he ever! There was Pat, who was pushing sixty-five easy, though he and Nan had never asked. In normal times, Pat had a figure most often covered appropriately with billowing tent-like outfits. Here was a transformation of the most shocking sort! Pat Veattle was all gotten up as what could only be described as a genie who'd been living off her wishes for an eternal supply of triple cheeseburgers, chili-slathered fries, and malted milks. She was wearing sheer, plum-colored pantaloons, with her exposed midriff hanging quite noticeably over the elastic waistband that was just barely holding them up.

Somehow suspended across her chest was a filmy mesh vest un-girded by anything in the foundation department, and which was decorated with little colored sequins doing a poor job of being strategically located.

At least she was wearing something on her head. That was good, since her hair had been thinning so dramatically that you could see the little bare spots from forty feet away. What passed for head cover was a precariously perched red fez trailing a fabric pennant at least three feet long that had embroidered on it *Pat Veattle Song Stylist Parties Weddings Call 642-888-1742.*

By twirling around in various directions, and at various speeds, and somehow keeping the fez from falling off, she worked that pennant so that you could usually see most of what was on it in one long twirl. A red bandanna was pulled, desperado-style, over her mouth and all the way up to her eyes, which George figured was probably the reason he couldn't understand whatever it was she was singing.

He saw Nan. She was standing in front, not more than five feet from Pat, and flinching to avoid the more extreme and wide-ranging of Pat's moves.

Pat made a spitting sound into the microphone, which, amplified, sounded like an old engine coughing and sputtering. George wondered whether this signified a sound effects routine, but then came another groan from deep within her ample abdomen. It was low, growling, and ominous.

Then, the groaning and castanet clicking stopped. With one swooping motion, Pat placed them on the table next to the root beer kegs and picked up her Jew's harp. As Pat began twanging away, George half expected her to break into a nasal rendition of "She'll Be Comin' 'Round the Mountain."

"Eeeehhaw!" he yelled.

But what Pat Veattle started singing was more like a chant. And, yes, the chant marked the debut of "The Men of Livia Are Drunken Wife Beaters."

Oh, you men.
Oh, you men.
Oh, you Livian men.
You drink too much.
You drink too much.
Yeah, you drink too much.
You get out the belt.
You get out the belt.
You get out the belt.
Yeah, you get out the belt.

Then, you let her have it.
Then, you let her have it.
Then, you let her have it.
Lord, Lord have mercy, you let her have it.

Whip her on her butt.
Whip her on her butt.
Whip her on her butt.
Yeah, you whip her on her butt.

Now, it's upside the head.
Now, it's upside the head.
Now, it's upside the head.
Yeah, it's upside the head with your naked fist.

Men are worthless bums.
Men are worthless bums.
Men are worthless bums.
Come to think of it, so are women.
Yeah, yeah, yeah.
Yeah, yeah, yeah.
Yeah, yeah, yeah . . . yeaaah.

She started to play her Jew's harp again, and a gasp rose up from the crowd. Several people, acquaintances from outside of the neighborhood, stalked off. George felt his face redden. His nerve ends sang out "Code red!" He looked over at Nan, who saw him, and jerked her head angrily toward Pat.

George steeled himself and walked over to the amplifier, which was throbbing from the noise of the Jew's harp, and which George noticed had been turned all the way up to 10. He yanked the microphone plug out of its socket with a staggeringly violent electronic squeal. Nan picked up the threadbare overcoat that Pat had brought with her and flung onto the concrete when her act began, and draped it forcefully over Pat's shoulders. She turned her away from the microphone and toward the steps leading down to the driveway, and gave her a little shove, but not before catching the full force of a vodka-fueled belch square in the face.

"Go away, and don't come back," she said. "You have thoroughly mortified me and George, and embarrassed our guests. . . . You're drunk! Do you need a ride home?"

Pat pulled the overcoat tightly around her, despite the eighty-five-degree heat, lifted her head up in a show of regal disdain, and silently began to negotiate the steps, further angering Nan by kicking her much-abused pea gravel this way and that with her dainty, pointed, red dancing slippers.

"The nerve of that woman!" she hissed to George, who was winding up the microphone cord and scanning the silently dispersing crowd for signs of shock and indignation. "Could you believe that?"

George could not, but he also secretly appreciated what he anticipated to be some of the ramifications of Pat Veattle's little display. For one thing, Pat had always been pompous and temperamental, even during the years when they called her a friend. With any luck, they would never have to endure that insufferable attitude again. Nor would they have to serve as sounding boards for her compositions. George's spirits were also lifted by the knowledge that his sorry little incident in the woods from a few weeks back would now be forgotten, to be completely overshadowed by Pat's rather sorrier one.

George and Nan, and a few others lingering in the back-yard, watched with mingled contempt and amusement, and even a little pity, as Pat wove down the side of Sumac Street to-ward her home, three blocks away. A block down the street, she stopped to adjust and readjust her overcoat. Then, she plopped down violently onto her rear end on the Atchinsons' lawn.

"Well, this party will go down in the annals of Livia his-tory," Nan said with a sigh. "I just hope the teachers were all gone before it started."

She surveyed what was left of the crowd. Most of the guests were straggling toward their cars or forming little pro-cessions down Payne Avenue and Sumac Street.

Those walking down Sumac, she noticed, were all crossing to the other side of the street to avoid Pat, who sat there clutching her overcoat, her head bowed down between her splayed-out knees. She considered asking George to walk down and offer her assistance, but his attentions were focused elsewhere at the mo-ment. He was gazing, worriedly, at the angel's trumpets, next to which two children and two adults were standing, their backs turned to George and Nan.

"Hey!" shouted George, flapping his hands wildly. "Hey! Get away from that plant! It's dangerous!"

"George!" Nan said. "What on earth are you doing? They're just looking at the plant. People do that when they come over here."

"But it's angel's trumpet, and it's dangerous, and I was going to tell you that something has gotten into the seeds, and

I tried to mash the rest of them into the ground, so it's dangerous to be walking there, too, 'cause you can get all that mash on your feet."

Nan sighed.

"Oh, don't be absurd. Jesus, George, you're so paranoid."

"Paranoid? You're the one who told me to wear gloves before I touched the blasted things!"

The clot of visitors slowly moved away from the angel's trumpets without having eaten any of them that George could tell. Still worrying that they had nibbled some leaves on the sly, he nevertheless turned to watch with Nan as the distant Pat finally roused herself, got up off the Atchinsons' lawn, and wobbled off toward home. A few remaining friends were gathering around now. They pressed in closer, smiling and sniggering, wanting to revel in the details of what had just happened.

"That woman was drunk as a skunk," said Juanita Winthrop, chortling as Steve beamed with mischievous pleasure beside her. "And what in God's name was she doing? And those lyrics! Did you catch those?"

"I thought it was pretty sensuous myself," blurted Steve to laughter as he caught a Juanita elbow to the rib.

"Quite the show this year," came a familiar voice from behind them. "Glad we didn't miss it."

George and Nan turned, startled. Alex and Jane McCandless were standing there, right behind them in their backyard instead of on the banks of Lake Louise, having appeared magically, it seemed, out of thin air.

"The McCandlesses!" cried a delighted Nan. "When did you get here? We didn't see you. We thought you'd be gone."

"And, boy, are we glad we got here in time," said Alex, whose tall, stooped stature, somewhat skewed wire-rim glasses, and clipped, rapid-fire speech made him the perfect complement to Jane, who was short, stood upright and rigid, had eagle vision, and spoke slowly, in very measured and complete sentences. "I was wondering when Pat was going to jump off the deep end, and jeez, did she ever do that or what! Talk about toasted! Have you seen her lately? She'll go down to the lake and do some kind of wacky Chinese exercise. She'll spend two hours down there doing that and dressed up like . . . like . . . well, once, she had a moose costume on."

"Alex!" said Jane. "You're just making that up. I never saw her in a *moose* costume. Maybe I saw her dressed up like a ballerina once, and come to think of it, in reverse drag, with a tux and tails once, but a moose? You're just making that up."

"Swear to God."

"He's not making it up," Steve said. "I saw her in that costume, too. It has goofy, antenna-looking antlers and everything. It's a really bad costume but if you look closely you can tell it's meant to represent a moose, maybe an abstract moose. It looked homemade. Anyway, when I saw her, she was walking down Sumac right over there."

Steve pointed to a spot just to the west of Sumac's intersection with Payne.

"Or *stumbling* would be a better word for it. I was driving along, minding my own business, when I saw this human moose kind of weaving along." The others were laughing now. "I saw this human moose, and I stopped because I was scared I was gonna hit whoever was in this human moose costume." More laughter. "So, I pulled up alongside and said, 'Hey, you need to be careful walking along the street like that.' She turned toward me, and I could tell looking at the holes for the orifices it was Pat. So I said, 'Pat, what the hell are you doing dressed up like a moose?' It was ninety degrees out there, and she was panting inside that costume. And she said . . . she said . . . 'I'm gonna go scare some fish. I'm gonna go scare some fish.' "

The laughter erupted across the patio and echoed against

the Grunions' house. The few other guests remaining in the yard glanced over, puzzled and smiling.

"Jeez, could I ever smell the liquor coming out of her mouth. Then, down the slope she went. I don't know how she kept from falling over. Down the slope she went, to scare some fish or small children, I guess."

"I saw her dressed up as a medieval lady once," said Juanita once the laughter had died down enough to be heard over it. "With the pointy hat and everything. She just stood there with her arms stretched out all crooked like tree branches. I guess she was trying to be a medieval lady tree."

There was another round of laughter. Nan was laughing so hard the tears were welling up and dripping down her cheeks.

"Well, it would have been nice if someone had told us about all those things," she said once she regained her composure. "Instead of letting us fall prey to her eccentricities, and causing a scandal right here in the backyard."

"What the hey," George said. "Scandals can be fun. But I sure as hell am not going to pay her fee."

"Fee!" the others cried.

"Yes, what was it, Nan, $150?"

"Something like that," Nan said. "And, yes, we're dissatisfied customers who have no intention of paying. I doubt she'll have the nerve to send us a bill or come by to collect."

"That's the scandal," Juanita said. "Actually charging for a performance like that."

The last few stragglers were leaving now. Several came over to say their good-byes to Nan and George, neglecting to offer any commentary on what had just transpired other than to make a few oblique remarks, such as "Quite a party," and "Interesting afternoon," and "Really enjoyed your gardens this time."

Once Hans and Robin Jerlick slurped down the remnants of their root beer floats and dropped the empty cups unapologetically on the grass as they strode off toward Payne Avenue, the Fremonts were left with a clot of bitter enders, their very best friends.

"Now that we've gotten all the rabble out of the way, how about if I break out some real drinks for the important people," George said.

16

The Good Life . . . and the Bad

Out came the Bombay Sapphire gin and Canada Dry tonic, the 2005 Sagelands merlot, and some chilled white wine George and Nan kept in the refrigerator for the McCandlesses, those poor, lost souls who didn't know what they were doing.

Then came the toasts. Those were mostly raised to friendship, conviviality, and life given over to joyful languor, although that's not how it was always phrased. Before they could clink glasses, Nan motioned to Steve and George to go easy on the first toast; last time, they had gotten so enthusiastic about a salute they proposed to a couple of cranberry-breasted purple finches that were visiting the feeder that they shattered their wineglasses.

These were times the Fremonts cherished more than any others, except maybe those occasions when they were so lost in admiration for their gardens as to be struck dumb. It was at impromptu gatherings such as these where they rehashed special old times, planned their children's' futures, and extolled the glories of the present. They did not broach sobering, unpleasant topics such as making ends meet or the decline of the silver maple—that lofty old patriarch—in the front yard. Occasionally, the McCandlesses and the Winthrops playfully tried to coax the Fremonts into traveling with them. The Winthrops planned to drive out to Oregon next summer. The McCandlesses fell in love with Banff; they wanted to go back. It was all in vain. Everyone knew that. The Fremonts could not be pried loose from their backyard and unhurried lifestyle.

"How about Fitchburg?" Juanita said. "Couldn't we lure you down to Fitchburg to do some biking? Great bike trail. Great bed and breakfasts. Antique shops coming out the wazoo, Nan. It'll be in October. The trees will be all blazing color. What else will you have to do here anyway?"

"Our own maples will be flaming," George said. "The ashes will be a brilliant yellow. The mums and sedum will be blooming. I really want to see what those mums look like this fall. We'll be having our last opportunities for grilling. The Muskies will be in the playoffs. . . ." That prompted a few chuckles and guffaws.

"What, you don't think so?"

"The Muskies are going nowhere this year," Steve said.

"They have a shot."

"No way. They're ten games out. How can you say that?"

What followed was what always followed when these three sets of friends got together. It started with the three males, who engaged in what seemed to the women to be an interminable and painstakingly detailed breakdown of the Muskies, in which every player's statistics and strengths and weaknesses were recited, and every minor leaguer with a chance to move up to the bigs was vetted. Then would come the breakdown of the other teams in the division, the other teams in the league, and even a few teams in the other league, especially if they had players of trade value to the Muskies.

The women at first listened politely, offering a few observations and posing some general questions. Then, they turned to their own topics: flowers, children, and the latest gossip relating to neighbors and friends. The Jensens were divorcing, Juanita said to gasps of surprise. Amy and Brad Phillips's eighteen-year-old son, Kurt, recently had a run-in with the cops, though Jane didn't think it was anything serious.

"Curfew violation right before graduation," she said. "He and a couple of buddies got caught tp'ing somebody's front yard. And gadzooks did they make a mess. It was the Bishops' place. You know the Bishops. Their daughter, Stacey, was in show choir last season."

In the meantime, George had gone inside to fetch the old portable radio that was now booming the voices of the Muskies, Milo Weavermill and Bernie "Bad Dog" Simpson. Third inning. Score knotted 2–2. Muskies up to bat. Bud Nichols at the plate.

"Automatic out!" Alex cried.

"No way," George said. "He's better in the clutch than most people realize."

Viewed from afar, the gathering around the patio table in the Fremonts' backyard would be judged accurately by most to be a joyful affair, graced with animated conversation, smiles that were genuinely worn and the true appreciation of alcoholic beverages as bright, yet measured, contributors to all of the above. As twilight gathered in the western sky, the friends chattered away and the game ebbed and flowed in its unrushed way into the seventh inning (Muskies 6, Brickbats 4). George and Nan reflected separately, but with a telepathic current linking them, that what they had here was the ideal life; there could be no better.

"We'll think about Fitchburg this year, Juanita," said Nan as things began to wind down, and spouses started patting each others' hands in the mutually recognized signal that it was time to go.

A few minutes after those dawdlers Alex and Jane left, Nan and George watched as a short, mysteriously clad figure ambled down Payne, stopping occasionally to stare into their yard. She was still wearing her sunglasses, which was odd enough at this hour of day, the sun having just set, and a bulky, hooded thing, which made her look like a monk or one of those bit-player aliens from *Star Wars*. How strange to be walking around in such a getup when it was 82 degrees, and so many others were clad in shorts and short-sleeve shirts. They waved at her, but she didn't seem to notice, apparently lost in thought and gazing down at the pavement as she was now. They waved a second time. Still, no response.

"Hi!" they both yelled. The woman finally looked up at them, then turned away quickly and double-timed it down the block, almost colliding with Ellis's Duster, and having to grope her way around it.

"Who the hell *is* that?" George said. "Pretty dang uncivil, if you ask me. Is she blind? I don't see a cane. And what the hell is she up to? Isn't that the same woman we saw running out of our yard just last week? She's got a camera. See it?"

"She's not blind," Nan said. "Otherwise she'd be crashing into a lot more things than just that car no matter how heightened her other senses might be. Secret agent. Probably that Dr. Sprout woman Earlene was talking about checking out the grounds."

"Sproot."

"That's right. Sproot."

"How can she check out anybody's grounds if she's wearing sunglasses at this hour of the day? I mean, really." George chuckled. "Ten to one it was that cowled person Cullen and Ellis have seen wandering around in the yard recently. They thought it was the meter reader. Hmm. Dr. Sproot. Ha-ha . . . uh-oh. Look what's coming."

Jim Graybill trudged up the slope toward them carrying

something heavy and metallic connected to a long rod with a spherical base that looked as if it were attached to his arm. He was wearing headphones.

"Hey, guys, how 'bout if I do that sweep now?" Jim shouted from a distance. George looked at Nan, who shrugged.

"I told him he could," she said. "What's the harm?"

"Then, of course, he'll be returning whatever he finds, like loose change that spilled out of people's pockets, to whomever the rightful owners are, correct?"

Nan nodded unconvincingly.

"I think he's looking for something bigger than that," she said.

Jim was now standing in front of them, proudly flaunting what he called his "TreasureTrove XB 255."

"Check this baby out," he said, swinging the rounded metal base toward them. "That's a ten-inch search coil. They say it can go down four-to-six feet for the big stuff. I could find a nickel buried a foot-and-a-half-feet deep. This here's my control panel. Look how it's right in front of me so I can take readings without having to look too hard."

"And if you find something?" said Nan.

"It beeps as you move the coil. I've got headphones, but you guys probably want to hear when it beeps 'cause it will signal some pretty exciting news that there's something down there."

Nan and George sipped their wine and smiled in a non-committal way.

"Glass of wine?" George said.

"Good Lord, no!" cried Jim. "Not while I'm treasure hunting. I need all my faculties operating at the highest pitch of performance."

"But of course. Silly me . . . Well, just to make sure, Jim, you need to bring any stray things of value over here so we can figure out who it belongs to. We just had a bunch of people over here—sorry you yourself couldn't make it—and they might have dropped some things. Anything valuable gets returned to the owner, okay? Just so we're clear on that. I guess if you're lucky you might find a few stray nuts and bolts."

"What?" Jim said. "You think I'm over here bothering you folks just to pick up the odd little worthless metallic object and some spare change? Wrong! I'm going big-time, looking for the bigger stuff!"

"There is no bigger stuff," Nan said.

"So don't be thinking about digging up our backyard," added George.

"Don't worry," said Jim as he positioned the metal detector so the search coil hovered on the same plane as the ground and a couple of inches above it. "I'll be sure to get your permission before I rent the bulldozer."

Twilight segued into dusk. There had been some beeping, and each time there was, Jim smiled and gave a thumbs-up to George and Nan, who responded with perfunctorily raised wineglasses. An hour after he began, Jim strode confidently over to the patio, where Nan and George were draining their last drops of merlot, and hefted the metal detector high in the air in a sign of victory.

"Strong," Nan said. "You been lifting weights?"

"Good news!" he said.

"Can't wait," said George. Jim chuckled.

"George, your humor is so understated. So dry. Isn't it, Nan?"

"You wouldn't believe it," said Nan in her most affected monotone. Jim laughed, then turned suddenly serious.

"Well, the good news is this: There are some hot spots in your backyard."

"Do tell," Nan said. Jim laughed some more.

"I've got more good news," George said. "Muskies win eight to six. Dawson got rocked, but Meredith picked up the save. Homer and triple for Nichols. I'll have to rub Alex's face in that. 'Automatic out' indeed!"

Jim ignored him.

"From what I can tell, they are big ones. Doozies. Might be, say, a chest down there . . . filled with . . . with . . . who knows?"

"I suppose it could also be just a big chunk of metal," George said.

"Maybe a pan," Nan said. "Or an iron skillet from 1900 at best."

"Well, I'm not adept enough at translating the information, I gotta admit," Jim said. "But I do know people who could. And then, if we've got something, we can dig!"

"No digging!" Nan said. "How many times do we have to tell you, Jim? There is nothing of any value buried beneath our property. And we have gardens to keep up, and a contest to keep in mind. We're not going to go messing up our backyard just because there might be a chunk of metal down there somewhere!"

Nan stopped abruptly, aware that she had gone too far. Jim looked as though he had just been slapped.

"Actually, Jim," said Nan, conciliation dripping from her now-honeyed tone. "Could you prepare a full report on where those hot spots are? Then, we'll get a better idea how to proceed next."

"Yeah, Jim," said George. "Put something down in writing for us."

"You don't mean it," Jim croaked. "You think this is all just a waste of time. Well, I won't be bothering you anymore."

With that, Jim tucked the metal detector under his arm, and stalked off into the gloaming. Nan and George watched, bemused, as the streetlight flickered on, illuminating a slumped, shaking form who dragged his curved metal detector behind him, allowing its base to bump and scrape noisily against the pavement.

Shortly after the Fremonts went inside, a dim figure appeared from behind one of the silver maples and moved stealthily toward the heart of the gardens. In the gathering darkness, Marta Poppendauber made a quiet beeline for some ornamental grasses she hadn't recorded yet and snapped their pictures with her silent and surprisingly unobtrusive flash providing the light. She was headed toward the back to shoot the paper birches and crab apples when a door hinge squealed and a screen door slammed shut. Marta froze, her arms thrust outward in the manner of a small tree. She was looking straight at the back patio, where someone stood illuminated by the glare of the motion-detector light. One of the Fremont kids!

"Hey! Who are you? What are you doing here and why are you trying to look like a tree?"

Marta took off like a shot, hurdled over the split-rail fence, and plunged into the nearby woods, careening off trees and small saplings. She emerged scratched, bruised, and panting for breath onto Jeri and Tom Fletcher's driveway on the other side. On went a motion-detector light. Within seconds the front door opened, revealing a gauzy, formidable figure standing on the front stoop.

"Can I help you?" It was Jeri Fletcher's booming voice coming from the top step of the cement stairway leading up to their front door. "Who are you and why do you look like a monk? Are you a monk? Do you listen to confessions? I haven't been to confession in at least twenty-three years."

Marta tore off down the driveway, across Sumac, and down the slope that lead to the shores of Bluegill Pond. Tripping over an exposed cottonwood root, she found herself lying faceup on the spongy ground at the edge of a cattail marsh and not particularly wanting to get up. She wondered whether that was because she'd suffered a debilitating injury from her fall. She gazed at the evening star, shining brightly above her. That must be Venus, she thought, then reflected sadly on how a cold-weather lover such as calendula could never flourish on that hothouse planet.

A loud sniffling and a belch interrupted Marta's cosmic reverie. Something loomed over her. All she could really see was a dark head-sized shape blotting out a small part of the sky. Also, there were a couple of things that looked like bent rabbit-ears antennae sticking out of it. Marta stifled a scream. She knew better than to panic when a wild beast was sizing you up for a nighttime snack.

"I'm a moose," said the figure. "And I eats little girls like you for dinner." With that, it lurched backward, plopping noisily onto the spongy ground. Marta jumped up, threw off her suffocating cowl, and ran a wind sprint across the sucking mud of the marsh to the other side of the lake.

For an hour, she wandered aimlessly, following one street, then another, until she had no idea where she was. Then, she knew. There was Dr. Sproot's house, smack in front of her. She had been drawn to it as if by a homing device. Marta rushed to the door and pushed the doorbell. Again. The door flew open and there stood Dr. Sproot, a wall of looming rigidity partially hidden by her screen door. Dr. Sproot squinted, then switched on her front porch light.

"Marta! What in the name of Hades-on-fire happened to you?"

"Dr. Sproot," Marta gasped. "Please help me. I was almost caught spying on the Fremonts, then a horrible moose-person almost ate me. Then I had to run across that lake, and all the gooey mud spattered all over me and . . . and . . ."

"And what? You look a disgrace, Marta! Don't you dare

cross this threshold with all that carnival tomfoolery slime all over you."

"But, Dr. Sproot, I need to wash up and get back to my car. I've got to get back home before Ham starts worrying. Please . . ."

"Where's your cowl, Marta?"

"I threw it on the ground somewhere, Dr. Sproot. It was so hot, and . . ."

"And your camera?"

"My camera? Oh, no! I must have dropped it somewhere. I must have . . ."

"You will go back and retrieve the cowl and camera, and make sure they are restored to their original condition. Do you understand me?" Marta stared at her blankly. "Otherwise, you'll owe me for them. Did you think I got them for free? That's $600 for the camera, conservatively. And the cowl? I'll have to figure that out. Were you discovered?"

"I don't think so, Dr. Sproot."

"Better not have been. Otherwise my name is mud, and rest assured, Marta, if my name is mud I will make sure yours is as thoroughly soiled as mine. Now, go find that cowl and camera!"

Marta arrived at her home around midnight worried sick that Ham might be frantically searching for her, calling out the police and volunteers and bloodhounds and whatnot. But he lay quietly in bed, in his pajamas, snoring up a storm, as usual. She jostled him gently awake.

"Honey? Honey? I'm home. Sorry I'm late. Were you worried?"

"Huh? Wha? Worried. What worries? Who's worried? Muskies over the Brickbats, eight to six, in thirteen innings." With that, he turned over and returned to his noisy slumber.

"Men!" Marta hissed.

As she got out of her wet and rumpled clothes and show-ered, she reflected on her humiliations of the night, and how that twisted Dr. Sproot had done nothing to help her. In fact, worse; she had heaped on scorn, which just added to her shame. For the first time, she felt an energizing fury rise up into her reddening face. Never again would Dr. Phyllis Sproot treat her like a poor dandelion getting pried out of the ground, roots and all.

Never again!

17

Bismarcks and Broomsticks

Dr. Sproot was getting impatient. Here it was ten thirty a.m., and she was still waiting in the back booth of the Hi-Lo Dough- nut Shoppe. She munched on her third gooey, chocolate-glazed Bismarck, which was giving her a stomachache, and slurped down her fourth cup of coffee, which was making her feel like jumping up and doing the jitterbug. Still no contact. It *was* the right place, wasn't it? Marta, that pathetic scatterbrain, had prob- ably told her the wrong place to go, or maybe the right place to go, but the wrong time, or the wrong part of the right place to seat herself.

She studied two customers sitting at the counter. One was a man, which ruled him out unless some sort of intermediary would be secretly employed to arrange the *real* meeting at yet another location. The other was a pimpled teenage girl, probably a high school freshman dawdling away the summer morning. Who knew? Dr. Sproot looked at the teenager, and, catching her attention, fluttered her eyelids as a sort of signal. The teenager blushed and turned her attention back to her cinnamon strudel.

Dr. Sproot suddenly felt extremely silly sitting around for a half hour, waiting for an assignation as if she were . . . as if she were . . . someone extremely silly. All this talk about spells and the supernatural, why, it was patently absurd, that's what it was. How could she ever allow herself to believe such nonsense? Huh? It was Marta's doing. Marta was trying to get back at her in her own little infantile way. She was being had, and, at some point, Marta and her cronies would burst in, surround her, and revel in her humiliation. Well, that simply was not going to happen!

Dr. Sproot was about to signal the proprietor—a short Vietnamese woman whose name she had never bothered to learn and who couldn't possibly be her contact—could she?—for the bill when the bell on the entrance jangled and one of the most absurd apparitions she had ever seen entered the doughnut shop.

Here was a rather large woman wearing a ridiculous outfit. Her hair was all bouffed up with wavy curls lapping at her cheeks and long bangs grazing her forehead. She wore a trim, short-lapeled green suit buttoned over a white translucent blouse, and white gloves. Three strings of pearls hung from her neck like a choker necklace. On top of her large mass of auburn hair rested a pillbox hat that matched her suit. From that hat dropped a black mesh veil that thinly covered a heavily made-up face, squinty and mascaraed eyes, and a pair of black cat's-eye glasses. Refugee from the sixties, and the early sixties at that, thought Dr. Sproot, who couldn't help but let fly with a deep-throated chuckle.

The proprietor still hadn't seen her, so Dr. Sproot signaled again with a curt wave meant to also signify impatience and an irksome sense that there was no accounting for the quality of the help these days. Her extremities tingling with caffeine, she couldn't sit still another moment. Just as she was about to bounce up from her seat, the sixties woman approached.

"Is anyone sitting here?" she said, motioning to the opposite side of the booth.

"No," said Dr. Sproot. She wondered why this odd duck had chosen her particular booth instead of four other ones, which were quite empty. "And I'm leaving now, so you could also sit on this side if you wanted."

"I hear the guacamole-slathered croissants are quite good here," said the looming human cartoon character. She threw up her veil, and peered at Dr. Sproot expectantly through those clownishly dated glasses, which Dr. Sproot noted had tinted lenses and thick frames inscribed with the initials E.M. in gold, cursive script. Dr. Sproot shrugged and frowned. She wasn't aware that they sold guacamole-slathered croissants at the Hi-Lo. If so, since when? Besides, who'd want to eat something like that! And who was this impertinent oddity anyway? Then, it clicked. The secret sentence! Marta had given her a secret sentence that was to be delivered to her . . . and to which she would respond:

"Yes, and the snapping turtle milk goes quite well with them."

The woman smiled slyly and slid into the booth across from her. The proprietor, whom Dr. Sproot had failed three times now to flag down, instantly appeared and took the woman's order for three toasted waffles with maple syrup on the side and a glass of orange juice.

"You wanted to see me, I understand, on a matter of . . . business?" The woman mouthed the words slowly and carefully, almost in a whisper. So this was the infamous Edith Merton.

"Is this how you really look?" said Dr. Sproot. She made no attempt to disguise her simmering contempt.

"Of course not. I go incog in matters such as these. This is my mother's outfit, which I'm proud to say fits me. I've lost twenty pounds in the past six months. Imagine what it was like trying to squeeze into it back when I was a much plumper witch. Mom's wig, too. What do you think of it, eh?"

"I could give a holy hoot what your stupid costume looks like," said Dr. Sproot. "And why should I? I don't know you from Eve. We've never met."

"Ah," said Edith. "But I know you. I know you quite well, and for all the wrong reasons. You're one of those awful nose-stuck-in-the-air gardening snobs who blackballed me from the Rose Maidens. Yes, indeed, I know you all too well, Phyllis Sproot. Oh, and how, may I ask, are your grounds looking these days?"

Dr. Sproot shuddered. She felt violated. Had Edith Merton been watching all this time from her little witch hiding places as she fussed and fretted over her moribund gardens?

"You know darned well how my *grounds* are looking because I have it on reasonable authority that you are the cause of it. You wouldn't be here trespassing on my neighborhood doughnut shop if you hadn't known that."

Edith Merton cackled in a way that Dr. Sproot had to admit sounded very witchy, but which she was afraid might mark her to the alerted doughnut shop crowd as a weird person who bore watching.

"Welllll," said Edith. "Let's get back to this wonderful disguise I've cooked up. It serves a dual purpose. No one will know I'm Edith Merton in this getup. The glasses, by the way, are my own touch. I find they strengthen the spells, and besides, I like them. But maybe I'm getting ahead of myself. I also need to wear this outfit to cast my spells. It channels the spirit of my poor dead mother and, for some reason I'm not sure I fully understand, the energy force of thousands of dead plants, into my extremities. It's quite intoxicating, actually."

Dr. Sproot guffawed.

"Oh, you don't believe me? Well, then, what are *you* doing here other than stuffing yourself with sweet rolls? I tell you what, we can always try a spell *without* the uniform. Then, I'll have the advantage of taking your money without having to work up a sweat, because the spell won't work. You don't want that to happen now, do you?"

Dr. Sproot, silently furious at being addressed in such a manner, sat there crossing and uncrossing her legs and fidgeting. Her much-abused bladder was sending out its distress signal.

"Do you have to go to the little girls' room, Phyllis Sproot?"

"I can hold it!" Dr. Sproot barked proudly. "I can do anything I put my mind to. Now, please continue. And please refer to me as Dr. Sproot. I must insist that you address me by my proper title."

"Very well, *Doc-tor* Sproot. You should know that, in our professional dealings, you're to call me Sarah."

"Sarah?"

"Yes, Sarah. Sarah Twiddle."

"That's about the dumbest thing I ever heard. Why can't I just call you Edith, tell you what I want, and then you can get on with it without all this super-secret shilly-shallying around?"

Edith Merton frowned.

"Marta warned me about you."

"Warned you about *me*? What did that silly little twerp say? What kind of calumny is it that's being flung in my face these days? Why, I'll—"

"You'll do nothing!" roared Edith so abruptly it startled Dr. Sproot into spilling some of her coffee, which had been re-filled yet again. "You will do nothing to hurt Marta, or anyone else for that matter. You've seen your gardener's delight turn into the fossil fuels of tomorrow. You and your other dried-up old Rose Maiden hags. I can make it worse, and will if you continue with this attitude. Get this straight: I'm only doing this for the money. Now, here are my conditions. . . ."

"*Your* conditions? I'm the one who's the customer here."

Edith held up her gloved hand palm out, directly in front of Dr. Sproot's face, causing her to go tongue-tied for the first time since she went into a deep coreopsis-induced reverie, and walked into the crowded men's restroom at Barnum's by mistake.

"My conditions are full payment in advance. That's number one. Number two, you are to sponsor me for membership in the Rose Maidens." Dr. Sproot twitched. "Three, you are never to reveal my identify to anyone, under any circumstances. Is that clear?"

Dr. Sproot, now reduced to what, for her, was a certain degree of meekness, nodded.

"Very well. I understand I am to reverse the spell on your gardens," said Edith, hungrily forking one big bite of waffle after another into her mouth, and revealing a set of crooked, pearly teeth smudged red where she had misfired on her lipstick application. "Is that correct?"

Dr. Sproot nodded.

"Then, I am to cast a spell over some other people, the Fremonts, at the corner of Payne and Sumac. This is to be a bad spell?"

"Yes. A bad spell."

"Good. I know the spot. I've already inspected it, not wearing this silly getup, of course, since people would suspect me as a mentally ill sixties throwback, but as simple old Edith Merton attending their lovely party of a few days ago. Did you go, by the way? That had fabulous ice cream floats. Oh, well, certainly not. You are probably persona non grata as far as the Fremonts are concerned."

"No, I'm not. They don't know me from anyone."

"What? You don't know these people and you still want to hurt their yard full of lovely creations? And they are quite lovely, I must say."

"Yes, I want to hurt their lovely creations, which are not *that* lovely."

"Well, you have your own reasons, I suppose, and I don't have to know them. And, as I said before, I'm only in it for the money. The good thing about casting a spell on strangers is that it helps us to cover our tracks. Not that anyone would suspect witchcraft as the cause of all this distress we're going to cause . . . except maybe the plants, and they're not talking. Ha-ha. Ha-ha. Now, enough of this levity. You have photographs to refresh my memory?"

Dr. Sproot nodded.

"For a simple, low-power spell, that should be sufficient. Not enough to wreak utter havoc, just dry things out a bit, to turn the spectacular into the merely average, or maybe slightly below."

"Yes, that should do the trick."

"Very well, my fee is this: $500 to release your gardens from the industrial-strength bad spell I put on them, and $350 for the mild little run-of-the-mill spell I will cast on these Fremonts. Since you're going for two, you get the bargain rate of $700. Could you give me the payment now, please?"

Having been told that Edith Merton did not accept checks because of the paper trail they created, Dr. Sproot had come prepared with a crisp wad of hundreds and fifties. She retrieved it from her purse, and was counting out the fee, one bill at a time, when she noticed the proprietor, coffeepot at the ready, standing next to her. Dr. Sproot froze, visions of bleak little prison flowerpots sitting on barred window slats flashing before her eyes.

"No more coffee, please," said Edith. "We're kind of busy here arranging for the sale of my antique armoire."

The proprietor moved away. Dr. Sproot was relieved to notice that she did not go immediately to the telephone on returning to her station behind the counter.

"Whew!" she gasped. "That was close!"

"Too close," said Edith. "After we leave this place, you are to avoid it for one year, minimum. Understand?"

"What? They sell my favorite Bismarcks here! And I get unlimited free refills on my coffee!"

Edith leaned menacingly across the table.

"That means they know you, which is bad. You are to avoid it. No ifs, ands, or buts. And once you are finished counting out my fee, we will leave together, smiling and chattering away as if we are the oldest friends in the world, which will take some very hard work on my part, I have to tell you. Oh, and on the topic of fees, there's the matter of a possible surcharge to be tacked on to your bill."

"Surcharge? What surcharge? Marta didn't tell me about any surcharge."

"It's in the eventuality that you win the Burdick's Best Yard Contest, which my sources tell me is a very good bet . . . assuming your gardens get un-spelled, that is."

"Of course it's a good bet. My gardens will *not* be beaten."

"Well, in that case, I see no reason why I shouldn't take my cut. I'll take ten percent of the prize money. That's the surcharge."

"That's outrageous!"

"Listen here, doc; you wouldn't even be in the running if it weren't for me. And, hey, if you don't win it's just the standard fee that applies."

"If you're such an accomplished witch, why don't you just wave a magic wand over your own garden and win the blasted prize yourself? Huh? And don't call me doc."

Edith chuckled silently, infuriating Dr. Sproot.

"You obviously know little about witchcraft. Let me explain: I can improve on something already good or knock it down. I can't create from whole cloth. I can only make my garden better within its modest confines. It's already perfect in its own little way. But its scope is far too small for the Burdick's judges to even consider it. That's why I'm depending on you. So, what's it to be, yea or nay?"

Dr. Sproot just sat there frozen in fury, a barely perceptible nod indicating her agreement with the new terms.

"I'll take that as a yea. Okay, here's what will happen now: I will study the photographs, which you will have Marta deliver to me in a plain brown manila envelope the day after tomorrow. I will then cast the spell. Precisely two hours and twenty minutes after that, I will pay a visit to your house and remove the spell on your gardens. I will not call in advance. Please leave your gate open to allow me access. The whole thing should take between one to two hours, and you are not under any circumstances to be standing around watching me, much less jabbering away while I'm trying to work. In fact, it would probably be better if you're not around at all. And I'm warning you that this will be hard work. I cast that spell in a passion, and those are the ones that usually work the best and are the hardest to undo. With any luck, you should notice marked improvement overnight, and complete recovery in two days. There are no money-back guarantees. I'm sort of like a doctor in this regard. If the spell and the anti-spell don't work that's tough tamales for you. I will give you no phone number. . . ."

Dr. Sproot chuckled.

"I could just call you at the liquor store or appliance mart, Edith."

"That's *Sarah!*" said Edith, pulling the mesh veil back down over her face. "I told you to call me Sarah! And if you dare to call me at my place of work where I am Edith to talk about my

Sarah business, then there won't be any spell undoing on your gardens. If you must contact me, you may do so through Marta.

"Now, one more thing before we leave—you're paying my bill as well as your own, of course—do you know of anyone whose dearly beloved little pet has passed away recently? I have a special on July pet séances. Offer ends at midnight July twenty-second."

18

Out of Season

There was one big obstacle facing the Fremonts in their efforts to make prize-winning improvements to their gardens: planting season had ended a month ago.

Sure, there were a few shriveled-looking things still sitting on the picked-over nursery shelves that could be stuck in the dry ground and, if they survived the trauma and heat, coaxed into putting forth a few puny blooms. Those would stick out in their obvious and pathetic distress to any judges who knew their business.

Instead, they would have to spruce up the things that were already there, pay Jerry to build them a new trellis, then sand and paint it. They would scour the antique shops for any knickknacks that could lend little artificial accents to those parts of the yard that needed more of an exclamation point.

Another problem: they still hadn't gotten significant rain. The mild temperatures that had made the dryness bearable through June and into early July were gone. Now they were suffering through the worst heat wave of the summer. Adding an unforgivable insult to that was the humidity level, which had soared as a heavy mass of moist air covered them like a dense, stuffy blanket.

"Dew point's at seventy-four," said George, panting from his exertions in the gardens, after an inspection of his weather station. "That's tropical. That's Amazon rain forest. Oh, and there's the regular temperature . . . ninety-four degrees."

Nan gasped, then glugged down a big glass of ice water. Her tank top, work shorts, and kerchief headband were soaked in oily perspiration. Exhausted, she plunked down into one of the patio chairs, her heart pounding, her body's near-depleted cooling mechanism on the verge of breakdown and screaming for her to stop.

"George. Take five. Take fifteen, even. You're gonna kill yourself." Trickles of sweat streamed down her dripping forehead to sting her eyes with their salt. "As much as I hate to say so, we gotta go inside and get some AC."

"I got a little more to do first. Fifteen bags down, ten to go."

George migrated toward the driveway, where they had dumped the twenty-five bags of moist-smelling cypress mulch picked up at Burdick's earlier in the morning. Eons later he was back, trudging uphill with a forty-pound bag of mulch slung over each shoulder. He stopped about midway, hunched over, and sighed.

"Sweetheart!" Nan moaned.

She watched in awe as George straightened up after a few seconds, then continued toward the fence line to dump his massive load with a deep, lingering groan. Just as Nan was all set to be lost in a dizzying cloud of admiration for this wonderful, indefatigable man, the man whom she would trade for no other, the man for whom no barrier proved too impenetrable, George slouched over to her, slumped forward, and let loose an appalling squeal of pent-up gas.

"George!"

"That's it," he said. "I quit. Inside for some air-conditioning, and maybe a nice cold gin and tonic for a little pick-me-up."

Halfway down the slope, the yellow Rain Train chugged

slowly upward, its grooved, plastic, white wheel fitted on its track—the garden hose—and flung curved jets of water across the swaths of bluegrass, rye, and fescue with its twirling aluminum arms. It was four p.m., the hottest part of the day, but they had the Rain Train going all day now, as well as an oscillating sprinkler in the back near the woods, alternating with two soaker hoses. They had to; two or three days without water in this kind of heat, and something, somewhere, would be drooping, the first sign of a swift descent into a dangerous plant coma from which there could be no return.

Their top competitors were doing the same thing. Some were doing it on a far grander scale. They observed yards and gardens hidden in clouds of drifting mists and spray. On closer inspection (they had grown more daring now when they sensed the homeowners were away) they saw endless coils of coarse, gray, water-beaded soaker hoses seeping their garden-boosting moisture directly into the ground. When breezes wafted those curtains of mist aside, wonderworlds of deep green grass, manicured shrubs, and bloom clouds of every conceivable hue were revealed to them.

That meant they had to redouble their efforts. Jerry had the new trellis built in three days. It was angled to hide the compost pile from virtually every point in the yard. They had it sanded, primed, and painted in a weekend, working early to avoid applying the paint to the pine in the heat of midday. Then, they screwed long hooks into the wood from which they hung a dozen birdhouses of various shapes, colors, and sizes.

"It's ugly," said George, inspecting their handiwork after hanging the last strategically placed, earth-tone-painted birdhouse. "Who hangs birdhouses from trellises?"

"It's distinctive. And it hides the ugly compost pile. And it's far enough away from the other trellises to avoid trellis clutter. I think it will make an impression."

They had been attending to the front yard with some half-hearted maintenance that probably didn't do much good anyway. Now, they ignored it altogether. Not that it mattered that much. The grass had gone completely to hell, cooked a medium-to-well-done brown, and possibly past the point of dormancy. That didn't matter to the Fremonts, whose only concern about their front yard centered on the ailing silver maple, the withering crown of which they could see from the backyard, towering over the roof.

"We should get rid of it," Nan said. "It's dying and beyond hope, and it really wrecks the view from here. Imagine a judge admiring what's on the ground, then looking up to get an eye-ful of that old thing."

A tree service was hired to cut down the silver maple. That cost the Fremonts $1,700, which included removal and grinding up the stump. Coming on top of the $500 it cost to build the trellis, that made George nervous. He knew the money situation was deteriorating rapidly. Stoking that concern into a white-hot panic was the letter they got from the mortgage company informing them that they were in arrears and would they please make payments immediately for this month, plus the three months preceding along with a sizable penalty fee before foreclosure proceedings began.

"So, we're going to lose our home," Nan said.

"Not necessarily."

"Not necessarily? What do you mean, 'not necessarily'? You think they might be joking or something?"

George stroked his chin and ran his hand over his bald pate, then picked at his ears, all the while avoiding direct eye contact with Nan. From long, hard experience, Nan knew these were signs that whatever he said next, which would often be with a great show of false bravado, would be absolute crap.

"It usually takes several more notices like this before they actually make a move," he said. "They don't want to lose us. This is just the first warning shot fired across the bow."

Nan stared at George, amazed by what great lengths he would travel to rationalize a bad situation, despite all her years with the poor, delusional slob.

"So, the next shot from the mortgage company does what, knocks down a mast, or puts a nice big hole in the hull, allowing the ship to sink? That's if you want to continue with your nautical analogy. And I'd have to guess, George dear, that this isn't the first warning shot . . . three months of no payments? What am I missing here?"

"Nan-bee!"

"Don't Nan-bee me. Tell me what the deal is."

George shrugged in that innocent, childlike way that always melted her in lesser situations. Now, it just made her madder.

"What?"

"I don't remember them. They must have just looked like junk mail. You know all the mail we get marked 'urgent,' and it just turns out to be junk mail."

"Yes, and I also know that there is mail marked 'urgent' that really is urgent, and you've got to deal with it right away. How much do you have?"

George cleared his throat, cueing Nan that what was to come would be straight and unpleasant, no deceptions.

"We have no savings, of course. In checking, jeez, not enough to come close to paying the mortgage bill. That's more than $4,000. I figure I've got about $450. That's with utilities and phone bill yet to pay . . . and cable . . . and the newspaper . . . and there is the small matter of a tuition payment for Ellis. And room and board. That's due next month. . . . Oh, and Cullen's first Dartmouth payment. That's a whopper!"

"Credit card balance?"

Another throat clearing.

"Pretty much maxed out thanks to the party, the trellis, and cutting down the tree. I just made a payment yesterday. Minimum."

"Greeting card prospects?"

George's face brightened. "Yeah, I forgot about that. I'll be getting a check for $300 any day now. Any day now. Ha-cha. I knew there was some good news I forgot to tell you."

Nan remained stolid, her voice cold and businesslike. "What about your inventions? Isn't it about time you came up with another world beater of an invention? We got oodles from that last one. But it's been, what, five years ago, or something like that. And no money left over from that? Unbelievable! You must have some other ideas cookin.' Huh?"

"Yes, well, I have ideas."

"Such as . . ."

"Such as the vibrating rake?"

"The vibrating rake."

"Yeah, you plug it in and it vibrates."

"Why would anyone want it to do that?"

"Automatic mulch. The vibrating teeth have little hammers on them that pulverize the leaves. Little wires connect each of the teeth to a main wire than runs down the handle to a fifty-foot cord that you plug in."

"Why not just run your lawn mower over the leaves? That's what we do."

"This is why the idea never got past the planning stages."

"Hmmm. Others?"

"Well, mounts that keep your snowflake collection permanently frozen."

"That has promise. . . ."

"And chewing gum that has adhesive qualities so you can use it as a sticky putty after it loses its flavor."

"That sounds okay. Why not try to market those ideas?"

"I haven't figured out how to make them work."

"Oh, well, let's move on along to your more regular gig, that of greeting card hack writer. Got any prospects there? I haven't seen you composing much of your schmaltz lately. Maybe you've been too busy looking at that lingerie stuff on the computer. Huh?"

"Nothing until the holidays," said the suddenly grim George.

"That would be the Christmas holidays?"

"That would be the Christmas holidays. You?"

"Well, I've got about $400 in checking and maybe $75 in my purse. Compounding the problem is my handbags aren't selling. I've got thirteen of them sitting on shelves in stores. If they magically all sell in the next two or three weeks, that's another . . . um . . . another $400 or so. Still way short. So far short. How did we get to this? We're going to lose the house! We're going to lose the house, the backyard, everything, and get thrown out on the street! We've been spending so much time on that blasted backyard we've lost sight of everything else. I could rip it all up right now!"

"Not necessarily."

"Not necessarily what?"

"We won't necessarily lose the house."

"Shut up with your not necessarily! We ARE going to lose the house unless we come up with a plan. What's your plan, George?"

"Winning the contest?"

"Oh, be quiet!"

"I'm serious. Haven't you heard? First prize just got jacked up to $75,000. Businesses all over Livia are chipping in money for it."

"Seventy-five thousand dollars?"

George nodded eagerly.

"Nobody ever gave that much money for a gardening contest . . . at least until now. Why didn't you tell me so?"

"I just found out at the party. Cullen and Ellis told me. I meant to tell you. It just slipped my mind."

"How do Cullen and Ellis know?"

"They must circulate more than we do."

That Wednesday's *Lollygag* carried the official news, which was a stunning revelation because the amount being circulated unofficially was short. According to the *Lollygag*'s front-page banner headline story, contributions continued to come in. As things stood now, first prize topped $100,000, with Burdick's trying to egg on more corporate sponsors to top off the contest at $150,000.

The paper quoted Mr. Burdick as saying this could be the biggest contest of its kind ever held . . . in the history of the world! He said he wanted to reward those folks who had given his store so much business over the years and that applications were cut off last week at 240 to prevent mercenaries from jumping to take advantage of the big prize money. This contest, he said, was for people who put their hearts into their gardens and would continue to do so even if no contest existed. He said he had ordered his staff to keep in touch with their landscaping sources and conduct regular patrols to make sure contest applicants weren't relying on professionals to shape their creations.

Mr. Burdick said he was in personal negotiations right now to line up a sponsorship with the nation's third-largest lawn care company, although numbers one and two had also expressed interest. He had also made sure his communications department had gotten the word out to not only the local but the national media as well. A major gardening magazine had already contacted him. So had a reporter at the St. Anthony *Inquirer*, though he had to swallow hard to mention that one, knowing full well that the stupid rag was infiltrated with semisocialist ultraliberals who wanted to nationalize the gardening industry.

George and Nan worked like gardeners possessed. They laid down more freshening cypress mulch, and checked and rechecked every blossom and leaf daily to make sure any browned and rabbit-nibbled clunkers got snipped off. To George's surprise, Nan gave up on the dusty miller and without so much as the faintest flicker of remorse dug out the offending plants and cast them with a cackle into the compost.

They gambled on a new plant, one that they could buy fully mature and in reasonably good condition, and scatter around the backyard, and that with proper watering and enough sunlight would guarantee them dozens if not scores of big, multicolored blooms. This was to be their go-for-broke trump card, the flower that would take them over the top, the one that would explode in the judges' faces like the floral version of nitroglycerin, and which nobody else that they could see was cultivating.

They gambled on the hibiscus.

19

The Wanton Flower

The tropical hibiscus is generally thought of as a denizen of the warmer, more moist Pacific climates, or of swampy areas of the United States untouched by snowflake or sleet pellet. It is most at home in places where heavy coats are stored more or less permanently in fragrant cedar closets, to be retrieved every three or four years when the mercury crashes through the freezing barrier, plunging maybe even to 29 or 28 degrees Fahrenheit, usually for about ten minutes, at about six a.m.

The plant can, however, live as a summer annual in the far northern reaches of the upper Midwest. The advantages presented by the tropical hibiscus are big blooms of garish yellow, orange, and salmon hues, often varying between the throat of the bloom and the individual petals. There is also the way it encourages otherwise semi-somnolent Midwesterners to break out the Hawaiian shirts and split open some coconuts.

For the more traditional gardeners prevalent in a suburb such as Livia, the notion of planting tropical hibiscus was something that had never even remotely occurred to them. A dignified magnificence was to be preferred. The garish opulence of the tropical hibiscus would, for them, be like putting neon signs on those quaint little bed-and-breakfasts in the picturesque towns along the Muskmelon River. You just didn't dabble in something like that and expect to be taken seriously. A tropical hibiscus would be much more in its element wedged behind the ear of some half-naked Polynesian wanton, or as the singular floral attraction at some pagan shrine to tastelessness, such as the Hanging Gardens of Babylon. Besides, they were transients, their blooms continually fading, to be replaced by gaudy newcomers. Such a rapid turnover would befuddle the average Livia gardener.

So, the Fremonts had their work cut out for them as they searched for the tropical hibiscus of the quality and in the quantity that they needed. No greenhouses or nurseries in Livia—of which there were four—offered such an extravagance. After an Internet search and a few phone calls, they were finally able to locate a greenhouse fifteen miles to the west, in Westmoreland, that had them, already four feet tall, and bursting with big blooms, with stiff stamens pointing straight out, and somewhat menacingly, at them.

The very sight of these large Day-Glo creations gave George and Nan pause. It looked as if they could morph into aliens at any second and shoot out a stream of noxious poison at them from their stamens. Or maybe the stamens sheltered long needles designed to immobilize victims. You should never go to sleep within striking distance of one of these, Nan reflected, as she stared, amazed, at one of the plant's fuchsia-colored flowers.

There was also a disturbing sexuality about them that reminded her of Georgia O'Keeffe's vaginal irises. These had a lushness and stench of immorality that eclipsed even those playmates of the plant world. They were also far more representative of the other sex.

"Look at the size of those stamens!" said Nan, caressing one. "And so stiff!" George slapped her hand away.

"Don't be handling the merchandise there, Nan-bee, espe-cially when your mind has obviously sunk into the gutter."

"C'mon, now. What's wrong with stroking a little plant tissue?"

"They certainly are rather obscene looking," said George, who was chagrined to note that Nan continued to caress one of the stamens with her fingertips.

"Who knows, that could be good," Nan said. "Look at it this way: they could appeal to the judges' subliminal, sexual urges. That could give us the psychological edge that can make us a winner. Daring! That's what the judges want."

The Fremonts cleaned the greenhouse out of its remaining plants. In two days, they had all eighteen tropical hibiscuses planted.

"I hope they're happy," said George, after he tamped down the last shovelful of dirt on hibiscus number twelve, which, along with the six others yet to be planted, would significantly brighten up the yard along its perimeter in four different clus-ters. "Because, God knows, this is their kind of weather." He wiped his face with an already dampened bandanna.

"It is," said Nan, gasping from the combination of the heat and having to kneel and stoop over for the past two hours "Can't you see how perky and straight and bright they look? It's like they're saying, 'Thank you, Nan and George, for find-ing such a nice, steamy home for us.' They love it here!"

"You're welcome," said George, blinking rapidly as the salty sweat dribbled into his eyes and wiping his forehead again with the drenched and useless bandanna. He scanned the backyard for their most recent handiwork and saw it speckled with at least thirty blobs of bright, ultraconspicuous color. "Damn, those things are so . . . uh . . . uh . . ."

"Unique," said Nan, finally getting her creaky knees to allow her to stand up. "No other garden in Livia has them . . .

at least, not that we've seen. This is just the kind of risk-taking choice that will give us an advantage over the competition. I feel good about this."

George, however, was being pricked by the harpies of self-doubt.

"I don't know," he said. "They really stick out. They might be a bit much for our conservative judges. Maybe they'll think they're gauche, sort of like a Las Vegas flower, or like dropping a clown costume in the middle of everything."

"We don't know that the judges are going to be conservative. They could be looking for something shocking, something they haven't seen anywhere else. Who knows, maybe your stupid Cervantes wood carving will catch their attention . . . or . . . or . . . Mr. Poison Plant over there."

George flinched.

Two days later, Nan discovered that the new hibiscus plants could converse with her in a telepathic sort of hissing/humming way. It took her just a few hours to master this plant lingua franca and the following day she was greeting them with cooing baby talk, asking them how they were doing, if they needed misting or other special ministrations. She told them they were beautiful and that they would grow into fine adults that would bring pride to the Fremont backyard. Occasionally, when George was loitering out of earshot, she would whisper things to them about George that weren't very flattering but which Nan had to tell someone or some-*thing*.

"I wish George would work harder," she whispered to them one morning while showering them with garden hose mist. "He's kind of a lazy bum, don't you think? Look at him over there, will you? No ambition."

Nan continued in this vein for several days, and the plants flourished, showing new growth and blossoms daily, and continually replacing the short-lived older blooms.

George approved, or at least didn't object, though he had at first been startled to observe Nan mumbling into what appeared to be thin air. But look at how well the new plants were doing! They were going great guns! Besides, he was gratified to admit that the hard-driving, passionlessly ambitious Nan who had emerged in the past couple of weeks—a Nan who had seemed a robotic stranger to him—had retreated, giving way to the Nan he was more accustomed to: gentle, relaxed, and okay, sure, a little bit weird in a touchy-feely kind of way.

Encouraged by Nan's gentle prodding, he began talking to the new plants himself. At first, he wasn't quite sure how to address a hibiscus plant, but Nan told him not to make it more complicated than it needed to be.

"Just say nice things to them in a soft or whispery tone," she told him. "Never scold or raise your voice to them. Don't ever tell them they are letting you down or not growing enough. And, by all means, don't threaten to freeze them; they hate the cold. Act natural. No need to be stiff or formal. And be sincere. They can tell if you're just going through the motions."

George, being a gracious, good-natured fellow not given to affectation, adapted quickly. Soon, he was making conversation with his new buddies, the hibiscus guys/girls, as natural a part of his day as watering and fertilizing them and inspecting them for bad bugs. One day, though, he noticed a problem.

"We've got trouble," he told Nan. "The other flowers are getting jealous. They think we're lavishing too much attention on the hibiscuses."

"Jealous?" said Nan. "What on earth are you talking about? What a ridiculous notion. How do you know they're jealous?"

"They told me so. And, by the way, what's this I hear about my being a lazy bum? Huh?"

20

The Gardening News

The so-called gardening expert sent over by the St. Anthony *Inquirer,* supposedly to fawn all over Dr. Sproot's gardens and write a hyperlaudatory puff piece about them, wasn't living up to Dr. Sproot's expectations. For one thing, he hadn't seemed all that bowled over on being introduced to her gardens. Dr. Sproot expected bulging eyes, exclamations of awestruck wonder, and a humble willingness to hang on her every word. Instead, he seemed confused. He even had the temerity to stifle a yawn.

What made his listless ignorance even more galling was the transformation the gardens had undergone. Evidently, Sarah the Witch's *un*spell was working because, my Lord, hadn't everything perked up so remarkably? And it had all happened four days ago. Overnight! Why, it was a miracle, that's what it was. If anything, it had done even better service than anticipated because, well, would you look at it all. Anything stronger and her flowers would have burst into a Maurice Chevalier song-and-dance routine.

So, why couldn't this lug nut of a journalist notice and do homage?

" 'Scuse me," he said sheepishly. "Not enough sleep last

night." Dr. Sproot shook her head in disgust at this lack of preparation. She would cut him some slack this once, but he'd better perk up quickly now that he was being led through the alpha and omega of Livia gardens. Why, such a floral treat should awaken the dead!

Roland Ready, suburban reporter of two years' undistinguished standing at the *Inquirer,* gazed over the grounds that Dr. Sproot introduced to him with a regal sweep of the hand. He had never seen so many flowers in one place in his life. Unimpressed, he was merely at a loss as to what to make of it.

"What are those?" he wondered, pointing to a bunch of large desery-looking plants with spiked leaves angling out in every direction and big white-flowered stems sticking up a good three feet. "They're all over the place. Are they cactuses . . . or should I say *cacti?*"

Dr. Sproot chuckled softly.

"Why, no, Mr. Ready, those are not cacti, those are yuccas, and, though you are right, they are quite at home in the desert, they can be cultivated right here in our upper Midwest, hundreds and hundreds of miles from the nearest desert. They are not common here, however, mostly because they require the nurturing of an expert who knows her business, such as myself, who has devoted her life to the care of plants and has her Ph.D. in horticulture."

"Hmmmm," said Roland in a way that didn't seem to Dr. Sproot to show sufficient deference. He was writing something down in his steno pad.

"That's *Dr.* Phyllis Sproot," she said, craning her neck for a gander at all those squiggly-looking hieroglyphics he was committing to paper.

"I'm writing about the plant," he said. "Describing it. Y-U-K-K-A?"

Dr. Sproot forced herself to emit a sharp little half-laugh that sounded more like a quack.

"No, it's Y-U-C-C-A."

"Got it. And those over there, more of the same?" He pointed with his pen toward another cluster of yuccas.

"Why, yes," said Dr. Sproot, not sure she liked his insouciant tone. "I may well be the reigning expert on yuccas in Livia, and perhaps even the entire St. Anthony metro area. So I have quite a few yuccas in the yard. There are some different varieties of yucca, as you will no doubt note."

"No, I didn't note that," he said.

Dr. Sproot frowned. How did someone such as this get to be a reporter if he couldn't even tell what a yucca was?

"The yucca, Mr. Ready, is the future of gardening in Livia. I have reason to believe that I am in the vanguard of a new gardening mindset in Livia."

Roland had perked up from his post-lunch torpor when his editor handed him the thick packet of contest press materials. His instincts shouted at him that this could make for a great feature story. It would have pathos without degenerating into bathos. It would have ethos. It would show sympathy and empathy, but would not, he hoped, lead to entropy. Laid before him was a story about how a single event can bind an entire community together. Extrapolate it across the nation and even the world and it could serve as the blueprint for harmony and prosperity in our time.

He also figured it might help his career, stuck as it was in neutral. For two years, he had been covering crappy city council meetings, sleep-inducing school board deliberations, and the latest lame initiatives of various public works departments. A story such as this, properly reported and crafted, could propel him out of the suburbs into a beat more befitting his talents—the Statehouse beat! So promising was this story that it was already writing itself in his head before he had done one phone call's worth of reporting on it.

Roland pictured an idyllic community of avid gardeners.

Their lawns would sprout pink flamingos and yard gnomes. They would spend every waking moment planting and transplanting, watering, seeding, digging away with little hand trowels hand-crafted by grouchy old guys in Maine who grew foot-long beards and smoked corncob pipes. Coarse work gloves would cover their hands, and baseball caps and spacious sun hats would shield their heads, as they bent down on their knees to do battle with the hated dandelion and all those other weeds with names he had neither seen spelled out or heard spoken. This contest would unite a whole community in one big beautification experiment. The town of Livia, heretofore an undistinguished bedroom burb with virtually no nightlife or cultural amenities to attract a full-blooded young man whose star would soon be in the ascendant, would become a model for mankind.

Roland had to look past some prejudices to concoct such a story line. The product of a well-to-do suburb himself, he was fresh from a world-renowned journalism school and six different internships at top-flight, unimpeachable newspapers across the nation.

Along the way, he had grown to see suburbia as a wasteland of unimaginative, middle-class morons who did little more than mow their lawns, go fishing, and hold Tupperware parties. He marveled at the bourgeois clownishness of such a yard contest. Wouldn't it be wonderful if he could spin the story another way? Deep inside, he wanted to turn it into a comic fable of how petty and inconsequential the masses could be in their quest for some trivial little acknowledgment barely worth noticing.

But that wasn't journalism and Roland was a true journalist now. He took pride in being driven by the most compelling story angle, and not by personal sentiment, however truthful and enlightening that might be.

He charged ahead to find the facts that would suit the particular angle he had chosen. He didn't call the source of the information, which had been passed on to him by his editor. That would be too easy and predictable. Instead, he called the chief custodian at the Valleydale Middle School, a nurse at the DoBeWell clinic, and the owner of Paws 'n' Stuff pet store, all of whom he'd profiled in past feature stories.

Much to his amazement, they knew nothing. At least, that's what they claimed. Here's where things got all messed up. It was where he needed to be nimble. Changing circumstances changed story angles. The good reporter could turn on a dime. What popped into Roland's mind suddenly had much more potential than the original angle, which now looked sappy and stupid. This reeked of a bigger story. Perhaps those sources were playing him for a fool. Maybe they were just pretending to know nothing. Corruption? Misplaced funds? Secret societies of moon worshippers defying zoning restrictions and performing perverted lunar rites on public property? When people got evasive on you, it could mean anything.

Roland wanted to probe further. He told his editor that he was certain there was something bigger here. He spent the next three days calling four more people in Livia whose positions should have assured him an entrée into the story he was pursuing. To his amazement, they didn't. This would be one of those tough nuts to crack. Where to turn next? He was about to call a sporting goods store owner whom his diligent research informed him was very likely the stepdaughter of the superintendent of schools from 1982 through 1983 when he sensed a looming and hunched-over presence.

"Have you ever thought about calling Burdick's?" said the editor, a wheezing, wizened old professional whom Roland saw as a coarse, burned-out old shell of a hack who didn't truly understand the time that was required to root out the big stories. "You might note that the number is right there at the bottom of the press release."

The Burdick's people were very cooperative, eager as they

were to get as much free publicity as possible. They furnished Roland with the rules of the contest and some background about Jasper Burdick.

They even gave Roland a list of the year's contestants, who had been asked to describe in general ways what any judges and other visitors might expect to see in their gardens.

Bingo! thought Roland. At least this is getting me *somewhere!* But which of these names to call? It was at that moment that a colleague, the terribly attractive yet resoundingly untalented and ditzy Midge waltzed up to his desk. Roland was sorry he couldn't remember her last name. He should remember it because he really liked the way her poorly hidden charms raised her blouse like tent poles pushing up a rain tarp.

"You're working on that Livia garden contest, Roland?" Midge asked as Roland forced himself to look up from her thrust-out blouse, and at her face. "My aunt's one of the contestants. Her name is Dr. Phyllis Sproot, Ph.D. She'll never let you forget it either. She's kind of a stiff, but she knows her stuff. You really should interview her."

"Sure," said Roland, eager to start off with someone he knew would talk to him and especially wanting to do whatever it took to please Midge.

Now why wasn't he paying attention? Dr. Sproot thought. Roland was ignoring her when she had important points to make. There he was, looking around again, all mopey and critical when he had no idea at all what he was witnessing. Why wasn't he listening to her and enthusiastically absorbing her sound arguments for why she was a shoo-in to win first prize in the Burdick's Best Yard Contest?

Dr. Sproot had done her darnedest to disparage every other gardener in the city and to pump up her own credentials to this Roland Ready fellow. But now here he was fumbling to understand something so far beyond his ken that it might as well have been quantum physics. Well, she supposed that was sufferable as long as it led to the end result: positive publicity that would convince the judges that she was the one to be crowned as Livia's gardening royalty.

"And those?" he said, pointing to one of several vast stretches of flora alive with blooms. "What are they? Are those roses?"

Dr. Sproot tittered insincerely. The buffoon!

"No, not even close. That is my coreopsis-salvia-hollyhock blend."

"Salivate?" repeated Roland as he scratched it down in his pad. "Saliva?"

Dr. Sproot clapped her hands together and pursed her lips, as she often did when confronted with ignorance of the most abominable sort.

"No, Mr. Ready! Salvia. S-A-L-V-I-A. C-O-R-E-O-P-S-I-S. H-O-L-L-Y-H-O-C-K. Got that, or am I going too fast for you? And, please, in the order of coreopsis first, and hollyhock last. It's important that you get them in the proper order." Roland frowned as he scribbled madly onto his pad.

"Got it," he said with a sigh that disturbed Dr. Sproot.

"You should know, Mr. Ready, that I am Livia's expert when it comes to the coreopsis-salvia-hollyhock blend. No one else in Livia even comes close, though there are a few that planted coreopsis, and maybe salvia, as a kind of sideline. For me, it is a passion."

"Along with yuccas," said Roland, scribbling furiously.

"Yes, they are separate, but intertwined as part of an overall garden design, and, oh, with a few other things just to leaven the mix."

"Others?"

"Roses and dahlias."

"Okay, roses and . . . how do you spell dahlias?"

Dr. Sproot was getting tired of serving as a plant dictionary for this undereducated bozo. She now realized that this was an unusually stupid person posing as an expert, and that he didn't know the difference between a rose and a pine tree, and might give some other, far less worthy contest entrant equal play. Her little dumbo of a niece, Midge, should have told her that.

What was he doing now? Roland retrieved and unfolded a wad of papers from his coat pocket and studied them intently. From the way the papers were tilted, Dr. Sproot could see the Burdick's letterhead. It was obviously part of the list of entrants that Burdick's had so unwisely been circulating despite her best efforts to put a stop to it.

"Would you like to go inside, Mr. Ready, and talk some more? I have an extensive background in horticulture, with my advanced degree and everything, and you might like to learn more about it."

"Actually, I need to visit some of these other folks," said Roland, peering at his list. "Some of these other gardens look really interesting."

How the hell would he know that? thought Dr. Sproot peevishly. Those other gardens are all rot! Stupid little plots scratched out by uninspired hardscrabble people who call themselves gardeners and have no inkling as to what they're doing! How could he even think of putting those amateurish efforts on an equal footing with her own masterpiece, created with the benefit of years of knowledge and study and hard— very hard—work?

"Mr. Ready, you would be making a very big mistake going to any of those other homes."

Roland looked up at her from his crumpled paper. "Why is that?"

"That is because they are very sad, very pathetic efforts at gardening by people who are only in it for the money. Mercenary people who haven't given to gardening the way I have given to it. You would be disappointed, and you would be unjust. They can't win. I have given you complete and unfettered access to my private property here and my private thoughts, and I, in all likelihood, will win this contest. Why do you need to go any further?"

"Ms. Sproot—"

"*Doctor* Sproot . . . D-O-C-T-O-R. Or you may put a comma and a Ph.D. after my name. The P and D are capitalized, with a period between the h and D."

Roland smiled at Dr. Sproot in a way she took to be patronizing.

"*Doctor* Sproot, in my business you have to talk to lots of people. You can't develop a good story without intensive reporting, taking in lots of information from lots of sources. Ooh, this looks like a good one." He was studying that wretched paper again.

"And who might that be?"

"Marta . . . uh . . . Marta . . . Pop . . . Pop . . ."

"Poppendauber?"

"Yeah. Yeah. That's it. Poppendauber."

Dr. Sproot flushed. Marta had entered her gardens in the contest! What a joke! She had specifically warned Marta that her feeble efforts would not be nearly up to the standards of the Burdick's Best Yard Contest, but now see what she'd done! Out of some little pique directed at her, no doubt.

It had been more than a week since she had seen or talked to Marta, whom she had tried to call three times, only to get the answering machine, and then no returned call. Marta was avoiding her on purpose. The ingrate! See if she would ever help her again with the scrubby little dirt pits she called gardens.

"I happen to know that the Poppendaubers are on vacation in . . . the Adriatic. Completely out of the country. They'll be out of town for two weeks. Probably too long for your article. Who else? Hmmm?"

"Ummm. Looks like the Fremonts on Payne Avenue. They seem to have lots of stuff in their garden. Do you know them?"

The Fremonts! Good God Almighty, how could he possibly have tumbled to those people? Why, they were just drunks who used gardening as an excuse to get soused, that's what they were. The problem was that they had shown just enough skill in working their grounds that they might bamboozle an untutored ignoramus such as Mr. Ready into believing they had something of actual merit to show off.

What was worse was that Edith Merton's little bad-girl spell didn't seem to have taken effect on their gardens yet. What was the story with that, eh? Next time, Dr. Sproot fumed, she would press harder for a money-back guarantee.

Seeing as how Marta seemed to have detached herself from her service, and was thus no longer submitting reports and photographs to her, Dr. Sproot had taken it upon herself to do her own sleuthing. She had done so unapologetically. Having determined that a certain amount of subterfuge could still be accomplished without resorting to disguises or slinking around when nobody was home, she strolled boldly through the Fremonts' backyard, examining every inch of ground, politely declining any offers of refreshment from those boozehounds.

"I'm just admiring your wonderful gardens," she told them.

"Be our guest, whoever you are," called the man from their patio. "No special permission required. Just remember, there's a glass of merlot always up here with your name, whatever that might be, on it."

Dr. Sproot wrinkled her nose and continued her inspection. New things here, either just planted or popping up through the ground. She sniggered at the sight of the hibiscus. What in heaven's name had caused them to plant those? Too much drink, perhaps? As she turned away to get a good, hard look at the roses smothering their arched trellises, she heard some-

thing. Was it just the breeze? Her imagination? No, it was
someone whispering. Someone very close by. She turned back
toward the hibiscus and there was the Fremont woman, kneel-
ing and muttering. Muttering to whom? To herself? No, for
heaven's sake, she was talking to her plants! Sweet little coaxings and blandishments in the most repugnant little baby-talk
voice.

Dr. Sproot shuddered. This was an outdoor asylum, that's
what it was! And she was in the presence of lunatics! She double-
timed it back toward the street, halfway convinced that she
would at any moment feel the sharp stab of a hurled pitchfork
digging its prongs deep into the small of her back, and wondering why the hell it took so long for Edith Merton's spell to start
earning its pay.

Now, she was dolefully reflecting on the glories of the Fremont's backyard. That hateful little voice inside of her kept ex-
tolling it as a work of genius, that could easily have been
designed by a top-flight landscape designer. Then there were
those angel's trumpets! What an inspiration! What if Roland
Ready saw them? Dr. Sproot told the nagging little voice to
put a lid on it. It was time to stop all this foolishness.

"Do not go to the Fremonts'!" she said in the most stentorian, threatening tone she could muster. Roland jerked his
head and frowned.

"Why not?" he said. "Why not go to the Fremonts'?"

Dr. Sproot quivered with anger and disdain.

"Why? Because the Fremonts are amateurs who should
never have been allowed to participate in a contest of this sort.
They are gardening parvenus."

"What's that?" said Roland, pen and steno pad poised for
action.

"Parvenus. I'm not going to spell that for you, and stop
writing what I say until I give you permission to do so. This is
all off the record."

Roland pursed his lips into a disagreeable smirk, clicked his pen, and put it back in his coat pocket.

"They also have criminal tendencies," Dr. Sproot said. "Although you didn't get that from me."

Roland moved to retrieve the pen from his pocket, but Dr. Sproot was quicker; she grabbed his wrist firmly and jerked it downward.

"Hey!"

"I told you this is all off the record. Do you want to hear it or not?"

Roland nodded grudgingly.

"All right. This is strictly confidential."

Dr. Sproot lowered her voice, cupped her hand over her mouth, and leaned close enough to Roland to get a whiff of what must have been the most powerful aftershave lotion ever created. Eau de musk oxen, she thought, as the powerful, chemical-laden fumes singed the hairs in her flaring nostrils.

"Mr. Fremont was caught a month ago in flagrante delicto."

"Where is that?"

Dr. Sproot rolled her eyes.

"It's not a place, Mr. Ready, it's a situation. He was caught . . . uh . . . um . . . relieving himself in the woods . . . outside . . . in broad daylight . . . with strangers . . . little strangers . . . present."

Roland jerked back from Dr. Sproot, not so much out of shock or outrage, but because she was emitting an overpowering odor that smelled like caffeinated paper plant effusions mixed with raspberry jam.

"Phew!" he said reflexively.

"That's right," Dr. Sproot said. "The police were there, too. His wife just stood by. Did nothing to stop it. They say she sunbathes nude back there and lets chipmunks and squirrels and all the other creatures of temperate suburbia crawl all over her when she is in a naked state. That's all I can tell you. You might think twice now about devoting any of your precious time to a couple of questionable characters like that."

But what seemed questionable or worse to Dr. Phyllis Sproot sounded enticing or better to the young journalist. He had been thoroughly bored by her; she struck him as a self-important, intolerant prude whose gardens didn't seem all that extraordinary to him anyway.

"I don't know; they sound pretty interesting to me. Well, I'll be on my way. Thanks for the time and the fascinating tour."

Dr. Sproot rushed to insert herself between Roland and the route to his car.

"Mr. Ready, if you interview those people over my objections, I will demand that you strike everything you heard and saw here from your record. I will simply not be in the same story with *those people*."

Roland wriggled his nose. That smell!

"Dr. Sproot," he said. "You will not prevent me from exercising my right as a journalist to talk to whomever I please. I will talk to the Fremonts if they consent to be interviewed, and will be more than glad to ignore anything I saw and heard here today."

He jerked quickly around Dr. Sproot, who stood rooted to the ground, fuming, and wondering what her next move might be, and strode swiftly to his car. As he slammed the door shut, he caught a glimpse of her, as unmovable as one of her plants, her face frozen into the malevolent scowl of a gardener scorned. He suddenly reflected, miserably, that he had just torpedoed whatever chances he might have had with the one bit of gardening that someone in the Sproot family had truly excelled at: Little-Miss-Tent-Pole-Tits.

21

The Plant Whisperer's Guide

George and Nan were meant to be plant whisperers. It came so naturally to them. Once they got the hang of talking to the erstwhile silent multitudes in the backyard, it got to be as routine as conversing with themselves, singing in the shower, and muttering monosyllabic mantras in the meditation bower.

And so rewarding! Say whatever you wanted to plants and they never failed to listen, often respectfully. George noticed the impatiens to be somewhat haughty, perhaps because they bloomed all season long, and the irises to be barely conscious when he was addressing them, though that might have been because their blooms had been gone now for well over a month. Or maybe it was because he had clipped a couple of them inadvertently while mowing the lawn. Amputees!

Both Nan and George hoped the flowers would grow to trust them enough that they could get a little more feedback about what was bothering them, especially in the area of bugs or funguses. That would just take time. Still, it was wonderful to watch them all perk up as they approached with the hose or watering can, or a special treat of fertilizer.

The Fremonts' friends watched them, amused and a little concerned. A few would indulge them by accepting their invitations to join them in some basic plant chitchat in the hope of getting a full-fledged backyard klatch going. The proviso was that they should expect no two-way social intercourse in the usual sense.

Whatever their friends might have thought, there was certainly no arguing about the results. Something had turned the Fremonts' backyard from merely wonderful into a paradise on earth. Though the heat wave lingered, alternately steaming and baking everything within its reach, the Fremont gardens were lush and iridescent. Blooms exploded by the score. Ruby-throated hummingbirds and butterflies alighted everywhere. Even the rabbits seemed to have noticed, and refrained from wreaking their usual havoc; no nibbled leaves or shoots turned up for an entire week.

Inspired to do even more, the Fremonts bought some coleus to plant among the rocks near the patio, and a serviceberry, which was placed at the base of the split-rail fence, near where it intersected with the chain-link fence, and just to the east of the hydrangeas.

Ellis, Cullen, and Sis were forced by sheer proximity to witness their parents' new talents, which they viewed as bemused spectators. It was the latest turn in a long history of bizarre behavior to which they had become accustomed. Plant talking, however, marked a radical shift that ratcheted the weirdo factor to a whole new level.

Still, they figured, if you were shameless enough, there was entertainment value in it. Ellis and Cullen even took some pride in knowing that their parents were unconventional, not the usual bourgeois types. At the same time, it was good that there were no signs that their feelings and actions as responsible parents had changed any, though this was not something either of them would have openly voiced.

Sis was more sensitive. She was easily humiliated by bizarre parental behavior. The day before, she had been publicly mortified when she and her friends Margo and Taylor were walking across the yard and chanced upon a laughing Nan, who, it turned out, was sharing a joke with some of the petunias. That was the kind of behavior no teenager could ever forgive. Knowing their parents' talents, and appreciating those gifts more than Sis, who could only pout about her genetic lot in life, Ellis and Cullen were beginning to realize that there could be positive benefits to their parents' eccentricities.

"It's lame," Ellis said. "It is truly the lamest thing I've ever seen them do, and I've gotta say that I'm concerned about their sanity. But, hey, this contest has over $100,000 in prize money, and everyone says Mom and Dad are the ones that can make a garden do what they want. If it takes yakking to the plant life, I'm all for it."

"Yeah," Cullen said. "Check out the way the backyard looks, even though the front yard is a pit. Man, it is something *else*. JoAnne and Mark said their parents don't think there's anything like it in town. And their parents should know. Hey, you've heard of horse and dog whisperers. So, Mom and Dad are plant whisperers. What's the difference? And one hundred thousand smackers could sure go a long ways toward a college tuition . . . am I right, Sis?"

"Don't call me 'Sis' anymore," said Sis. "I'm Mary now, please. I am a fully formed woman now at the age where I can bear human fruit."

"Human fruit?" Ellis said, chuckling. "You mean like half-baby, half-tangerine?"

"You're not telling us you're *with child,* are you, Sis?" Cullen said.

"*With child?* You mean pregnant? Good God, no! I don't even have a boyfriend. I wish I had a boyfriend, but I don't. I mean I'm old enough to *get* pregnant, so I am a woman, and you can quit calling me Sis. That is so juvenile."

"Okay, Miss Sis, then," said Ellis.

Mary flushed strawberry-vanilla and sputtered, trying to spit out a bad word that wouldn't quite escape. She turned abruptly and stormed out the back door. Outside, Nan and George were bent over, locked in a very casual, pleasant conversation with the alyssum. Mary boldly walked up to them.

"This is, like, the weirdest thing I've ever seen anyone's parents do," she said. "You're, like, kidding, right? You just do this as a joke. . . . If it's not a joke, will you please stop?" Nan and George beckoned Mary to bend over and lean closer to the alyssum.

"We promised to introduce you," Nan said. "They've been asking about you." Mary stomped off in a huff, muttering something about parent aliens and drug use in the sixties. She brushed past Ellis in the doorway. He was holding the phone.

"Hey, plant whisperers!" he yelled. "Telephone." Nan took the phone. It was a fellow named Roland Ready from the *Inquirer*.

"Sweetheart!" she yelled at George, who was still absorbed in his little chat with the alyssum, whom they had both found to be a bit too loquacious.

"What?" said George, excusing himself politely from a conversation that seemed to be going around in circles.

"There's a fellow from the *Inquirer* who wants to interview us. Shall we let him?"

George gasped.

"About . . . that? Tell him I have no comment."

Nan laughed.

"Not *that*," she said, cupping her hand over the receiver's mouthpiece. "It's about our backyard, and the contest. He's doing a story about the contest."

George heaved a sigh of relief, and winked at the roses, who were eavesdropping. They were so *prying*.

"I guess so. Why not?"

★   ★   ★

Roland Ready arrived a half hour later with a photographer, who was snapping away rapid-fire as soon as he set foot in the backyard. Here, truly, was Eden, thought Roland as George and Nan showed him around the grounds. He had never seen anything so lush and colorful in his life. Where was that fragrance coming from? It might be the sweetest thing ever smelled.

Nan and George proved to be wonderful guides, so pleasant, answering all his questions with smiling and unevasive aplomb. Roland could not help but draw a distinction between these laid-back and welcoming gardening wizards and that flinty, smelly old bitch, Dr. Sproot, who had sneered at him, and accosted him, and had falsely made herself out to be the greatest thing that ever happened to plantdom.

Unlike Dr. Sproot's yuccaland, here was a vast variety of different plants with exotic names he had never heard of: hosta, phlox, petunias, monarda, clematis. How were they ever able to find and nurture such a motley assortment? Why, it beggared description! Nevertheless, Roland scribbled furiously in his notebook, asking for the spelling of every plant name, which Nan and George furnished without complaint. And such humility! As the framework of the story began to rise in his head, Roland saw this as only a slight variation on his original theme. It would be a suburban idyll, a story about a couple of carefree suburbanites removed from the travails of city life, creating their own Nirvana in the form of a peaceful plant kingdom, where beauty and tranquility reigned supreme.

The screen door flew open with a bang. Out charged Sis, wailing for George and Nan, and screaming back at Ellis and Cullen, whose taunting voices could be heard following her from the dining room.

"Mom, Dad, make them stop! They keep teasing me about getting pregnant. Make them stop! And they keep calling me 'Sis'! I'm Mary now. Mary, Mary, Mary!"

George and Nan smiled wanly as Roland and the photographer, attracted by the commotion, walked over after making a brief detour to inspect one of the rose trellises.

"Oh!" said Sis, suddenly burying her burning face in her hands to hide her embarrassment. "Sorry. I didn't know we had guests. Jeez, I'm sorry."

"Excuse us," said Nan as she put her arm around Sis and ushered her back into the house. George smiled self-consciously at Roland and the photographer.

"Trouble in paradise, Mr. Fremont?" said Roland.

"Teenagers," said George, wondering ruefully whether Sis really was pregnant.

At this point, Roland's story construct had crashed into a pile of dust-choked rubble. New story foundations began to rise. One portrayed the Fremonts as a dysfunctional family where some kind of abuse—physical or mental, but it made no difference—was going on, forcing the family to seek escape and redemption in the solace of their gardens. Another put the onus on the teenagers; they could be terrors beyond the control of their mom and dad, manufacturing drugs in the basement, holding sex parties in the bedrooms, driving their poor parents to seek shelter in an ersatz outdoor paradise.

"Lemonade anyone?" said Nan, pushing through the door with a tray of glasses and a pitcher of rich pink lemonade with pieces of lemon pulp still floating around in it, just the way Roland liked it.

"Yes, absolutely!" said Roland, so glad to get some refreshment on such a steamy day that he draped a mental drop cloth over his story ideas to be uncovered sometime later. He and the photographer then sat down to enjoy some of the best lemonade they'd ever tasted.

"Sorry about the disturbance," Nan said. "Sis's older brothers were teasing her a little too cruelly. And, for the record, she is *not* pregnant! Three teenagers—uh, I mean two teenagers and one twenty-year-old—can be a handful, Mr. Ready."

"I can imagine," said Roland as the photographer jumped up to snap some photos of two goldfinches that had landed on the feeder perches, and promptly scared them away.

"Wow!" said Roland. "That was the yellowest bird I ever saw. What was that?" He whipped out his pen.

"Goldfinch," said George. "G-O-L-D-F-I-N-C-H."

"Hey," said the photographer, who had sat back down and lifted his camera with its big lens to his squinting eye. "Check out the blue bird at the other feeder. Pure blue."

"Wow! And that is . . ."

"Indigo bunting," said George. "I-N-D-I-G-O B-U-N-T-I-N-G. And you've gotten a treat there. It's the first time we've seen that guy around this summer."

Orange-and-black monarch butterflies fluttered over the monarda, which were starting to show signs of life, and lighted on some daisies.

"Monarchs?" said Roland. Nan and George applauded.

"You've done your homework, I see," George said.

As Roland and the photographer were getting ready to leave, Nan told them to wait for a moment and ran back into the house. She emerged carrying two plastic bags filled with Asiatic lilies in full bloom.

"A parting gift for you as a thank-you for showing interest in our humble efforts," she said. "You, in turn, might want to present these to your girlfriends or wives. Women are suckers for lilies."

The story Roland wrote appeared three days later, in the Sunday edition. It got centerpiece display on the front page of the metro section with a beautiful photograph of the indigo bunting and another of the smiling Nan holding her daylilies.

Roland, in what he considered to be his best effort to date, described in effortless prose a suburban wonderland, a refuge from the roar of the crowd, a haven from the troubles of our time. He also made sure, at the insistence of his editor, to insert a couple of paragraphs with more prosaic details about the Burdick's contest. As his fingers flew on his computer's keyboard, he barely recalled the unruly teenager who had run, wailing, toward her parents, and what that might portend.

Praise was fulsome. The Fremonts called to thank him. Readers called and e-mailed to laud his writing and the positive light it had shed on gardening. Even old grump Joe Edwards, his editor, gave him one of his rare "tip o' the hat" praises. There was one jarring note: Dr. Sproot called in a fury.

"I can't believe I went to all that effort, and then you don't even insert me in the story . . . not at all!"

"You told me not to."

"Yes, but I didn't mean it! I didn't mean it! Couldn't you tell that was just a gambit, and I didn't mean it?"

"No, I couldn't tell."

"And those Fremonts. Ha-ha. What a blunder to focus on them! Why . . . why, did you know they pretend to talk to their plants? *Talk* to their plants. . . ."

"Hmmm."

"They also grow psychedelic plants."

"What?"

"Psychedelic plants. You know, plants that make you crazy if you eat or smoke them. That's probably why they talk to their plants."

"Hmmm."

"Don't you 'hmmm' me, Mr. Stupid Reporter. You just gave free publicity to a couple of people who are not only drunks but certifiably insane. Didn't you realize that? Didn't you do any fact-checking on this? Furthermore, if I lose this contest, I will threaten to sue you. I will threaten to sue over the loss."

"Thanks for your time, but I am very busy," said Roland.

He hung up with Dr. Sproot's voice still crackling over the receiver and turned his attention to his next assignment: a triple homicide that looked like a love triangle gone bad just reported in from the sleepy bedroom community of Triace.

22

A Watering

Rain was finally on the way!

A vigorous cold front charged down from the north and collided with the moist, slovenly soup-air that had been loafing over Livia. The prospect of atmospheric combat lured the Fremonts into the front yard. It was distasteful to them, but what could they do; the front yard, with its panorama of Bluegill Pond and open sky that stretched for miles, was the only place on their property where they could take in the full measure of weather in the making. On this morning, it was still sultry ("Dew point in the mid-seventies," George reported), and clouds were piling up overhead and to the west, into ungainly stratospheric columns. Some were tumbling outward and darkening at the base.

"Pretty impressive buildup," George said. "We should get something good out of this."

Nan nodded.

"Let's water anyway, just in case. . . . I hope we don't get any hail or worse."

Little dust-settling showers came and went throughout the morning and into the afternoon. By three, the mercury stood at 94, and it appeared that the rain was going to be a no-show.

Either the moisture in the air was insufficient or the temperature aloft wasn't cold enough to spark the thunderstorms they had anticipated for the past three days, when the weather forecasters had first predicted them.

That evening, things changed. Their backyard was unusually animated. Either the Fremont flora were anxious about something or joyfully anticipating it; George and Nan couldn't tell which. Their queries around the backyard went unanswered, even by their favorite backyard informants, the spirea.

"They're not telling me jack," George said.

"Me neither," said Nan. "It's like they're keeping a big secret. Maybe they want to surprise us."

"They must know the rain is coming," George said. "Somehow they can feel it and they just can't stand the anticipation."

"Either that or they're afraid. They sense the big wind, the downpours that wash away before they can get a decent drink, or the hail that could slice them into bits."

Pondering the ineffable vagaries of the plant world, George and Nan ended their work day by uncorking a bottle of Sagelands and toasting their successes in the backyard over the past week and a half.

They were imbued with a new confidence that victory, and, with that, financial solvency, was within their grasp. It was less than two weeks now before the judging began. It would start with seven judges doing three days' worth of quick inspections, winnowing the entries down to seven finalists. On the third day, reserved for a Saturday, all the judges would tour the gardens of the finalists, consult with one another, and announce the winner at the new Livia Arts and Culture Center that evening.

As George and Nan refilled their glasses, and waved to the Boozers passing by at an unusually brisk pace, they settled into a peaceful euphoria brought on by alcohol and a wonderful premonition that what had started as a mere hobby and a way to keep busy, and which had morphed into this magnificent obsession, would now truly become their life. A distant growl startled them out of their reverie.

"Thunder?" Nan said.

"Too far away to tell. Might just be traffic."

The stillness was absolute. Not a leaf or a petal stirred. A second growl, this time closer, got them up out of their chairs, ambling slowly toward the front yard. Far off to the north, there was milky sky punctuated by cloud pillars and few gray masses with cauliflower tops. Directly above them and off to the south haze gauzed over the sky, giving it a coppery tint. In the west, the sun shone thinly through a screen of ice clouds.

Farther west, just above the horizon, was the source of the noise: a dark, distant smear brightened with intermittent flashes. It was moving fast. Five more minutes and the cloud blotted out the sun. Then, the oppressive stillness was gone, whisked away by the fresh breeze that preceded the storm. The thunder was doing its impersonation of field artillery now. Nan and George stood there, entranced, as the flashes turned into ragged white lines ripping across the clouds, and the sky erupted in the crash of flying electrical charges. The sky to the west turned a purple-black, and the first fat rain-drops of the storm came splattering down.

"Good rain for sure," George said. "We're right in the bull's-eye of this one."

"Anything besides rain, Mr. Meteorology?"

"Don't think so," said George, taking a long, slow sip of merlot as the rain spattered against him. "Sky's not that black. No straight-line winds. We would have had them by now. Looks like a nice light show and a garden-variety thunder-storm. Just what the doctor ordered. Let's just hope it's more of a steady rain than a deluge."

A couple of cyclists zipped by on Sumac. Then came a

jogger with a dog straining at its leash. The elderly Smiths were walking along the sidewalk and paused to stare at the purple sky descending on them, and the ripples and puckers covering Bluegill Pond. They turned to wave at the Fremonts.

"You can shelter here if you need to," yelled George, knowing that the Smiths had two blocks to go.

They smiled and shook their heads, then continued walking. That was when the apparition came hurtling down the sidewalk, a block away. It was a bicycle, a racing bike from the look of it, and bearing down fast on the Smiths. The rider had a freakishly tall and pointed head and was wearing metallic-looking robes sparkling with multicolored glitter that billowed out behind her.

"Eeeehh! A conehead!" cried Nan. "And it's going to run right into the Smiths!"

The Smiths were moving in the slow, deliberate, hunched-over way of the elderly, oblivious to the bicycle kamikaze heading full-tilt directly for them.

"She'll veer off or slow down before she hits them," said George. "Won't she? What the hell is a conehead doing on Sumac? And on a racing bike? What the—?"

"Hey!" Nan yelled. "Look out!"

Lightning shot through the sky like flashbulbs, followed almost instantly by ear-splitting peals of thunder that bounced around the clouds for the next ten seconds. The Smiths pushed on faster as the downpour started. Right behind them, the conehead hunched down low over the handlebars for the final approach toward what could only be a terrible collision with one or both of the Smiths.

Suddenly, the bike veered to the left and jumped the curb, sending it rattling into the street, and its rider sprawling on top of the curb, just above the storm sewer, into which rivulets of rain were already beginning to drain.

"Whoa!" went Nan and George.

The Smiths, scurrying for all their creaky old appendages were worth, had already disappeared around the curve. The conehead got up, apparently unhurt, and leaned over with some effort to pick up the bike and what proved to be a flesh-tone, foot-and-a-half- long rubber cone, which had been jarred off her head, and lay crumpled up on the sidewalk. Now, a bedraggled, stringy-haired woman, her silvery robe pasted onto her ample body by the rain, gazed up at them.

"Good Lord!" Nan gasped. "It's Pat Veattle!"

George guffawed, and, after a second, Nan laughed, too. Through the curtain of pouring rain, Pat stared at them. Then, she raised an arm and an index finger in their direction. She held that pose for an entire minute. At first, George and Nan thought she was flashing them a V for victory sign or signaling for help. Then, it dawned on them.

"She's giving us the finger!" Nan cried. "Why, the nerve of that woman!"

Pat Veattle put her prosthetic head back on, then tried to get on her bike. The wind and the rain pushed her down before she could straddle the seat. She tried again with the same result, then gave up. Walking her bike down Sumac, she was eventually swallowed up in the rain. Nan and George dumped the water out of their wineglasses and ran for the front porch.

"What the hell was she doing in that conehead thing?" said George, as they took one last look at the blur of Pat Veattle and her bicycle disappearing around the curve.

"I still want to see her dressed up like an elk, or whatever it was Steve saw her dressed up as when he almost hit her," Nan said. "The poor woman must be mad."

The storm quickly lost its intensity, and the purple sky lightened into a steel gray. The rain continued, but at a steady and moderate rate. It finally stopped in the middle of the night.

*　　*　　*

When the Fremonts woke up the next morning, the sun shone down, and there were one-and-three-quarters inches of water in the rain gauge. The backyard luxuriated in the deep breath of moisture that remained after the rain. Even the front yard was showing signs of life.

"Million-dollar rain," George said as he and Nan inspected their happy gardens. "No watering necessary for at least three more days."

23

When Garden Spells Go Bad

"Sarah says the spell isn't working," said Marta. She accepted a mug of steaming coffee, as they sat on Dr. Sproot's patio, their Adirondack chairs positioned to take in the full glory of the coreopsis-salvia-hollyhock blend. "She wanted me to come over and tell you in person."

"Is that so, Marta? Is that really so? I can tell that with my own eyes. I've known for an entire week and a half that her stupid spell isn't working!"

"Well, at least she undid the spell on your gardens. I'm so glad to see it. They're glorious!"

"Of course they're glorious!" barked Dr. Sproot. "But that's only half the job. The other half isn't happening, and I demand my money back. Otherwise, I'll have to expose Edith Merton as the witch she is."

Marta lifted the mug gingerly to her lips, puckered them, and set the mug back down on the glass-topped patio table.

"What? Too hot for your liking, Marta?"

"Yes, just a touch too hot, thanks, Dr. Sproot. I'll let it cool off a little."

Dr. Sproot sneered.

"Gee whiz, Marta, I made it especially hot for you, knowing how much you like scalding drinks. C'mon, don't be a fraidy cat. Take a big swig out of that mug."

"No, thank you," said Marta, noticing once again that Dr. Sproot was apparently able to drink hot coffee without any adverse effect.

"I see you are able to drink hot beverages again."

"Eh?" said Dr. Sproot between slurps.

"I take it your throat is healed and you are able to drink your hot coffee again."

"Yes, isn't it lovely," Dr. Sproot cooed. "It is the best coffee ever grown, and I have to special order it. Apart from gardening it is my only vice. I mean, I mean . . . no . . . no! My throat is not healed. Not healed at all. I still have to make an appointment with a specialist. Yikes! Now that you mention it, this coffee is a little hot."

Dr. Sproot set her mug back on the patio table, and made a big show of waving at the steam curling up from its contents.

"Wow! I really shouldn't be drinking this with my throat condition, should I? It's not nearly as hot as your wretched tea, anyway. Listen, Marta, what are you implying here? I took a big glug of your tea, which was hotter 'n blazes. I'm just sipping this coffee, which is nowhere near as hot anyway. It's too hot for *you,* isn't it?"

"Not really," said Marta. She picked up her mug, pointing her rigid pinkie straight toward the sky, and downed a long, noisy draft. "It's just that I wanted to see your reaction when I said it was."

"How dare you, you . . . you . . . you little shrimp! You accuse me of trying to scald you with my coffee because of the damage you inflicted on me? Is that it?"

"Yes, Dr. Sproot."

"And then . . . and then . . . and then . . ." Dr. Sproot was screaming now. Marta discreetly formed her hand into a canopy over her coffee mug in case the spittle started to fly. "And then

you accuse me of faking an injury after I scalded my poor
throat and can no longer sing, and must see a specialist? Huh!
And why would I do that, Marta? Why?"

"Easy. So you could scare me into thinking you could sue
me for damages. I am somewhat gullible and a little timid, Dr.
Sproot. You know that and take advantage of me. And we used
to be friends. For a long time. It's hard to let that go, even
when your good friend is treating you like freshly turned topsoil and stomping all over you. And you did help me *so* much
to learn our wonderful craft."

"But you ignored me! You ignored my best advice, and
now look at what you've got. It's nothing but a nuthouse, plant
cuckoo-land, an anarchy. It's like you wanted to create a little
United Nations of gardens. You'll never win anything, Marta
Poppendauber! Nothing! I can't believe you had the temerity
to enter that contest! Why, the very nerve! I know the judges.
They'll either burst out laughing or vomit when they get a
good, hard look at your place."

"I'll take my chances, Dr. Sproot."

Dr. Sproot was standing now, sputtering grunts and various
vowel and consonant sounds. Her face was contorted and aged
in hatred and disdain and self-righteousness. Her shirttails had
gotten yanked out of her shorts and were fluttering in the
breeze, revealing an occasional flash of bare, pale midriff. Marta
noted that that somehow made her seem laughably pathetic.
Dr. Sproot collapsed back into her chair, throwing her elbows
across the patio table and cradling her head in her hands. Marta
found whatever residue of pity she had left for her now mingled with scorn. She was exhilarated to discover that, for the
first time in years, she could deal with Dr. Sproot without fear.

"Let's get back to Sarah," she said. "Sarah said the Fremonts' gardens must be strong because they are resisting the
spell. The only option left is a much stronger spell, which will
create havoc and destruction. Stronger even than the spell she

cast on your gardens. To do that, she will have to take additional steps, which will include a personal nighttime visit to the Fremonts', without their knowing it, of course. This will cost much more—$1,200—and, as before, there are no guarantees. I strongly advise that you not do this, Dr. Sproot."

Dr. Sproot downed a slug of coffee, which revived her, and sat bolt upright.

"And why not?"

"Because it is evil. It is bad. It contradicts every standard of morality."

"It does not!" said Dr. Sproot, to whom another long draw from the coffee mug had returned the old dominating, offensive assertiveness. "You tell that stupid old witch that I will pay her $700 and no more for this . . . this . . . super-spell. You tell her that. Do you think she'll do it?"

"Yes, I know she will. I was authorized by Sarah to go down to precisely that amount if necessary. It's her returning customer discount. You will be assessed additional dry cleaning costs should her uniform get all messed up. That's a distinct possibility when doing fieldwork. Now, if you will give me the cash, I will deliver it to Sarah. Another thing: from now on I'm having nothing to do with either you or Sarah."

"What? Why, I'll destroy you, you little mouse."

"I don't think so, Doc Phil."

Dr. Sproot shook with rage. "I told you never to call me that! I'm telling you again! Don't call me that horrid little nickname! D'ya hear me!"

"Just give me the money, Doc Phil, and I'll be on my way. If you need to contact Sarah anymore, then you'll have to figure it out on your own. I will also be letting her know that I'm no longer making myself available as an intermediary between you two.

"As for you, I'm no longer going to be spying for you, or taking notes, or committing your 'death-by-a-thousand-cuts' by sneaking over there way past my bedtime—Thank God Ham is such a sound sleeper—and trespassing on private property like some thief, and snipping off blossoms, three or four at a time. That really was the low point, Dr. Sproot. That's destroying life. But no more."

"I always knew you were a fraidy cat," Dr. Sproot said. "You cut off how many little monarda stems on your two or three little nocturnal visits to the Fremonts' before chickening out, and you call that work! Why, that's nothing. 'Death-by-a-thousand-cuts' requires numerous trips over time. It requires dedication, which you obviously don't have. It is the slow, subtle torture of a garden that is hard to spot, and almost impossible to resolve, unless you're the most observant of gardeners."

"I'm sure the Fremonts noticed."

"Those drunkards! Of course they didn't."

"They know exactly what's going on, Doc Phil."

Dr. Sproot trembled in the presence of this new, more assertive Marta. "And my camera and cowl?"

"I've recovered them. I'll have them cleaned and ready to return to you by Thursday."

"Just put it on the doorstep. And guess what, you bumbling bumpkin: I don't have the cash on hand right now to pay that demented chucklehead of a sorceress. I'll have to bring it by your house. Don't worry, you won't have to sully yourself by dealing directly with me. I'll just put it in an envelope in your mailbox. And, by the way, don't count on any more advice from me about your wretched gardens. And . . . and . . . don't you dare come whining for help when you don't even get an honorable mention."

Marta got up and left without saying anything. She secretly pledged to do everything in her power to ensure that the Fremonts and their gardens came to no harm. That meant using her newly improved intelligence-gathering skills to keep careful tabs on both Dr. Sproot and Edith Merton. When they were on the move—and that would have to be soon—then she would have to be right there with them.

Dr. Sproot felt a sense of triumph as she watched Marta go, flipping her the bird when her back was turned. How does someone like that make any friends at all? she wondered. Freed of Marta's squeamishness and overdeveloped sense of fair play, she could now take her campaign to a new level of ruthlessness. Depending on that quack of a witch, Edith Merton, wouldn't be enough. She would have to act on her own. She would hold back nothing and give no quarter! Destroy! Destroy! Destroy!

But first, something a bit more subtle. After all, Marta Poppendauber wasn't the only person in town who had sources.

24

A Proposition

A man George and Nan didn't know, and dressed for business besides, parked his shiny new Honda on Payne Avenue behind Cullen's Camaro. He spotted them lounging in the backyard and walked up the steps leading to the patio with a smile and a casual wave. He was carrying a satchel, which appeared to be made out of fancy leather. It gleamed a rich, unblemished brown and had a gold clasp that shot reflected flashes of sunlight right at them.

"Turn off those brights," said George, shielding his eyes. The upscale briefcase struck George and Nan as strange, as the religious proselytizers they had entertained from time to time never seemed to carry such an accoutrement. Neither did they wear sport coats. Come to think of it, the mirror-lensed aviator sunglasses, blue Oxford-cloth shirt, and striped tie looked kind of out of place, too. They wondered whether this might be some high muckety-muck associated with Burdick's Best Yard Contest, or maybe a salesman of encyclopedias or laxatives.

"Greetings!" said the man as he stepped onto the patio purposefully. "Great day to be lounging around. Taking the day off, I see. Vacation?"

"We're not taking the day off," said George, who took an instant dislike to the man and his patently disdainful attitude toward sloth. "This is our work. We sit and watch our gardens, and drink a little wine. Besides, it's almost noon. Aren't most self-respecting epicureans relaxing around this time of day?"

The man chuckled self-consciously.

"Sure," he said, reflecting uneasily that he had somehow in-sulted the Fremonts. "Sure. After this, I'm gonna go play golf, for instance. I know a guy who sits around and drinks during the day. He got laid off work and just went through a divorce, though. Ha-ha. Ha-ha."

George and Nan grimaced.

"We never drink to excess if we can help it," Nan said firmly. "At least not too much to excess. We have not been fired by anyone and are not contemplating divorce. Are we, George?"

"No, unless you make me do the laundry today."

"Ha-ha, ha-ha," went the man. "Brother, do I know how *that* goes."

"Can we help you, Mister . . . Mister?"

"Abelard. John Abelard." John Abelard laid his briefcase on one of the patio chairs, and plucked a business card out of his billfold to present to George.

"Schwall's Dry Cleaning? I didn't know dry cleaners made house calls."

"We don't have anything that needs dry cleaning now any-way," Nan said. "Usually, we take it to Jocelyn's Dry Cleaners right here in Livia."

Mr. Abelard slapped the heel of his hand against his fore-head.

"A thousand pardons," he said, holding his hand out for George to return the card to him. "Wrong card." He put the card back in his billfold, wondering if the trick, which veteran colleagues told him was a great ice-breaker for cold-call visits, would work. He pulled another one out and handed it to George.

"This is the genuine article. Well, gee, at least that helped me remember I've got something to pick up on the way home. Ha-ha, ha-ha."

George inspected the card and raised his eyebrows.

"Hmm, a realtor, huh?"

"That's right," said Mr. Abelard, straightening up and smiling proudly as he removed his sunglasses to reveal sunken, beady, darting eyes that reminded Nan of whatever animal it was that had sunken, beady, darting eyes. She could understand now why he might want to wear sunglasses, even in the dark. "One of the best around, and specializing in Livia properties. I made the $1,350,000 club last year. Not too many in my business do that well."

"How nice," said Nan.

"What brings you to us?" said George. "Glass of merlot?"

Mr. Abelard paused, his eyes shifting furiously, and tilted his head as if in careful reflection, pretending to consider the offer.

"Gee, I'd love to but I can't," he said. "Not while I'm working. But thanks so very much for the offer. How 'bout a rain check? I'll take you up on that someday when *none* of us is working. Ha-ha."

George and Nan nodded stiffly, hoping that he would never return to take them up on that offer.

"Well, I'll get right down to brass tacks." With that he opened up his satchel and removed a sheaf of papers, then pulled back one of the patio chairs. "May I?"

"Certainly," said George.

Mr. Abelard sat down and leafed through his papers for a moment. He put on a pair of reading glasses, not because he needed them, but to impress prospective clients with his supposed erudition.

"The old vision's not what it used to be," he said. "Ha-ha, ha-ha."

Mr. Abelard went through the papers again, then laid them on the table. In doing so, he allowed his coat sleeve to pull back, revealing a very expensive Rolex watch gleaming in silvery splendor from his wrist. Such a tactic, he had learned, impressed and intimidated possible clients. Intimidation, he had been told by those in the know, was the fifth of the seven keys to success in business. But it couldn't be carried too far. A little pushing, a little feigned surprise when someone turned him down, and a fast-paced, let's-get-'er-done approach when someone showed the slightest inclination to sign on with him was how you hooked a prospective seller.

"A client of mine who lives right here in Balsam—"

"Livia."

"What?"

"You're in Livia now, Mr. Abelard. Balsam is twenty miles away."

"Ah, certainly. So sorry. I have an appointment in Balsam tomorrow. You know us busy realtors. No time to think! Uh, as I say, my client, who lives right here in Livia, is interested in your property and would like to buy it . . . or, at least, *use* it for a few days. What do you say?"

George shifted uneasily in his chair. Nan quickly drained the rest of her wineglass, and just as quickly filled it back up again.

"My client is willing to pay you more than the market value for your house—within reason, of course. Or, if you prefer, keep your house, and allow her use of the grounds for, oh, three to four days. She, of course, would pay for that use. We call that an easement."

"How much more than market value?" said George.

"I don't have an exact figure at this point. Within reason,

as I said. Hmmm, you could be looking at ten to fifteen percent over market value."

"How much for using it?"

"Two thousand dollars a day."

George cleared his throat.

"Should you sell, a condition would also be that she have immediate access to the property. Not the house. You can continue to live there until you find a new place. She would just need access to your backyard for three to four hours a day."

"Why?" said Nan.

"Why?" said Mr. Abelard as he pulled out a sheet of paper from his sheaf and laid it on the table in front of George and Nan. "She is an archaeologist who is interested in this property for historical reasons. You see, my client is convinced that your house rests on an old Indian burial ground. Hundreds of years old, but with skeletons still moldering away not more than ten to twenty feet under your backyard. If she owned this property, she would be able to study this Indian graveyard without the constraints of time or having to seek permission to dig it up."

"Burial ground!" George and Nan cried.

"Certainly. The Indians in the vicinity may well have buried their dead right beneath your property."

"Hmmm," said George, as laconically as if he had just been told something mildly interesting about the digestive tract of a manatee. Nan figured he must have suddenly sampled semi-somnolent ennui from his rather limited emotional palette.

"You should know that Indian spirits are renowned for looking after their old stomping grounds . . . and protecting them by whatever means necessary."

Nan shivered.

"My client, a member of our august state archaeologist's office, has asked me to urge you to do nothing to disturb the grounds. Otherwise, the spirits might take offense."

"Don't disturb the grounds!" Nan cried. "Why, we've been doing nothing *but* disturb the grounds for the past six years! What about the house? Somebody built the house on the burial grounds and there it stands, as sturdy and safe as ever."

"My client informs me that the probable burial site is not under the house itself, but under the yard; indeed, under where many of your remarkable gardens are now located."

"But what about all the work we've done on our gardens?" said Nan. "Isn't it possible that the dead approve of what we're doing and have been blessing them in whatever way dead Indians bless things?"

"My client said the spirits are probably really mad now and will get even madder if you so much as lay a hoe edge to any of your gardens. She asks you to please refrain from any future improvements that will disturb the souls underneath. Don't even water the grounds. Let nature take care of it, is what my client counsels. Sell or rent the property to a trained archaeologist, of course, and she will know exactly how to placate these restless spirits."

"Who *is* this client of yours anyway?" said George.

"You've probably heard of her," Mr. Abelard said. "Dr. Phyllis Sproot?"

"Yes, that name *does* sound familiar," Nan said.

"Wait a second," said George. "Isn't she one of those gardening nuts I overheard Earlene McGillicuddy telling you about?"

"Why, yes, George, I believe it was . . . the *trespasser!*"

"And she's an archaeologist, too?"

"Yes, indeed," Mr. Abelard said. "My client is a woman of many interests, gardening being second only to archaeology. But she would never stoop to trespassing. Never! I would stake my professional reputation on that. Just so you know everything is on the up-and-up, I've got an official document here attesting to the probable archaeological value of the property signed by Dr. Sproot herself."

Mr. Abelard pushed the paper he had separated from his pile toward George and Nan. It bore the letterhead of the state's "Department of Archaeological Research," and, at the bottom, the signature of one "Dr. Phyllis Sproot, Assistant Director in Charge of Indian Artifacts and Burial Grounds."

"Looks official enough," said Nan, pushing the document back to Mr. Abelard after she and George perused it. "But I wonder if this is that same woman running around in a monk's cowl or whatever it was she was wearing?"

"And who supposedly will do whatever it takes to win the Burdick's contest. Or, hey, maybe that woman who's been poking around in the yard and won't even come over to make a little polite conversation."

"That's right, George! That's right!"

"I can assure you that is just some libelous rumor being passed around the neighborhood," said Mr. Abelard as he leafed through his pile of papers and retrieved another document. "My client does not run around masquerading as a monk and trespassing on people's private property, though I suppose she might have taken a gander at your backyard at some point. I mean, after all, she wouldn't be doing her job as an archaeologist if she didn't do a little site inspecting . . . hee-hee. Now, we can get this done in a jiffy." He pointed his pen at the bottom lines on the document.

"All you need to do is sign right there, and that will get the process rolling. Or, if you prefer a rental arrangement, I have that document right here, too. There will be more to sign and get notarized later, but this will do for now. Need a pen?"

"The house is *not* for sale . . . at least not yet," said Nan.

"It's not? What do you mean it's not?"

Neither George nor Nan liked the tone of this response.

"Just what she said," George said. "It's not for sale, perhaps never for sale."

"She said not now."

"Take that to mean never."

"Mr. Froebel . . ."

"Fremont."

"Huh?"

"Fremont is my name."

"Oh, dear, yes . . . Fremont. So sorry. Too much to do today. Ha-ha, ha-ha. You are being offered a price for this property that you could probably not ever get for it, except from my client. Who knows, maybe she would even go twenty percent over market. If that's not generous enough, why not sign the temporary use agreement? That could give you a quick $6,000 to $8,000. I'm thinking my client might even go up to $3,000 a day, but no more than that. Certainly, no more than that." George and Nan looked at each other in silence. Mr. Abelard sensed an opening.

"Sign now," he said, thrusting the pen toward George. "I have the two documents here. The sales agreement merely promises that you will sell the property to my client for an agreed-upon sum. We don't have to talk about an actual amount now. That can be agreed on later. Or, if you wish, I can take any amount you have in mind, take it to my client, and return today with your answer. Or, if you sign now, and no amount is agreed on, the deal is kaput, and the document is voided. I will tear it up with no hard feelings."

Mr. Abelard picked up the paper and made a tearing motion across it.

"But, as I said, a condition of the agreement would be that my client is allowed to begin her exploration of these historic grounds immediately."

"You mean, to wreck our gardens?" Nan said.

"Ah . . . I don't think *wreck* is quite the word. There are a few spots where Dr. Sproot said she must do exploratory digs. Ummmm, some slight damage, perhaps, but only minimal. She'd just be scratching the surface of what she'd *like* to do. Then, as I said, you can back out if you change your mind . . . so could my client, for that matter. . . . I have here the rental document as well. Think about it, thousands of bucks for a little disturbance to the soil, and you keep the property anyway."

"You can tell your client that the property is not for sale, or rent, and that we will take our chances with the spirits underfoot," Nan said. "And that is final."

"And tell her to quit snooping around in our backyard," George said.

Mr. Abelard shook his head solemnly.

"In that case, my client will ask you to sign a document attesting to the fact that she has warned you of the dangers imminent to your property, and that she is absolved of any damage to property or loss of life that can result therewith."

"We won't sign anything of the sort," George said.

"Absolutely not," Nan said.

Mr. Abelard snapped his briefcase shut with a menacing abruptness.

"Of course, you know that eminent domain proceedings might apply here should the property be shown to be of incalculable value. In which case, you would have no choice. The state would buy your home at a price it deems to be fair. That would probably be much less than what my client is offering. You realize that, don't you?"

"We'll take our chances," George said.

Mr. Abelard leaned across the table toward them. His lip curled up. He exhaled a big breath full of garlic that a hundred pieces of Dentyne gum couldn't cover up. He appeared to be on the brink of a snarl.

"If I may ask, Mr. and Mrs. Fremont, what is your mort-gage status?"

"What do you mean?" said George.

"I mean exactly what I said. Are you able to keep up with your mortgage . . . or is there a little payment schedule prob-lem here that we need to resolve? It could be that a mortgage company will be at your doorstep any day now to claim your property. Am I right, or perhaps I'm misinformed?"

George felt his resolve suddenly turn into a mass of quiver-ing jelly. Nan wasn't quite as unnerved, though Mr. Abelard's garlic breath was making her queasy. She sat up, fully erect, and summoned up the requisite amount of indignation.

"That," she said, "is none of your damn business!"

"Look," Mr. Abelard said, suddenly shifting into reason-able, avuncular helper-guy mode. "I know I said I wouldn't throw out any figures, but . . . well . . . I guess I can. You could get $300,000 from my client for this home. That lets you avoid foreclosure, pay off the rest of your mortgage, and have plenty left to play around with. Let's do some quick math here. . . ." Mr. Abelard pulled a calculator out of his briefcase and punched some buttons. "How much do you have remaining on your mortgage?"

"That would be none of your business," Nan said. "And I'm getting gosh-darned sick and tired of saying that."

Mr. Abelard looked up from his calculator and pursed his lips.

"Well, of course, you're right," he said. "I'll just put this thing away. . . . I don't need a figure. Let's just say that you would surely be able to pay off your mortgage, and have lots to put down on another house . . . a much nicer house, probably."

"No deal!" said George, startling both Mr. Abelard and Nan with the firmness of his voice.

"What?"

"No deal. NO DEAL, and that is final!"

"You can't be serious?" said Mr. Abelard in his best tone of disbelief. "The deal of a lifetime and you want to pass it by."

"Yes, I do. Now, will you please leave, Mr. Abelard, and we will wish you a good day."

Mr. Abelard left them his card, encouraging them to call the minute they changed their minds, and warning them that the offer would likely be taken off the table at a moment's notice if he hadn't heard from them. Then he stomped off, muttering, down the steps. Nan watched him to see if he would be the latest in the line of miscreants who disturbed her pea gravel. Sure enough, on the last two steps, his shoes scuffed the surface too hard, and tiny rocklets went flying everywhere.

"Jerk," she muttered. She looked over at George, who was studying the card intently. What the hell is he thinking? she wondered. George put the card down on the table and sighed, then picked it up again.

"Maybe we'd better keep this around," he said. "Just in case we have second thoughts about our contest prospects."

25

Backyard Maelstrom

Dr. Sproot realized she looked ridiculous, maybe even dangerous.

Here she was, having parked her car two blocks away, strolling down Sumac Street at two thirty-two a.m. in the middle of a violent thunderstorm with a gas mask clamped to her face, and wearing work gloves, a wide-brimmed, moisture-repelling safari hat, and a lime-green, billowing rain slicker. She carried a hatchet and a tomahawk, both unsheathed and honed to razor-edged sharpness, in her right hand.

What else could she do? There was a job to be done, and it had to be done now. There was no point pussyfooting around about it anymore. That idiot Abelard had failed miserably. She should have known it, as he was from Mort's feckless side of the family.

As for Edith, she had gotten word to Dr. Sproot via an anonymous, whispered phone message that she would make her spell-casting foray into the Fremonts' backyard sometime late at night, preferably when the weather was unsettled and therefore more favorable for the casting of spells. Dr. Sproot hadn't placed much stock in that, and hadn't even bothered to tell her of her own mission. And why should she have? Edith's powers apparently extended no farther than the Rose Maidens' gardens, where they worked remarkably well. Dr. Sproot found that disconcerting. It meant they would have to be really nice to Edith for the rest of their lives, or run the risk of facing perpetual blackmail.

What was even more troublesome was that she had just fleeced Dr. Sproot out of another $700, and for what? She was beginning to suspect that Sarah the Witch was a fraud, a charlatan, a newbie in the realm of the supernatural who had had a little beginner's luck, which then fizzled when she got too big for her broomstick.

"Ha-ha, ha-ha!" Dr. Sproot chortled into her gas mask, clouding up the lenses with vapor.

What it came down to was this, she figured: if you want the job done and done right, you've got to do it yourself. She clenched her heavy hatchet and tomahawk with a new determination that she would not flinch from this task. If the police, say, were to cruise by on their late rounds, she already had her alibi; she would explain to them that she was the owner of the Acme Pest Control Company out on an emergency call to remove some very large rodents infesting a home down the street, and would they please let her go about her business.

Still, she was relieved to be able to branch off from the street and begin walking up the hill on the edge of the woods that lead to the Fremonts' backyard. Her gas mask was doing good service. It was keeping her from getting dizzy and lightheaded or seeing strange things. She had heard that the intoxicating perfumes of the angel's trumpet were especially potent at night and had taken no chances, pulling the gas mask over her head and yanking the straps taut to make sure it fit as snugly as possible before even getting out of her car. She knew that even the teeniest amount of hallucinatory plant gas entering her nervous system could wreck tonight's mission.

As she toiled up the hill, thunder crackled above her, and

the rain came down even harder. She stopped halfway up the slope to tighten her straps. Moisture was getting into the gas mask, causing the lenses to fog up. But she didn't dare take it off; the angel's trumpets were too close by.

She continued on, barely able to see through the curtain of rain and her clouded lenses. She would have to feel her way along. A big gust of wind came up, lifted the hat off her head, and carried it off toward the invisible, churning lake. There was nothing to be done about that. Dr. Sproot steeled herself and pushed on. Drenched, and with her hair matted into heavy strands, she transferred the hatchet to her left hand and waved it and the tomahawk in front of her so she wouldn't crash into anything.

Shortly after the ground leveled off, she made a sharp turn, barely missing the arbor in front of her. The gauzy shape of the house loomed to her right, and she was relieved to notice with what little visibility remained to her that there were no lights on.

Her waving weapons didn't prevent her from colliding with a fence post. She groaned upon making contact and swiveled to the left to find the opening in the fence. Another good thing about this mask, she thought: nobody could hear that groan. The tomahawk scraped against something, the outline of which she could barely make out. She felt along it with the hatchet, found the top, measured its diameter with the tomahawk, and swung down hard with it. The first blow met nothing but thin air and just missed slicing across her right leg. The second merely glanced off the object. Dr. Sproot screamed into her gas mask. The third attempt paid off, and she sank the tomahawk deeply enough into the object to be lodged in it. Her right hand now freed, Dr. Sproot reached into her raincoat pocket for a vial, popped its top, and poured the contents around the stuck tomahawk. With any luck, the partial protection of a tree canopy above would keep it from washing away.

Her job accomplished there, she backtracked toward the split-rail fence, found her way through it without hitting the post this time, and worked her way toward the looming fence that separated the Fremonts' yard from their neighbors'.

She could barely see now. She held out her gloved right hand so she could feel the plants. Pulling back suddenly when she felt a branch pushing against her gas mask, she sighed with relief to know that, without the mask, and its protective rubber, she would have had angel's trumpet emissions slathered all over her face now. The plant waved frantically in the thunderstorm as she felt for its stems. Another gust of wind almost blew her over as she attempted the first stroke and missed. Another stroke missed, though it connected with a thwack against the fence. The angel's trumpets gyrated wildly in the storm as Dr. Sproot pulled the hatchet out of the wood and swung wildly at them, shifting the hatchet from one hand to the other, and occasionally hitting the plants, but never able to deliver a coup de grace. Finally, her arms limp from exhaustion, she stopped to regain her strength.

What were those piercing noises? Those noises that weren't storm noises? They were coming from close to the house. Startled, Dr. Sproot turned her head and found she could see nothing through the waving curtain of rain but a bulky, balled-up shape at the base of the house. What the hell was that? There they were again, this time barely audible above the roar of the thunderstorm. Incantations or some other such cant! That was what it was. Edith . . . uh, Sarah the Witch . . . was here! And would she be in that ridiculous costume, with no raincoat, no umbrella, no nothing to protect her from the elements? Well, figured Dr. Sproot, witches can probably weave their little no-sick spells to protect them from catching cold or pneumonia. And it was about time she started earning her pay!

★   ★   ★

And what an awful way to earn my pay! thought the cowering Edith Merton, who by that time had morphed from Sarah the Witch into a shivering, sopping lump of mortal vulnerability sitting on the Krossa Regal hosta bed underneath the eaves of the house.

Edith had parked her car two blocks down Payne Avenue just before the full fury of the thunderstorm struck. Her dead mother's wobbling high heels precluding even a semblance of speed, she tottered down the street, then turned before reaching the driveway to climb cross-country up the slope into the heart of the Fremonts' gardens.

The recent rains had made the ground spongy. Her spiked heels sank in with sucking sounds at every step. She had also gained weight in the past few weeks, making her mother's girdle and tightly cinched skirt feel like a straitjacket. Finally, breathless and sweating, she reached the patio.

Careful to stay out of the range of the motion-sensor lights, she faced every direction of the compass and whispered the chants the dead flowers had taught her. Then, she tossed a handful of talcum powder mixed with Butch McDougal's "Spicy Ricey" seasoning up into the air. The howling wind whisked it away instantly. Edith took that to be a good sign. The flower spirits and Mother were listening. Then, as she rotated in a slow, full circle, she raised her arms skyward and wiggled her fingertips and toes, which she could only semi-wiggle within the confines of her high heels. Once she completed her circle, the spell was cast and her work was done.

Edith had just turned back toward the street when a flash of lightning blinded her and a clap of thunder ripped the sky apart. The rain drove down with a roar, soaking her within seconds. She'd have to find shelter quickly; that much was clear. Unable to see more than a couple of feet ahead through her rain-spattered cat's-eye glasses, she groped her way toward cover. Her feet found a bed of big-leafed hosta edged up against the house, then her hands found the slickened panels of siding. Edith flattened herself against it, gaining the partial protection of the eaves. She would just have to wait out the worst of it right there.

Moments later, just when the storm seemed to slacken, she thought she saw a vague gray shape emerge from behind the house and move toward her. She leaned forward, wiped off her glasses with a gloved forefinger, then froze. What else could she do, especially in those high heels, which she hadn't had the presence of mind to kick off? The shape stopped. Then part of it moved suddenly. Then again, and again. What was it doing? Edith instinctively shrank down into an agonizing crouch, lowering her head as far toward her knees as her bulky frame would allow, and hoping that would shield her from detection.

What was that *swack?* Edith looked up to see something sticking out of the Fremonts' weird tree sculpture. The lightning was continuous now. Its stuttering strobe effect showed her that some kind of hatchet or axe had been planted in the head of the sculpture. Despite her best efforts to make herself inconspicuous Edith shrieked. Once, twice, then one last modulating time for good measure.

The gray shape had moved away to the limits of visibility, then began flailing at something she couldn't see. Edith began to moan, which at least wasn't anywhere near as loud as shrieking. The thing turned to face her. Edith watched, transfixed as the lightning illuminated it. It was hideous, and it had big opaque eyes and a snout! Louder and louder moans were pushing themselves out of Edith's mouth without her even knowing it and became mingled with barely intelligible pleas for mercy.

Edith was saying something Dr. Sproot couldn't make out. Were those her so-called spells? And what was she doing crouching down over there, stapled against the side of the house? Slackass!

"Stop this storm, dad-blast-it, Edith, before we all get killed!" she yelled, but all that did was fog up her gas mask even more. Dr. Sproot struggled to suck in oxygen, which seemed to be coming through the mask filter in shorter supply than she was accustomed to breathing in. What was worse was that she was hearing some other sounds now. Something was coming up the slope, behind the northeast corner of the house, which she couldn't see anyway through her fogged-up gas mask. Something *else* was making a racket in the woods. Deafening thunder crashed just above her. The wind howled and the rain came down even harder, drowning out all the other noises, and plunging the world into the relentless chaos of the storm. Wracked by miserable wet discomfort and a new sensation—paralyzing fear—Dr. Sproot summoned just enough energy and strength of purpose to prepare for her last stand. She turned toward the house and raised her hatchet, which gleamed sharp and deadly in the blinding flashes of lightning, to present-arms level. Then, she whimpered out a solemn promise to some unknown deity that she would forever follow the path of righteousness if she could somehow survive this dreadful night.

The racket coming from behind the house was Earlene McGillicuddy and her twenty-two-year-old intern, Shirelle, trudging up the slope from Sumac Street. Earlene had parked her black Chevy on the street about a block north of the Fremonts', being careful to find a spot in the shadows to avoid the incriminating blue glare of the streetlamp. As they emerged from the car, they had closed the doors quietly and pulled the hoods of their rain slickers over their heads as the heavy, slanting rain drove down on them.

"These are good for disguise," Earlene shouted to Shirelle, a floriculture major at the university who was between her junior and senior years, and was looking for some hands-on experience with a local gardening expert. "Besides, they come in handy in this pouring rain."

Raindrops crackled against their slickers as the wind picked up and cascading peals of thunder rumbled overhead. Shirelle stood rooted to the pavement, staring at the flashing sky above her.

"Don't be frightened," said Earlene, sidling up next to Shirelle so as to be heard above the wind and the rain. "Storms are good for this kind of work."

Shirelle shivered and wrapped herself tightly in her arms.

"I don't know if I should be doing this, Mrs. McGillicuddy. It seems kind of . . . illegal."

Earlene snorted.

"Nonsense," she said. "It's expected. Everybody does it. Just you watch. These people will be doing the same thing to someone else directly. They might even hire me, tee-hee-hee. Besides, we're professionals. The only reason I'm getting a job of this magnitude is because I'm the best. That's what you have to think. Gardening scruples are for the little people who have tiny vegetable patches and some pansies. Only top-notch pros know, accept, and practice the fine art of gardening sabotage. Besides, we're getting paid $600, of which your share is $25. Not bad for a night's work, eh? Now, let's get on with it. Quietly, now. Shhhh."

They both wore sneakers especially modified by Earlene with foam packing materials glued to the soles so as to be extra quiet.

"Don't jangle the cages," Earlene said.

Shirelle unlocked the trunk and retrieved two large cages with old bedsheets covering them, and handles with big handgrips sticking through rips in the sheets. Violent rustling from within them almost knocked the cages out of her hands, but she held on tight.

"That's the girl," Earlene said. "Now, let's get moving. We're only a block away. Do you remember what to do if you see a car coming?"

"Run down the slope to the right until I'm out of sight."

"Good girl. Now let's go."

Earlene, carrying a large, filled-up paper grocery sack, guided Shirelle, with a heavy, bouncing cage in each hand, about a hundred yards down the sidewalk, then across the street to a slope that bordered a fringe of woods. Up the slope they climbed as the rain slammed down.

"Don't pant so much!" Earlene shouted to Shirelle as they crested the rise. "You're making too much noise!"

The sound of raindrops on plastic-coated rain slickers boomed like cannon shots to Earlene. Even the storm couldn't completely muffle it. That was a factor she had not taken into consideration when she planned the job. She cast quick, worried glances at the house, wondering whether, any minute, the lights would go on and the alarm get sounded before her task was done. And those cages, squeaking and squealing like all get-out. Someone forgot to oil the hinges! Earlene figured she could dock Shirelle $10 for such a gross transgression.

"Can't help it!" grunted Shirelle. "Too heavy!"

"We're almost there. Just a few more steps."

Their eyes were accustomed to the dark now, and they got occasional assistance from the staccato flash of lightning. They carried no flashlights; Earlene figured they were too risky.

"Right here," she said. "Set the cages down."

Shirelle gingerly set down her jiggling loads and moaned in relief.

"Now, take off the sheets."

Shirelle tugged at the sheets, which the rain had dampened into a heavy clinginess.

Inside the cages were masses of blurred gray motion. Earlene and Shirelle had stuffed six fully mature cottontail rabbits into each one, and they struggled and pushed against one another, biting and scratching, in anticipation of escape and something to eat. Earlene looked down at them appreciatively, then peered into her bag, which contained a special blend of spinach leaves, carrot shavings, and celery shoots, all irresistibly flavored with Earlene's not-yet-patented rabbit-nip.

"Now, I'll go spread the contents of my bag around the yard. When I come back, you can release the rabbits. If everything goes right, they'll make mincemeat of these gardens within a week."

Shirelle smiled uneasily as Earlene stuck her hand in the bag, pulled out a fistful of special rabbit mix, and began walking away from her, flinging the rabbit treats wherever she could make out the outlines of a garden and giving her special attention to the arbor, which she hoped would soon be utterly fouled with rabbit feces.

Shirelle trembled with fear and guilt. She thought she had signed on with Mrs. McGillicuddy to learn the deepest and most arcane secrets of the gardener's craft. So far, all she had been doing was starving rabbits, cramming them into cramped cages, and preparing to destroy someone's else's gardening handiwork.

It wasn't right, but what could she do? She needed the experience an internship would provide. As for these particular distasteful tasks, she would have to gloss over them on her résumé.

The fury of the thunderstorm and the potential criminality of it all fueled the adrenaline that honed Shirelle's senses to the peak of performance. She heard the squeal of tires that could have been five miles away. She sniffed at something faintly oily and metallic, the ozone-y smell of charged particles careening into one another and yanking one another apart.

Then came a noise that was neither thunder nor the hammering of millions of raindrops on roofs, leaves, and metal gutters. It was unmistakable: some human or beast was moving through the woods behind her, crashing into branches and saplings, and snapping twigs underfoot. Shirelle turned to see a dark form struggling through the woods. It was grunting and breathing heavily; she could hear that now. It was coming straight at her.

"Mizz McGillicuddy!" she squealed in a garbled, high-pitched voice that made it sound more like "Masma Golidoddy." "Mizz McGillicuddy!"

Mrs. McGillicuddy couldn't come right then. As she strode through the Fremonts' gardens, sowing the seeds of havoc and discord, the sky lit up, revealing something that made her blood curdle. Off to her left and separated from her only by the split-rail fence, the hydrangeas, and about ten yards of open lawn was a darkened form next to a couple of bushes. It had something in its hand.

"Jesus-Mother-Mary-Christ!" she whispered, her heart pounding away like John Bonham's bass drum. Thunder rent the sky. Then came another flash of lightning. The figure faced her. It was all rubbery and green with a protruding snout, and huge goggly eyes. A monster! Its arm was upraised and sticking out from it, glinting in the illumination of the lightning, was . . . a hatchet!

Earlene screamed as she had never screamed before. Hidden in that scream was a prayer that the wind and the thunder would stop so someone could hear her and come to the rescue. She stood there, petrified into immobility, only to be assaulted by new terrors. These came from her right. She turned her head. Lightning flashed. Earlene screamed again. This time she kept it going for a while, like a banshee's wail, or Livia's civil defense sirens on the first Tuesday of the month, at one p.m.

There, no more than ten feet from where she stood, was a tomahawk stuck in somebody's head. He was just standing there as if nothing had happened, a little short guy holding something, and with that awful thing protruding from his head! The sputtering, violent light showed that blood had gushed out all over the poor fellow's head, shoulders, and torso. His eyes were so wide open in death! Maybe he was alive, using his eyes to plead with her for succor. They stared, unblinking, at her.

"I can't help you," she moaned once she had stopped screaming to catch her breath. "Sorry. Please pray for me."

It was then she noticed that on the other side of the hideous tomahawk victim was Jackie Kennedy all wadded up in the middle of a hosta bed and staring at her, mouth agape, through rain-spattered cat's-eye glasses. Jackie Kennedy never wore cat's-eye glasses, Earlene suddenly realized. That's an imposter! A dead person impersonating another dead person! Oh, the perfidy! She shrieked again. Jackie Kennedy howled as if all the voices of the underworld were being funneled through her mouth.

Earlene began to run. Her legs pumped furiously as she panted from the exertion. But what was this? She wasn't going anywhere. She looked down at her feet as the distant thing with the hatchet approached the fence stealthily, but inexorably, and saw that she was running in place. Her feet were going up and down, up and down like pistons, giving her plenty of vertical lift, but nothing in the way of horizontal motion. The figure with the hatchet gurgled something, then did its own little high-pitched squeal, which sounded unnaturally quiet and contained, almost as if it were screaming underwater. Jackie Kennedy was still howling away, her pillbox hat loosened and tilted to the side of her head at an awful, Satanic-looking angle, and all Earlene could do was this stupid little in-place workout. Earlene screamed again. The horrible figure next to the fence flinched and raised its hatchet.

"Move, feet!" Earlene shrieked. "Move, feet! Move, you piece-of-shit feet!"

"Earlene?" gurgled the figure in its underwater voice.

"Earlene McGillicuddy?" But, to Earlene, that just sounded like guttural monster talk. She shrieked a cry for help, and continued running in place, alternately cursing and pleading with her feet to do what used to come so naturally to them.

Shirelle heard the screaming above the din of the thunder and watched in horror as the lightning lit up shapes in a mad dance of confusion. Completely bewildered and utterly panicked, she began to hallucinate. She looked down at the cages and imagined the rabbits were Toby and Turner, the two hunting dogs her family owned when she was growing up. She flung open the gates to the cages. Twelve rabbits half-crazed with fright and hunger bolted out, running and hopping in all directions.

"Sic, Toby! Sic 'em. Sic 'em, Turner!"

Shirelle turned back toward the woods. She was instantly sorry she did. The shape thrashing through the brush and small trees was an animal, one of the biggest she had ever seen. It had weird-looking antlers, too; more like some alien's antenna ears, come to think of it. Lost in a hallucination whirling madly out of control, Shirelle reflexively reached into her pockets for a fistful of shells, and grasped in the air to crack open the breach of a twenty-gauge shotgun, just like she used to do as a little girl back home in Waydeen, sitting with her daddy in a blind waiting for geese to show up. Not finding either, she ran screaming back down the slope, into the street, then to the south, in the opposite direction of where Earlene's car was parked.

26

Battleground Backyard

"We should call the police!"

"Call the police and tell them, what, that there are Indian spirits disturbing the peace in our backyard?"

The thunder crashed overhead as George and Nan huddled together in their bed and hoped that the chaos erupting outside their bedroom window was just a communal invention of their febrile imaginations.

"Maybe the thunderstorm will scare them away," George said.

"The thunderstorm won't scare them if they're spirits," said Nan, who was shivering. She clung closer to George and pulled the bedsheet up over her head. "If they're spirits, they're probably the ones who are *bringing* the thunderstorm."

Then came an unmistakable cry for help.

"That's definitely a human," said Nan. "And it sounds like someone we know." But what the heck was somebody they knew doing hanging out with a bunch of wailing, dead Indians?

Nan flung the sheet off her, sat up, and strained to hear more above the barrage of rain and wind that threatened to drown out everything else. "You know, that sounded sort of like that Earlene McGillicuddy." Then came more screams, a pause, thunder, a piercing shriek, and an unearthly howl from right outside the window.

"That's it. I'm calling the cops."

Nan reached for the phone and fumbled with it. She dialed three wrong numbers before she finally got the 911 operator. By then, George had shot out of the bedroom, his Smokestack Gaines bat at the ready. A shape approached him coming fast down the hallway. George stopped, leaned back, and cocked the bat, trying to remember how to turn his hips to get the proper torque and let one hand go after the swing the way Smokestack did. Here it comes, right down the pipe. Get ready to pull the trigger and . . .

"Daddy! Daddy! Don't hit me!"

"Sis?" George dropped the bat. Sis flung herself at him, crying.

"Daddy, what's going on outside? Something terrible is happening. People are screaming."

"Don't worry, honey," said Nan, poking her head through the bedroom doorway. "It's only the spirits of dead people buried here a long time ago." The telephone was clamped between her scrunched-up shoulder and cheek as she waited for the 911 operator, who had put her on hold to field three calls about a bunch of rampaging kids driving around in a Duster and Camaro and tp'ing yards indiscriminately.

"The police should be right over. I mean, what else do they have to do in Livia? Just get back in your room. Your dad's going to go check it out."

"Be careful, Daddy!" said Sis. She darted back into her room, then slammed the door shut and locked it.

"Don't open that door unless it's for us," George said. "We'll have a secret knock. Four long ones, three short, two long, a pause, two short knocks, then one long one. Got it?"

He picked up the bat and walked through the darkened hallway and into the dining room. He hesitated before looking out through the back door window. There was nothing but the tumult of a thunderstorm going on now. Everything must be all right. He looked outside. The motion-detector light hadn't even been activated. What seemed like an hour passed.

"Get out there, George!" He almost jumped through the ceiling. It was Nan, who had crept up quietly behind him.

"Get out there! Someone might be getting murdered, and you're just going to stand here waiting for the cops?"

"The thought had occurred to me."

"Get out there! I'm coming with you."

George threw open the door, then the screen door, and charged into the rain and the blinding glare of the motion-detector light. Bat at the ready, he did a 360-degree turn to make sure he wasn't walking into an ambush. Outside of the floodlit patio, the whole backyard was in motion. In fact, it was pandemonium. Rain poured down. Thunder crashed. The wind howled. A series of lightning flashes revealed a terrifying sight: strange forms writhing and careening aimlessly in the darkness.

Zombies! George thought, then banished it as irrational nonsense, then accepted it as a distinct possibility. Dead people coming up from the grave to harass you at best, and eat you alive at worst, are zombies. That was a pretty well-established fact.

Two rabbits emerged from the darkness and hurtled past him. George swung and missed both. Then came the scream from the woods. Something took off in a mad dash toward the street. A large, hulking, shadowed shape emerged from the distant blackness.

George squinted through the rain to try to make out what it was. Sensing his vulnerability in the blinding illumination of the floodlights, he sprinted out of their reach and dove behind the trunk of one of the silver maples.

"Made it!" he whispered.

Nan hadn't followed him. She was standing in the lighted

dining room, peering through the screen door, and holding a butcher knife. The shelter of the tree steadying his frayed nerves, George scanned the backyard through the sheets of rain. A sopping woman-y-looking thing in a hooded poncho and clinging to a big grocery bag stood in the middle of the yard next to the rose trellis. Her screams were being turned into really loud gargling by the rain falling into her upturned mouth.

What's a bag lady doing out here at this time of the night? wondered George. And running in place? Or is she something else indeed?

More lightning revealed the glint of a metallic object over to the right and farther toward the back, just beyond the fence and hydrangeas. A hatchet! And one of the zombies—this one *really* scary looking—holding it! Making weird noises, too, or was that just the storm? So, what was the deal here? Was the bag lady-thing a human, and, ergo, an ally, about to be sliced up by the hatchet-wielding zombie? Or were they both zombies just engaging in a pre-dinner howl?

"Hey!" George yelled, more to give himself courage than anything else. "Knock it off!"

He wondered whether anything could hear him above the din of the thunderstorm, and shivered as the cold, driving rain soaked him. It occurred to him that he would have to make his move because of two things: (a) He would die of hypothermia just lying there getting drenched behind the tree, and (b) the darkened form wielding the hatchet was turned in the direction of the screaming bag lady. It would soon lift itself over the low split-rail fence, crash through the hydrangeas, and march straight on an unobstructed path toward her and him.

It was time to show those zombies what a Smokestack Gaines bat can do when it means business. Just as he stood up and gripped his bat in the Smokestack Gaines style, with the pinkie of the right hand swinging loose like a broken gate, a racket sounded from the street: honking horns, sputtering engines, and the clattering of a loose muffler bouncing off the street that George had told Cullen at least a thousand times to have fixed. It was the Camaro and the Duster, and they were loaded with zombie-hating high school and college kids.

"Reinforcements!"

George gripped his bat with a new determination. He recalled from something he had seen or read that zombies could be thwarted by the sound of teenagers honking horns. Didn't that turn them into rocks if they heard it two hours before dawn, or something like that?

On further reflection, as all the shrieking and yelling subsided into a sort of moan chorus coming from three distinct points in the yard and the form carrying the hatchet stopped (turned to stone?), George wondered whether Cullen, Ellis, and their friends might be walking into a fiendish zombie feeding frenzy, with all these whatever-they-weres just waiting to spring their trap.

He tried to get a closer look at the bag lady. A series of lightning flashes lit her up. Her rain poncho hood had slipped off and her head was bowed back at an unnatural angle. Stringy hair hung, mop-like, all over her head, which appeared somewhat shrunken from this angle. The bag she was holding was turning to cellulose mush in the rain. Too ugly to be a bag lady, George decided. Spirit from the depths, no doubt, in distorted human form.

Kids were piling out of the cars. He had to do something and do it now. Where were the goddamn police when you needed them most? He prayed fervently that they carried a few silver bullets with them for just such an emergency as this. There they were; he heard a siren in the distance. By the time they got here it would be too late! His course of action was clear; he would have to sacrifice himself to save the rest of his family. And he would have to do it now. Now? Hmmm . . . now! George turned toward the street.

"Danger!" he yelled, his voice turned into a croak by the terrible knowledge that he could be on the wrong end of a fast-food feast in a matter of seconds. "Danger! Go back! Go back!"

It was no use. They couldn't see or hear him as they scurried through the rain into the house through the garage door. Kids! George moaned as he dove back for cover behind the tree, his resolve having morphed into abject, immobilizing terror.

Suddenly, he smelled wool. Warm, wet wool. And close. Very close. Something touched his shoulder. George jolted into the tree trunk, slamming his cheek against the wet, scaly bark.

"Jesus-fricking-Christ!" he cried, pain for the moment trumping fear and decorum.

Caressing his bruised cheek, he turned to see a cowled monk leaning over him. The monk, really short—more like a hobbit, really—held a long, rather crinkled and crude cross that looked in the lightning flashes like aluminum foil wrapped around joined sections of PVC pipe. In fact, George could see the hollow end of PVC pipe sticking through the bottom of the cross. He knew it perfectly, having made exactly the same kind of cross for last year's Christmas pageant. And that cowl. Hadn't he seen it somewhere before?

"Do not fear," said the monk in a curiously feminine voice. "I'm a friend here to help you."

George suddenly understood. Casting aside his suspicions concerning the makeshift cross and familiar-looking cowl, he whispered a heartfelt prayer of thanks that a force of good—an angel, no doubt—had been sent down on a moment's notice to do battle with the evil jerks assailing their home.

"What is your bidding, O Great Spirit?" George said. His voice quaked with worshipful amazement that he and Nan had made the right decision fourteen years ago in joining the Please-Redeem-Me Lutheran Church just down the street.

"I'll take the one on the right," said the voice. "Old rubber face. You take the two on the left. When I count three. . . . One . . . two . . . two and one eighth . . . two and a half . . . two and three quarters . . . two and four fifths . . . two and seven eights . . ."

When the count of three finally came, George raised his bat and started twirling it, more in the style of a samurai warrior than Smokestack Gaines. He charged toward the thing with the disintegrating bag, which he could now see bore the imprint of Curman's Carnival Foods. The appropriate brain signals finally having been telegraphed to her feet, Earlene lifted her head, shrieked, and ran off toward the woods. She then collided with the vertical fence post and the weather station that sat on top of it and got twirled through the gate like a pinball ricocheting off a bumper paddle.

George turned toward the house. There was Nan. Brandishing her butcher knife and a flashlight, she charged out the door.

"Over there!" shouted George, pointing to another screaming figure who was cowering under the bedroom window. "Guard that one! And be careful with that thing!"

Nan shone the powerful beam of her flashlight into the face of a disheveled figure who looked up at her in abject terror and whom she could now see must have lost her way to an old-timers' fashion show.

What's with the veil and grandma glasses? Nan wondered. And how many consignment stores did she have to visit before finding that getup?

Nan could see there was little about this person, who was smushing her hosta as she crouched there all balled up in a fetal position, that anyone could consider to be terrifying. Here was just a scared relic of a bygone era, possibly trying to find her way back to another time and another place. But how? Was there some kind of time warp residing in their backyard?

"Don't worry about this one, George!" she yelled. "She's just a lost time traveler."

Nan turned back toward Edith Merton, who was squeaking out weak protestations of apology now that Nan was pointing the tip of the butcher knife at her Adam's apple.

"What the hell are you doing mucking around in our backyard at this hour of the morning, and right under our window, no less? Huh? You stay right there, and don't move or I'm gonna slice your little pillbox hat to ribbons!"

Nan made a mental note to ask her, once everything had calmed down, where she had made such a find, and with a mesh veil and all. And those gloves!

Out of the corner of her eye, Nan noticed something amiss. She pointed her flashlight slightly to the right. There was Miguel de Cervantes's tree trunk likeness, its maple skull cloven by an Indian tomahawk. There was red all over his poor head. Someone had obviously doused the wood carving with paint, or ketchup, or . . . maybe even merlot. Oh, the sacrilege!

"Eeeek!" Nan screeched. "George! George! Someone has defaced Miguel something awful! Eeeek!"

"Wasn't me," moaned Edith, who was gesticulating wildly toward the hatchet-wielding figure on the other side of the fence. "Wasn't me. Wasn't me. I swear! It was *that!*"

"I said stay still and shut up!" Nan said, holding the knife over her left shoulder in a downward-stab position and shining the flashlight at her. Edith quieted down and stopped gesturing. She shifted her tightly girdled haunches over onto some as-yet-untrampled hosta. "You want what happened to Miguel to happen to you? Don't mess with me, bitch, 'cause I'm just the gal who can do it, too. I've chopped chicken, steak, salami, hard-as-a-rock cheese, and roasts with this thing, and I'm not afraid to use it on some worthless live meat. What really burns me up is that you're squishing some of my Krossa Regal hosta!"

Edith jumped up instantly and stepped gingerly out of the hosta bed. It was then that Nan noticed she was wearing high heels.

"Where the heck did you think you were going in those things?" she said.

The siren was getting louder. George, now driven to an absolute fury by the desecration of his beloved wood carving and emboldened at the sight of zombie *numero uno* taking flight at his approach, twirled his bat like a baton and searched the backyard for a new target. Looking to his right, he saw the angel-monk. Cross raised, she (he? it?) strode solemnly toward the fence shouting religious-sounding things.

"No help needed in that quarter for now," George mumbled. "The forces of good are girding for battle."

"Mr. Fremont!"

It was the really ugly, green-faced, and horribly disfigured zombie at the fence screeching at him, but in a very muffled way that made it hard to hear.

"Mr. Fremont! This has been a terrible mistake! Please forgive me!"

George caught a stray word here and there, then a glimpse of the hatchet dangling from the dark form as the angel-monk approached it slowly, still chanting.

"Droppeth it!" the angel-monk shouted. "Droppeth the hatchet now or thou shalt be turned back into the mulchified muck from wherest thou camest. How darest thou rely on the black arts instead of prayer? How darest thou?"

"Mr. Fremont!" the zombie screeched. "I'm Dr. Phyllis Sproot, and I can explain everything. What in God's name is going on here? Please help me!"

"Eh? Phyllis Sproot?"

George ignored the barely audible pleas. Zombies were well-known mimics, and would often pretend they were people you knew—or, in this case, people you barely knew, but had heard of—in order to catch you with your guard down. He wasn't falling for it.

"Go back to stoking the fires of hell, zombie!" he yelled. Three half-crazed rabbits went zipping past Dr. Sproot, causing her to break into a continuous moan-yelp.

Listen to that! thought George, eager to take advantage of his ringside seat at a once-in-a-lifetime faceoff of good versus evil. Zombie for sure. But pretty darned bad voice projection. And, check this out: hell is unleashing its pestilence in the form of rabbits. Wow! More rabbits scurried over the patio. There was a blinding flash of lightning, followed by the loudest peal of thunder in Livia's recorded history.

"George! Look out!"

The figure that had emerged from the woods had made a very slow and ungainly transit across the northern part of the yard, rattling through the leaves of the arbor trees, tripping over the bench, then clumsily picking itself up. It had taken a swipe at Earlene as she flew by and was now lumbering toward the gate in the fence, arms and head swinging wildly. It was braying something awful.

"That's no zombie!" yelled George, who, having been thwarted twice in his efforts to hit something with his Smokestack Gaines bat, was not about to be deterred this time. "That's a goddamn moose! Standing on its hind legs! And it has terrible eyesight."

"Zombies?" Nan said. "What zombies? Who said anything about zombies? That zombie who just took off wasn't a zombie. That was Earlene McGillicuddy. This pathetic wretch here doesn't look like a zombie. She looks like . . . like . . . Jackie Kennedy, only with weird glasses on. Wait a second; Jackie Kennedy's dead. Isn't she?"

"I'm not a zombie," burbled Edith, who was drenched and

shivering, and watching very carefully where she put down her high heels, which she had barely been able to keep from collapsing under her all this time. "I'm human. I might look like Jackie Kennedy with glasses, but I'm human. I swear it on a stack of bibles; I'm human!"

"Aaaaaaaah!" Dr. Sproot yelled at the angel-monk, whom George noticed was a heck of a lot shorter than the zombie she was confronting.

As the angel-monk lowered its cross, which for all anybody there knew was made of highly electrified, brain-scrambling heaven stuff, Dr. Sproot quickly ducked out of the way. Attempting to vault the fence like a champion high-hurdler, she caught a foot on the top rail, and fell facedown on the sodden ground with a smack even the thunderstorm couldn't drown out. It barely fazed her. She got up and, still clutching her hatchet, tore off, full tilt toward the street. She missed the two silver maples, but crashed into the side of the Duster. Even that didn't stop her. Scrambling across the hood in a millisecond, she disappeared into the street.

"George!" screamed Nan, who was still holding her prisoner at bay, though half expecting her to vanish into the time warp at any moment. "The moose!"

What happened next occurred in a washed-out blur of violence and confusion. George grunted and charged headlong toward the moose, which he quickly toppled with one big uppercut to the chin from his bat. As the moose lay dazed on the ground, with George stooped over it, ready to let loose with another power stroke, he suddenly realized that the siren had stopped. So had all the shrieking, screaming, and moaning. Even the thunderstorm was spent. The rain, thunder, and lightning were retreating toward the east. The moose, however, was singing.

"Tall and tan and young and lovely . . . the girl from Ipanema goes walking . . ."

"What tha . . . ?"

"And when she passes, each one she passes goes 'aaah.' "

"Hey!" came a petulant croak from the other side of the fence. "Hey! What the hell is going on over there? Are you Fremonts having an orgy, or what?"

Four more rabbits scampered across the yard. As George studied the figure more closely, he could see now that what lay beneath him, croaking out "The Girl from Ipanema," was no moose, but an unreasonable facsimile of a moose. In fact, it was the worst moose costume he had ever seen. He was startled to see two more figures standing over the faux moose and looking down at it. It was Jeri and Tom Fletcher. They were each armed with pool cues, the tapered ends of which were pointed straight down at the moose thing.

"Burglars are coming up with some pretty weird costumes these days," Jeri said.

Burglars! But of course, George reasoned; these were burglars, not zombies. There were no such things as zombies! What was he thinking? Still, who the heck was it who deposited that tomahawk in Miguel's head, and why?

"All I know is that this is the worst singing burglar of a moose I ever heard," George said. "Who'd want to bossa nova to that?"

"That's no moose . . . and I don't think it's a burglar."

Nan, still holding her butcher knife, stood over the recumbent moose form and shone the flashlight down at it.

"George, how could you ever think that was a moose, even in the dark? I mean, look at it; that's Pat Veattle. And you must have broken her jaw, or nose."

"Pat Veattle!"

"Of course. The moose costume matches what Steve told us about. And the insane behavior. And she's singing 'The Girl from Ipanema.' That was the first tune she ever recorded, that polka version of 'The Girl from Ipanema.' Besides all that, she's very drunk. Can't you smell the fumes?"

The other three stooped over to within a few inches of the groaning mouth of the costume.

"Phew," said Jeri, flapping her hand dramatically in front of her squinched-up nose. "Now that you mention it."

"Then who is . . . that?" said George, turning and pointing his bat accusingly at Edith, who had stealthily slipped through the gate and was trying to make her way, high heels dangling from her hand, down the slope and to the road.

"Hey, you!" yelled George. "Hold it right there. You've got a lot of explaining to do."

"You heard him!" said Jeri menacingly as she and Tom ran to interpose themselves and their pool cues between her and the escape route to the road. Edith instantly complied and threw up her arms.

"Hey!" came the voice from the other side of the fence. "Hey! I told you to shut up. I'll sue you. I'll sue you Fremonts for disturbance of the peace."

"Oh, shut up yourself, Grunion!" Jeri yelled. "Or I will sue you for being a first-class jerk and a public nuisance to the neighborhood as such."

There was the squawk of a police radio. Down on Payne Avenue, a police cruiser with flashing light had pulled up behind the Duster and Camaro and an officer with a flashlight was inspecting the license plates. Another one, with the radio, approached them, her own bobbing flashlight marking her progress up the steps and across the patio.

"A little late for a party, isn't it, boys and girls?" she said. Nan instantly recognized the voice.

"Sergeant Sneed!"

"Smead! Sneed's back at the cruiser checking those tags."

"Sergeant Smead! How nice to see you. You were just out here last month. How can we help you, Sergeant Smead?"

"Well, you will have to tell me that. It appears every call we've had tonight has involved this particular address. We had a call from a neighbor about excessive noise. Make that three neighbors. All reported repeated screams, which must have been very loud on account of the thunderstorm that was going on at the time. Then, there was a young lady running hysterically down Sumac, screaming something about a moose, also at this address. Then, there was a call about murderous spirits rising from their burial grounds. We didn't take that one too seriously. . . ."

"That was me," said Nan, sheepishly.

"Rising from the dead?"

"No . . . no . . . of course not. It was me who made that call."

"Hmmm. Now, it appears we have found the vehicles belonging to two young men who reside at this address that have been linked to a certain amount of mayhem in the surrounding neighborhood. And what's this?"

Sergeant Smead shone her flashlight down at Pat Veattle, who was still mumbling what must have been verse seventeen of "The Girl from Ipanema." "Ah-ha, and here is our moose . . . or someone dressed as a moose. Gee whiz, that's a bad moose outfit."

"Isn't it, though," said Jeri.

"Hard to believe someone actually thought this was a moose. . . . I mean, the snout looks pretty moosey, but those antlers, sheesh! Those are just a couple of beat-up old rabbit-ears antennae. You can get those Styrofoam antlers, you know, over to Jumpin' Judy's Party Store. Uh, sir, could you drop the bat please, sir?" George, without thinking, had begun practicing his Smokestack Gaines swings.

"Huh?"

"The bat, sir. Could you lay it down, please? You make me nervous swinging it around like that."

"Sure," said George, propping it carefully against the fence.

"Sir and ma'am, please drop those pool cues." Jeri and Tom instantly let the cues fall to the ground. "Ma'am, your knife, please." Nan turned and flung the butcher knife expertly into the fence post, burying its point with a vibrating thud one inch into the wood.

"Wow!" said George, unaware until now of his wife's knife-throwing skills.

"Sergeant," Nan said. "Bullwinkle here and the woman holding up the high heels are trespassing on our property. They are the ones who started all this mess."

Sergeant Smead heard a noise along the fence line. She pointed her flashlight directly into the eerily glowing eyes of four rabbits.

"Looks like you've got a little rabbit infestation problem here," she said. She then swung the arc of the light over toward the woods. "And what's that over there?"

"Cages," George said. "Maybe that's where all those rabbits came from."

"Backyard sabotage!" Nan snorted. "So that's what Earlene McGillicuddy was doing here. Did I hear that Dr. Sproot cat-erwauling away . . . and where did she go? Is that the same Dr. Sproot who's the archaeologist, and who wanted to buy our house?"

"She's no archaeologist," Jeri said. "Obsessive gardening nut, and a first-class . . . well, I won't say what. She's black-balled me twice from gardening clubs. Even more obsessive than you guys, but without the wine and good graces. She was out here, too?"

"Aha!" George said. "So that really *was* the infamous Dr. Sproot. And with a hatchet, no less! At first, I thought she was a—"

"George!"

"Well, she sure looked like one. Did you get a look at that puss? Uuuugly."

"What on earth was she doing here?" said Nan, eager to steer the conversation away from George's zombie fantasies as quickly as possible. "More snooping?"

"If I know Phyllis Sprout, she was here on a sabotage mission herself, maybe to chop something down," Jeri said. Another rabbit went whizzing by.

"We had a report of a woman in hysterics with a hatchet walking down the street not five minutes ago," Sergeant Smead said. "She was wearing a gas mask. That must be the suspect in question. Another patrol just picked her up. There was another woman in a black car who was speeding down Sumac and hit a telephone pole a couple of blocks from here. She was babbling about some kind of disturbance. She come from here, too?"

"Must be Earlene," sniffed Jeri. "That's just like her. The first whiff of trouble and she goes to pieces."

Sergeant Smead's radio crackled with the voice of Officer Sneed.

"Hey," George whispered to Nan. "What happened to the angel-monk? I don't see the angel-monk anywhere."

"The what?" said Nan through teeth that had begun to chatter. "Brrrrr!"

"The angel-monk. Sent from on high to save us from the forces of darkness. Didn't you see the angel-monk?"

Nan clamped her hand over George's mouth.

"Please keep your yap shut, George," she hissed. "No more talk about zombies and angel-monks. Pul-eeeze!"

"Officer Sneed," Sergeant Smead barked into her radio. "Why don't you join me up here in the backyard. This is getting complicated. Hurry up. These folks are all soaking wet and cold. Oh, and bring the plastic cuffs."

"You know what?" Nan whispered to George. "I wonder if Pat Veattle is one of the creatures who got into those angel's trumpet seeds. Talk about freaked out!"

"Hey!" George gasped. "What about the kids?"

Nan snorted. "The kids? Don't worry about them. I checked on them before I came running out. They hadn't heard a thing. They were all downstairs playing *Guitar Hero*. You wouldn't believe the din down there!"

27

Restitution

George and Nan had no desire for vengeance. Neither did they show any particular interest in pursuing the sort of justice the fellow from the county attorney's office mentioned. That would mean gross misdemeanor charges carrying penalties of perhaps a few weeks in the workhouse, a pretty hefty fine, or both.

But when he suggested something called restorative justice, they perked up. What that involved was a frank conversation with the guilty parties—well, four of them—about what they had done to undermine the Fremonts' health and well-being, and how they might make restitution. Should they be able to reach some sort of agreement on that, then the charges would be dropped. That would also help to unclog a court calendar that had gotten very crowded at a time when many of the judges had scheduled their vacations.

So it was that they all gathered in the Fremonts' backyard, where Nan served her pink lemonade, gin and wine having been regretfully passed over as inappropriate for the quasi-judicial nature of the gathering.

Dr. Sproot was defiant and restlessly unrepentant, or maybe that was just the eight cups of coffee she had downed so far.

The cringing Earlene McGillicuddy fretted over the collapse of her surreptitious sabotage-for-hire business. Earlene's intern, Shirelle, was bowled over on seeing the Fremonts' lavish gardens in broad daylight. She plotted to sever her ties with Earlene so she could hitch on with the bona fide gardening savants of Livia. Edith Merton was the most contrite, or at least pretended to be so. She pleaded with the Fremonts to keep her participation in the sorry affair out of the newspapers. She also pleaded with her fellow petty criminals to pledge themselves to secrecy concerning the whole sorry mess.

"Fat chance of that happening . . . *Sarah*," Dr. Sproot sneered.

"Now, now," said Nan. "No arguing, please. We want this meeting to be constructive. If we can arrive at some kind of settlement satisfactory to George and me, then there's no reason why this matter should go any further."

Missing was Pat Veattle, who had been deemed a poor candidate for restorative justice. The thick rubber skin of her costume had protected both her and the Smokestack Gaines bat from George's powerful blow; her jaw had only been slightly bruised and the bat wasn't even scuffed. She was, however, intoxicated to a degree Officers Smead and Sneed had not seen before in a living person. She was turned over to the custody of her daughter and son-in-law in St. Anthony after spending the night in the drunk tank and was scheduled for a thorough psychiatric evaluation.

Dr. Sproot confessed proudly to masterminding her own personal attack with specific targets in mind. She blamed her fogged-up gas mask and the general mayhem of the night for thwarting her destruction of the angel's trumpets.

"You will notice that they are fully intact, with the exception of three or four stems," she said. "Another five minutes and I'd have cut them down to the ground."

"And why did you go to such great lengths to do that?" Nan wondered.

"The angel's trumpets were, to me, the sign of genius, which you, however, probably just blundered upon," Dr. Sproot said solemnly. "I was convinced that they would win you the prize that I cherished for myself and which would crown my efforts in discovering the importance of yucca and the coreopsis-salvia-hollyhock blend. But I'm so far ahead of my time, and I was afraid my pioneering would go unnoticed. So, I decided to cut them down."

"And the gas mask?"

"Angel's trumpets are hallucinogenic. A big whiff can cause brain damage and a warped sense of reality. Maybe that's what happened to you."

"How dare you!" Nan hissed. "Are you bucking for jail time or what?"

I told you, George's inner milquetoast whispered nervously to him. I told you those things are deadly. What more proof do we need?

"I had a coconspirator, too," Dr. Sproot said. "She was much worse than me. She was actually out here cutting up your flowers."

"The midnight snipper!" George exclaimed.

"That's right," said Dr. Sproot. "Do you want to know her name? It's Marta Poppendauber, that's who. She lives at 1452 Waveland Circle. She should be sitting here right now, and you should be nailing her hide to that trellis over there."

"In due time," Nan said. "Let's stick to you for now, Miss Stool Pigeon. What about the archaeology thing?"

"That was a clever ruse."

"Yes, we figured that out. Your realtor, by the way, was really obnoxious. Next time, pick somebody better. He had really bad breath, too."

Dr. Sproot rolled her eyes.

"Yes, the sleazy idiot is a shirttail relation, but he charged me anyway, the fink! Just for paying you a visit! Not completely aboveboard, as you were probably able to tell. But for what I had in mind, he was exactly what I wanted. Anyway, if you had agreed to sell or rent the property, the transaction would have been perfectly legitimate."

"And if you had bought it?"

"If I had bought it, I would have done enough damage to the gardens in the name of archaeology to have wrecked any chances for your winning first place. Then, once the sale was finalized, I would have made some improvements—your front yard is really sorry looking—and flipped it. No more Fremont backyard to worry about."

"Just turned around and resold it?"

"Yes. Or I could have reneged. The contract wouldn't have bound me as buyer, or you as seller, for that matter. It was a preliminary agreement, a memorandum of understanding that would have allowed me immediate access to the backyard as a condition of the prospective purchase. Of course, if you had agreed to an easement, I would have done pretty much the same thing: inflict substantially more damage than I had initially led you to believe, and then apologized profusely for wrecking your handiwork. You would have made a few thousand dollars and had the consolation of knowing that there was no Indian burial ground under your backyard."

"That's a lot of hard work just to win a gardening contest," George said. "And, by the way, the property is *still* not for sale."

"*Just* is not the word, Mr. Fremont. This is the alpha and omega of my gardening career. I deserve to win the contest. And I still shall."

"And the $150,000 that goes with it."

"More," said Earlene, gesturing with her thumbs up. "Much more."

"Really!" said George and Nan.

"They're up to $200,000 now." George whistled. "And that's just for first place. Second is $50,000. Third is $25,000. It kind of goes downhill from there. Fourth through tenth gets you a few packets of seeds."

"Money is not the main object," Dr. Sproot huffed. Earlene laughed out loud. "Reputation is all that matters. Why do anything if you can't be number one at it?"

"Some other questions for you, Dr. Sproot," George said as Nan refilled the glasses and graciously accepted compliments on her lemonade's sugary tartness. "How did you manage to ferret out private information about our tardy mortgage payments?"

"It's the talk of the town, Mr. Fremont. Besides, I have my sources but I'm not at liberty to divulge them. I ask to be granted immunity in that respect."

"Ha!" said Earlene. "She's got a nephew in the state archaeologist's office and a sister-in-law who handles a lot of the paperwork at Homestake Mortgage. Isn't that true, *Phyllis?*"

"Dr. Sproot, if you please, *Mrs.* McGillicuddy."

Edith Merton had been quietly sipping her lemonade, trying to project an air of shame and resignation that she hoped would get her off easy and without revealing the secret she needed so desperately to harbor. Now was the time for her preemptive strike.

"I need to make a confession," she said tremulously. "Uh, I was working for Dr. Sproot and freely admit my complicity in this sordid affair. But listen to what I'm saying, and pity me. Dr. Sproot blackmailed me into doing this job. Blackmailed me!"

"What?" Dr. Sproot shot up out of her chair, knocking over her glass and spilling sticky lemonade all over the table and concrete patio. "What?"

"Sit down and shut up, Sproot!" barked Nan. "You're in enough hot water as it is. You can add cleaning up this mess to your restorative justice tasks, and you will do so before all the yellow jackets arrive to make life miserable for us. Now, do continue, Mrs. Merton."

Edith took a long draw of lemonade as if fortifying herself for what lay ahead.

"As I said, Dr. Sproot blackmailed me. This is a horrible secret I'm about to divulge, but I want to make a clean breast of everything."

George and Nan leaned forward. During the pregnant pause that followed, and except for Dr. Sproot angrily chomping on an ice cube she had picked off the tabletop and popped into her mouth, you could have heard a chickadee sneeze.

"Excuse me," said Edith, who was emitting low sobs and wiping away make-believe tears with the back of her hand. "It's a hard story to tell."

"Try," said Nan.

"About three and a half years ago, Dr. Sproot found me in a . . . a . . . compromising position with her husband."

Dr. Sproot gurgled something that was unintelligible since she was still working the ice cube around in her mouth and was about to jump up from her chair again, but Nan pinned her in place with a stare that would have frozen over Kilauea Volcano.

"I've never forgiven myself for that, but if you knew him, then you'd know why I had fallen so hopelessly in love with him. I was stricken by guilt. I guess Dr. Sproot didn't want any public scandal, so, at first, she contented herself with merely hating me and hoping I'd die a very painful death someday.

"Anyhoo, she eventually told me she'd keep the secret and let me alone as long as she could call on me sometime when she needed help . . . help in anything. She would call on me, and there would be no questions asked. If I did that, helped her get out of some really big fix, she'd consider my adulterous debt paid off in full. It so happened that she was bent on destroying your gardens, though I am just now finding out the reasons why, and ordered me to help her in her wretched scheme. As you can imagine, I demurred, but there was no way out. I had to do it. Oh, yes, she made me wear that stupid costume as the mark of my sin. Sort of like being branded with the letter A, but a lot more ridiculous and a lot less permanent. So, there you have it."

"That's a lie! Lie! Lie! Lie!" Dr. Sproot, having chewed up her ice cube by now, was shrieking and pounding on the table, shaking it violently and almost upsetting the two glasses and the half-full lemonade pitcher sitting on it. "Why, you don't even know the name of my husband, Edith! What was his name, huh? What was it? You probably don't even know that he died three years ago! Huh!"

Edith merely shook her head, seemingly reluctant to be drawn into such a scene as was now unfolding.

"You want to know the truth?" Dr. Sproot continued. "Well, here it is. Edith Merton is a witch who casts spells on gardens. I hired her to cast a spell on yours and that's what she was doing here that night. Casting a spell. Okay, so her putrid spell hasn't worked, but she did try. Oh, and she has her little witch name, too: Sarah. Sarah the Witch."

Edith stared down into her lemonade. George quickly looked Dr. Sproot up and down to make sure she wasn't carrying any weapons. He quietly wished Nan had frisked her before admitting her to the backyard. Earlene went all bug-eyed and was gasping for air. Shirelle wasn't paying attention; she had turned her chair around to study the hibiscus and was all in raptures over them.

Nan studied Dr. Sproot in a calm, measured way for a moment. Then, she pushed back her chair and stood up, picked up the pitcher of lemonade off the table in a slow, deliberate fashion, and calmly poured the remaining contents over Dr. Sproot's head.

"There's some more for you to clean up," she said. "And I'd do it soon. Those yellow jackets are going to love all that sticky, sugary sweetness all over you."

Thoroughly spent, Dr. Sproot collapsed back into her chair and dropped her head onto her splayed-out arms. Convincing sobs racked her body and all present had to admit that, for all her faults, Dr. Phyllis Sproot was either a very compelling nutcase or a darn good actress.

"And now, for you three," said Nan as the others nervously sipped their lemonade. "You might notice that a number of plants and flowers have already been nibbled at by the Mongol horde of rabbits that was unscrupulously unleashed in this yard, to say nothing of those crushed by frantic people running around all over the place. Your job will be to trap those rabbits and dispose of them in any way you choose except by releasing them in someone else's yard. You're also to dig up our damaged plants and replace them with those from your own gardens. It will have to be soon because the judges will be coming by in five days. Tomorrow would actually be good. This includes you, Dr. Sproot."

Dr. Sproot raised her head and gasped in despair.

"You wouldn't ask *me* to do that! Why, already I almost died of fright that night. I was actually on the verge of a nervous breakdown. And then to be humiliated by being dragged off to the city jail! And now to have to rebut these terrible lies and none of you believing me, and you dumping that awful lemonade on me, and here's a bloody yellow jacket buzzing around me already. I damaged nothing—well, almost nothing—and I'm here to tell you how sorry I am. I'm sorry. Okay? I didn't release the stupid rabbits anyway. Those two did! Besides, I have my own yard to worry about. I'm a contest entrant, too, you know."

"You broke the law, Sproot," said Nan. "You came here to

do damage, you trespassed on our property, and you frightened us all out of our wits. We have reason to believe that you have trespassed on our property before. What you were prepared to cut down, or why, is not a huge concern for us. As you said, little damage was done. But you would have wreaked havoc in our gardens if you hadn't been stopped by circumstances. So you need to do what we are asking you to do, or you can damn well go to jail! In fact, I'm leaning toward turning you over to the county attorney as a restorative justice reprobate."

Dr. Phyllis Sproot lurched forward in her chair.

"All right!" she said sharply. "Please don't send me to jail. I will do it. But I might not have the plants necessary to replace what's been damaged. I specialize in coreopsis-salvia-hollyhock blend and the yucca, though I dabble in dahlias and roses. I was only going to cut down those damnable angel's trumpets. Well, and maybe a few other odd stems and blossoms . . . I mean, since I was here."

"All right," Nan said. "Everyone just do your best, go shopping for what you don't already have, and we'll forget about it."

"Uh, by the way," said Dr. Sproot. "Who was the weirdo who attacked me with the cross?"

"Zip it, Sproot," said Nan. "All the weirdoes have been accounted for as far as we're concerned. Your job now is to keep quiet."

"We'll get on with the rabbit control promptly," said Earlene, who had assumed the attitude of fawning penitent. "And my cursory inspection of your lovely gardens shows that your hosta has suffered the most damage. We can, and will, replace those with the finest specimens from my own garden."

"Before you start, there is one little mystery that needs to be cleared up," said George. "That is the matter of the tomahawk planted in the skull of our wood carving. That is a very precious wood carving, fashioned with chain saw and chisel, of the great Spanish novelist, Miguel de Cervantes. Who put it there?"

"No idea," Earlene said.

"Ummmmm," said Edith.

"Hold on," said Nan. "It seems to me, Edith, that I recall you fingering Sproot as the culprit here. Or were you doing that to cover your own tracks?"

"I *think* it was her," said Edith. "I have no actual proof. It was *not* me. Who else could it have been? I mean, everything was so scrambled up, and the rain was pouring down soooo hard."

"C'mon," said George. "Level with us. All is forgiven, though we might ask for a little settlement to clean off the carving and fill in that nice little groove that was made in the top."

"Okay, it was me," said Dr. Sproot, who was tugging at a strand of her sticky hair and licking the lemonade off it as one yellow jacket alighted on her left ear and another on her right shoulder. "I did it when I first got here, before everything went all to hell. It kind of went along with the Indian burial grounds theme. I thought it would be a nice touch. As for the tomahawk, I found it in the history center gift shop over there in Bemis; you know, down near the old restored Indian village. It's just a cheap replica. You're welcome to keep it."

"And the *blood* gushing out of poor Miguel's head?" Nan wondered.

"Gobby oil paint that's been sitting around in my basement for months. Lucky for me it didn't wash off." Another yellow jacket hovered two inches over Dr. Sproot's head.

"Lucky for you it wasn't merlot," Nan said. "Otherwise we would have nailed *your* hide to that trellis over there. Now, let's get you cleaned up before our little visitors start using you for a pincushion."

28

Genocide and Retribution

A pickup truck pulled up along Payne Avenue. Out of the bed of the truck jumped Shirelle, who opened the tailgate and pulled out a couple of cages. Earlene emerged from the driver's side of the pickup and waved at the Fremonts, who were sitting on the patio. The passenger door opened to reveal Dr. Phyllis Sproot, who only smirked in their general direction. Edith had been dispatched to comb the gardening stores in St. Anthony for those replacement flowers none of them had in their own gardens and which Burdick's no longer had in stock. She was also assigned to work the odd-day watering shift. Dr. Sproot and Earlene, deemed the most culpable of the four, got the even-day shift in addition to their transplanting and rabbit-catching duties.

"Now, George," Nan said. "No more gin. We're in a sort of a law-enforcement situation here, and we have to keep our wits about us to properly supervise this mish, these mish . . . these . . ."

"Mish-creants?" said George.

"Thank you, dear," said Nan, patting George's hand. "Now, no more for me either. And by no means offer *them* anything to drink. They've got work to do."

For the next three hours, with the vocal, gesticulating, and good-natured encouragement of George and Nan, who had switched over to ice water, Earlene, Dr. Sproot, and Shirelle baited and set rabbit traps, dug out the damaged hosta and a few petunias that had gotten trampled, and replaced them with their own, then watered the transplants.

"Don't they have anything better to do than just sit there and watch us?" said Dr. Sproot to Earlene as they tamped the loose soil into place around the last transplanted variegated hosta. "It's as if they're mocking us. And they're nothing more than drunks. And the *hibiscus!* Who came up with *that* idea?"

"Oh, keep your shirt on, Sproot. Look at it this way, you and I are now criminals in the eyes of the law. If it weren't for the indulgence of the Fremonts, we'd be cooling our heels in the workhouse now. So, just put a lid on it."

"I keep wondering who the idiot was who hired an incompetent like you," said Dr. Sproot. "Who could be that stupid?"

"You didn't exactly succeed either, did you, Sproot."

"I would have if it hadn't been for you, and your stupid *intern,* as you call her. Who was your client?"

Earlene was about to drop a shovelful of dirt on Dr. Sproot's shoes when Shirelle yelled from the edge of the woods, where the four baited traps had been placed.

"You need to see this, Mrs. McGillicuddy!" Shirelle yelled. "You too, Mr. and Mrs. Fremont! Come over here!"

Once everyone except the subdued and sneering Dr. Sproot was gathered next to the excited and panting Shirelle, she pointed into the woods.

"Over there," she said. "See it? And over there, too."

"I don't see anything, dear," said Earlene, squinting. "What exactly is it you're pointing at?"

"Rabbits. At least they look like rabbits. Why are they so still?"

"Then you must have the eyes of an eagle, Shirelle," Nan said. "I don't see anything."

"I do," George said. "There's a ball of gray, right over there."

He pointed toward a clump of underbrush about halfway through the woods. "And there."

George swung his arm in an arc over to the left, about 30 degrees, so that he was pointing at a little clearing in the woods.

"There's a couple of gray clumps right at the base of that buckthorn you've been after me to cut down for the last five years."

"You have buckthorns in your woods!" cried Earlene. "Why, I never would have guessed the Fremonts would have allowed such a noxious, invasive species onto their grounds, even if it is in the wild woods."

"I see them!" cried Nan. "What are they?"

"Ohmygosh!" Shirelle gasped. "There's two right behind your shed."

The group walked over to the shed. George stooped over into the woods to pick up a long branch that had fallen off one of their silver maples during the last storm, and poked it at one of the clumps, turning it over.

"Well, it *is* a rabbit, and as we can see, it is quite dead. No sign of any wound."

"And that appears to be a young rabbit in its prime," Earlene said. "Not old and sickly."

"There's another!" said Shirelle, pointing to a sixth motionless gray form about ten feet into the woods in front of them.

"Dead rabbits everywhere," said Nan somberly. "Why?" She turned to look at Earlene. "Why, Earlene? Is this something you know about?"

"Yeah, Earlene, what's the story here?" said George. "If you let a bunch of sickly and diseased rabbits into our yard to spread something around, you are in for a lot more trouble than you reckoned for. . . ."

"Really, Earlene, it's one thing to damage plants. It's completely another to start messing around with people's health."

"I . . . I . . . I . . ."

"Spit it out, Earlene!" barked Nan. Earlene cringed.

"I . . . don't have any idea what's going on here. No idea. I swear it. I would never, never do anything like that. Never in a million years. Those rabbits were healthy when we brought them over. Healthy! Weren't they, Shirelle?"

"I don't know what they were, Mrs. McGillicuddy," said Shirelle, who had now decided she would instantly cut all ties with Earlene and turn state's evidence against her if necessary. "All I know is you wanted to half starve them so when we brought them over here they would eat everything in sight."

Earlene blushed. Nan, arms folded, glared at her.

"We should have let you go to jail, Earlene. And to suck an impressionable young woman into your devious schemes . . . why, it defies belief! And, by the way, who was it who hired you, Earlene? Who would stoop so low as to hire a garden assassin to do her dirty work? Was it that Yelena Diggity you claimed to hate so much? Huh? Or Vanessa Stevenson? Who was it, Earlene?"

"It was me."

"What?"

"It was me," said Earlene, her lip curling and cheeks twitching. "I was working for no one. I only pretended to have a client so my reputation would spread. That way, word would get out about what I had done, and lady gardeners would be lining up to pay for my services. A sort of publicity stunt, I guess you might say."

Shirelle gasped.

"Mrs. McGillicuddy!"

"That beats all, Earlene," Nan said with a snort. "It really does."

"Please!" begged a sobbing Earlene, who had dropped down on her knees. "Please don't send me to jail! I'll do anything! Anything! Just don't send me to jail!"

"Here's what you will do," said Nan, glowering down at the cringing, crumpled form. "You will go home now, inform Livia Animal Control of the situation here, have them or someone else haul away the carcasses, and make sure someone tests them for rabies or whatever."

"Those rabbits weren't rabid!" cried Earlene, who had dissolved into a writhing, howling, pathetic human representation of woe. "What kind of monster do you take me for?"

"You will have them tested!"

With the help of George and Nan, Earlene stood up. She wiped her face with the sleeve of her work shirt, and beckoned to Shirelle to follow her back to the pickup.

"Mr. and Mrs. Fremont," said Shirelle. "Is it okay if I stay here and look at your gardens for a while? They are so AWESOME! I can get a ride later."

"Sure, Shirelle," George said. "Stay as long as you like and look around to your heart's content. I'm sure Mrs. Fremont will be happy to give you a guided tour."

"You won't be needing me anymore, Mrs. McGillicuddy," Shirelle said. "You will have to find another intern."

Earlene absorbed this news silently, her eyelids and lower lip twitching. She slouched off toward Dr. Sproot, who, all this time, had been sitting on the patio bench, mulling over the inequities of life, and wondering why the fickle gardening fates had chosen her—the estimable Dr. Phyllis Sproot, Ph.D.—as the victim of their cruel whims this year.

She was also beginning to fret that planting the hibiscus was not as gauche a move as she initially believed. In fact, it could be another stroke of genius that, along with the angel's trumpets, could be the Fremonts' passports to victory. Too bad she hadn't gotten a few more whacks at those things!

"What was all that bawling about?" she said as Earlene retrieved her shovel and steel-toothed rake, which were propped against one of the ash trees. "My goodness, you'd have thought they were demanding your firstborn the way you were carrying on."

Earlene glared at Dr. Sproot. Then, without a word in response, she took off at a trot toward the pickup truck.

"Hey!" yelled Dr. Sproot. "Wait for me!"

She bounded down the steps, flinging Nan's pea gravel everywhere, but was too late; by the time she got to the street, Earlene had tossed the shovel and rake in the bed of the pickup, peeled out with a shriek of tires, and screeched through the intersection of Payne and Sumac. Then, she slowed down.

With her home two miles away and with no intention of further debasing herself before the Fremonts by asking them for a ride, Dr. Sproot took off at a sprint in pursuit. Earlene, cackling maniacally, had slowed down enough to allow her to catch up. Then, she stepped on the gas, shooting ahead about fifty yards before stopping. Dr. Sproot jogged toward her. This time, Earlene let her get to the passenger door and blurt out something about really having to go to the bathroom before gunning it, leaving Dr. Sproot standing in the middle of the street, screaming something inaudible and shaking her fist.

On the way home, Earlene tabled her resolve to follow the straight and narrow gardening path from now on. She would take the high road, but not until she had done one more sabotage job. It would be the crème de la crème of garden destruction, a no-holds-barred, damn-the-torpedoes suicide assault.

No real planning required for this one. No effort to cover her tracks here. Everyone would know she did this job and it would go down in Livia lore. She'd launch her assault on the first day of the judging for the contest.

What better way for Earlene McGillicuddy to go out in a blaze of glory than by taking down Phyllis Sproot's gardens.

29

Devastation

"I think I can solve our dead rabbit mystery," George said.

Nan was only half listening. She was too busy balancing herself on the pedestal onto which Shirelle had lifted her. Over the past two hours, Shirelle had treated Nan as the golden goddess of gardening, lavishing upon her the kind of fulsome praise she had not heard since performing a flawless rendering of "Chopsticks" at the age of twelve on the family piano. Nan had given Shirelle the full, heavily annotated tour of the gardens, complete with anecdotes and silly asides about George, and the young woman lapped it up, bug-eyed and panting for more.

And all the questions! Why didn't she plant zinnias? When would she prune her climbing roses? What did the bridal wreath spirea look like in full bloom? Would she start planting more ornamental grasses mixed in among the rocks? How had she managed to turn her backyard into paradise? Did she have a daughter? How would she feel about acquiring another one? Well, that last question really didn't get asked but it might as well have been. By the time Shirelle called her brother to come pick her up and take her over to Earlene's to get her car, a bond had grown between the two women that it takes some friends ten years to seal. There were proffered good-byes and hugs and promises to keep in touch. Shirelle wondered if she could come work for the Fremonts as a gardening intern.

"Well, we wouldn't be able to pay you anything," said Nan. "And there's not very much left to do now but maintain everything and keep our fingers crossed for the contest. But we should have a burst of new blooms any day now. Come see them! You're welcome to come over any time, Shirelle, and I will teach you whatever I can!"

Shirelle was beaming from ear to ear as her brother pulled into their driveway and honked his horn long enough to spoil the mood a little; she waved her way out of the driveway into the intersection and along Sumac until she passed out of sight.

"Earth to Nan. I think I've solved our dead rabbit mystery."

"What? Oh . . . really? Why bother? The animal people will do their tests."

"Just bear with me," George said.

Still walking on a cloud, Nan followed George over to the angel's trumpets, which had suffered a couple of glancing blows from the ineptly wielded hatchet of Dr. Phyllis Sproot. Seeing the wounded plant again brought Nan right back to earth with a thud.

"Gosh darn her!" she said. "Look at that gash! We'll have to prune it now, pronto."

"That's not really what I'm looking at," George said. "Look at this."

The ground around the plant had been disturbed. The seed pods he thought he had ground deeply enough into the earth seemed to have been uncovered. Dangerous, mutilated seeds now lay strewn around the plant. Not only that, but carrot ends and lettuce and spinach traces littered the area around the seeds. Something else caught George's eye. A few feet away, lying in the fresh cypress mulch between the variegated dogwoods and chain-link fence, was another rabbit, curled up, still, with a couple of paws extended out at unnatural angles from its body and obviously quite dead.

"The rabbits have been gorging themselves on angel's trumpets seeds," George said. "That's what killed them all. They were running around the yard, famished, found this, and gorged themselves. Death from rabies or some other awful and sudden scourge? I don't think so. But what I don't get is I mashed all this stuff into the ground. Did the rabbits dig it up? And a meticulous observer will note that additional seed pods had been cut off the plant and, perhaps, scattered around its base. I wonder who might know something about this. What I figure is this: a couple of those rabbits died from what we put down here before. But someone—who could it be?—must have added a little supplement recently to make sure the job was done right. Hmmm?"

"Hmmm," said Nan, irritated that her buoyant mood had been disturbed by George's petty neuroses. "Well, if that's the case, then it worked, didn't it? I mean, didn't we scatter that rabbit food around here anyway as a form of pest control? I just added a little booster shot to the mix, and sprinkled on a little rat poison—just a little teensy bit. Okay, maybe not so teensy—and, *voilà,* it solved our sudden, unexpected infestation. And gee whiz, George, I didn't know what killed those rabbits . . . at least not for sure. It *could* have been rabies. It *could* have been something else. Besides, I didn't want to let Earlene off the hook on a little technicality. What's important is I was able to detach the seeds with a minimum of disturbance to the rest of the plants. Why, look, you can barely tell they've been altered except for that gash, damn that Sproot! And, if you ask me, it's worth it. Those bloody rabbits were going to nibble us out of contention. All this reminds me that we need to police this area a little bit before the contest. It's looking a little messy, to say nothing of this mutilated stem."

"When? When did you do this?"

"Oh, a couple of days ago. You were gone somewhere for a few hours. What's the problem anyway? You wanted to kill rabbits and I wanted to kill rabbits and that's what we did. Besides, you wanted the damn seed pods cut down anyway!"

"I wanted to *control* the population, not commit genocide!" moaned George, visions of those orphaned rabbits beginning to populate his imagination once again.

"I say good riddance," said Nan. "Now quit being so goddamn squeamish. You're the one who smashed a rabbit's head in, not me!"

"I know, but that was a horrible thing to do, and you can't imagine the guilt. . . ."

"For Chrissakes, quit being such a hypersensitive geek. Look at it this way: they died with full stomachs."

"They died in pain, and hallucinating, not able to tell fantasy from reality. It would have been a long, lingering, crazy-as-hell death."

"Well, obviously we didn't do the job as thoroughly as I would have liked."

"Huh?"

"Look over there."

Nan pointed to where the compost pile touched the woods. A small, silent, and still ball of fur gazed, unblinking, at them, twitched one of its ears, then, when they moved toward it, bounded off in three big leaps into the woods.

"Thank God! There are survivors!"

Thunder grumbled in the distance.

"I didn't know we had thunderstorms in the forecast today."

"Forty percent chance," mumbled George through the hands that cradled his anguished face. "With the possibility that a few could become severe."

There was more thunder, this one a long, distant roll, followed shortly by a louder crack. That brought George out of his funk and sent him and Nan racing through the twilight into the front yard.

There was no mistaking that they were in the crosshairs of this thunderstorm. Looking across the lake, they could see a black sky alive with ragged strings of lightning. What especially alarmed them was some of the black was turning a sickly green. A burst of wind from out of nowhere collided with them, almost knocking them over.

"Straight-line winds!" George said. "This will be big!"

"We have to cover the plants! We have to protect them!"

They sprinted to the shed to get the plastic tarps with grommeted borders and the ropes. The hail had already begun to rattle against the roof and vinyl siding of the house by the time they threw one madly flapping tarp over some of their newest little darlings—the hibiscus—and had just started to pass the rope through the grommets. Then, as thunder crashed above, the skies opened up, hurtling a blizzard of hailstones the size of marbles earthward. It wasn't long before bigger ones—some as large as ping-pong balls—came crashing down. Glass shattered somewhere. It sounded as if artillery rounds were crashing into the walls and roof of their house.

George and Nan finally had to drop their rope ends and run for the eaves that sheltered that part of the patio immediately adjacent to the back door. There, they sat silently and grimly watched as chaos engulfed their beautiful gardens and tore them to ribbons. In ten minutes, it was done. The furious wind subsided and the hail gave way to a steady downpour of rain. The backyard was covered more than two inches deep with white hailstones of all shapes and sizes, as well as several large and medium-sized branches, and dozens of smaller branches and twigs that had been sliced off the trees. One large branch came crashing down onto one of the rose trellises, cleaving it in two. It wasn't a half hour before the rain ended and the clouds gave way to a moonless night darkened even further by a neighborhood power outage.

The next morning it looked as if a hurricane had roared through. In addition to all the branches lying everywhere, leaves had been stripped from most of the trees. Many had been plastered to the sides of the house. They stuck there as if they had been glued on. Much of the siding was dented and puckered from the pounding it had taken from the hail. Scores of broken shingle pieces were lying around the yard. Others had probably blown off into neighbors' yards. The glass in one of the front windows had been shattered, as had the rear window in Cullen's Camaro and the front passenger side window of Ellis's Duster. The electricity came back on around four thirty a.m. with blasts from the radio and TV, which had been left on by the kids when the power shut off.

As Ellis, Cullen, and Sis gathered the branches into several big piles, George and Nan surveyed their backyard gardens, which had been crumpled, sliced, battered, and broken. The shrubs and bushes were still standing, but what was the point? Their leaves and blooms had been shredded. At least, George noted with grim satisfaction, the hated angel's trumpets hadn't made it; their leaves and flowers were pulverized.

"There are a few survivors," Nan said glumly. "The alyssum's okay. The hosta under the eaves. Gosh, one of the hydrangeas seems intact. It's close enough to the house that the way the hail was angling down, it must have missed it. That's about it. Everything else's torn to pieces."

A small crowd of neighbors and friends had gathered on Payne Avenue to survey the damage. Several had their hands clamped around their faces and their mouths open in shock. Here were the Boozers, the Rodards, and the Mikkelsons, Deanna noting happily once condolences were offered and an appropriate moment of silence was observed that she was due in late August and that it was going to be a boy. Then came the McCandlesses and the Winthrops walking gravely up the steps. They stood next to the Fremonts and for several quiet moments surveyed the damage.

"All that work!" Jane McCandless said, her voice breaking as she wrapped her arms around Nan. "All that hard work!"

"The insurance should cover this," said Alex McCandless. "I can't imagine that they wouldn't."

"I don't know," George said. "Who could put a price on what we lost here?"

The Fremont children crisscrossed the yard, gathering up debris in stony silence as if they were collecting the bodies of plague victims who had died overnight.

"What happened to you guys?" Nan wondered.

"Power out, that's all," Alex said. "A couple branches down. Nothing that bad compared to you guys."

"We didn't even get hail," Juanita Winthrop said. "And our power never went out. It was you guys right next to the lake that got the brunt of the storm. Go down the street two blocks and there isn't any damage at all."

Someone carrying a clipboard and holding a pen had stealthily joined their group, and was also looking around the yard.

"The homeowners here?" The Winthrops and McCandlesses pointed to the Fremonts.

"That was quick!" said George. "We just called two hours ago." The insurance adjustor smiled, and handed him his business card.

"Quite a mess you got here," he said. "I've already looked at the home. Looks like you'll need new siding in the front, a new window, and maybe a new roof. We'll have to work out some figures and get back to you. You'll have to call your auto insurance for the cars, assuming those parked on the street are yours. Anything damaged inside?"

"We had some frozen ice cream cakes in the freezer," Nan said. "And several gallon-sized buckets of Rocky Road. *Extra-creamy* Rocky Road. They're all mush now. Melted ice cubes. The limes are probably warmer than we would like. Thank God we don't drink chilled white wine."

"Make a list," the adjustor said. "Funny. The rest of the neighborhood barely got touched. Just little stuff. Never seen anything like it. You guys were at the epicenter."

"What about all this?" said Nan with a sweep of her hand.

"All what?"

"Why, our beautiful gardens. They've been wrecked."

"Hmmm. We probably won't give you much for that. We're already covering the house and roof. I see your thing over here. . . ."

"Trellis."

"The trellis is wrecked. We might give you something for that. But don't count on much for plants. We might give you a few hundred. No more than that, I would think."

"A few hundred! These gardens are virtually priceless!"

"Sorry. You can submit a list to us of the plants damaged and destroyed and their approximate greenhouse value. We'll see."

"You need to fight them on that," Alex said as the insurance man walked around the yard. "You should get thousands for that."

"Even thousands won't make up for it," said George. "Maybe $200,000."

"Two hundred thousand?" said Juanita. "How come that much exactly?"

"That's how much the Burdick's Best Yard Contest first prize is up to now. You know, the contest we just lost."

"Maybe all the other contestants suffered damage, too," Juanita said. Nan and George forced wan, unbelieving smiles.

"What's worst is it's like losing your friends," said Nan, a tear sparkling in each eye. "This was such an animated place.

Now it's so quiet. Even the ones that are still living aren't talking. They're hurting too much. And to think that we had really just gotten to know them. Listen." The McCandlesses and Winthrops earnestly pretended to listen.

"Hear that?"

"Mmm–hmm," said Juanita.

"I hear something," Steve said.

"No you don't!" retorted Nan sharply. "Don't patronize me. There's nothing. What you hear is the sound of silence. What can something say if it's dead?"

Juanita and Jane hugged Nan, while Steve and Alex nodded sadly.

"Well, I guess it's about time to call Jerry and get him and his chain saw over here," said George after the Winthrops and McCandlesses made their slow, somber way down the steps, stopping and swiveling their heads halfway down as if not believing the damage they had witnessed and having to check again to prove it to themselves. Nan noticed appreciatively that, as always, they managed to negotiate the steps without disturbing any of her pea gravel.

Another visitor was climbing up the steps toward them, stopping halfway to the patio to pivot and survey the carnage spread out before her with a long sigh. Short of stature and middle-aged, she carried herself with the familiarity and confidence of someone the Fremonts figured they should know. She stopped directly in front of them, smiled meekly, and offered her hand.

"I just wanted to tell you how much I feel your pain," the woman said softly. "I'm just distraught at what happened here. Well, you don't really know me, but I've been a big admirer of your gardening skills for a long time. I wanted to offer you the solace of someone who cares a lot more than you might realize."

The Fremonts looked on, puzzled, but accepted the woman's

proffered friendship. Her tiny hand had the firm, purposeful feel of someone who meant what she said.

"I'm sorry," Nan said. "But your name is . . . ?"

"Marta."

"Marta what?"

"Just Marta's enough."

"Sounds familiar. Don't we know you?"

"I don't think so. But, as I said, I know *you.*"

"Wait a minute!" said George, snapping his fingers. "That voice. I know that voice. I *know* who you are."

Marta winced and held her breath, hoping that she wouldn't start hyperventilating.

"You're the voice of Kurt's Karamel Kandies! On the radio. Between innings during the Muskies games! The one that does the Kurt's Alerts, then finds somebody at the ballpark eating your caramels and gives him a year's supply if he can eat ten at one time. 'Eat Kurt's Till It Hurts.' I love that promotion. I never mistake a voice. That's you, isn't it?"

Marta almost fainted with relief.

"No, not me. Sorry."

"Dang," George said. "That's the first time I've mistaken a voice."

"Well," said Marta, "I won't waste any more of your time. I did want to tell you that I know what happened to you and may be able to make it right."

"You *what?*" Nan said.

"That's all I can say for now," said Marta, who had turned and was about to make her way back down the steps. "I'll do whatever I can to help you. Be patient."

"Hang on, there, Mrs. . . . Poppendauber." Marta stopped dead in her tracks. "A little bird told us that you might have had something to do with all the trouble we've been having."

"And that little bird would be correct," said Marta,

wringing her hands. "But I didn't want to. I was weak and Doc Phil . . . ah . . . Dr. Sproot had been my best friend for many years. She had helped me so much to become the gardener I am now, not as good as she is, of course, or you. But I *did* break loose eventually. I am my own woman now, and I have actually already helped you."

"The woman in the robes!" George cried. "The spy!"

"Correct again," Marta said. "But I never did any damage other than snipping off a few of your monarda."

"And that's what you call *help?*" said Nan. "Strange definition of the word, if you ask me."

"Hang on!" George said. "You're the angel-monk with the cross that night. The one that vanquished the zom . . . uh . . . Dr. Sproot! You *did* help us."

"Oh, jeez," Nan moaned.

Marta sighed.

"You wouldn't happen to have any of that wine of yours handy, would you?" she said. "I'm afraid you haven't heard the whole story of what has happened here. If you don't mind, I'd kind of like to fill you in."

30

Garden Renewal for Fun and Profit

"I don't believe a word of it," Nan said. "Not a word. I mean, really. A witch's curse on our property? This is some kind of joke . . . isn't it, George?"

"Pretty hard to buy," George said. "But she seemed sincere. She seemed sane. And, Nan-bee, you might have noticed that some people have been wondering about *our* sanity, what with us yakking it up with the plants and all. And you and your *sentient* flowers. I mean, if this was Salem, Mass, circa 1690, you'd be toast. Besides, she's as old as we are, maybe older. When you come right down to it, how many people our age get their jollies telling people lies about spells being cast on them? Huh? There must be something to it. And it's the same story Dr. Sproot was trying to tell us."

"That's hardly a reliable source," Nan said acidly, peeved that George would stoop so low as to connect her proven techniques of cross-cultural contact with such a dark, superstitious absurdity as witchcraft. "And sane? This Marta Poppendauber is the same woman who's been dressing up like a monk to spy on us. I'd say she's got a side to her that's certifiably wacko.

"Let's say it's true, which it is not for one thing, and for two, it would be blaspheming. But just for argument's sake, let's say there's something to all this hokum. Okay? Here goes: 'Edith. Edith Merton. I know you can hear me with your witch powers. Edith, please call up one of your good spells and plunk down a check right here in front of us to cover the damages. A check for, um, $100,000 or so would work quite nicely as a starter, thank you.' Okay, where's the puff of smoke and the check? Nowhere, of course. You know, it really burns me up that I haven't heard that Marta Poppendauber or anyone else stepping forward to offer *that* kind of restorative justice."

"She said be patient."

Nan snorted.

"Well, I've had it up to here with patience," she said.

George and Nan were sipping diet Cokes as evening rolled around, wine and gin not really seeming appropriate considering what they had been through. They gazed abstractedly into the meaningless jumble of torn, knocked-down plants that was their backyard. A light breeze wafted their way, carrying with it the scent of charcoal and lighter fluid.

"Somebody's firing up the grill," said George unenthusiastically.

"The Cadawalladers," said Nan. "Whatever it is they're cooking, they'll vaporize it. We'll be smelling carbon and ash soon."

George smiled joylessly.

"I guess it's about time we figured out whether we have misspent the last six years of our lives indulging in a fruitless, unproductive hobby at the expense of our livelihood," said Nan. "We need to get off our hindquarters and start looking for jobs, full time and permanent. That means we start pounding the pavement tomorrow. Time for you to freshen up the old résumé, bud."

"Freshen it up with what?"

"Good point."

A week later, after their first unsuccessful rounds of job interviews, George and Nan settled in on the patio, pinching pennies by reluctantly tolerating the cheapest merlot they could find.

"Damn if this rotgut doesn't work fast," Nan said, puckering her lips. "You sure someone didn't bottle one hundred percent grain alcohol in here and just add a little sour grape juice for flavoring?"

Just after they had waved halfheartedly to the Boozers, who waved back and said something inaudible, a black BMW pulled up on the side of the road, leaving enough room between it and the leper Duster to avoid any chance of contamination. Out stepped a serious-looking man wearing a dark suit and carrying a plain but tasteful briefcase.

"Uh-oh, another jerk realtor," growled George. "It's okay. One more glass of this stuff and screw propriety; we'll just keep insulting him till he leaves."

"Now, dear, be civil. We *are* the Fremonts, after all."

The man walked briskly up the steps, making a good impression on Nan by not mussing up her pea gravel and disarming George with a serious mien that didn't even hint of phony neighborliness.

"Mr. and Mrs. Fremont?" George and Nan nodded. "I am Jasper Burdick, owner of Burdick's PlantWorld as well as any number of other enterprises with which I won't bore you this evening. You may have heard of me and I am quite certain you've heard of our big contest. The results were announced Tuesday, you know."

"We know," Nan said with a hiccup. "So, you're here to tell us we didn't win? We know that already. Just look around. We know Marta Poppendauber won first place and our heartfelt congratulations go out to her."

Mr. Burdick chuckled.

"Glass of budget merlot?" George said halfheartedly, motioning for their unexpected guest to seat himself.

"No," Mr. Burdick said. "I want to get down strictly to business here. And I think you will find my visit to be quite a pleasant surprise."

"How might that be?" Nan said.

Mr. Burdick cleared his throat.

"How that might be is that we've awarded you first place in the Burdick's Best Yard Contest. Your first-place sign will be delivered to you later this week. I, however, am here to personally deliver to you your official certificate of congratulations and a check for $200,000."

For a minute, the earth stood still. No bird twittered. No tree rustled. No plant photosynthesized.

"I'm sure this comes as something of a shock," said Mr. Burdick as George and Nan stared vacantly at him. "A good shock, I would think, but I can see you're flummoxed."

George grabbed one of the bottles of merlot, which came from a small town in Utah, and not too far from a big uranium mine, and squinted at the label.

"I don't see anything here that would unduly speed up brain cell mutation," he said. "But it sure is very bad wine. Could you repeat what you said, Mr. Burdick? My wife, as you can see, has gone apocalyptic . . . I mean, ha-ha, *apoplectic* on us."

"I said I have a check here for $200,000—tax-free, I might add, since we prepay the taxes on the total amount—for winning the first-place prize in the Burdick's Best Yard Contest."

"But how can that be?" cried Nan, suddenly alert and feisty. "These gardens were destroyed two days before your judges came by. And when they did come by they looked for five minutes and we told them what happened. They said, 'Sorry, tough tequila,' and they left. Poof. *C'est la vie.* Et cetera. Et cetera. Besides, Myrtle Pupildinger won anyway."

"No, Mrs. Poppendauber did not win."

"Mr. Burdick, I know this must be fun for you playing your little joke here and taking advantage of a couple of folks who're on the verge of getting shit-faced, but could you please explain what exactly is going on? Nan and I are on our third bottle of very, very cheap merlot and our senses—well, Nan's especially—are a little scrambled. At this stage of the evening and considering the extent of our alcohol intake, we confuse easily."

Mr. Burdick chuckled again with what seemed to the Fremonts to be genuine mirth.

"Okay, then. I'll tell you the whole story. Marta Poppendauber did indeed win first place, but when I paid her a visit to deliver the news, she explained everything to me. A sad story, certainly. And I was indignant to hear that unscrupulous persons would stoop so low as to sabotage one of our contestants and stain our competition with corruption. But when you've got $200,000 at stake, well, you know how people are.

"At any rate, Mrs. Poppendauber insisted that we give first prize to you, not just because your efforts had been so cruelly undermined, but also because you so richly deserved it."

"A little of our wonderful vintage wine, Mr. B?" said George, shakily dangling a half-empty wine bottle in front of him. Mr. Burdick waved it away with a smile.

"Not now, thank you, Mr. Fremont. I'll just finish my story. So, as it turned out, Mrs. Poppendauber had hundreds—yes, hundreds!—of photographs of your gardens. Not only that, but she had made schematic drawings of your grounds, down to the tiniest little flower. I must say, no landscape designer we employ could have done better. Well, I took the matter under

careful consideration. The judges were consulted and yesterday the decision was made: You get first place! You know, of
course, that Dr. Phyllis Sproot's gardens were also destroyed."

"No!" said Nan.

"How?" said George.

"Oh, didn't you know? Well, that's for someone else to say.
All I can say is any prize she would have won would have been
nullified posthaste. Though the initial thought was to disqualify Mrs. Poppendauber from any prize at all, she did get points
for her honesty and forthrightness and mostly for her willingness to forfeit her first prize. With all that in mind, the judges
decided that awarding her the second-place prize would be
quite reasonable. Plus, we offered her a job as special gardening
and landscaping consultant to Burdick's."

During all this time, George and Nan had been getting
thoroughly potted. George once again waggled the wine bottle at Mr. Burdick, and, once again being waved off, flourished
it at Nan, who somewhat shakily held up her glass for a refill.

"But, Misther Budwink, how would any person want to
see some firsth place gardens that don't exist?" Nan hiccuped
and perched her fingertips daintily on her lips.

"I've thought about that, Mrs. Fremont."

"Nan-bee. You can call me Nan-bee, just like Georgie
does."

"Don't call me *Georgie!* Not ever again!"

"Okay, Nan-bee, I have given that some thought, and the
way I see it is this: people love to see disaster and devastation.
Then, they love to see the comeback, the phoenix rising tri-
umphant from the ashes. Do you know what I mean?"

George and Nan stared at Mr. Burdick.

"Please don't be taxing our brains too much, Mr. Beatwash,"
said George. "Just tell us up front what you're getting at."

"Well, they'll want to see the devastation first, then they'll want to see the resurrection when the gardens look even better. It's what happened after Mount Saint Helens blew its top. It's what happened after forest fires ravaged Yellowstone. It's what happened to . . . Jesus."

All three instinctively bowed their heads for a moment in respectful silence.

"Now it's time for it to happen to the Fremont gardens of Livia."

Nan giggled. George frowned at her.

"I've even seen a vision of what will happen." George and Nan swayed from side to side. "I've seen your future gardens being more resplendent than ever, and people making pilgrimages to your backyard and returning to their homes awestruck and inspired. I have these visions sometimes, you know." Mr. Burdick was looking up into the sky, so, to be polite, Nan and George looked up there, too.

"I don't see nuttin'," Nan gurgled. "And it's right about at the stage when I should be starting to, whether there's sumpin' there or not."

Mr. Burdick decided it was pointless to push the mystical element of the story any further. He lowered his eyes and adopted his most businesslike tone.

"I have to tell you that we've received certain inquiries from the press about this matter. I ordinarily disapprove of the press, but seeing as how the contest did get quite a bit of publicity that we actively sought in the first place, I'm not sure it does us any good to say no. It's up to you how you yourselves want to deal with this."

"Bring on the goddamn newshounds!" screamed Nan.

"We agree!" shouted George. "But under one condition . . . one eentsy little condition."

"Which is?"

"Which is to call the guy who can do the story right. His

name is Roland Ready and he works for the . . . he works for
the . . . whacha name of that shtupid rag downtown? . . . Oh,
yesh . . . oh, yest . . . the . . . the . . ."

"I'm familiar with Mr. Ready," Mr. Burdick interrupted
gently. "And he's done a very fair job in his coverage, I must
say. Not so much as a whiff of socialist bias. I will contact him
at the *Inquirer* and let him know you're willing to be interviewed. I'm hoping, by the way, we can leave some of the more
sordid elements out of this. However, Mrs. Poppendauber's
confession can be an inspiration for gardeners everywhere."

As Mr. Burdick got up to leave, George and Nan took
turns hugging him four times each. Nan stumbled her way
through two flower knock-knock jokes, praised the clematis
for its stoicism, and insisted on introducing her pea gravel
while the bemused Mr. Burdick listened politely. George got a
quarter out of his pocket, grabbed Mr. Burdick's hand, and
slipped it into his palm.

"Thasha tip," he whispered into his ear. "For alla good
works you do. . . . No . . . I inshist."

Mr. Burdick finally managed to slip away, with the Fremonts waving good-byes like maniacs and George crying out,
"Y'all come back now, heah!" six times.

As George and Nan strolled around the backyard on a
mid-August Saturday morning, they were astonished at how
quickly their gardens had shifted into full recuperation mode.
The lilacs, their leaves machine-gunned by the hailstorm, had
dropped their damaged leaves and generated new ones. Hostas
poked their clumped, giant, asparagus-tip points through the
soil. The crab apples were crowned with clouds of white and
pink blossoms, unusual for August, to say the least. Everywhere
were new shoots, new leaves, and new blooms that were paying no attention to what the calendar told them they shouldn't
be doing.

"This is a miracle!" Nan cried. "Scientifically speaking, none of this is supposed to be happening!"

"If I didn't know any better, I'd say someone cast a spell on our property," said George. "A really good spell. Or maybe it was somebody's vision."

"Oh, c'mon, George," said Nan. "You don't believe in that kind of nonsense, do you? It does appear that we're going to have another go-round this summer with the gardens. And next year, we can work both sides of the house, not just the back."

George groaned. This was the coffee-fueled Nan talking here.

"The prize money gives us enough to do the entire yard. And, at least for the foreseeable future, we'll have nothing but time. But, George, the money won't last forever, you know. We can probably live off our winnings another year and a half, maybe two years at most. Lots of college expenses coming up. Shouldn't we start looking for at least some regular part-time work?"

"Nah. Let's put that one off a little longer. I've got this idea anyway that I'll get around to someday: SpellCheck greeting cards."

"Go on."

"These greeting cards would have computer chips implanted in them that would be sensitive to the impressions your pen makes when you write your little notes. Your card would beep when you misspell a word. No more misspelled words for birthdays, graduations, get-well events, et cetera. Eh?"

"Sounds lovely, George."

"Hey, Fremonts!"

George and Nan turned to shake hands with Roland Ready, who had parked his car on the street and walked up quietly behind them.

"Back for more flower drama, Mr. Ready?" Nan said. "You

must be a glutton for punishment. Haven't you had enough of our little garden soap opera to last you a lifetime?"

Roland laughed.

"I see you've still got your Burdick's sign up. Pretty nice touch."

"Yep," Nan said. "We can keep it up all the way to Halloween, they said. Someone must have known we were going to have this late-season resurrection here. They'll bring it back next spring and we can have it up for a few weeks in May. Then, I guess they save it for the next winners, whenever that might be. All they have to do is change the names. You won't believe this, Mr. Ready, but we actually saw people pull up and take their pictures next to that sign. We must have had at least three hundred visitors; isn't that right, George?"

George shrugged; he figured it was more like seventy-five, and even at that he was ready for the visitations to start tailing off.

"It was a big deal."

"That it was," Nan said, sighing, then laughing.

Roland's contest story had run on Sunday 1A a week and a half after the Fremonts got the news of their contest victory. It had been thorough and accurate. George and Nan admired the way Roland conveyed the seediness of the sabotage conspiracies against them without making it the entire focus of the story. Marta came across as a beacon of righteousness, converted to the straight and narrow by an inner courage and determination to thwart evil. And Dr. Sproot, as it turned out, had gotten her comeuppance.

The first day of the judging, Earlene had brazenly tramped across her yard in broad daylight brandishing a McCulloch "Pro Series" chain saw that she could barely carry, and which would come in handy if you happened to have a stand of Douglas fir needed to furnish structural framing for a few subdivisions. She plowed through three beds of coreopsis-salvia-hollyhock blend, amputated every yucca in sight, and almost took off one of her legs before the police came and had to draw their service revolvers to get her to "Put down that chain saw, ma'am."

Dr. Sproot had refused to be interviewed but Earlene had not; she and Marta were the ones who spilled the beans on the entire debacle. Those interviews and the police report of the night's incident gave Roland enough to name all three culprits and flesh out his story nicely.

For this second, and more serious, infraction of the law Earlene had to do a week's worth of time. She also had to part with a few thousand dollars and would probably be talking to Dr. Sproot's lawyers before long.

When she got out of jail, Earlene decided to embark on another career. She signed on as manager for the newly rehabilitated Pat Veattle, who had burned all her silly costumes, emptied out fifty bottles of hard liquor, and was looking for a recording contract. Pat didn't make it into Roland's story because of space restrictions. Plus, Roland noted, as outrageous as she'd been, she had no direct bearing on the contest or the gardens.

The part about Edith's spells never made it into Roland's story, either, but for a different reason. Edith had categorized herself to the police as a mere accessory to Dr. Sproot's diabolical plot. Those with direct knowledge of her part in the scandal either kept quiet about it because they didn't believe it themselves, or believed it but didn't want anyone else to know they did. At least as far as any public notice of the affair was concerned, Sarah the Witch remained unreported and, therefore, nonexistent.

The Fremonts, whom Roland had interviewed for two hours, came across as the victims of fickle fate whose gargantuan and magnificent efforts received their just desserts despite getting a good, hard swat from Mother Nature. They talked about "the phoenix of hope rising out of the ashes of tragedy" (Nan's words), and made clear their esteem for Marta and their willingness to forgive all, even Dr. Sproot. Besides, whose fault was it that some mysterious power—perhaps even God's—had decided to act up and visit a plague of hailstones upon their garden?

"What was weird was how localized it all was," Roland said. "Your property bore the brunt."

The Fremonts could only shrug their shoulders and marvel at the capriciousness of Livia weather. Roland was amazed at how easy it was for them to laugh it all off and extend the hand of friendship to one and all. They had immediately invited Marta and Ham Poppendauber over for an appreciation dinner, gushing gratitude and plying them with Sagelands and Bombay Sapphire and offering them a one-fifth share of their first-prize earnings, which Marta and Ham graciously declined. They even gave them two bottles of Sagelands to take home with them. When Roland pressed them they admitted that, sure, it was a little easier to let bygones be bygones when you had a check for $200,000 in your pocket and a first-place sign in your front yard.

"And Marta Poppendauber," Roland said. "I confess I was mystified as to why she would so willingly give up the $200,000, no matter how good-hearted she might be . . . until I discovered something."

"Discovered what?" Nan said.

"How strong her desire was to completely discombobulate Dr. Sproot. She knew Dr. Sproot would be absolutely stricken when she found out what she'd done. So, Marta's Good Samaritan gesture wasn't quite as saintly as it seemed. Besides, her husband's long-lost aunt had just died and, much to their surprise, left him a pretty good-sized inheritance. They probably didn't need the money."

"Aha!" Nan cried.

"Hmmm," said George.

"They just found out about that inheritance a few days before the judging. In fact, it was the day before your storm."

"She never told us that!" Nan said. "But she *did* want the honor. I think we can attribute *that* to the goodness of her heart. So, why wasn't the inheritance stuff in your article?"

"My decision. Marta Poppendauber is an honest person and told me in the interest of full disclosure, though I couldn't persuade her to tell me what that inheritance is worth, except that it was 'generous.' I didn't push it. But then I figured why spoil a wonderful story of redemption with mere facts? Besides, she was already helping you before she knew about the inheritance.

"Did that make it a little easier for her to forfeit first place? Sure, it did. Still, I think we can agree that Marta Poppendauber is at heart a good person. It wouldn't surprise me if she turned most of that inheritance over to charity anyway."

"I'd like to think she would have given up first place no matter what," Nan said. "In fact, I *will* think that."

"Well, I do want to do a follow-up on your gardens sometime before the summer ends."

"Sure," said Nan. "Anytime you want. I'll mix up a pitcher of that lemonade you liked so much. If you look around, Mr. Ready, you might just find your material popping out of the ground even as we speak. Everything's coming back from the storm already . . . in August!"

"It won't be for the paper this time," Roland said. "I quit my job there. I'm working as the editor of *St. Anthony Gardener.* I've decided to devote my professional efforts full time to gardening now. I think we'll be able to give your yard and its comeback a nice spread."

"Well, you'd better hang on until you see how much more actually comes up," George said.

"I don't think there will be a problem there," Roland said. "I have full confidence in the Fremont magic at work here."

"Glass of merlot?"

"Nope. Was in the neighborhood and just wanted to

check in. Gotta be off. I've got our next big edition to edit. I'll
be in touch. So long, Fremonts."

"Look who's coming," said George after they waved Roland
out of the driveway and out onto Payne Avenue.

Bounding his impatient way up the driveway with those
long, loping strides of his was Jim Graybill, lugging along with
him his TreasureTrove XB 255.

"George! Nan!" shouted Jim.

"Jim!" they shouted right back.

"I have a proposition," said Jim, breathless from excitement
and his semi-trot over the length of two blocks. "Let me sweep
your *front* yard. I have this feeling there might be something
down there worth finding. Call it my gut instinct, my nose for
treasure."

"Oh, yeah?" said Nan with a chuckle. "Well, what happened to that gut instinct in the *back*yard, huh?"

Their backyard destroyed, the Fremonts had allowed Jim to
root around where his metal detector had signaled hot spots.
What he came up with was a couple of flattened cans, a pad-
lock, and a few large rusted screws that were undoubtedly very
old. Jim went all sheepish and shy, and stared down at his shoes.

"Yes, that didn't work out. Sorry. False alarm."

"No harm done," said George. "Perk up there, Jim. Nan
says we're digging up the front yard next year for new gardens.
So, by all means, have at it. Not now though, Jim; we've got
guests coming over."

Once Jim loped off toward home, George retrieved two bottles of Sagelands from the wine rack; the McCandlesses and
Winthrops would be arriving soon. So as not to put on big
award-winner airs, George changed from the expensive polo
shirt he had bought when he and Nan went on a shopping spree
into his navy-blue Jethro Tull 2005 American tour T-shirt,
and donned his sweat-stained Muskies hat.

Nan sat down on one of the new patio chairs she had

bought on a separate shopping spree and cast her frowning disapproval upon the Miguel de Cervantes wood sculpture. Much to her dismay, George and Jerry had rescued Miguel from what she hoped would be a mortal wound, sanded out the dinks caused by the hailstorm, filled in the tomahawk groove with faux-wood putty, and repainted it to make it even more conspicuous than before.

George appeared, open wine bottle in hand, filled the four glasses placed on their new wrought-iron-and-tile-topped table, then gave the bottle that no-spill little wrist turn he could do as deftly as any maître d' worth his salt in a four-star restaurant.

A couple of short beeps announced the return of Sis and Shirelle in Sis's new 4x4. Spurred by the resurrection of the backyard, they had just been to Burdick's to get a few more gardening supplies. Shirelle was eager to get to work as Nan's new helper.

And what about that Sis! Look at how much she'd matured since the storm, thought George and Nan. No longer the pouty, oversensitive Sis, she had become Mary, their invaluable helper, throwing herself into their renewed gardening efforts with a verve that put them both to shame. Nothing like a little disaster to get the gears of maturity grinding, thought Nan; George could really benefit from Mary's example. One thing was for sure: neither one of them would ever call her Sis again.

As for Cullen and Ellis, they kind of took after their dad, didn't they? Nan reflected with affection. Winsome, heroic when they needed to be, and, like most men, no help at all when the situation allowed it.

After Mary and Shirelle dumped their last bags of potting and fertilizer next to the shed, Shirelle headed back to the truck.

"One more thing," she said. "A surprise."

Mary tittered. When she returned from the truck, Shirelle carried a small shrub about six inches high, its roots encased in a large black plastic container. As she got closer, Nan began laughing.

"What's so funny?" said George. "A little too much Sage-lands there already, Nan-bee. Don't gag on it, please. What could be so funny about a plant, especially one that hasn't learned to communicate yet?"

"This is our very special gift to you," said Shirelle. She hoisted up the plant for George to get a good look at it. "A new angel's trumpet. It's what your wife and daughter said you wanted more than anything else. So, on behalf of Mary and Mrs. Fremont and myself, let this be a token of our wishes for many, many wonderful gardening years to come. Oh, and please use gloves and safety goggles when handling."

Acknowledgments

Here are some of the folks who bear the burden of making *Backyard* possible. Should you find this book riddled with inaccuracies, misconceptions, and notions that defy the conventions of accepted gardening behavior, blame them!

Many thanks go out to my editor at Kensington, Martin Biro, whose suggestions have invariably made this book better, and whose meticulous attention to detail continues to amaze. My agent, Peter Rubie, at FinePrint Literary Management, salvaged *Backyard* from his agency's scrap heap of orphaned manuscripts, then promptly made selling it seem effortless. It all began with my former agent, Marissa Walsh, who charged right in where so many others feared to tread and steered *Backyard* onto its proper course. Even though I never got to speak with her, thanks also to Kensington acquiring editor Audrey LaFehr, who, thank God, bought the book shortly before deciding to leave Kensington for the Rocky Mountains.

If it seems as if I'm an expert gardener, that's because there are some true experts who helped me pull off this masquerade. Special thanks go to master gardener and former colleague Mary Jane Smetanka, who fact-checked the manuscript, one draft after another, and served as my horticultural sounding board on more occasions than I can count. My mother-in-law,

Joyce Sandahl, endured many an early-morning flower question as I drained her coffeepot and perused her endless supply of gardening catalogs. Finally, the greatest tribute of all goes to my dear wife, Jennifer, who is also my favorite gardener and most accomplished teacher.

GREAT BOOKS, GREAT SAVINGS!

When You Visit Our Website:
www.kensingtonbooks.com
You Can Save Money Off The Retail Price
Of Any Book You Purchase!

- **All Your Favorite Kensington Authors**
- **New Releases & Timeless Classics**
- **Overnight Shipping Available**
- **eBooks Available For Many Titles**
- **All Major Credit Cards Accepted**

Visit Us Today To Start Saving!
www.kensingtonbooks.com

All Orders Are Subject To Availability.
Shipping and Handling Charges Apply.
Offers and Prices Subject To Change Without Notice.